To ashley,

ARMS OF GRACE

Enjoy!

Cheers,

ARMS OF GRACE

Eleanor Chance

Darlington Publishing

Published by Darlington Publishing, Williamsburg, VA
ISBN-10: **099812740X**
ISBN-13:**9780998127408**
Library of Congress Control Number: 2016915895

To Mike, my extraordinarily patient, supportive, and loving husband, partner, and friend

ACKNOWLEDGMENTS

Thank you to my family for putting up with this indulgent dream of mine. I couldn't have done it without your continued love, support, and motivation.

Thank you to my friends, who were sometimes more excited about this than I was. I feed off your energy, and it strengthens me in times of doubt.

Finally, thank you to all the editors, doctors, nurses, lawyers, and social workers for taking the time to talk with me and teach me. Your assistance was invaluable.

CHAPTER ONE

Johnny blew into my life on a hurricane. It happened in early September. The Category 1 storm made landfall in the Chesapeake Bay and roared up the James to Richmond. Meteorologists predicted our certain doom, but few others seemed concerned about the danger. The governor called for evacuations, but most chose to ignore him. Most came to regret that choice.

It wasn't the wind so much as the rain that wreaked the havoc. The storm stalled over downtown Richmond, and lower parts of the city flooded within hours. All avenues of escape were soon underwater. I was trapped with those who'd decided to stay and ride out the storm, but I wasn't there by choice. I was considered essential personnel at Richmond City Hospital where I worked as charge nurse on the internal-medicine floor, so escape hadn't been an option.

I trudged ahead, working long after my shift ended. At forty, I couldn't pull thirty-six hour shifts like I used to, so I snuck away to my office at nine for a break. I had no idea how long the flooding would keep me from my cozy brick rancher in the suburbs, so I needed to pace myself.

The phone rang two minutes after I sat down. I grabbed the receiver and said hello. Daniel Kinsley's voice answered back. He was my boss and least favorite person at the hospital. Just when I thought my day couldn't get worse.

Without greeting me, he said, "They need you in the ER. They're swamped. I can't force you, but with the hurricane, it's all hands on deck."

That was Kinsley's way of telling me it was optional but expected. My aching body begged me to say no, but since Kinsley and I were in a perpetual state of battling wills, I hoped to gain some ground if I agreed to go. I knew the ER staff would be glad of the help too. I told Kinsley I'd go and made my way to the ER for round three.

⊷≼⊹⊹≽⊶

Five grueling hours later, I went to the nurses' lounge for a break. I closed my eyes with a sigh and propped my throbbing feet on the cluttered coffee table. As I did, a flash of lightning flooded the room. Thunder boomed three seconds later and rattled the walls. Wind howled between the buildings only feet from where I sat. I'd been too busy to notice the storm while I'd helped treat a never-ending stream of patients, but I couldn't escape it in the quiet of the nurses' lounge, so I downed a bottle of water and went back to work.

I peeked into the waiting room as I passed by. It was full, but not overflowing like earlier. As I turned to go, a young couple stormed in through the sliding doors and thrust a baby into the arms of the receptionist, Amanda. They were talking in a rush. The only words I caught were "drowning" and "mouth-to-mouth." The receptionist tried to hand the baby back so she could help them, but they wouldn't take him.

"I can't understand you," she said. "Slow down. Tell me what happened."

"We were evacuating in our boat," the man said between gasps. "When we got to shore, we spotted him floating in the water. I pulled him out, and we ran to find a cab. He wasn't breathing. I gave him mouth-to-mouth on the way here."

I didn't wait to hear more. I tucked my hands under the infant and carefully lifted him into my arms. "Announce a code blue," I said to Amanda and asked the couple to follow me.

The man ignored me and yanked on the woman's arm. She tried to fight him off with one hand and grabbed the child's foot with her other hand. She looked to me for help with anguish in her eyes, and I wondered why she refused to leave some random infant. The man grabbed her wrist and dragged her toward the entrance. He gave her a shove, and they disappeared through the curtain of pelting rain.

I tore my eyes from the scene and rushed the baby to the nearest trauma room. I laid him on a gurney and studied him for the first time. He was blue and unconscious, taking shallow, choking breaths. A swollen bruise covered the left side of his forehead. I examined his body for other superficial injuries but found none. I estimated his age at about six months. Doctors and nurses came flooding in from all directions and crowded around the gurney.

As I removed my little patient's wet clothing, I described the scene from the waiting room. The attending physician took his place, and I stepped back to let his team work. He fired questions at me without looking up. I recounted what little I knew.

"Go ask Amanda if she has any more information, and hurry," he said as I ran out of the room.

⊷⊶

The waiting room was calm when I got back, but Amanda was staring wide-eyed at the entrance. When I asked if she had any details

3

about the incident, she held her hand up to my face, and said, "Look, I'm still shaking. What was that?"

The ER was always unpredictable, but even I had to admit that what that couple had done was bizarre. I smiled reassuringly at Amanda and repeated my question.

"They wouldn't tell me anything, not even their names. All they wanted was to get away. I'm sure they were lying, and did you see the way the woman hung on to the baby?"

I nodded, but tried again to get the information we needed. "You didn't notice anything else?" I asked, hoping something would come to her.

She just shrugged. "You saw the whole thing, Ms. Ward. You know as much as I do."

"We've got to get those people back here," I said and rubbed my forehead.

"The orderly gave the couple's description to two cops who'd been dropping off a DUI patient. They took off after them," she said.

"Hopefully they'll find them," I said, knowing it wasn't likely. "We don't even know how long the infant was in the water or how his head got injured."

The attending wouldn't be happy with so little to go on. As I turned to go, Amanda asked about the baby.

"Not good," I said. "They've got him intubated. Hopefully the cold water slowed his circulation and need for oxygen. He has a head injury too. I need to get back and report."

"Poor little guy," Amanda said and shook her head. She was about to say more, but a man stepped up to the counter cradling his bloodied hand, so I made my exit.

By the time I got back to the trauma room, the baby was lying silently in a hospital crib. The blue tinge in his skin was gone, but the bruise was bigger and more swollen. He had an IV running and a collar to stabilize his neck. Whips of his blond hair peeked out of the blue knitted cap on his head. The attending came in and shined a light into the baby's pupils to check his response. I recounted what Amanda had told me.

"It's not enough, but it'll have to do," he said, pulling off his gloves. "We'll keep a close watch on his intracranial pressure. The next few hours will be critical. They're making room for him in the PICU. They're slammed like everyone else. What a night, and it's not over."

I volunteered to stay with the child until he was moved to the pediatric ICU. The attending thanked me for my help and walked out, shaking his head as he went. I dragged a chair next to the crib and rested my arms on the rail. He was an adorable little boy. Despite his ugly wound, he was peaceful and oblivious to the fact that his life was in danger. I wondered again at how he'd ended up in the river. If he'd been my child, I'd have protected him with the fierceness of a lion.

It had been a long, exhausting day, and my eyes became heavy as I watched him. I leaned back, resting my head against the wall to let sleep come. The next thing I knew, the trauma nurse supervisor was shaking my shoulder.

I sat forward and rubbed my eyes. They felt like sandpaper. "What time is it?" I asked. "And how did you get to the hospital?"

"Five thirty. I walked. I live close by. We just finished our shift change, such as it is. Why don't you take off? We'll keep an eye on him," she said, cocking her head toward the baby.

I was reluctant to go but knew I'd need sleep to brace for the rest of the day. "I'll go crash in my office," I said. "Call if there's any change."

"I'll let the PICU know. We're getting ready to transfer him. Now go," she said and shuffled me out the door.

I took a last longing look at the baby and headed for my office.

⊨⊨ ⊨⊨

I spent what remained of that night haunted by dreams of that pale little face. After tossing on my office sofa for three hours, I gave up and went to the staff showers to clean up. After my shower, I pulled my wet hair into a band and threw on some scrubs. By then, it was almost ten. My stomach growled, and I realized I hadn't eaten anything but cheese sticks and yogurt since around five the day before.

I gave the cafeteria a shot, but wasn't surprised to see that there wasn't much of a selection. I choked down cold cereal and a day-old doughnut and then went back to my office to tackle charts. That was a total waste of time. The words and numbers danced on the screen in an incomprehensible jumble, so I gave up and decided to give sleep another try. As soon as I was snuggled in on the sofa, the phone rang. Assuming it was Kinsley again, I was tempted to ignore it but knew I'd get an earful later if I did.

I reached for the receiver and said, "Grace Ward," without trying to hide my irritation.

"Hi, Grace, it's Walt," my cousin said.

My irritation vanished at the sound of his voice. Walt never called me at work. He rarely even called me at home. I swallowed and braced for the bad news about to come.

"Hello, Walt. It's great to hear from you," I said, trying to mask my dread.

"You won't say that when you hear why I'm calling. I'm sorry to bother you at work with the hurricane and all, but you didn't answer your cell. There's no way to soften this. Andrew Whiting passed away this morning. Heart attack. Mom called me with the news but didn't have the heart to tell you. I'm so sorry. I know he was like a father to you."

I gasped and didn't trust myself to speak for several seconds. When Walt asked if I was still there, I said yes and swallowed again. "Thanks for letting me know. When's the funeral?"

Walt didn't know but said he'd call back with the details. "I really am sorry. Talk to you soon," he said and hung up.

My thoughts reeled, refusing to accept that Andrew was dead. I'd talked to him two days earlier. We'd been making plans for Christmas. How could he be dead?

Andrew had been much more than a father figure to me. He'd been my savior. If not for Andrew, I wouldn't have become a nurse. If not for him, I would have died twenty years earlier. I hadn't even told him how much I loved him when we last talked. I didn't tell him he was everything in the world to me. Had he felt that? I'd never know. He was gone too soon, like everyone I'd loved.

I gazed at the framed photo of Andrew that sat on my desk. I had taken it at my nursing-school graduation. That was the first day I had allowed myself to believe I had a shot at a normal life. Andrew had encouraged that, and he'd been so proud of me.

I was startled out of my thoughts when thunder rattled the windows. I'd forgotten the hurricane in my grief. I wished I could forget my grief so easily. I'd faced loss in the past and knew what was coming. I longed to run and hide, but long experience had taught me that grief is a relentless stalker we can't escape. I hugged Andrew's picture to my chest and curled up on the sofa in a futile attempt to cry away the pain.

I drifted off at some point and woke three hours later with drool running down my cheek. It took several seconds for me to get my bearings and figure out why I was sleeping on my office couch. When my head cleared, I looked for Andrew's picture and found it lying face down on the floor. I picked it up and was relieved to see that the glass wasn't broken. I wiped it clean with my sleeve and sat it on the blanket next to me.

Desperate for a distraction and change of scenery, I decided to check on the abandoned baby in the PICU. He'd looked so defenseless and vulnerable the night before. With the storm, I knew the PICU staff wouldn't have time to give him the love and care he required. I had time and love to give. And I needed to be needed. I tenderly set Andrew's picture back on the desk and went out, locking the door behind me.

I was afraid of what I might find. The last thing I needed was news of another death. Working with critically ill patients wasn't new to me, but having trouble maintaining my professional detachment was. My patients had always mattered to me, but I rarely gave them a second thought once they left my department. For the first time since becoming a nurse, I began to understand how families felt about their loved ones lying in those beds.

I trudged ahead in spite of my trepidation. The supervising nurse blocked my way at the PICU entrance and started to say that only authorized personnel were allowed, but she stopped when she recognized me.

"What do you want?" she asked, sort of suppressing a scowl.

"I'm here to see the infant who came in last night with the head injury," I said, trying to appear calmer than I felt.

"You and everybody else. He's in six." She gestured with her thumb toward his station.

Relieved by the good news, I nodded and went to room six. Marci, a nurse who'd once worked for me, was taking his vitals. She raised an eyebrow at me but didn't say anything. When she finished with her patient, she faced me and said, "I heard you were subbing in the ER when he came in."

"That's true," I said, not in the mood for small talk.

"What happened?" she asked, not taking the hint from my tone.

"Probably just what you've heard. How is he?" I asked, hoping to change the subject.

"Still comatose. Intracranial pressure's stable but still high. We've lowered his O-two sat. Dr. Carter hopes to take him off the vent in a few days if his ICP comes down. We're watching for pneumonia too."

The improvement in his breathing was a good sign, but the brain pressure wasn't. If the swelling didn't go down or continued to increase, they'd have to open his skull to drain it. With his other injuries, he probably wouldn't survive the procedure, or he'd have significant brain damage. I cringed when I imagined his precious little skull cut open.

"Thanks, Marci," I said, softening my tone. "I'll keep an eye on him if you have another patient."

"I don't, but I do need a break, so I'll take you up on your offer."

Once she rounded the corner, I pulled the curtain around us and peered at the baby. The bruising had spread down to his cheek, and his eye was swollen shut. Even with his injuries, I was smitten with him. I wanted to cuddle and kiss him and make it all better. Ignoring protocol, I brushed my gloveless finger across his chubby palm. He gripped it and squeezed, making me jump. He shouldn't have reacted. I tried to pull away, but the baby tightened his hold. My training cried out that it was only an instinctive reaction, but my heart refused to listen.

I stepped closer and wrapped my other hand around his. His warm hand in mine sent shivers up my arms, and I wanted to cling to him forever. After checking that no one was watching, I put my lips to his ear and whispered, "That's right, my little man; I'm right here. Hold on tight. Fight for your life."

My tears welled up as we clung to each other, and I didn't fight them. I cried for the baby. I cried for Andrew. I cried for myself. I cried until I couldn't mask the force of my sobs. The curtain rustled behind me, and I turned to find Alec Covington staring at me through the opening.

Alec was my second least favorite person at the hospital, and there'd been bad blood between us since she'd been hired to work in my department. Alec was everything I wasn't. She was five nine, with dark wavy hair and perfect skin. I was five one in shoes, and

I had a slight limp and thin, flat blond hair. Her nursing degree was from UCLA on a full scholarship, and she'd been recruited to a top-rated hospital in San Francisco straight out of school. I'd had to work full-time while I was in nursing school. I wouldn't have been able to do it if Andrew hadn't paid my tuition.

I'd secretly nicknamed her Spoiled Rich Girl, even though she'd never actually done anything to deserve the name. I let pettiness and jealousy affect the way I treated her, and it drove her away. She had transferred to the ER six months earlier. I hadn't seen her until the previous night in the trauma room, and I was mortified that she'd caught me bawling my eyes out in the PICU.

I wiped my face on my sleeve and said, "I just came to check on him." It sounded so lame.

She gave me an indecipherable look and said, "Me too. Have the police taken your statement?"

I turned back toward the crib to escape her scrutiny. "No. I'm meeting them this afternoon."

Alec came closer and leaned over the crib. "I gave mine this morning. I didn't have much to say. How's he doing?"

"Still critical. Our biggest concerns are pneumonia and his ICP," I said.

Alec looked at me again. "You said, 'our biggest concerns.' Have you been assigned to his case?"

I couldn't tell her that I'd designated myself as his caregiver, so I said, "I meant the hospital staff in general."

"Doesn't sound good," she said and looked at the baby. She brushed a wisp of hair from his forehead and sighed. "The whole situation is so strange. I guess he could have been swept away by the floods, but who would have had him down by the river in the first place?"

"That's the million-dollar question. Maybe his parents were evacuating. Hopefully there'll be news today," I said, glad the conversation had turned back to the baby. It was the first time I could remember carrying on a civil conversation with Alec. She was popular around the hospital and probably a perfectly nice person, but we'd always kept our conversation to work matters.

I needed someone to talk to, but as I was about to open up to her, she said, "I'm sorry to be nosy, but why were you crying when I came in? I thought maybe he'd died."

Marci came back before I could answer, so I motioned for Alec to follow me out. While we watched from the nurses' station, her question hung in the air between us and gave me the perfect opening.

"He's so alone. He doesn't have anyone to care for more than his physical needs. I guess the sight of him so defenseless broke my heart," I said and turned to face her. "Who's going to love him, Alec? We all need to be loved." Tears threatened again, so I let my words trail off.

"True. Thanks for telling me. It's none of my business," Alec said.

"I probably would have asked too. We both know this isn't like me. I got some bad news yesterday, and I haven't slept, and with the hurricane and all…" The words tumbled out before I could stop them, and I wondered why I was making excuses to her.

Alec hesitated before saying, "I'm sorry to hear that." The words fell flat. She didn't sound sorry. We fidgeted for a few seconds before she said, "I'd stay and talk, but my break is over. The ER's still swamped. I'd better go."

I almost laughed at how fast she tore out of there, desperate to be free of me. I stayed with the baby for another hour before I got word that my nurses were turning the hospital upside down to find me. I pulled myself away from my new little friend and took the elevator back to my floor. An unhappy crowd awaited me at my office door. I took a deep breath and charged in.

The rest of that day was filled with petty irritations and micro-crises. By the end of my shift, Kinsley insisted I go home. He told me that the national guard was escorting people out of the city. I checked in on the baby before I left, but there wasn't any change. I promised him I'd be back in the morning and kissed his forehead when no one was looking. He didn't react, but I was certain he'd felt it.

I pulled into the garage never so happy to see my house. I went in and heated a frozen lasagna. My block hadn't lost power like some of the surrounding neighborhoods, so I'd gotten lucky in that at least. After dinner, I took the best bubble bath ever and climbed into bed. I snuggled into my cocoon, certain I'd be asleep in minutes, but each time I closed my eyes I was plagued by memories of Andrew and anxiety for the baby.

I'd learned that the best way for me to combat insomnia was to get out of bed. I went to the hall closet and hunted for a box of letters from Andrew. When I found it, I sat on the hallway floor and pulled out the precious contents. Several of them spoke of my bright spirit and capacity for good, but I'd never found those qualities in myself. I thought again of how I'd treated Alec when she worked for me and cringed. I'd never told Andrew about Alec or how I'd treated some of the other nurses. He'd have been so disappointed. I imagined him in some afterlife, looking down at me and shaking his head.

I pulled out another letter. In it, Andrew had encouraged me to open myself up to the good in the world. I had no trust in that world and didn't believe it existed. I'd never seen it, and I'd learned early on that trust was dangerous. Since the death of my mother when I was ten, I'd trusted only Andrew. With him gone, my choices were to continue alone, trusting no one, or to learn to trust in the world Andrew spoke of.

I thought of the poor baby in the PICU. I could make his world a loving place for as long as he needed me. It would be a good place to start. I put Andrew's letters away and went back to bed, where I drifted into the best sleep I'd had in months.

CHAPTER TWO

My gut tightened as the plane touched down at the Lincoln Airport four days later. I hadn't been to Nebraska for many years. I wouldn't have set foot there for any reason other than Andrew's funeral.

His cousin Jessica picked me up at the airport. I'd gone to grade school with her daughter and caught up on their lives during the ride to my hotel. Jessica walked me to my room and said she'd give me an hour to get settled before she returned to get me for the viewing. I was about to tell her I didn't want to go to the viewing, but she was in the elevator before I could.

I sat on the end of the bed, staring at the ugly curtains that blacked out the clear, blue sky beyond. I walked to the window and started to open them but changed my mind. The dreary darkness in the room matched my mood. Facing the reality of Andrew's death was bad enough. I hadn't figured out how I'd find the strength to face my relatives, many of whom I hadn't seen in more than twenty years.

Andrew and my mother had grown up and gone to school to-gether, and our families had been friends for generations. I dread-ed the interrogation I'd get about where I'd been for so many years. I made a mental list of evasions and started unpacking.

I only glanced into Andrew's coffin as I walked past at the viewing. I didn't want my last memory of him to be that lifeless body in the casket. On my way into the chapel, I decided that when my time came, I wanted to be cremated so no one would be forced to view my corpse.

Andrew had been well loved in the community, so the chapel was already full when I walked in. I took a seat in a back corner, hoping I hadn't been spotted by anyone who knew me. The fu-neral was lovely and was more a celebration of Andrew's life than a dreary memorial. Andrew would have insisted on that. After hear-ing stories of his selfless service to anyone in need, I felt honored to have been considered one of his closest friends.

The instant the pallbearers were out of the chapel, I made a beeline for the exit. I was almost through the doorway when I heard Aunt Jenny's voice behind me. I took a deep breath before turning to face her. She had been my surrogate mother when I was a teenager. The sight of her as an old woman shocked me until I realized that I'd aged too. Mama and Aunt Jenny had looked so much alike that I could picture Mama at her age. Aunt Jenny broke me from my thoughts by giving me a tight hug. I hugged her back gently, afraid I'd break her.

When we stepped apart, she said, "Is this what it takes to get you here, Gracie?"

The years vanished at the sound of my childhood nickname, and I reverted to the timid and vulnerable child I'd once been.

"I'm sorry, Aunt Jenny," I said. "It's hard to get away from my work. I'll try to get up to Des Moines soon." I had no intention of ever going to Des Moines, but it was all I could think to say.

"See that you do, sweetheart. We've missed you. Walt was just talking about you at Sunday dinner the week before Andrew died. How are you doing?" she asked.

They missed me so much that none of them had ever bothered to call and say that. I let the comment drop and said, "I'm good. Busy. We just had a hurricane."

Walt and Uncle Thomas stepped closer to join the conversation. Soon, other old friends and family crowded around. The conversations drifted away from me, so I took the chance to duck out. I had gone to the funeral to honor Andrew and console his daughters, not to satisfy my family's curiosity.

I hoped to find Andrew's daughters in the foyer but only caught a glimpse of them as they climbed into the limo to go to the cemetery. I found Jessica and asked if she'd mind taking me back to the hotel.

"You're not going to the cemetery or family luncheon afterward? You're invited, you know," she said, looking concerned.

"I know, and I appreciate that," I said, "but I got up at the crack of dawn to catch my flight, and I have a bit of a headache. I need to lie down."

She started to protest, but I put up my hand top stop her. "It's fine, really. I'll catch up with everyone later."

She shrugged and followed me out the door to her car. I told her that the hotel had an airport shuttle, so she wouldn't need to give me a ride in the morning.

"It's no trouble," she said. "I'm retired now, so I don't have anywhere else to be. I wish I could talk you into staying for a few days. Everyone wants to see you."

"I really can't. Things are crazy at work with the hurricane and all," I said, never thinking I'd be so grateful for a hurricane.

"I understand, but don't be such a stranger. You know you're welcome anytime," she said.

I nodded but didn't say anything for the rest of the drive.

I ordered dinner at the hotel restaurant and ate it in my room. No one called or came by to check on me for the rest of my time there. I assumed that Jessica made my excuses for me, but I thought Aunt Jenny would have called to check on me. I should have known better.

As my plane took off the next morning, I realized that Andrew had been my only tie to the past, and they'd just put him in the ground. As the fields below faded away, I let my past fade with them. My only hope for happiness lay in what stretched before me, so that's where I set my sights.

By the time I got back from the funeral, the inflammation on the baby's brain had receded, so he'd escaped a craniotomy. He was also breathing on his own. Dr. Brad Carter, the pediatric neurologist in charge of his case, had removed the breathing tube and transferred him to a private room on the pediatric ward.

I brought a rocking chair to set next to his crib and bought him a blue quilt with blocks on it. I spent as much time as I could spare with him.

The name on his chart read Baby John Doe. I couldn't bring myself to call him that. It made him sound like a homicide victim. I named him Johnny, and the entire staff soon started calling him that. All that was left was for him to wake up.

I had to skip my morning time with Johnny three weeks later when Kinsley called me to his office. He rarely asked to meet with me unless there was a problem, so I dreaded going to see him. All he cared about was the bottom line and didn't seem to comprehend that patients were people, not products. He had to deal with increasing costs and dwindling budgets, but he made no effort to find a middle ground. I was sure that was why the board had hired him.

I'd nicknamed him the Hyena, and not just because of his behavior. His wide-set, soulless eyes were in constant motion. It unnerved me, and I was cautious to never turn my back on him. His opinion of me was less than stellar too, so there was no love lost between us. He was perpetually irritated by my refusals to implement his cost-cutting initiatives. I feared most of them might put patients' lives at risk. The rest I ignored out of spite.

Kinsley wasn't the only one who didn't like me. Most of the staff was more than a little intimidated by me and called me Attila the Hun behind my back. I ignored them, because it pretty much gave me the run of the place.

As soon as I sat down in Kinsley's office, he said, "I'll get right to it, Grace. We're both busy people."

Our meetings had historically started with, "We have a problem," so I felt a glimmer of hope that he hadn't called me in to chew me out.

"The NIH has chosen this hospital, in conjunction with the university, to create an infectious-disease unit. I'd like you to head the nursing team."

It was a good thing that I had a firm grip on my chair, or I would have tumbled out of it. I easily thought of four people he could have chosen over me. I wondered if they'd all refused, and he had been forced to ask me.

"I'd be honored," I said before he could take the offer back. "What's involved?"

He gave me the details and told me he had a replacement for me on the IM floor. He said I had four weeks to put together a nursing team. I could have anyone on staff, pending his final approval. Alec Covington came to my mind as soon as the words were out of Kinsley's mouth. I went straight to my office after the meeting and called the ER. I asked Amanda to have Alec come see me on her break.

"May I tell her what this is about?" Amanda asked.

"No," I said and hung up.

I wasn't sure Alec would come, but she tapped on my open door two hours later, looking like she'd been summoned to the principal's office. It made me wonder if I was her Hyena.

"Come in," I said, motioning to the chair on the opposite side of my desk.

She hesitated for a second but then came in. I explained about the infectious-disease unit and repeated what Kinsley had said. "The position will require spending long hours with patients in isolation. I know you like working in the ER, but I'd like to offer you a position with the unit," I said.

Alec blinked a few times and said, "What?"

I was confused by her confusion. "I'm offering you a chance to work for me on the ID team," I said to clarify.

"Oh, I got that," she said. "I just can't believe you had the gall to say it. The answer is no," she said and jumped out of the chair.

"Alec, wait," I said. "Don't you want to think about it? It's a great opportunity. It could really enhance your career."

She stopped in the doorway and turned. "I'm sure it would, but no career advancement is worth having to work with you. I couldn't wait to get out of your department the first time. I won't make that mistake again."

I sank into my chair and put my head in my hands. "I deserve that. Please, let's talk about this. Don't miss this opportunity because of me. You'll regret it."

Alec folded her arms but didn't move. "The only time I regretted moving to Richmond was when I met you. Your demand for perfection was intolerable, and you were constantly riding me. I respect your abilities in spite of that, and I've even learned from you, but that's not enough to make it worth working for you again."

"I was only trying to help you reach your full potential. I didn't want to coddle you," I said.

"Coddle me? No one would mistake what you did for coddling. Besides, you treat everyone that way. It's who you are."

That stung. I closed my eyes and rubbed my temples, desperate to figure out how to convince her. I didn't just need her on my ID team. I wanted to make up for the past and gain her trust. I wanted her as a friend.

I raised my head and said, "Listen, Alec, you have one of the quickest minds of any nurse I've known. The way you interact with the patients is impressive. Your name was the first one on my list."

She leaned in and put her hands flat on my desk. "Are you kidding me? I'll make this simple and not waste our time. I'm not leaving a position I love to go back to working for the resident tyrant."

Her comment was so unexpected that I did something rare for me: I laughed.

Alec stepped back and said, "What's so funny?"

I went to her and put my hand on her arm. "I've owed you an apology for my behavior since the day we met. You didn't deserve the harassment I gave you. You are a skilled nurse, and you worked hard for me. I'm sorry. Give me a chance to make it up to you."

"You're only saying that so I'll agree to work on the ID team," she said and pushed my hand off her arm.

"No, I'm not. Three other nurses jumped at the chance, and there are other nurses I could ask. I do want you on the team. Things will be different. I'm different."

"Why should I believe you?" she asked, and I could tell I was getting to her.

"Because I'm tired of being the 'resident tyrant,'" I said and smiled. "I don't deserve your forgiveness, but I give you my word:

I've changed. Do you remember when you saw me with Johnny in the PICU? Did that seem like the old me?"

Alec squinted at me for a few seconds. "Not at all. Honestly, it freaked me out."

"I know it's asking a lot for you to trust me, but that's what I'm doing. Will you please reconsider?"

I tried to read her eyes, but she looked away. "Maybe. I am intrigued, and not only about the job."

"Take three days to decide. Training starts next month. That will be enough time to replace you," I said.

"Fine. I'll contact you either way in three days, but I'm still leaning toward no." She started to leave but turned in the doorway. "How is that baby, anyway? I heard you're taking care of him. I didn't believe it. That didn't sound like something you'd do."

"The rumors are true. See? I've changed. To answer your question, though, he's still comatose but stable."

"Why do you care about him? I'm sure the peds staff has it covered."

I wanted to tell her the truth, but it was too soon. "It just seems right," I said.

The look on her face made me laugh again, but I caught the hint of a smile on her face before she turned to go.

Waiting to hear from Alec was torture. I was dying to find out if I'd gotten through to her. She found me in Johnny's room three days later.

"I'd be honored to accept the position," she said, "with two conditions. First, I'm daring you to show me that you've changed. And second, teach me everything you know."

"It's a deal," I said, extending my hand. "I'll send the paperwork over tomorrow. The orientation information's in the packet."

Alec walked to the crib and gently scooped Johnny up. "How's he doing today?" she asked.

"Not much change. He must have been strong and healthy before the accident to be doing as well as he is. I wish he'd regain consciousness so we can see if, or how much, brain damage he has. Dr. Carter thinks it'll be severe."

"I wish they'd find out who he is. Most people say his parents drowned in the flood, but they haven't recovered any bodies from the river. You hear about stuff like this but never think you'll see it in real life."

I just nodded, wondering how she'd react if she knew the truth about *my* "real life."

"I have to get back to work," she said. "I'll let my department know about the transfer. They won't be happy. We're already shorthanded."

"If you have any trouble, have your supervisor call me. The department heads are aware that this program is a priority, so it shouldn't be a problem."

She turned to go, but before she got away, I said, "Want to get to dinner tonight after work to celebrate? My treat."

It took longer than I liked for her answer. She looked me up and down and said, "Sure, I guess."

"Great. Call when you get home. We'll decide where to meet."

"Talk to you then," Alec said and waved on her way out.

Alec called that afternoon and suggested an Italian restaurant she liked. I didn't eat out much, so I was glad she knew a good place. I loved Italian food, but I'd never told Alec that, so it was a lucky coincidence.

The restaurant was small, but not very crowded since it was a weeknight. I was relieved she hadn't picked one of those huge, noisy chain restaurants. They usually had the music so loud it was impossible to carry on a conversation without shouting.

Once we ordered, I took advantage of the chance to find out why she'd come to Richmond. "Can you tell me, or is it too personal?" I asked.

"It's not too personal, but it is boring, so you've been warned. I was running away from my mother."

I laughed and said, "Weren't you a little old to run away?"

"You wouldn't ask that if you knew my mother," she said and grimaced. "My father was a lawyer and later a California state senator. He's retired now and writing his memoir, not that anyone cares enough to read it. My mother's a tenured sociology professor. My parents pride themselves on being part of the Bay Area elite. My two older sisters are more than happy to follow in their footsteps. The oldest is a commercial real-estate lawyer. The other's a bio-medical engineer."

"There's nothing wrong with wealth and success," I said.

"There is if you sit perched in your hilltop mansion smugly watching the minions scurrying about below. I've never wanted any part of that world. I used to wonder if I'd been switched at birth, because I'm so different from the rest of my family. I'd lie in bed at night imagining what my 'real' family was like. I look exactly like my grandmother, though, so that ended my hope of being a changeling."

I took a bite of bread and chewed slowly before saying, "I know what it's like to wish you'd been born into a different family."

Alec looked up from her plate. I could tell she wanted me to say more, so I shoveled a spoonful of pasta into my mouth.

She took the hint, and said, "After I graduated from UCLA and passed my boards, Mother interfered to get me that job in San Francisco so she could keep me under her thumb. I took the job to shut her up but immediately began planning my escape. I applied for jobs all over the country. I was ecstatic when I got the offer here. I didn't know anything about Virginia, but moving here meant I could put a continent between Mother and me. One day I packed my bags and boarded the plane without telling anyone where I was going."

"Sometimes running away is the only option," I said without looking up.

"My family doesn't feel that way. Even my friends thought I was crazy for leaving my cushy life. Luxury often comes at a price, and you can't understand another person's life until you've lived it."

I looked into her eyes and nodded. No one understood that better than I did.

Alec stared at me for several seconds before she said, "I probably sound like a whiny coward, but I did what I had to do."

The server stopped by the table to ask if we needed anything, and Alec ordered cannoli for our dessert. Even though I loved cannoli, I wasn't sure how I'd fit it in if I finished the pile of pasta on my plate.

When the server walked away I said, "Give yourself credit. You have a right to the life you want. Not many women would jump off into the unknown like that. I admire it."

Alec's eyes widened when she said, "That's high praise coming from you. Now it's my turn to ask you something."

I stopped with my forkful of linguini in midair, and my gut tightened. I wasn't ready to expose my past life like she had.

"What's happened to cause this change in you? It's pretty drastic. I couldn't have pictured us doing this even a month ago."

I relaxed and finished chewing. That was a question I could answer. "I lost a dear friend from childhood the same day Johnny was abandoned here. With the hurricane, it was literally the perfect storm."

"I remember you saying you'd gotten bad news. I'm sorry I was so abrupt with you, but we weren't exactly on friendly terms."

I smiled at her. "That's an understatement, but I understood. Can I tell you about my friend? I haven't been able to talk about him since the funeral. Taking care of Johnny has helped with the grief, but that's not the same."

"I'd like to hear about your friend. What was his name?" Alec asked and seemed genuinely interested.

"Andrew. He was like the father I should have had." It felt good to say it out loud. "He got me through some of the most difficult times in my life, and I've had difficult times." I shook my head to chase away the memories and folded my arms. "I owe him more than you can imagine. When he passed away, I remembered lessons he taught me about finding happiness and friendship. He was the best man I've ever known. In fact, he's the only truly good man I've ever known."

My throat tightened, and I had to stop. I didn't want to break down in front of her. I looked up when she put her hand on my arm, and I saw compassion in her eyes.

I took a few deep breaths and said, "After some serious soul searching, I realized how miserable I've been and how miserable I've made everyone around me. I behaved that way for over twenty years, but that's not who I was before. I need to let go of past pain and bitterness. Even though Andrew knew my reasons, it disappointed him when I drove people away. I don't want to do that anymore. I'm starting over. Making peace with you is the first step."

"*Hic locus est ubi mors gaudet succurrere vitae*," Alec said.

"Here, death happily serves the living," I said.

"You speak Latin?" she asked with surprise.

I nodded and said, "I studied it while I was in nursing school, but what does that quote have to do with this?"

"One of my anatomy professors recited it on our first day working with cadavers in the lab. He was referring to people who donated their bodies to science, but I've learned that it has a wider meaning. Grief over Andrew's death could have driven you further inside yourself. Instead, it was the catalyst for positive change. Wouldn't he be happy to know that?"

"I know he would be. Thinking about his death like that does ease the pain some," I said.

"I'm sorry you lost your friend, but I'm glad he opened the way for us to become friends, if you're planning to consider me a friend."

"It's what I'd hoped even if I don't deserve it. That old Grace isn't who I want to be. When you know me better, maybe you'll understand why I acted that way, but for now, I hope you can accept me as I am. I have a hard time trusting people. I hope you'll be patient."

"I tend to trust everyone—well almost," she said and winked. "It gets me into trouble too. We'll make a good pair, but take all the time you need. I'm not going anywhere."

"To new friendship, then," I said and lifted my glass.

CHAPTER THREE

When I got back from dinner that night, I heard on the news that the FBI had taken over the investigation into Johnny's case. Agents thought they'd found the couple's boat, but it was an untraceable fishing boat. Rain had long washed away any finger or shoe prints. Even the tire tracks were gone. Officials set up a tip line for any information and offered a reward.

I walked into Johnny's room the following afternoon to find a man leaning over his crib. "Excuse me, may I help you?" I asked.

He flinched and turned toward me. He looked me up and down, and said, "Who are you?"

"You first," I said.

"Fair enough. I'm Special Agent Grant Erikson." He reached into his pocket and pulled out his credential, flipping it open inches from my nose. "Now, I'll ask you again, who are you?" He stood taller and straightened his shoulders. He was over six feet tall and had a broad build. He was trying to intimidate me, but he had a friendly face, so it didn't work.

"I'm Grace Ward. I'm a nurse here. I've been looking after Johnny."

He sniffed and stuffed his credential back into his pocket. "Who?" he asked.

"Johnny. The baby," I said and motioned to his crib.

"You don't look like a nurse. Where's your uniform and badge?"

I looked down at my clothes. I'd forgotten that I'd changed into my street clothes after work. I reached into my purse and took out my ID badge and held it inches from his nose like he'd done to me. "I was coming to visit Johnny before I go home. Why are you here?"

I wasn't sure he'd answer, but I was dying of curiosity. Maybe they'd found out who Johnny was. Maybe his parents were about to walk through the door.

"I've been assigned to his case. I've been here to see him before. You said you're looking after him. Why? Does he have some relation to you?"

I decided the best way to answer was to give the simplest explanation. "I was the nurse on duty in the ER when those people abandoned him. I gave the police my statement."

"Ah, I thought your name sounded familiar," Erikson said and nodded. I was surprised he remembered me out of the hundreds of people the police had questioned. "So you actually got a look at the man and woman?"

"Yes, I did. I gave a description with my statement," I said.

"Yes, I read it, remember? Not much to go on."

"It happened so fast, and I was more focused on the baby." I don't know why I felt I had to explain. I'd always been observant and loved murder-mystery shows. I thought I'd given a good description.

"I'm not criticizing. Sometimes people remember details after the fact. Probably wouldn't matter by now. They're long gone. It's a frustrating case."

"Do you have any leads?" I asked.

"I have my own theories," Erikson said and leaned against the wall. He looked like he wanted to say more but just shook his head.

Erickson came closer to Johnny's crib and silently studied his face.

"What is it?" I asked.

He shook his head and said, "Nothing. Doesn't matter. We found the couple's house from a tip, but neighbors say they took off the night of the storm and haven't been back. We haven't found anything else that's useful."

"So, what happens now?" I was glad they were making progress, but it sounded like they were still a long way from finding the truth.

"Johnny will become a ward of the state. If his parents aren't found, he'll enter the foster system if he's ever well enough to leave here. Then he'd be available for adoption. Aside from that, we'll keep investigating until we have nowhere else to look."

The word *adoption* stuck in my mind. Since that day in the PICU, I'd known that I would do whatever it took to protect and care for Johnny in the hospital, but on some level, I assumed he'd go home with someone else if he survived. If he could be adopted, who better than me to do it? I loved him in a way no one else at the hospital did. The thought of him becoming my son thrilled me. I looked at my poor unconscious boy in his crib.

"Thanks for telling me," I said. "Do you have a card so I can contact you?"

He took a card from his wallet and handed it to me. "Call if you think of anything else," he said and left.

I went to Johnny and caressed his silky cheek with the back of my forefinger. He was already mine. I didn't need a piece of paper to tell me that.

Life settled into a routine of sorts. I continued to spend every minute I could with Johnny. He was the little angel who had blown into my life and transformed me. I rocked him and sang lullabies that my mother had sung to me. More importantly, I talked to him. I told him things I couldn't tell anyone, things I hadn't even told Andrew.

Work on the ID unit took more of my time away from Johnny than I liked, but I was enjoying the work. Once the program was up and running, the physicians, nurses, and researchers congealed into a cohesive unit. Team members were becoming friends and began socializing outside of the hospital. They often met in the staff lounge after a grueling shift to blow off steam. I was glad to see it happening but wasn't interested in being a part of it. I watched from the edges, like a lone planet orbiting around them.

Alec found me in Johnny's room one day after work. She sat in the chair opposite me and glared. She'd been upset with me for the past few days, but I'd been doing my best to avoid her.

"Hello, Alec," I said cheerfully, pretending I hadn't noticed her frowning at me.

"Don't give me that. We need to talk," she said.

"So, talk."

"What's going on? Why are you avoiding everyone? What happened to 'I'm going to change my life and be nice to everyone'? Was that just talk?"

"That's not what I said. But I've been nicer, haven't I?"

"To me. You're tolerable to everyone else. People are talking. They think you're a snob or worse, that you don't trust them."

The truth was, I didn't trust them, or more accurately, I didn't know them. I wasn't even sure I wanted to. Being part of their social group wasn't for me. "I can't change overnight. I told you it would take time."

"But you're not even trying. You spend all your free time with Johnny. It's admirable, but you need to be around real people too."

"Johnny is a real person," I said and frowned, irritated at her comment.

"Fine. But you know what I mean, like grownups who can talk back to you, not a comatose baby."

I lowered my shoulders in defeat. "What do you want, Alec?"

She perked up and said, "Do you have plans tomorrow night?"

"Yes, with Johnny."

"Someone else can take your place for one night. I'm sure you'll both survive."

Not wanting to know, I asked her why anyway.

"Caroline, Angela, and Kimberly are coming to my apartment tomorrow to hang out. You know, pizza, beer, and girl talk."

It sounded like the last thing I wanted to do, and Alec knew it. "Doesn't sound like my kind of fun," I said.

"What is fun for you? So you don't drink. Who cares? If you want to socialize with grownups, you'll have to be around people who do. I rarely drink, but it doesn't bother me if other people do. They're not going to get drunk. We all have to work the next day."

She had made a good point, so I racked my brain for a valid excuse but came up empty. "Fine," I said, "but do you have to invite Angela? I know she's part of your posse, but that girl doesn't know how to think before she opens her mouth."

"My posse? Really? But if you feel that way about Angela, why did you want her on the ID team?"

"She's good with the patients. She puts them at ease, and she has an endless supply of energy."

"You could use a dose of comic relief. Besides, I can't uninvite her."

Ignoring her comment, I said, "I'm too old to 'hang out.' I could be Angela's mother."

"Not quite, and no more excuses. It'll be good for you."

"I doubt that, but since you won't take no for an answer, I'll come. Just promise to leave me alone after this."

Alec jumped up and pinched my cheek. "No, I won't promise. You won't regret it."

I shook my head at her. She obviously didn't know me very well.

I had that familiar knot in my stomach for the following twenty-four hours. I tried to back out the next morning, but Alec wouldn't hear of it. I knew if I wanted to keep her as a friend, I had to go. She'd been great about not pushing me. I owed her.

I followed the directions she'd given me to her apartment. She lived in a popular, historic part of Richmond called Shockoe Slip. Her apartment building was a converted warehouse in Tobacco Row. I wouldn't have chosen to live there, but it was a nice area. It was too busy and trendy for my tastes.

I had bought my house in the suburbs five years earlier. It was easy to keep my anonymity there. I didn't know any of my neighbors, and I was invisible to them. I was sure Alec knew every one of her neighbors on a first-name basis.

I stood outside her door for a full three minutes before knocking. I could hear the women talking and laughing inside. I was tempted to turn and run, but then I'd have to explain to Alec the next day. I squared my shoulders, took a breath, and knocked.

"Grace is here!" I heard Alec shriek from inside.

Here we go, I thought. She opened the door and hugged me, something she'd never done. I wondered if she'd been drinking. I tried to smell her breath, but she rolled her eyes at me.

"Stop it," she said and pulled me into the room.

The other three stared at me in dead silence. They'd never seen me outside of work. They must have been thrilled when Alec had told them I was coming. Angela, the impetuous one, was the youngest in Alec's posse. She had fiery Italian eyes and a brilliant smile to match. The rest of us had made a game out of guessing what her hairstyle *du jour* would be. Kimberly and Caroline were both thick-haired blondes in their midtwenties, but their person-alities were polar opposites. Kimberly was independent and opin-ionated even though she always conceded to Alec, who was the clear leader. Caroline was reserved but confident. She had a much sweeter disposition than the other three.

"I wasn't sure what kind of pizza you like, so we got four kinds," Alec said to break the silence.

Four large pizzas sat on the counter. There was almost enough for each of us to have our own! "You know me. I love all Italian food. What have we got?" I followed Alec into the kitchen. The oth-ers relaxed and started talking again. I exhaled loudly, and Alec laughed.

"You work with these people every day. They aren't going to bite you," she whispered.

She handed me a plate and told me to get a soda. I obeyed and followed her back into the living room. Angela was sitting on the floor telling a story, mostly with her hands. She stopped for a sec-ond when I came in but went on after I sat next to Alec. Everyone laughed when she finished. I laughed too, even though I had no idea what she'd been talking about.

I took the chance to look around. Alec and I had always met on neutral territory, so we'd never been to each other's houses. Her apartment was contemporary and sophisticated but comfortable. It wasn't my style, but I liked it. It told me a lot about Alec too. Even though she'd rejected her pretentious parents, she'd learned the good parts from them too. She noticed me admiring the room and winked.

When I put my plate down, Caroline said, "How's Johnny doing? I've wanted to visit him, but my boss works me so hard that I never have time."

Angela gasped, and Caroline's face turned as red as the sauce on her pizza.

"That must stink," I said. "My boss is a sweetheart."

They all knew I was pretty much my own boss, so that got a laugh.

"Good one," Alec said and patted my back.

"Let me get this out from the start. We're not at work. I'm just Grace here. To answer your question, though, Caroline, Johnny's the same. Dr. Carter's baffled. It's been three months, but he still has no idea why Johnny hasn't come out of the coma."

We talked about Johnny for a few minutes before the conversation returned to normal small talk. Alec tried her best to include me in the conversation, but I wasn't making it easy. I answered their questions in as few words as possible and turned the conversation away from myself. That accomplished, I melted back into the sofa and listened. In one attempt, I said something about Dr. Emerson, and that got the attention off me.

Dr. Adam Emerson was an internal-medicine resident in his early thirties, just a few years older than Alec. He looked like a model for an outdoor magazine. He was a common topic of conversation with the nurses, and they constantly competed for his attention. Alec had confided in me that she loved his sense of humor and relaxed, easy manners, but she wasn't interested in a romantic relationship. She agreed that he was attractive, but she only wanted his friendship. That was hard to believe when her face lit up every time he walked into a room. I knew that if I brought him up, it would take the heat off me.

At the end of the night, Alec asked me to stay after the others had gone. She shut the door behind Caroline and turned to face me. "What was that?"

"What was what?" I asked, shrugging my shoulders.

"Don't play innocent. You know what I mean. I wanted this to be about you relaxing with everyone. You ended up making them more uncomfortable."

"Hey, I tried."

"Did you? Was that you trying?" She waved her arm toward the sofa for effect.

She was right. I regretted spoiling her plans. She didn't deserve it. "That wasn't fair to you. I'm sorry," I said. "I mean that, but I'm not like you. This is hard for me."

"Excuses," she said. "At some point this friendship has to go two ways. Right now, it feels pretty lopsided to me. Are you ever going to make an effort?"

"When you know me better, you'll understand," I said.

"You keep saying that, but how am I supposed to know you when you won't let me in?"

I looked at the floor, ashamed to meet her eyes. "Give me another chance. Now that the first time's out of the way, it'll be easier. Don't give up on me."

"I'm not, but you're making it tough."

I raised my eyes to hers. "I warned you."

"You weren't kidding," Alec said and smiled. "I know there's another you buried in there. I'd like to get to know her. It's time for you to get past whatever's standing in your way."

"I will. I promise. Soon."

Alec led me to the door and hugged me again. "I'm holding you to that," she said as I went out.

CHAPTER FOUR

Dr. Emerson was telling a story about his cousin's ex-husband when I walked into the staff lounge a week later.

"He'd been smacking my cousin around for years," he said. "One day, she'd had enough. She packed up their kids without a word and moved in with her brother's family. She called yesterday to tell me that her ex was arrested for slamming a crowbar over someone's head at the local raceway. He's nothing but filthy white trash."

"I think I dated that guy once," Angela said and everyone laughed, except me.

"At least you were smart enough to get away," Dr. Emerson said. "We all tried to stop my cousin from marrying him, but she was 'so in love.' Why do women always ignore the warning signs with losers like that?" He looked directly at me as he said it.

My uncle had leveled those words at me twenty-five years earlier.

I stepped back, trying to escape before anyone saw me. As I did, Caroline came up behind me. I bumped into her and sent her lunch tray crashing to the floor. The hit sent me off balance, and I fell, dropping my tray too. So much for getting away unnoticed.

I apologized to Caroline and started cleaning up the mess. Alec jumped up to help and tried to catch my eye. I avoided her, not ready for her to see what was there. When we finished, she cleared a chair and guided me to it.

"Are you all right, Ms. Ward? You look pale," Dr. Emerson said.

"I'm fine, and call me Grace."

"Grace, then. I'm Adam," he said. "Seriously, I think you're in shock." He knelt next to me and grabbed my wrist to take my pulse.

I pulled my arm away. "This is what I get for working with doctors. I'm fine. I just didn't see Caroline, and my blood sugar is low. I need to eat." Before he could say anything, I stuffed a bite of sandwich that I'd salvaged into my mouth.

Alec's eyes bored into me. She wasn't buying my story. I wolfed down the rest of my lunch and left without my tray. I had to get out before the interrogation started. I made it as far as the nurses' station when Alec grabbed my wrist and spun me around.

"Where do you think you're going?" she asked.

Even though she had eight inches on me, I wasn't about to let her push me around. I made myself as intimidating as my five feet allowed and said, "You work for me, remember? You can't talk to me like that. Let go of me."

I pulled my arm free and rubbed my wrist. We were in front of the nurses' station and every eye was on us: nurses', doctors', and patients'. For someone trying to avoid attention, I was doing a terrible job. I motioned for Alec to follow me into an empty patient room.

"I'm sorry. I forgot where we were. That was unprofessional."

I nodded and went on rubbing my wrist.

"Did I hurt you?" she asked, taking my arm to examine it.

"I'm fine. Forget it. I'm just being a baby," I said.

She squinted at my arm. "I don't see any redness or marks. I *am* sorry. I was just trying to catch you."

"I know. Like I said, forget it. Let's get back to work."

I reached for the door, but she put out her hand to block me. "Not until we talk. What happened back there? You don't have low blood sugar."

"What Adam said hit close to home, that's all. He caught me off guard."

"Because of your ex-husband, you mean?" Alec asked and crossed her arms.

I stared at her and wondered if everyone was reading my mind that day. "How do you know about him?"

"Just what I heard from old-timers who were here back in the day. Not much."

I leaned my head against the cool tile wall and closed my eyes.

"What happened to you? Why won't you tell me?"

In answer, I pulled the hair back from my forehead. "See these scars?" I asked and pointed to the web of white lines at my hairline.

Alec examined my face and nodded.

"I have more. I keep them hidden, but the physical scars aren't the worst ones. They've healed. The scars on the inside, the emotional ones, those are the hard ones to cover up. I can't hide them very well sometimes."

I slid to the floor and sighed. I was tired of hiding, tired of lying, tired of pretending.

Alec sat next to me and waited. When it got too quiet, she said, "Have you ever gotten help for it? You know, talked to anyone?"

"You mean therapy? Oh, I've had therapy. Andrew insisted on it, for all the good it did. I said what they wanted to hear until they declared me healed. The problem was, I didn't trust them, so I only told them half-truths. I couldn't allow them to have that kind of power over me."

I hoped my answer would satisfy Alec, and she'd let it drop, but that wasn't Alec's way. I should have known better.

"Then you did it wrong," she said. "Or maybe you had the wrong therapist, or maybe you needed a friend instead."

"Alec, I don't think there's a right or wrong way."

"Maybe, but either way, you're different, and I'm here. You're not leaving this room until you spill."

"It's not the time. We do have to get back to work," I said to deflect her.

"We have ten minutes left in our break, and you're the boss. You can tell everyone we were treating a patient. It's true, isn't it?"

I smiled. Alec had an easy way of getting to me.

"Fine. If it will get me free of your clutches, I'll tell you," I said with a lightheartedness I didn't feel. I wrapped my arms around myself and shivered, not from the cold, but from the ghosts that had haunted me for those endless years. I thought of Andrew's letters again and decided it was time to banish the ghosts.

"My ex-husband was abusive, but it didn't start there. My father abused me too. The first time was when I was four. He stepped on one of my blocks and took it out on me. When I was seven, he nearly killed me." I lifted my foot and said, "That's where I got my limp. It took months for me to walk again. He went to prison for attempted murder."

"Good Lord! Didn't anyone try to stop him?"

"Mama tried, but she was small like me, and he was a giant. At least that's how I saw him, like the evil giant from *Jack and the Beanstalk*. I have two older brothers. They tried to run interference too, but Pop swatted them away like gnats. I wouldn't have survived if he hadn't been stopped."

I held myself tighter as the darkness of that time enveloped me. Alec left the room without a word, but came back seconds later with a warm blanket. She wrapped it around me and sat on the end of the bed.

"Now someone's going to have to change that bed," I said.

Alec rolled her eyes and said, "Can't you stop being you for five minutes? I'll do it. What happened when your father went to prison? Please tell me your life got better."

I closed my eyes, wishing I could tell Alec that my life had been all butterflies and rainbows after Pop went to prison, but I would have been lying.

"For a while, until Mama died of cancer when I was ten. We lived with our grandparents after that, until they died within six months of each other when I was fifteen. My brothers had joined the army by then, so I had to go live with Mama's brother and his family. I hardly knew them. I was born and raised in Lincoln, Nebraska. They lived in Des Moines. I was torn away from my last connection with Mama."

I stopped, reliving the profound abandonment I had felt at the time.

Alec moved next to me on the floor and put her arm around my shoulder. "Didn't they want you?"

"Andrew and his wife tried to adopt me, but my uncle fought them. He thought I should be with blood relatives. I've fanaticized so many times about how my life would have turned out if I'd stayed with Andrew and Sarah."

"Don't live in the past. It only makes it worse," Alec said.

Before I could respond, the door flew open and Angela stepped through. "Here you are. We've been looking all over for you. Dr. Crawford wants you fifteen minutes ago. We have a protocol breach. Kimberly's been infected."

We followed Angela to Dr. Crawford's office. He was the chief physician on the ID team. On the way, she explained that Kimberly had spiked a high fever and was coughing. She also had a rash on her torso.

When we got to the office, Dr. Crawford was leaning against his desk with the rest of the staff crowded around him, all talking at once. He held up his hands and said, "Listen," to quiet everyone.

"I'm no happier about this than any of you, but there's nothing we can do, so we need to settle in and get to work. Grace, it's about time," he said when he saw me standing in the back. "Stay behind so I can fill you in. The rest of you have your assignments. Get going."

Everyone filed out. Dr. Crawford motioned for me to take a chair next to his desk.

"What's going on?" I asked.

"Where have you been? We've been looking for you for more than half an hour," Dr. Crawford asked.

"I was tending to a patient," I said, being deliberately vague.

He eyed me suspiciously but let it go and repeated what Angela had told us. It was the worst-case scenario we'd feared most on the ID team. Dr. Crawford leaned back and rubbed his temples. He was in his early fifties and the only member of the ID team who was older than I was. While he was a brilliant physician and skilled leader, he wasn't known for his patience. He didn't have much of a sense of humor either, kind of like the old me. In spite of that, he'd been the perfect choice to lead the project. Seeing him so concerned made my gut tighten.

"Why are you so sure this isn't a common influenza or something similar? I saw Kimberly when she came on this morning. She seemed fine," I said.

"Here's her chart," he said and handed it to me across the desk.

With one glance at the test results listed in the chart, I could see we were dealing with more than the flu. It was the exact situation we worked hard to prevent.

"I'm convinced it's viral, and it may be a flu strain," Dr. Crawford said. "If it is, it's a new one. I've never seen symptoms like these. I suspect it came from Mrs. Morrison in one twenty-one who was medevacked here from North Carolina three days ago. The pathologists haven't even had enough time to determine what the infection is. We're throwing everything we have at Kimberly and her, but they're both still deteriorating."

I was shocked by the short incubation period and quick contamination speed. "How did this happen? Kimberly knows the protocols as well as anyone."

"That's what I want you to find out, even though knowing won't change the situation. We're trying to ascertain how many were exposed to the zero patient before she came to us," he said.

"And how many Kimberly infected before she exhibited symptoms," I added.

"Exactly. There's still a chance we can contain this, but we need to prepare for a full outbreak. I've alerted NIH and the CDC. They're setting up a temporary center in Chapel Hill, and two other teams will be here tonight. For now, we're all under quarantine until further notice."

Even though I'd expected that, my heart sank. Patients and staff alike would be trapped at the hospital for who knew how long. Some of them had spouses or children waiting for them at home or expecting to be able to visit. For me, it meant I'd be barred from Johnny. He'd be alone. I'd promised to never leave him alone. I was frantic at the thought of getting sick, not for my own sake, but for his.

I pushed my thoughts aside and listened while Dr. Crawford reviewed the emergency protocols that we'd hoped never to implement. After that, I left his office and went in search of my nurses. We were already down by one. Nurses often become infected first since they spend the most time with the patients. If we lost any more, I didn't know what we'd do until the CDC team arrived. I revised the shift schedule and reviewed the emergency protocols with the nurses.

I asked Alec for an update on Kimberly. "Not good," she said. "Whatever this thing is, it hits fast. We're not sure if one twenty-one will make it. She's gone downhill since this morning."

"Don't call her that. She has a name," I said, snapping at her.

"Sorry. Margret Morrison might not make it," Alec said and held up her hands in surrender. "We're looking for similarities between the two patients."

All thoughts of my earlier conversation with Alec had vanished. I lifted my hands to rub my temples as Dr. Crawford had done, but stopped myself just in time. Face touching is the fastest way to spread disease. I dropped my hands, took a few slow breaths and said, "I'm sorry too, Alec. The pressure is getting to me already. I'm worried about Kimberly, and I can't stop thinking about Johnny. How did this happen on my watch? I've pounded the protocols into all of you."

"This just happens sometimes, in spite of everything we do."

"I won't accept that. We're here to prevent infectious disease spread, not contribute to it. I'm going to dig until I'm satisfied with an answer. In the meantime, please help me administer the antibiotics and antivirals to everyone. Let's pray this isn't some new resistant super bug."

⋙ ⋘

Twelve hours later, I was in my office going over my breach investigation notes, but I wasn't getting anywhere. It was my assigned time to sleep, but I hadn't been able to. The CDC and NIH teams had arrived four hours earlier and had taken another hour to set up. By then I was too keyed up to sleep.

An orderly named Tony, along with Patrick, one of my nurses, had already started showing symptoms. Patrick was the last one I'd expected to get sick. He was as meticulous as I was about the protocols, and he was as strong as an ox. I'd checked on him before going to my office. It had taken all his strength to lift his head off the pillow. If the infection could take him down like that, the rest of us were doomed.

43

The CDC team director told us to expect the quarantine to last at least three weeks. That was the best-case scenario. Three weeks. It felt like an eternity, but I knew it would likely last much longer. I pushed my notes to the side and laid my head on the desk. People I cared about were facing their own mortalities, and I couldn't stop worrying about Johnny. The nurses in the peds wing were getting irritated with my calling every two hours, but it comforted me to know they were taking care of him. Calling helped me feel closer to him.

I'd been at the hospital for over twenty-four hours and hadn't slept. I decided a shower might help. I filed my notes and headed for the locker room. I turned a corner to see Alec heading toward me.

"You're supposed to be sleeping. I went to your room looking for you," she said.

"I couldn't sleep, and why, if I'm supposed to be asleep, were you coming to bother me?"

"To tell you that Margret Morrison died."

Alec went blurry for a second, and I had to lean on the wall to keep from falling. "Who?" I asked.

Alec grabbed a chair and made me sit. I didn't resist. "The Zero Patient, from one twenty-one. I thought you'd want to know. Are you all right?"

"Oh, when?" I said, ignoring her question.

"Twenty minutes ago. They're doing the autopsy. You didn't answer my question."

"I'm just exhausted. I thought I'd have a better chance of falling asleep if I took a shower first." I stood, and my legs felt like cooked spaghetti.

Alec put her hands under my arms to stabilize me.

"Don't touch me. We're not supposed to touch," I said and pulled away.

"I'm more worried you cracking your head on the tile than getting germs on your scrubs. Are you getting sick?"

"You know I'd tell you if I had symptoms. The news about Margret Morrison shocked me I think. She went so fast. This is bad."

"We don't know enough yet to decide that. Let me walk you to the showers. Then I'm going to make Adam prescribe you a sedative. You have to keep your immune system strong."

"I know. I taught you that, remember?" I said. My legs were feeling stronger, so I took a few steps. "I'm fine. Let's go."

While we walked, I asked about Kimberly. Alec told me there wasn't any change. The fact that Kimberly was stable was good news. I was relieved, but it was early on. We had no idea what we were dealing with or how to treat it. I'd seen patients rally and then go downhill fast too many times to trust what was happening with Kimberly. I shook my head. Alec had been right. It was too soon to tell, and I couldn't let it defeat me. I had too much to lose.

A shower and a few hours of sleep were what I needed to clear my head. The next step was food. The last time I'd had more than a power bar was my abbreviated lunch the day before. I went to the meal-distribution area and grabbed a sack lunch. I could just make out members of the support staff on the other side of the heavy plastic curtains separating us. A gowned and masked woman gave me a wave and went back to work.

We were supposed to avoid congregating as much as possible, so I ate in my office. Being alone was never a problem for me, and I needed to go over charts. I turned my chair to look out the window while I ate. The sun streaming in felt nice, but all I could focus on was the people hurrying by a few feet away. They were free to come and go as they pleased. Even the woman who'd waved at me would be free to go home or to her hotel at the end of her shift. Thirty-six hours earlier, I'd been one of them. In a day, I'd become a prisoner whose only crime was the desire to help sick people.

I turned my chair back to my desk. I had to stop feeling sorry for myself and concentrate on helping those suffering much more than I was. I remembered Kimberly and my promise to fight. I had an obligation to those under my care. I had to protect those people outside my window and keep the infection from breaching the unit. Most importantly, I had to protect Johnny.

I put on a pair of gloves and opened the top chart on my desk. Before I could read it, Angela stuck her head in the door and said, "You'd better come."

Visions of the day before came to my mind, and my gut tightened again. I followed Angela to the nurses' station, where the on-duty staff circled around, talking in hushed tones. Alec was there even though she was supposed to be sleeping. She winked at me over her mask. When Dr. Bhandari cleared his throat, she turned her attention to him.

"Now that everyone's here, I need to update you on our situation," he said. "Dr. Crawford and Caroline are exhibiting symptoms, as well as two members of the CDC support team."

He stopped while we absorbed the implications of what he'd told us. Not only was the chief of the ID team down, but Caroline too. The CDC team members had only been there for twenty-four hours. That meant a lightning-fast incubation.

"Kimberly is stable, but Patrick and Tony are critical. Until further notice, I'll be acting chief of the unit. Dr. Emerson will be acting assistant chief. Admin is working on getting us additional help, and, of course, we have the CDC and NIH teams to rely on too. Any questions?"

No one spoke for a few seconds, but then Angela's hand shot up. I cringed at what she might say. I shouldn't have worried. The seriousness of our situation had sobered everyone, even Angela.

"Yes, Angela?" Dr. Bhandari said.

"Is anyone making progress on finding out what this is or how to treat it? We're like sitting ducks. I'm totally freaked out."

"Understandable, but the answer is yes, to a certain extent. The infection is a similar strain to *Streptococcus pneumoniae* but appears to be vaccine and antibiotic resistant. Even worse, it has manifested exclusively in our cases here as *sepsis bacteremia.* Each infected patient had been vaccinated, including Margret Morrison, who, by way of information, was a nurse who had recently traveled to Haiti with Doctors Without Borders. Amazingly, no one else from her group is ill, but a team is traveling there to investigate. Unfortunately, her husband is being treated in Chapel Hill, where they currently have seven confirmed cases, including Mr. Morrison."

When Dr. Bhandari finished, Adam reminded us that our only defense was strict adherence to protocols. "Our hope is that the infected patients were exposed before we were aware of it."

"How does that explain the CDC workers?" Alec asked.

"They could have been exposed before they got here. For now, our focus needs to be on stopping the spread instead of worrying about where it came from. We all need to be overvigilant, especially considering our extra workload, until more help gets here. Let's get back to work," Adam said.

I called Alec and Angela over to adjust our assignments. "I guess it's just us. I'll take Kimberly and Caroline myself. I'll get back to you in thirty minutes with your new assignments. Until then, split the other patients between you and get their vitals. I want up-to-the-minute info on them."

"How can the three of us take care of all these patients? I'm at the brink now. I don't think I can handle more," Angela said.

I was going to tell her to quit whining but stopped when I saw the look on her face. I must have looked just like that twelve hours earlier. I tried to reassure her with my eyes and said, "I know you're tired, and you've been working hard. This is only until we get reinforcements. After you take vitals, go catch an hour nap and eat something. Maybe we'll have more help by then."

She stared at me stone-faced for a few seconds before her face lit up. I could see her smile even behind her mask. That was the Angela I recognized. She nodded and headed off to carry out her assignments.

Alec eyed me and said, "She doesn't know how to handle a kinder, gentler Grace."

"Very funny. It worked, didn't it?"

"Yes, and what do you have in your bag of tricks for me?"

I searched her face for the signs of fatigue I'd seen in Angela, but they weren't there. "When was the last time you slept?" I asked, softening my tone.

"I slept some before they called us here. I'm taking care of myself. Don't worry. What choice do I have with Adam riding me?"

I raised an eyebrow at her. "Umm hmm, I'm sure he is."

"That's not what I meant. Wait, what did you mean?" she asked.

I just laughed and told her to get back to work. I could feel her glaring at me as I walked away.

CHAPTER FIVE

I found a puzzle buried in a cupboard behind some games and cards. I dumped it out on the lounge floor and started putting it together. After three weeks of reading lame books and watching the same TV shows, I needed something new to do. I'd always loved puzzles. They'd been a perfect way to escape the horror of my life when I was young. As I was finishing the frame, Alec came in and sat on the floor behind me and sighed.

"What's the matter?" I asked without stopping my work on the puzzle.

"Who says there's anything wrong?"

"The huge sigh gave it away." I put in the final corner and turned to face her. She was leaning against the wall with her arms wrapped around her knees. "Come on, spill," I said.

"You mean aside from the fact that Patrick, Tony, Dr. Crawford, and…" Her voice caught, and she took a few breaths before she said, "And Kimberly are dead? That's not even counting the seven other people not from the ID team. You mean, aside from the fact that we've been incarcerated for three weeks for no reason? Aside from the fact that they won't let us near the patients, so there's nothing to do? I feel like crawling out of my skin," she said and put her forehead on her knees.

Alec had been keeping me sane, so it was hard to hear her talk that way. I had nothing to say because she was right. I crawled to her and put my arm around her shoulder. We'd given up wearing the masks and gloves all the time since we were keeping to ourselves. The CDC director had decided to keep those of us first exposed away from the patients in case we carried the infection without symptoms. We thought it was overkill, because our blood work kept coming out clean.

Losing anyone from the ID had been painful, but losing Patrick and Kimberly had been devastating. We hadn't had time to grieve when they died, but being sidelined gave us nothing but time. Fortunately, Caroline was recovering. We put all our energy into making sure she survived. The mortality rate was running at 50 percent, but the number of overall cases was declining. The infection was weakening too, which helped, even though the pathologists hadn't found an effective treatment.

"It'll be over soon," I said. It became my mantra even though I didn't believe it myself. I hoped if I said it enough that it would become true.

"You keep telling yourself that," she said without lifting her head.

Adam came in and sat on the other side of Alec, laying his arm around her other shoulder. "What are we doing?" he asked.

"Feeling sorry for ourselves," Alec said.

"Now, none of that," he said. He got up and reached out his hands to help us up.

Alec smiled and obliged without hesitating.

I shook my head and crawled back to my puzzle.

"Let's help her," he said and sat across from me.

"I don't have the patience for puzzles, but I'll watch," Alec said. She lay down and put her head in Adam's lap. After a few minutes, she said, "You never finished telling me your life story. Tell us now. It'll help pass the time."

"This is the worst possible time," I said. "You feel bad enough already."

"Then how much worse can I get?" She caught my glance at Adam and said, "Don't worry about him. He already knows." When I glared at her, she shrugged and said, "I was bored. He's cool with it."

I stared down at the puzzle piece in my hand and thought, what the hell? Our lives had been turned upside down. Things from the past didn't matter much anymore. It seemed like a year had passed since my talk with Alec. I placed the puzzle piece and sat back against a chair.

"I told you about having to go live with my aunt and uncle in Des Moines. They're good enough people, but they weren't prepared to have me thrust upon them, even though that's what my uncle thought he wanted. I had my cousin Walt too. He looked out for me. Unfortunately, he was the one who introduced me to Danny Clemson. Walt couldn't have known. No one could have known."

My words trailed off as I relived the terror from that time in my life. I hadn't said his name in so long because I tried to convince myself he'd never existed.

"Who's Danny Clemson?" Adam asked.

I jumped at the sound of his voice. "Danny is my white-trash ex-husband," I said and smiled, reminding him of his comment in the staff lounge.

He chuckled and nodded.

"Now it all makes sense," Alec said.

"It's about time," I said. "Danny and I started dating when I was sixteen. He was a senior and the most popular boy in school. I was honored he chose me over all the other girls. It wasn't until later that I realized that, to him, I was the weakest member of the herd. Easy pickings."

"Men stink," Alec said. When Adam pretended to shove her off his lap, she said, "Present company excepted."

Adam put his arms down and motioned for me to go on. I wasn't sure I could. I stared at a print hanging on the wall above Adam's head to avoid his eyes.

"Danny raped me on prom night, and I got pregnant. He was furious and blamed me, like it was my fault. His dad forced Danny to marry me. In my naiveté, even after everything that had happened, I thought Danny loved me."

"Why didn't your aunt and uncle stop it?" Alec asked.

"They said I got what I deserved and that I had to take responsibility for my actions. I think they were just happy to be rid of me. I didn't care. It meant I could keep my baby. For the first time, I'd have someone I could love unconditionally who would love me back. Nothing else mattered. If I hadn't married Danny, I would've had to give the baby up for adoption. That's just what people did in my world."

"But you don't have a child, do you?" Adam asked.

The answer caught in my throat. I studied my shoelaces for several seconds before I said, "I miscarried six weeks after our shotgun wedding. Danny had gotten used to the idea of having a son by then, but I'd denied him that. The beatings started shortly after that. My life went on like that for four years and three more miscarriages, even though I tried to get away a few times. Danny always managed to get me and drag me back, saying I was his woman and belonged to him. With my fourth miscarriage, I had an emergency hysterectomy. I lost the chance of ever becoming a mother at the age of twenty-two."

Alec crawled over and wrapped her arms around me. "There aren't words," she said with her head on my shoulder.

Tears dropped onto her sweater, but I didn't cry. I couldn't cry anymore. I felt nothing. I gently pushed Alec up until I could see her eyes. "It was a long time ago," I said. "Don't cry for me. I have you, and I have Johnny. My life is full."

"How did you get here?" Adam asked.

"One night, Danny started in on me worse than ever, and something snapped. He had me pinned against the kitchen counter. I pulled an arm free and reached behind me. The cast iron skillet was there. I grabbed it and banged him over the head. He went down like a sack of bricks. I thought I'd killed him. Part of me hoped I had."

"Way to go, Grace!" Alec said softly.

"I make it sound like I was strong, but I was terrified and pretty beat up. I took Danny's emergency cash from behind the toilet tank, grabbed my few possessions, and got a taxi to the bus station. After I bought a ticket, I walked to the back of the bus and curled up on a seat. The other passengers stared, but no one offered to help. I leaned my bruised and bloodied forehead against the cool glass and let the darkness swallow me whole. It was the darkest and brightest moment of my life. I was free, but I had no idea how I'd survive."

Instinctively, my hand went to the scars on my face. While I stroked them, I closed my eyes, and the memories washed over me. I became that scared and battered young wife on the bus. When I opened my eyes, I searched my surroundings and remembered that I'd overcome all that. Even if I hadn't always done it right, I had conquered. Nothing would ever be as bad as that was.

"When I got to Richmond, I called Andrew, and he came to my rescue. He got me settled and helped me get my GED. He even insisted on paying for nursing school. Without him, I wouldn't have survived. Now you understand why I owe him everything. Losing him was devastating, but that was also when you and Johnny came into my life. I've wondered if he had something to do with that. Anyway, that's my story. You know the rest."

Alec stared at me like she was seeing me for the first time. I gave her a weak smile and squeezed her shoulder.

"You're an extraordinary woman," Adam said. "Most people wouldn't have survived that, let alone thrived like you have."

Alec sat up and said, "He's right. You're amazing. I would have crawled in a hole and waited for death. Compared to yours, my life feels frivolous and self-absorbed. I'm embarrassed for going on about myself that first time we had dinner."

"Don't say that. My tragedies don't diminish your trials. You did what you had to, and there were days when I wanted to crawl into a hole. Most days, in fact. That was twenty years ago, and I've only been truly coming to terms with it in the last few months. You deserve most of the credit for that. I don't know why I resisted telling you. I'm glad you know. Now we understand each other. I feel closer to you."

Adam cleared his throat, reminding us he was there.

"And you too," I said.

"Thanks for including me. I promise to keep what you've said a secret." He stood and stretched his legs. "But I need some sleep. I'll see you two later."

Alec's gaze followed Adam from the room. When she turned back and caught me watching her, she said, "Don't give me that look. There's nothing going on."

"Yes, so you keep saying."

"It's true. Stop it," she said and crossed her arms.

"I'm just teasing. He's a good man, Alec. You should go for it."

"We're just friends, and this would be the worst timing ever. Now, back to you. You can't drop a bombshell like that on me and expect me to let it go. I'm reeling. I have millions of questions."

I held up my hands to stop her. "Listen, Alec. I've told you all you need to know. It was a long time ago. You're the one who keeps telling me to let it go."

"Fair enough." She searched my eyes and said, "I was premature when I said everything made sense. Now it all makes sense, especially Johnny. It makes what you're doing for him even more noble."

"Anyone would have done the same thing, but it's not only about what I'm doing for him. It's what he's doing for me too. Being away from him is driving me crazy. I don't know how much longer I can take it."

"You sound like I did when I got here," Alec said.

I nodded and said, "I just came in here to do a puzzle. We'll all survive this," I said, "but Adam had the right idea. I'm going to bed."

Alec sighed. "If you're all going to abandon me, I guess I will too. See you at breakfast so we can get started doing nothing all over again."

⚜

I had no intention of sleeping when I got back to my room. All the talk about my past and Johnny got me too keyed up. The inactivity of the previous three weeks hadn't helped. I straightened up my room, read, and did some sit-ups. Nothing worked. What I wanted was to see Johnny. Three days after the quarantine started, I'd given up calling the pediatric ward several times a day. It hadn't been fair to take the nurses away from their work. I forced myself to only call once every twenty-four hours, but it wasn't enough. My arms still ached to hold my boy.

I was certain that I wouldn't get the infection. I was as frustrated with the CDC director and admin as Alec was. I knew it had to be Kinsley's doing since protecting his own self-interest was his guiding principle. He never cared how his decisions affected anyone, as long as his butt was covered.

I'd always been the good little girl who followed the rules. My father beat that into me. Obedience had been a matter of life or death for me, and Danny had picked up right where my father left off. I had become incapable of disobeying. Rules became my parents, and pleasing them consumed me. That behavior seeped into every aspect of my life, especially my work. I'd evolved since Johnny had come into my life though. I wasn't that scared little girl anymore. I was a mother who had to get to her son. I took a page from Kinsley's book and decided it was time to protect my own self-interest. I chucked the rule book and made my plan.

I took a long, sanitizing shower and put on sanitary scrubs. Next, I threw on fresh gloves, a mask, and a gown. It was late, so the halls were quiet. When I knew the nurses would be done with rounds, I walked confidently to the ID-unit entrance. Since the epidemic was slowing down, the guards had become lax. When they saw me in my mask and gown, they let me pass without question.

I was elated—and a little disturbed—that it had been so easy. I worried that adherence to protocol had softened in other areas of the hospital. No one paid the least bit of attention while I made my way to pediatrics on the opposite side of the hospital. I shouldn't have worried. A pediatric nurse named Rebecca Wilson swooped down like a vulture as soon as I set foot in her unit.

"What are you doing here? Aren't you still in quarantine?" she asked.

I was ready with the answer I'd rehearsed on the way over. "They notified us tonight that we'd be released in the morning. I decided to get an early start so I could visit Johnny. Don't worry. My blood test was clean today. The guards let me pass with no problem. How is he?"

I had to force myself to not rush and stay calm. I was anxious to see Johnny, but I didn't want to make her suspicious so she'd check my story.

My reputation as a stickler was in my favor. She stared at me for a few seconds before going to look up Johnny's chart. I took my first breath since I'd seen her and went to Johnny's room. There lay my sweet boy, as still as always. His hair had grown. I was tempted to brush a lock off his forehead, but stopped myself. I didn't want to touch or hold him until I changed my gloves and gown.

As I was pulling the gown around my shoulders, Rebecca came in to report on Johnny. "Not much has changed. He's put on some weight, so that's good. Here, I printed a copy for you." She reached out her ungloved hand for me to take the report.

After three weeks of hypervigilance, I was reluctant to take the report, but when I remembered where I was, I took it and thanked her. She left while I pretended to read it. The instant the door closed behind her, I threw the papers on a chair and ripped off my gown and gloves. I was grateful that I'd always insisted on having extra gowns in Johnny's room. Once I was wearing the clean ones, I ran to Johnny. I scooped him up and cuddled his warm body to my chest, careful not to let my tears drip onto his skin.

I stayed for an hour, rocking and singing to him. I explained why I'd been away and told him everything that had happened while we'd been apart. When it was time to go, I gently laid him back in his crib but then clung to the rail, reluctant to leave. When I finally tore myself away, I thought of the woman who had abandoned him in the ER. I remembered the anguish in her eyes at leaving him. I knew exactly how she'd felt.

No one spoke to me or even noticed me on my way back to the ID unit. I thought again that it had been too easy. I made plans to see Johnny the following night, going at a different time to avoid seeing the same guards or having to face Rebecca. I knew I wouldn't be able to keep up my nighttime escapes for long.

I discarded my mask and gown when I got back to my room and climbed into bed. My visit with Johnny had left me relaxed and calm for the first time since the quarantine had begun. I fell asleep to the memory of him resting in my arms.

⋇ ⋇

I woke two days later to Alec shaking my shoulders. When I opened my eyes, she said, "Wake up. What's gotten into you? It's nine. You never sleep this late."

I pushed the hair from my face and squinted at her, trying to make sense of what she was saying.

"If I didn't know you better, I'd say you were out tying one on last night." She threw her head back and laughed.

"Well, you're in a much better mood. Maybe you're the one who's been drinking. Why did you wake me up?"

"Great news. We've been paroled! We get to go home. They just told us." She did a dance of joy and told me to get up.

She didn't have to say it twice. I couldn't believe it. The story I told Rebecca had turned out to be true. I wondered if I had psychic powers. "I'm out of here," I said and started stuffing my things into a tote bag. "Is the quarantine over? Do we have to sign papers or anything?"

"No, the quarantine's still in effect. They're just letting us go. We can't come back to work until the quarantine is lifted and the CDC clears out. They're giving us paid leave. I'm going to take a trip. I've earned it."

"Not me. I'm going to spend every minute with Johnny to make up for lost time," I said, thrilled to be getting sprung from our quarantine prison.

"I get you wanting to see him, but I was hoping you'd come with me. Caroline's still too sick and Kimberly…" Her lips quivered, and she teared up. "How can I be celebrating when Kimberly's gone? What's wrong with me?"

I took her hand and led her to sit with me on the bed. "What would Kimberly have done if one of us had died? She wouldn't have sat around being miserable. She'd have gone out and done the things she enjoyed. She'd want you to do that."

"Or she'd have ignored it, pretending it wasn't real," Alec said and crossed her arms. "She was that way sometimes."

"Maybe, but that's not what I'm asking you to do. I don't have to tell you how unpredictable life is. Honor Kimberly by making the most of today. A wise friend recently said, '*Hic locus est ubi mors gaudet succurrere vitae.*'"

Alec gave a weak smile. "Way to throw my own advice back on me, but thank you. You may be right."

"Good. Now, about your trip. Why don't you invite Angela?"

"She's going to spend some time with her family to appease her mom. She's been going crazy."

"Take Adam then."

"Don't start that again," Alec said and rolled her eyes.

"If you're just friends, what's the harm?"

"I can't invite a man to go on a trip with me as friends. It'd be too weird. You'd never do that. I'll just go alone and have some me time or keep on trying to talk you into it."

I stood and picked up my bag. "Don't bother, but go and enjoy yourself, whatever you decide to do."

She nodded but didn't say anything as I rushed out to get back to Johnny.

CHAPTER SIX

I spent as much time with Johnny as I could for the following two days, but the time came to return to reality. I spent an hour with him on the third day before going home to clean my house, sort through piles of mail, and pay bills. The worst part was getting rid of the spoiled food in the fridge. After making a trip to the grocery store, I ate dinner in front of the TV, satisfied with what I'd accomplished. I was sore and grimy but grateful to be getting back into a routine.

A commercial with a woman soaking in a bubble bath came on while I was eating. The idea of a luxurious bath sounded perfect after three weeks of disinfection showers. The phone rang while I was filling the tub. The caller ID number was from pediatrics. I'd left word to contact me whenever Johnny showed any change, good or bad, but this was the first time they'd called. A woman whose voice I didn't recognize said, "Is this Grace Ward?"

"Yes, this is Grace," I said and sat on the edge of the tub.

"This is Karen Simmons. I'm filling in for Rebecca. She started running a high fever today and had to go into quarantine. I found the note to contact you with information about Johnny. He started running a fever too. He's in the ID unit. Do you want his last set of vitals?"

I hung up, turned off the water, and threw on clean clothes. I was in the waiting area outside the ID unit twenty minutes later. I called Alec on the way to meet me there. She lived much closer to the hospital and was waiting when I arrived.

"Why isn't he in the PICU? What have you found out?" I asked after giving her a hug.

"I'm so sorry. Johnny's infected. They got him over here with lightning speed. Maybe that'll give him a chance. They couldn't risk infecting the PICU. He'll get better attention here."

I dropped into a chair and put my head in my hands. Without looking up, I said, "He won't survive. He's susceptible to pneumonia under the best circumstances. Even Patrick couldn't fight it. How will Johnny?"

Alec sat next to me and said, "He's beaten the odds so far. Let's get more info before we start making predictions."

I nodded but not because I agreed with her. I knew it was the end for Johnny, and I blamed myself. From the moment I'd gotten the call, I knew I had to have been the one who'd exposed him. Not just Johnny. Rebecca's life was on my head too. Alec put her hand on my shoulder, but I shrugged it off, not deserving her comfort.

"What was that for? It's not my fault he's sick," she said.

"I'm not mad at you. I'm furious with myself. It's my fault."

"How? You didn't see him until they cleared you. You were clean."

I stood and grabbed Alec by the arm. "Come on. We need to talk," I said, and pulled her toward the exit.

"Let go of me." She freed her arm and straightened her sleeve. "Look. You stretched it out," she said and held out her sleeve to show me.

I ignored her and walked toward the parking lot to search for a clean strip of curb. Alec hesitated before sitting next to me.

While I searched for the words to tell her what I'd done, she said, "Did you drag me out here to admire the parking lot? Let's go in and find out what's going on."

I shrugged her off. I was struggling with whether I should tell her because it could put her at risk if word got out. My secret was tearing me apart, though, so I decided to tell her. She could always deny she knew if anyone asked her. I'd back her up so I wouldn't drag her down with me.

"I visited Johnny before they cleared us from quarantine."

Her eyes widened as I described my nighttime jaunts to pediatrics.

"I can't believe you did that. You, of all people. That's something Angela, or anyone else, would do. Never you. Why'd you risk it? You only had to wait a few more days."

"I didn't know—didn't know then that it would only be a few more days. The first time was the puzzle night. After our talk, I couldn't stop thinking about Johnny. I had to see him. Now he and Rebecca are going to die, and it's my fault. I killed them."

I put my face in my hands again and broke down. A car door closed near us, and I looked up. A man stood next to the car, staring at me.

"Keep your voice down. People might misunderstand," Alec said.

"So what?" I said through my tears. "I don't care what anyone thinks."

"You'll care if someone calls 911 to report the woman who just confessed to murder."

I glared at the man, and he scurried away.

"I still don't understand. You survived three weeks without seeing him. Didn't you stop to think that you could've infected him or risked losing your job, or worse, if they caught you? How'd you get away with it anyway?"

"No one even questioned me. Rebecca was suspicious at first. I thought she'd report me."

"See, right there. That should've been enough to stop you the next time," Alec said and shook her head. "It makes no sense."

I looked into her eyes, debating with myself whether or not to tell her the real reason. I knew she'd never understand if I didn't explain. I'd wanted to tell her since before the quarantine, but hadn't been sure if I could trust her. So much had changed in three short weeks. We were in a different life. Alec squirmed next to me, so I said, "I have something else to tell you, but you'll think I'm crazy."

"I already do," she said and winked. When I didn't respond, she said, "That was a joke."

"Oh, I know," I said, and shook my head. "It's about Johnny."

"What else? I'm not your father confessor, you know."

"You told me once that our friendship was lopsided because you didn't know anything about me. If I tell you, that will change. It's the final piece."

Alec rubbed her forehead. "I'm already wishing you'd kept your little escapades to yourself. I'll have to 'fess up if I'm questioned." When I nodded, she said, "But I get it about Johnny. You've always wanted a child. He fills that desire, that void, right?"

I raised my eyes to hers and said, "It's more."

"It can't be worse than what you just told me. I'm still here."

She was right. I'd worried about revealing my past and breaking quarantine to her, but it hadn't fazed her. With nothing to lose, I said, "It's not worse. It's different. I want to ask you a question first. Do you believe there's more to life than this?" I made a wide sweep with my arm toward the parking lot.

"Random question. What's wrong with you tonight?"

I laughed at her confusion. "Just answer."

She pulled her sweater sleeves over her hands and squinted while she considered what to say. "I wouldn't call myself spiritual. Our family went to church every Sunday when I was growing up, but it was mostly for show. You know, the family pew and all. For me, it was just something we did. I haven't gone to church much since I left home. It gives Mother another reason to be disappointed in me," she said and rolled her eyes. "I suppose I believe in a god of some kind. Life's got to have some purpose, right? I hope there's more than this." She waved her arm like I had. "I don't pretend to have the first clue what it is."

"I went to church when I was growing up too, but it held deep meaning for me. Before Pop went to prison, church was my safe place. He never went to church with us, so I was free for a few hours. It was more than that though. I loved the idea of a god on a cloud, watching out for me. I thought of him more as a magic prince who would sweep in to save me someday. Maybe he did, through Andrew."

I closed my eyes as the only happy memories from my childhood washed over me. I recalled sitting on the pew in my pretty dresses, swinging legs too short to reach the floor. I remembered the Bible stories in Sunday school. I loved them. They taught me there was good in the world, somewhere.

I sighed and said, "Danny beat those hopes and dreams out of me. After I left him, all I believed in was the here and now. Andrew tried hard to renew my faith. He failed. All I knew was that pain and disappointment lay down that road."

"Where's this going, and what's it got to do with Johnny?"

I stood and paced the sidewalk, searching for words to help her understand what I hardly understood myself.

"Grace," Alec said.

I jumped at the sound, and turned around.

She patted the curb next to her. "Come back."

I obeyed and sat down and then took a deep breath and said, "Do you remember the day you caught me crying by Johnny's crib?"

"I always will. It all changed for us that day."

I studied her face. "I didn't know you felt that way. I didn't ask you to be on the ID team for several more weeks."

Alec huffed and said, "You wouldn't have done that without what happened in the PICU. It was the first time I saw you as a person with emotions and not as some automaton."

I smiled before saying, "Not just our relationship changed that day. My entire life changed. There was the hurricane. I'd lost Andrew. I was alone and terrified, so I went to see Johnny, not even knowing if he'd survived the night. When I saw him, I reached into his crib, and he grasped my finger. That was when it got a little strange. I heard a voice say, 'This child needs you.' It was more than a thought. It was whispered words in my mind. I looked around to make sure no one was there. We were alone."

"So, you were hearing voices? There's a clinical term for that, you know," Alec said, only half joking.

"Alec, please. This is serious."

"I'm sorry. Go on," she said.

"My anxiety and grief cleared. I became calm. My life came into focus. I just knew. I knew my life had prepared me to rescue Johnny. His spirit cried out to me, as if he'd been waiting for me to come save him."

Alec got up and turned toward the door. "I'm cold. Let's go inside," she said with her back to me.

I stood and stepped in front of her.

"What're you doing?" she asked, still avoiding my eyes.

"Not letting you leave until you talk to me," I said.

"I'm just cold."

I stepped aside and motioned for her to go. She went in, but passed the row of chairs we'd used earlier. I followed, hoping that was what she wanted. Alec continued down the hallway toward my office and somehow convinced the guard to let us through. She held out her hand for my key when we reached my door. I dug it out of my purse and pressed it into her palm. When we got inside, I stopped to look around. I hadn't been there for several days. It felt foreign to me even though everything was where I'd left it.

Alec dropped onto the sofa. Still without looking at me, she said, "So you're saying that being abused by your father and Danny was necessary because Johnny would need you someday? That's crazy. Are you sure you didn't convince yourself that's what you heard? That's what you wanted, right? You were vulnerable because of Andrew's death."

Alec's reaction didn't surprise me. If it hadn't happened to me, I wouldn't have believed it either. I wanted to convince her, but it wouldn't have changed my conviction either way. I valued her friendship, but I valued the truth more. I sat down and took her hand, but she didn't look up.

"I spent twenty years angry at a god I wasn't sure existed. I got up every morning forcing myself to survive just one more day of my rotten life. Johnny changed everything. He gave me a reason to live, but it's not about me. Johnny deserves a chance. For some cosmic reason, he needs me."

Alec stared down at our clasped hands, so I couldn't gauge her reaction. I pulled my hand free and sat back, hoping she'd say something. When she didn't, I said, "Now I've screwed it up. The best I can do is be there for Johnny in his final days. I have to cope with the fact that I'm responsible for his death, but that doesn't change what I know. Does that make any sense?"

Alec looked up with tears glistening in her eyes. "Perfect sense," she said. "I'll need time to process this. For now, I'll have to trust you. I am sure of one thing, though. If God needed someone to love Johnny, he found the perfect person in you."

My voice caught when I said, "Thank you for that and for not thinking I'm insane. I warned you about becoming my friend."

Alec wiped her eyes and stood. "I should have listened. Enough of this, though. We have to get back to our reality. You're going to need me when this hits the fan. Even though I understand why you broke quarantine, it doesn't make it right. Aside from the fact that we could lose Johnny and Rebecca, they may have exposed others. You could be in serious trouble. Still think it was worth it?"

I would have given my life to take back what I'd done. I'd tried to rationalize that it had been an act of love, but it had been pure selfishness. My act could cost lives, including the one I loved most in the world.

"You know the answer," I said finally. "The first time I thumb my nose at the rules, I end up killing people."

"Stop that. They're both still alive. Let's make sure they stay that way."

I appreciated her optimism, but that hadn't worked with the people we'd already lost. "I'm going back to Johnny," I said. "No one but you and Rebecca know what I did. It won't take long for the truth to get out. Once Kinsley gets wind of it, he'll come after me with everything he's got. I'll stay with Johnny until then, but you need to go home. I appreciate your offer to help, but you need to distance yourself from me. I won't drag you down and have that on my conscience too."

"Then you shouldn't have told me. I'll be here to relieve you in the morning. You're going to need to keep your strength up for what's coming," she said.

"No, Alec, I mean it. Stay away."

"See you in the morning." She kissed my cheek and was out the door before I could protest.

⊷ ⊶

I convinced Johnny's doctor to let me put a recliner in his room. He agreed after I promised to stay masked and gowned and not touch Johnny. I dozed on and off during the night but gave up at six and climbed out of the chair when the nurse came in to take his vitals. His condition was critical, but it hadn't worsened. I honestly hadn't expected him to survive the night.

The nurse left after she cleaned and changed Johnny. I ached to hold him but refused to break my promise. I had learned my lesson about ignoring the rules. I sang to him instead, so he'd know I was by his side. My stomach growled an hour later, and I realized I hadn't eaten since six the night before. I was heading to the cafeteria when Alec came in.

"What are you doing here? And how'd you get in? I practically had to sell my soul to get them to let me stay last night," I said.

Alec didn't move, but her mask couldn't hide the anguish in her eyes.

"What is it?" I demanded.

"Rebecca didn't make it."

My legs gave out, but Alec caught me before I hit the floor. She helped me to the recliner and knelt beside me. "There's more. Kinsley sent me to find you. He wants to see you in his office. He wouldn't say why."

"Did he need to?" I leaned forward and put my head between my knees to fight off my rising panic.

"I'll tell him I couldn't find you. You're in no condition to face him," she said.

I sat up and said, "Thanks, but he'll know you were here, and you'd just be delaying the inevitable." I stood and grabbed the chair arm to get my balance. "I brought this on myself. What Kinsley has to dish out can't be worse than the punishment of knowing I'm responsible for Rebecca's death."

When Alec didn't argue, it was all the proof I needed. I left the room without looking back at Johnny.

⚔︎ ⚔︎

Kinsley's door was open. He was bent over some papers, so he didn't notice me in the doorway. He looked as hyena-ish as usual, but I detected a slight sense of glee in his demeanor. He raised his head and set his predator eyes on me.

"I see you got my message. Please, take a seat."

He'd never used the word *please* with me since the day we'd met. It was going to be worse than I thought.

"You've heard about Rebecca Wilson?" he asked.

He said the words as if he were asking about a change in hospital policy, not about the death of an employee. The fact that Rebecca's death hadn't affected him enraged me. I nodded, refusing to show him the loathing that seethed inside me.

"I know you're aware Baby John Doe is infected as well."

"Johnny," I said.

"Excuse me?" he said, looking directly at me over his reading glasses.

"I said Johnny. Call him Johnny."

He rolled his eyes and said, "Very well, Johnny's infected as well." Sarcasm dripped from his voice.

I had to grab my chair to keep from belting him in the nose.

When I didn't respond, he said, "The CDC director and I found it odd that the infection had jumped from the ID unit to pediatrics. Without much investigation, we discovered that you paid a visit to Johnny the night before being cleared from quarantine. Is that information correct?"

I nodded again, and his eyes lit up like he'd come upon a kill. I gripped the chair tighter.

"As you know, willfully breaking quarantine is a punishable offense. Pending completion of the investigation, you are hereby suspended. During that time, you are prohibited from setting foot on hospital grounds. In addition, Rebecca's family is pressing charges. You'll be hearing from their attorney. The hospital does not intend to defend you in this action. I suggest you find a good lawyer. Now, please clean out your office and vacate the premises."

I left Kinsley's office without a word. Arguing or fighting for myself was pointless. That one action had wiped out twenty years of faithful service to the hospital. My nursing career wasn't the only casualty. I'd destroyed my entire life. I made my way to the ID unit to say good-bye to Johnny, knowing that even if he lived, I'd never see him again.

━◁⊹ ⊹▷━

After I put on my mask and gown, I reached for the sign-in sheet before putting on my gloves. As I did, one of the guards who'd let me pass without a word the night I'd gone to Johnny's room stepped up, blocking my path.

"Can I help you, ma'am?" he asked.

"I'm going to visit Johnny," I said, fighting to keep my composure.

"I have orders not to allow you in." He moved closer and squared his shoulders. I wondered if he expected me to fight him. He was at least six-four and had shoulders that filled a doorway.

I took a step back and said, "I'm only going in to say good-bye. I'll just be a minute."

"I'm sorry, ma'am, but you're not going in."

I couldn't believe he was the same man I'd greeted almost every morning for the past month. I'd even brought him snacks a few times. One word from Kinsley, and he was treating me like a criminal. Even if Kinsley's actions were justified, I wasn't going to let him keep me from Johnny. I smiled at the guard and slipped into my kind mother persona. "No one is around to see. I won't even sign the sheet. I'll be in and out in two minutes."

I might as well have been talking to a wall. He stood at attention and stared at something beyond me. Refusing to leave without seeing Johnny, I swallowed my pride and resorted to my last desperate weapon. I dropped to my knees and began sobbing. It wasn't only a trick. The impact of Kinsley's sentence had finally hit me. When I could get the words out, I begged the guard to let me in to Johnny. He stood stone-faced, ignoring me.

I tried to find the strength to stand, but before I could, I felt a tug on my elbow. I looked up to see Alec and Adam standing over me. Alec pulled me to my feet and wrapped her arms around me. Adam asked the guard what was going on. After he explained, Alec released me, and she and Adam each took an arm to lead me away. I struggled to get free, but I was no match for them.

They took me to my office. Adam made an excuse to get away and left us alone. Alec pulled me toward the sofa, but I pulled my arm free and went to my desk. I leaned over it with my palms flat on the surface for support.

Alec waited for a full two minutes before speaking. "What's going on? Adam and I went to see Kinsley but didn't get anything out of him. I figured you would have gone back to Johnny."

Without turning, I said, "You don't have to stay. I'm fine now."

"Yeah, you look fine, and that's not going to work."

If I spoke the words, the nightmare would become real. I was terrified that I'd break down and never come back. I'd lost everything, and for the first time in my life, I had no one else to blame. I was back on that bus to Richmond, but I'd created the darkness consuming me. No Andrew would be there to rescue me at the end.

Alec got up and leaned on the corner of the desk. When she put her hand on my shoulder, I flinched, but she didn't move her hand. "Tell me what happened so I can help fix this. Maybe it's not as bad as it seems."

"Really, Alec? Is that how your world works? We talk it out, you say some kind words, and it's all better? Will that bring Rebecca back? Will that cure Johnny? Will it keep Kinsley from suspending me, or Rebecca's family from pressing charges? You think you have all the answers. This time you're just wrong. Nothing will make it better."

Alec stood and took a few deep breaths. "I may not have all the answers," she said softly, "but I can still care about you. Who else do you have? Why do you insist on pushing me away after all we've been through?

"I guess it's just classic Grace," I said.

"Fine, go ahead and try to drive me away. Crawl back to your miserable old life. I'll be here when you've figured out you've come too far to creep back into your hole."

The only sound was the tapping of my tears on the desk blotter. I heard a rustle and the squeak of door hinges ten seconds later. I fought the urge to go after her; severing our tie was right. She'd see that in time. I took my purse and the picture of Andrew from my desk. I left the rest for Kinsley to deal with.

CHAPTER SEVEN

My trip to the store the day before my suspension saved me from having to leave the house for a week. Without a reason to get up, I stayed in bed watching mindless TV and avoiding the news. I was afraid I'd see something about myself, or worse, about Johnny. Instead, I escaped into a fictional world where the reality outside my walls didn't exist.

I had no need to consider my future. I had twenty years' worth of savings in the bank. My old solitary lifestyle had meant no nights at the movies or trips to coffee shops with friends. There hadn't been parties, vacations, or birthday gifts to buy. I estimated that I had enough to live on for a year. I certainly had enough to live on until I went to jail.

Alec called and left several messages during that time, but I didn't bother to check them. I was afraid those would be about Johnny too. If I avoided the truth, Johnny could go on living exactly as he had been the last time I saw him. The lawyer for Rebecca's family called too. I ignored those too. If they wanted me, they knew where to find me.

The need for food finally forced me out of the house the following week. I went to the warehouse store first and stocked up on boxed dinners and canned goods. After that, I went to the grocery store for the few perishables I needed. When I had enough food to last a month, I went home to start the long chore of putting it away.

Alec's car was parked in my driveway when I drove up. I was tempted to keep driving and wait for her to leave, but I decided it was better to face her and convince her to forget about me. When I pulled into the garage, she got out of the car and followed me in. I started carrying my groceries into the house. She joined me without a word.

When the last of the perishables were in the fridge, she leaned against the counter and crossed her arms. "Why did you let me in if you aren't going to talk to me?" I didn't answer, so she said, "I'm relieved to see you didn't do yourself in. Looks like you're preparing for the zombie apocalypse."

I bit my cheek to keep from smiling. Alec always knew how to get to me, no matter how dire the situation. To shut her up, I said, "I'm glad you're here. I was going to call you today and tell you, again, to leave me alone. I appreciate all you've done. I do. You've been an amazing friend, but that's over. Find a new pet project. There's nothing you can do for me now."

"Nice speech, but wrong on most counts, except that I've been an amazing friend." She smiled at me and winked, and I wondered how she could be so glib given what I was facing. Before I could say that, she said, "Aren't you going to ask about Johnny?"

I went to the living room and sank into my favorite chair. I covered my face with my hands because I couldn't bear to look at her. Hearing Johnny's name had undermined my show of indifference. "Don't tell me," I said. "Dealing with Rebecca's death is too much. Having Johnny's death on my hands will kill me."

"All right, I won't tell you he died, because he didn't. He's recovering. He'll be back in his old room in pediatrics in a few days."

I lowered my hands and stared at her. She wasn't cruel enough to joke about Johnny. My brain struggled to process what she'd said. My subconscious was already grieving for Johnny.

"But how?" I stammered. "He couldn't have survived."

Alec smiled wider and said, "The epidemiologists are theorizing that roughly thirty percent of the population has a natural immunity. That doesn't mean people in that category can't get sick, but they have a far greater chance for survival. That's probably why you, Angela, and I didn't get sick. Johnny's an extraordinary little guy. A miracle really, if you believe in that kind of thing."

She winked again, and I couldn't hold back my tears. I hadn't killed Johnny. No matter what happened, he still had a chance at life, even if I wouldn't be a part of it. I wiped my face with the back of my hand and said, "It *is* a miracle. It doesn't solve my other problems, but knowing makes all the difference."

Alec took my hand and said, "I get why you've been acting crazy. You shouldn't have been dealing with it alone."

I pulled my hand away. "This doesn't change what I said earlier. The only thing you can do is promise to take care of Johnny."

"I already am, but soon, you'll be doing that yourself. That's the other reason I'm here."

"Alec, I don't know what you think you know, but I'm finished at the hospital, and I'm probably going to jail. Don't fool yourself into thinking that won't happen. Rebecca is dead, and it's my fault. No one can change that." The smug look on Alec's face made me want to shake her. "Are you listening to me?"

"Every word. How can you say I'm the one who thinks she has all the answers? Things have happened in the past week. If you'll shut up for two seconds, I'll tell you."

It was my turn to cross my arms. I tried to match her smugness, but my curiosity was piqued. "I'll listen, but then will you promise to go and not come back?"

"No," she said without hesitation. When I rolled my eyes, she rubbed her hands together and said, "Adam badgered Kinsley until he told him what was going on. Adam can be as obnoxious as I am when he wants to be."

"Oh, great. There are two of you," I said.

"Funny. Listen. When Adam was leaving Kinsley's office, Kinsley said that you'd better get a good lawyer. It reminded Adam of his friend named Paul Pierno, who's a lawyer here in Richmond. They were undergrads together. He's adorable by the way. If you were ten years younger and he wasn't married, I'd fix you two up."

"Glad I'm not and he is, then. Why are you telling me this?"

"Adam and I went to see him about your situation. He said there isn't much you can do about the fact that you broke quarantine, but he and Adam looked into the regs. He says you can appeal to the board if Kinsley fires you. Given your hospital service record, you might get off with a fine and a slap on the wrist. You'd probably lose your position on the ID team too."

"I killed Rebecca, Alec. None of that's going to matter when I'm in jail."

"It wasn't you. Adam talked Paul into investigating at the hospital. You're not going to believe what they found."

Nothing could absolve me of Rebecca's death, but I was willing to hear her out since Paul and Adam had gone to so much trouble.

"Four days before you broke quarantine, a child with cystic fibrosis was admitted. His room was three doors from Johnny's. His condition deteriorated rapidly, so they transferred him to the PICU. No one suspected that his symptoms were anything but CF. Poor little guy passed away three days later. The results from that morning's blood test came minutes after his death, positive for *Streptococcus pneumoniae*. This happened before you went to see Johnny. Two PICU staff members are in the ID unit. CDC considers that as the source of the new cases, not you."

"But how did the boy get sick?" I asked. My mind was reeling. How could Kinsley not have known when he suspended me? I kicked myself for not answering Alec's calls. I could have saved myself a week of anguish.

"Paul wants to meet with you tomorrow to go into the details. He needs you to sign papers. He needs the information on the attorney for Rebecca's family too. He says that from now on, you need to pass them off to him whenever they contact you. Don't discuss anything with them."

I went to the answering machine on the kitchen counter and pushed the play button. Alec raised an eyebrow when I skipped through all the messages from her. I wrote down the attorney's information and stuffed the note into my purse.

"What time does Paul want me there?" I asked.

Alec took a business card from her pocket and handed it to me. "Call first thing in the morning. He's not in court tomorrow, so he'll rearrange his schedule to make time for you. Tell his receptionist who you are. She'll put you through to Paul."

I nodded but didn't say anything. I studied my empty calendar hanging on the far wall, too ashamed to meet Alec's eyes. She, Adam, and even Paul were sacrificing their time, and maybe their reputations, to offer me a gift I didn't deserve. Who was I that they were willing to help me?

"Grace," Alec said, and I flinched. When I looked at her, she said, "Please tell me you're going to call Paul."

"I will if you help me understand why you're all taking this risk for me. My problems don't involve you."

"Don't involve us? You're our friend. Anything that happens to you involves us. We care about you because you're worth caring about."

Her answer touched me even though the last thing I felt was worthy of their help.

"You'd do the same for us."

"I hope I would," I said softly.

"What you've done for Johnny proves you would," Alec said. "Whatever the reason, just accept what we're offering with grace."

"Clever," I said and smiled at her. "I'm not sure I know how, Alec."

"Start with 'thank you.'"

"Thank you," I whispered, but the words caught in my throat.

She hugged me in true Alec fashion. It was the perfect reply.

❧ ❧

I met with Paul the following day. I was almost late for my appointment. His office was downtown, and I'd forgotten how hard it was to find parking. I relented and pulled into an expensive parking garage. The price was worth it to be on time.

I walked the half block to Paul's office building. The décor was elegant, with marble floors and leather furniture, definitely out of my price range. I hoped the appointment wouldn't be a waste of time for both of us.

The receptionist took me to Paul's office without making me wait in the lobby. Alec had been right about him. He was adorable, although stunning would've been more accurate. From his last name, I guessed he was Italian. If he and Angela ever had a baby, it would be the most gorgeous child on earth. His eyes were blue instead of dark-chocolate brown like hers. It was striking with his dark coloring.

He greeted me with a confident handshake and a warm, honest smile. He smiled a lot. I trusted him in seconds, which was rare for me. After introductions, he got down to business. "I'm sorry, but we'll have to make this short. I have an appointment in fifteen minutes. We'll schedule to meet later this week so we can go into more detail."

"Don't apologize. You don't owe me anything. Can I ask why you're doing this? It's clear you don't need my business."

"It started out as a favor to Adam, but when he told me that you had taken precautions before visiting Johnny and that your blood tests had all come out clean, I was curious. I wanted to find the source of the infection. By the way, Kinsley isn't cooperating. He sure has it out for you. What happened between you two?"

"Long story for another time," I said and glanced away.

"I think we need to talk about it now. Your relationship will have a bearing on his decision. You're facing anything from a warning to a dismissal. If he tries to fire you, I'd advise you to appeal, based on what you tell me," Paul said.

"Can we discuss your fees first?" I asked and looked down at my clasped hands. "I have money put away that I can use to pay you, but I don't even know your rates. I'm not sure I can afford you."

Paul smiled and leaned back in his chair. "Don't worry about that. Adam and I are working out a deal. I owe him."

His cryptic answer made me wonder what he owed Adam. I tucked it away in the back of my mind to ask Alec later.

"In that case, I'll tell you about Kinsley," I said. "He and I have this long-standing war of wills. He resents that I don't kowtow to every one of his cost-cutting policy demands, most of which ignore patients' best interests."

"Is this more than a difference in perspective and differing responsibilities? You're in the trenches with the patients every day. Does that make it hard to see the big picture?" Paul asked.

"No. It's more than that. A hospital is a business—I get that—but Kinsley is heartless and maybe even a little dangerous. There's something about him I don't trust. In reaction to my behavior and attitude toward him, he does whatever he can to make my life difficult, which is why it made no sense that he chose me to head the ID unit. Maybe he thought I'd fail and that would give him a chance to get rid of me. If so, his plan succeeded," I said.

"I'm not criticizing you. I just needed to be clear on your relationship," Paul said and smiled reassuringly.

"I appreciate that. What happens now?" I asked.

Paul rummaged through sloppy stacks of paper that covered his desk. I wondered how he ever found anything.

"I can't think unless my desk is tidy," I said. "I've never understood how people function with an unorganized workspace."

"There's actually a method to my chaos," he said and handed me the forms he pulled from the pile. "I need you to sign these if you'd like me to represent you. I'm not pressuring you into this. You're free to seek other representation."

I snatched a pen from his desk and started signing before the words were out of his mouth.

When I handed the papers back, he smiled and said, "I'll call the Wilsons' lawyer before the end of the day. I'm not sure if they're aware of the new information. The family has pressed charges, but the commonwealth's attorney is still deciding if there's enough evidence to go forward. I'll turn my evidence over to him. I'm anticipating they'll drop the charges."

"And the civil suit?" I asked.

"Civil suits normally come later. If they drop the criminal charges, there won't be a civil suit. All you need to worry about right now is Kinsley. He'll make his decision soon. Once he does, we'll go from there."

I gave him a weak smile and toyed with a stray thread on my sleeve to avoid his eyes.

"You don't look like someone who's just received great news," he said.

"I appreciate what you're doing for me. It's not that. It's just that this all turned out nice and tidy for me, all tied up in a bow. People died. Loved ones who were left behind won't ever be the same. Soon I'll go on with my life, the same as before. I'm grateful, but it doesn't seem right. A few days ago, I was certain that I'd be going to jail for killing Rebecca and Johnny. Now the worst that could happen is I'll have to find a new job."

Paul leaned back and eyed me for several seconds. When I squirmed under his scrutiny, he said, "That first night, when you broke quarantine to see Johnny, did you think about what would happen if you were caught?"

I searched my memories of that night. I'd planned my actions but hadn't given the consequences much thought. "I guess on some level I knew that, at worst, I'd be fired."

"Were you worried about infecting Johnny or anyone else?"

I didn't have to think about that answer. "No. Absolutely not. You can't ever say a hundred percent, but I wouldn't have gone if I thought it would put Johnny in danger."

"Adam and Alec explained your relationship with Johnny to me. They said what you just told me too. I'm saddened by the lost lives too, but how do their deaths differ from past patients you've lost?"

I considered his question and shrugged. There was no difference, but it didn't feel that way.

"You broke the rules and you feel guilty, as you should, but you're not responsible for these deaths. You didn't cause them. You couldn't stop them. It's all happened so fast. Give it a few days." He stood and walked around the desk. "My next appointment is probably here. Set another appointment on your way out. In the meantime, cut yourself some slack. This will all work out."

I nodded and thanked him again. I thought about what he'd said on the way to my car. Logic told me he was right, but it would take time for my heart to believe it.

⇒+ +⇐

After viewing Paul's evidence, the commonwealth's attorney didn't press charges. The Wilsons were reluctant to accept the decision. When I met with Paul a few days later, he told me it was because they were grieving and wanted someone to blame. I felt for them and wished I could ease their grief, but I knew nothing but time would do that.

I didn't have time to dwell on it, because Kinsley wanted me in his office the following day. I didn't bother trying to sleep that night. The Hyena had my future in his hands. It was enough to give anyone insomnia.

⇒⊢ ⊣⇐

Kinsley stared at me over his desk with the tips of his fingers pressed together. If he was trying to intimidate me, it worked. I would have preferred to face a jury. I had too much at stake to let him get the best of me though, so I refused to look away.

We glared at each other for several more seconds until he said, "While I'm relieved that you weren't the cause of Rebecca Wilson's death or any of the deaths that followed, that doesn't make what you did any less egregious."

Sure you're relieved, I thought. He would have loved nothing more than to see me go to prison for involuntary manslaughter. In spite of that, I said, "I agree."

It was obviously the last thing he expected. He sputtered a few incoherent words before saying, "You agree?"

"Yes, I agree. What I did was unconscionable. I did it out of my own selfish desire to see Johnny. I was as certain as I could have been that I wouldn't infect him or anyone else. I wouldn't have risked going to see him otherwise."

Kinsley opened he mouth to say something, but I held up my hand to stop him. "Not that I'm making excuses. What I did was wrong, and I'm truly sorry."

I reveled in the satisfaction of throwing the Hyena off his game. He shuffled through the papers on his desk as if searching for his next words. I'm sure he expected me to be groveling at his feet by that point. He picked up the stack of papers and tapped them on the desk to straighten them, and then slowly laid the stack back on the desk.

He pressed his fingers back together, and said, "Your agreement makes what I'm going to say much easier. Breaking quarantine would be a serious offense by any employee, but from the head nurse on the ID team, it's inexcusable. Therefore, your employment at this hospital is terminated." He stood and pulled the top few sheets of paper from the pile.

I willed my hand to stop shaking as I reached up when he held them out to me across the desk.

"You have the right to appeal my decision. Instructions on how to do so are included in the papers I just gave you. Once you leave this office, you'll be a private citizen. That means I can't prevent you from visiting Baby John Doe, but I hope you'll see that doing so will tarnish the reputation of this institution. Now, if you agree to this action, please sign on the line indicated on the top sheet."

Part of me wanted to sign so I'd never have to see that despicable man again, but I wasn't ready to abandon my life at the hospital. Accepting Kinsley's decision would also make it nearly impossible for me to get another job in Richmond, maybe even Virginia. Paul had recommended that I appeal. He said there were several steps between a slap on the wrist and dismissal. I realized that I had nothing to lose with an appeal. If I lost, the result would be the same.

I stood and shoved the paper into Kinsley's chest. "I do not agree with this action. I agree that I should be punished, but not fired. I've given twenty years of my life to this hospital without a single infraction. How many other employees do you have that can say that? So I'm appealing your decision. See you at the board hearing, Kinsley, and you enjoy the rest of your day."

My heart pounded so violently as I made my dramatic exit that I was sure Kinsley would notice, but it was the first time since the quarantine that I felt like the old Grace again.

⊨≒+ +≒⊨

The wheels of hospital bureaucracy turned much slower than I wanted. It took three weeks for the board to schedule my hearing. Since I wasn't allowed to work, I spent as much time I could with Johnny. During that time, he'd been moved from the ID unit to the PICU and finally back to his room in the pediatric ward. Seeing him back in his room with his block quilt was such a comfort to me. It was my first glimmer of hope that life might return to normal.

I spent my evenings during that time researching Johnny's condition. I started in the university's library but didn't find much that helped. After that, I scoured medical journals and online medical message boards. The last step was checking all the latest studies related to traumatic brain injuries in babies. None of it was encouraging. Traumatic brain injuries were still somewhat of a mystery, even with all the latest diagnostic tools. Johnny's case was even more difficult because of the circumstances.

By the time I exhausted all my resources, the three weeks had passed, and it was time for the hearing. I met with Paul a few times for prep work, but mostly he reminded me that it wasn't a trial, just a hearing with the board. That did little to calm my fears.

Since the hearing was a personnel issue and not a medical one, no one was allowed to come in with me for moral support, but Alec and Adam showed up to wait outside the boardroom during the hearing. Paul was allowed to attend but couldn't offer counsel or make statements. He was mainly there to make sure the procedure was conducted properly.

When the receptionist came to tell me it was time to go in, I was much calmer than I thought I'd be. I knew Kinsley would be present, but I doubted he'd have much to add. I'd admitted my guilt, so the hearing was more about what my punishment would be.

Paul sat next to me at the end of the long oval table. I recognized some of the board members from fundraisers and special events. I was relieved to see the two female members there. They both had children, and I hoped their maternal instincts would make them more sympathetic to my situation.

Kinsley was near the head of the table. I assumed he'd arrived early to make himself look more important than he was. He looked at me stone-faced, but I could feel him thinking a sneer.

The chairperson cleared his throat to start the hearing. I directed my attention to him, glad to get my focus off Kinsley.

"Ms. Ward," the chairperson said, "to begin, we'd like to thank you for cooperating during the investigation."

I nodded but remained quiet and wondered what choice I'd had but to cooperate.

"Each of us has had a chance to read your appeal statement, and we've come to a decision. Before we continue, is there anything you'd like to add to your statement?"

I nodded and stood. "Thank you for allowing me this hearing, sir. I do have something to add. As I've admitted throughout this process, I take full responsibility for what I've done, and I make no excuses. My actions were reckless and could have put lives in danger. All I want to add is that I acted out of deep concern for Johnny. I've come to care for him like a son."

I stopped to let that sink in and gauge their reactions. A few raised their eyebrows, and one man shifted in his seat, but that was it. Encouraged, I said, "I know it makes no sense that I would endanger him, but I took every possible precaution before going to his room. I made a promise to him that I'd never leave him alone. I had to keep my promise."

I expected Kinsley to pipe up at that point, but he sat like a statue staring at the wall on the opposite end of the room.

The board member who had squirmed said, "Ms. Ward, what difference would it have made to the child if you made a promise? He's too young to understand, and he's in a coma."

"You're right," I said. "He may not understand, and it might not matter to him, but it matters to me. He's alone in the world.

He needs me to look out for his best interests. If not for that, I never would have broken quarantine." I squared my shoulders and looked the chairperson in the eye before I added, "My spotless twenty-year record is a testament to that. I have nothing more to add."

"Fine, Ms. Ward. In light of your statement and the evidence in this matter, we've concluded that you may continue in your employment here."

I'd been so sure they were going to fire me that I could only stare in stunned silence.

When I didn't respond, he said, "There are stipulations to your continued employment, however. The first is that, for obvious reasons, your involvement with the ID unit is terminated, and there will be a permanent notation in your file. You'll return to internal medicine as a floor nurse. When the current internal-medicine charge nurse goes on maternity leave in three months, you'll return to that post. She'll be given a position of equal responsibility in another department upon her return. We'll consider the intervening three months as a probationary period. If there are no further infractions, you'll resume your former position. Mr. Kinsley was notified of our decision prior to this hearing and has agreed to comply. I hope that this matter is concluded to everyone's satisfaction."

I couldn't believe what he was saying. I'd thought that on the slim chance they decided not to fire me, they'd have me stocking supply cabinets. Instead, I was going back to my old job in just three months. Tears welled up, but I fought them back.

"Thank you all," I said and looked at each of the board members. "I can't express how grateful I am, and I promise that nothing like this will ever happen again."

As the words came out of my mouth, my eyes landed on Kinsley. His expression hadn't changed, but his face was redder, and a vein throbbed on his forehead. It was one of the best moments of my life. I could only imagine how he'd reacted when the board had given him the news. He'd come so close to getting rid of me. I only hoped he wouldn't try to find new ways to make my life miserable. I decided to tuck that thought away for later. I had won, and, for the moment, I was going to enjoy my victory.

I stood, and everyone at the table followed. I shook each of their hands and thanked them again before I practically ran out of the room. Adam and Alec stood when Paul and I came out of the boardroom.

"Well?" Alec asked.

I answered by smiling and throwing my arms open for a hug. Alec ran at me, nearly knocking me over. When I broke free from her, I explained the board's decision and said, "I'm relieved and grateful, but I still I don't feel like I deserve it. I broke a big rule. They had every right to fire me."

"Stop torturing yourself. One bad decision doesn't wipe away a brilliant career," Alec said.

"She's right," Paul said. "Trust me; these corporate boards always err on the side of caution. They wouldn't have kept you on if they thought you were a risk."

"I appreciate that, Paul, but with Kinsley going against me, I was sure I was gone."

"Kinsley's their puppet. They see him for what he is, which is probably why they hired him," Adam said. "That doesn't mean they feel the same way about you."

"Forget Kinsley. Let's just go enjoy this," Alec said.

I nodded. The board's decision meant more than keeping my job. It also meant I'd have access to Johnny that I'd have been denied if they'd fired me.

"You win, Alec. I'll let it go. Let's get brunch to celebrate, on me," I said.

"I have to be in court, but I'll take a rain check," Paul said.

"I'm going to hold you to that since you won't let me pay you. It's the least I can do. I can thank you though. Seriously, thank you, all of you."

"You're welcome," Alec said. "Enough of that. If I remember, there was talk of brunch."

Alec linked her arm through mine and pulled me forward. As we passed the open boardroom door, I saw Kinsley closing his briefcase. He caught my eye and stared me down with glacial contempt. I shivered and turned away. Even though I'd promised Alec to put the incident behind me, I'd thrown down the gauntlet for Kinsley. Our battle was far from over.

CHAPTER EIGHT

I was rubbing lotion on Johnny's legs when Alec found me in his room three weeks later. I was doing everything I could to keep Johnny from getting bedsores or losing muscle tone. I massaged his arms and legs two or three times a day. I wasn't sure it did him much good, but it was my favorite time of day.

Alec dropped into the rocking chair and said, "Come over for dinner tonight?"

Since I'd been banished from the ID team, we hadn't seen much of each other. I couldn't remember the last time I'd been to her apartment. "I'd love that. Can I help?" I asked.

We stared at each other for a few seconds and then burst out laughing. My less-than-stellar cooking abilities were no secret. My offering to contribute when she cooked for me had become a running joke.

"I'm good, but you can pick up dessert," Alec said. "I won't have time to fix anything."

"I'll run by Juliana's on my way over."

Alec had introduced me to Juliana's Bakery before the quarantine. I'd become so hooked that I had to limit my visits to special occasions. I always considered dinner at Alec's a special occasion.

"Perfect. Get enough for three," she said.

"Three? Who else are you expecting? Adam maybe?" I asked, teasing her.

"Yes, it's Adam, but it's not what you think."

"When are you going to admit that it's exactly what I think?"

"Oh, I've admitted it, but that's not what I mean. I told him about your research on Johnny's condition. He's done some too. I thought you could compare notes."

"That'd be great, but what do you mean you've admitted it?"

Alec moved closer, clearly thrilled to talk about Adam. "He's the perfect man."

"Perfect? No one's perfect, especially not men."

Alec rolled her eyes. "Well, perfect for me, I mean," she said.

"Even with all the time we spent together during the quarantine, I don't know that much about him. He's a good person though. Give me the juicy details."

"He came here from Colorado for medical school and ended up staying, so we're both transplants."

"Those are the opposite of juicy details."

"I'm getting to it," Alec said and put up her hands to shush me. "I've always considered myself an independent career woman who didn't need a husband or children to be fulfilled. I've learned that sometimes *independent* is just another word for lonely."

"I'd never describe you as lonely. You're constantly surrounded by people, and you have me, of course."

"And I'm grateful for that, but you know what I mean."

"More than most," I said.

Alec nodded and said, "You know how I felt about Adam when we first started working on the ID team. I thought of him as more of a brother. My feelings now are anything but brotherly."

"It took you long enough to come around. It was obvious how he felt from the first second he saw you."

"I was clueless. It started when he came over after our shift, and we talked for hours. I'd never had a relationship like that. I would have been happy to go on like that forever, but eventually Adam decided he wasn't content with our 'sibling' relationship. I had a group of friends over one night, and Adam 'accidentally' forgot his wallet when he left. He came to get it, and when we were saying good-bye in the doorway, he put his hand under my chin and kissed me. I was speechless, which, as you know, is rare for me. That played into his plan, because he kissed me again. I was ready the second time."

Alec's eyes glistened as she remembered the encounter. I could only wonder how she felt. Any memories of my affection for Danny were dead and buried. I'd come to grips with the fact that I'd never have romantic love in my life, but I didn't begrudge anyone else. I nudged her to go on.

"He told me he'd wanted to do that for a long time. He said it was better than he'd imagined."

"Sounds like a keeper," I said and smiled.

"You don't have to tell me. We have so much in common. Sometimes I think of him as the male version of me. Anyway, we've tried to keep it secret because we thought it might make things weird on the ID team. I'm glad you're okay with it."

"I'm thrilled, and I'm glad you've found out that there's more to life than nursing."

"Look who's talking!" she said and gave me a gentle shove. "About tonight, though, come over around six thirty." Alec looked at the white board on the wall and frowned at Johnny's latest stats. "At least he's put on weight."

"What does that matter? He's still not reacting to stimuli or moving," I said and frowned too.

"It's improvement. We need to take what we can get. He doesn't seem any worse from the infection."

I appreciated that she was trying to be positive, but even her news about Adam couldn't erase my disappointment. "It's been more than four months. He doesn't get better. He doesn't get worse. He just goes on sleeping. You know as well as I do that his prognosis is poor, especially since what happened during the quarantine. I've never seen anyone in Johnny's condition survive without severe brain damage. I'm trying to be positive, but I have to be realistic too."

"Four months already? It feels more like a few weeks," Alec said, ignoring my comment.

I picked Johnny up and carried him to the rocking chair.

Alec caressed his cheek and kissed mine. "I've got to run, but don't get discouraged. We'll talk to Adam about it tonight," she said and gave a small wave on her way out.

I was discouraged, as much as I tried to fight it. I was tired too, tired of waiting for some sign that the previous months hadn't been a waste that would end in Johnny's death. I swallowed my doubts and kissed the top of his head. Even if he didn't survive, I was comforted in knowing that I was doing my best to love and support him during his last days. At least he wouldn't die alone.

The sweet aroma of Italian cooking wafted over me as I reached Alec's apartment, and my mouth watered. When Alec met me at the door, I asked her how an upper-class Californian had mastered Italian cuisine.

"I had a roommate at UCLA whose grandmother emigrated from Venice as a young woman. I spent many weekends at her house learning to cook. I'm glad I have such a willing subject to hone my skills on now," she said.

I breathed in deeply and said, "What's on the menu?"

"Chicken parmesan, mushroom risotto, and sautéed peppers with green beans. What's in that beautiful pink box you're holding?" she asked.

I lifted the box to show her. We said "cannoli" at the same time and laughed.

"What else?" Adam said as he came around the counter. He kissed my cheek and took the box from me.

"Those are for all of us," I said and sat down.

Alec sat a plate piled with her aromatic food in front of me.

I took a bite of the risotto. It was the most delicious food I'd ever tasted. "You're in the wrong line of work."

"I think I was a chef in a former life," Alec said.

"It's the only reason I like her," Adam said.

Alec snapped him on the arm with a dish towel and sat next to him. We talked about Johnny during the meal. I told them about the research I'd done and how discouraged I was.

"Did Alec tell you about my connection to Johnny?" I asked Adam.

"Yeah, she told me. I hope you don't mind," Adam said.

"No, I'm glad. I won't give up on Johnny, but I understand that I should prepare for the worst. Alec told me about the research you've been doing. I hope your results have been more positive than mine. Most of what I've read makes it sound like I shouldn't expect much," I said.

"The fact that Johnny is an infant is in his favor. Most cases of infant drowning that occur before the age of one happen in the bathtub. Johnny's case is unique because it's coupled with a brain injury. Keep in mind that infant brains develop and recover at a much faster rate than older children or adults. Johnny's progress may not look promising, but we can't only base our judgment on current information that's out there. None of us can make an accurate prognosis, but I'm not giving up hope by any means, and neither is Brad Carter."

"I'm relieved to hear that. Kinsley's been giving me grief about my attention to Johnny, especially after the whole quarantine thing. Even though Johnny is a ward of the state, the complete cost of his medical care isn't covered, and the bills are piling up. The possibility that he may be here for years is making the board nervous. I've thought of going to the private sector to raise funds, but it's too much to take on with longer shifts on the IM floor and caring for Johnny," I said.

Adam wiped his mouth on a napkin and said, "That reminds me: Brad is working on getting Johnny transferred to Baltimore Regional as part of an ongoing research study there. He should know soon if they'll accept Johnny."

"Baltimore?" I asked feeling relieved and disappointed at the same time. It would be great to know more about Johnny's condition and possibilities for treatment, but I hated the thought of his going away and being all alone. "How long would it take?"

"Probably months, but don't worry about that for now. It may not even happen. The best thing you can do for Johnny is give him as much loving care and attention as possible. He needs stimulation and human contact," Adam said.

"Trust me, she gives him plenty of that," Alec said.

"It's my favorite thing. Alec's cooking is second," I said and licked my fingers.

Alec got up and started picking up our dirty dinner plates. "Don't forget that I'm here to help. You don't have to do this alone," she said.

I stood to help her. "Then will you come with me to meet Serena Davis tomorrow? I want to talk to her about the legal aspects of Johnny's future. I could use the moral support."

"Sure. I don't go on until three," she said.

"Who's Serena Davis?" Adam asked.

"Remember, you met her when Johnny was in the ID unit. She's Johnny's caseworker," Alec said.

Adam gave a suggestive smile and said, "Oh yeah, I remember her." When Alec flicked his ear, he flinched and said, "What was that for?"

"I know that look." Alec glared at him. "That look is reserved for me now."

Adam laughed. "You can't fault me for admiring a beautiful work of art."

"As long as you admire from afar," Alec said and kissed him.

He wrapped his arms around her and pulled her onto his lap. I smiled at their exchange.

Serena had grown up in the Mississippi foster system until an aunt and uncle from Virginia found her and adopted her. They told her that her mother had come into the United States illegally from Haiti. She was arrested a few times on drug charges before getting deported. They never knew anything about who her father was. Serena told me her story one day not long after Johnny came to the hospital. She'd wanted me to know that she understood what it meant to be abandoned. She'd grown into a beautiful and accomplished woman who was living proof that the system worked well sometimes. I was grateful she'd been assigned to Johnny's case. I knew she'd fight for him.

"I'm going to take off and give you two some alone time. I'll pick you up around nine, Alec," I said and got up to leave.

"I want to ask you something before you go," Alec said. "A few of us have been talking about throwing Caroline an engagement party, but none of us have room. We were wondering if you'd be willing to have it at your house. We'd do all the work. You just need to provide the space."

"I'd love to do that, but I insist on helping."

Alec clapped and said, "She'll be so excited."

"Come over Saturday, and we'll start planning," I said and waved on my way out.

⊨⊨ ⊨⊨

The phone rang at three that morning, and I bolted upright in bed. "Grace, it's Marci. I'm sorry to wake you. Johnny has pneumonia again. He's back in the PICU."

"I'll be right over," I said, dragging my warm feet out of bed and putting them on the cold hardwood.

"You don't have to come. I just wanted you to know," Marci said.

"I'll be there in twenty."

⇒⊱ ⊰⇐

Marci had a gift with children, and I was always relieved to see her tending to Johnny when I got to the hospital.

"Fill me in," I said while glancing at Johnny's chart.

"It's grim. He has fluid on both lungs. We *thought* he was past this. I have to be honest; if he's not going to make it, I'd rather it be sooner than later. I hate seeing him suffer like this, and I'm worried about you getting so attached to him."

"Don't worry about me. Just focus on Johnny," I said.

"Why do you do this? I doubt he knows you're here. You've seen his EEGs. I hope we aren't keeping a body alive, delaying the inevitable," she said and brushed a lock of hair off Johnny's forehead.

"If there's even the slightest chance I'm making a difference, isn't that worth it? It won't hurt Johnny. I'm the only one who'll get hurt, and I'm willing to take the risk."

"I respect you for that, and I'll do whatever I can for Johnny. You know that, but medical science only takes us so far. I've done this long enough to see lots of things I can't explain, but there's a fine line between faith and false hope. The tough part is trying to decide which side of the line to stand on."

"For now, I'm standing on the side of hope."

Alarms started going off on Johnny's monitors. I moved back to let the staff do their work. I'd called Alec from the car and asked her meet me in the PICU. She walked in at that moment.

"What's happening?" she said, still half-asleep.

"Full arrest," I said. We watched in silence until I tugged on her arm and said, "I can't stand to watch this. Let's go to the waiting room."

While we were waiting for word, I said, "I don't know how to repay you for this. You have to work today."

"I told you at dinner I'm here for you. I know how I'd feel in your place."

Fifteen minutes later, Marci came to tell us that they had resuscitated Johnny, and we could see him. He was so still and peaceful. It was hard to believe he'd been through a life-threatening ordeal only moments before. Alec went home, but I stayed through the night and postponed my plans to meet with Serena. With Johnny in critical condition, I couldn't see the point.

CHAPTER NINE

Johnny spent a week in the PICU but was soon back in his old room. I woke up a week after his recovery with a smile. It was the day of the engagement party. I'd never thrown a party before. I was nervous and excited. Alec and I scoured magazines and the Internet to get ideas. I wanted to get it perfect. Alec prepared most of the hors d'oeuvres, but we also ordered some from the restaurant where we had our first dinner together.

I got up and had a quick breakfast before running off to pick up the food and supplies. I had to get the tablecloths, flowers, and cake. There were so many details I was afraid I'd forget something. Alec teased me about my mountain of lists, but when the day arrived, I was glad to have them.

Adam and Alec drove up just as I was pulling back into the garage.

"How many people did you invite to this thing?" Adam asked when he peeked into my backseat.

"Wait until you see the trunk," I said and popped it open.

Adam gasped. "I hope I'm only the first of the army coming to help."

"Nope. Just us and Angela," Alec said.

"Oh, great." Adam grabbed an armload of tablecloths. "Can't think of a better way to spend my first day off in ten days."

"And we've been sitting around eating bonbons with our feet up," Alec said. "Put those on the sofa and come back for another load."

"Yes, ma'am. I see how it's going to be," he said and went off grumbling under his breath.

We worked for about four hours until everything was ready. I stood back to admire our work and couldn't believe we were standing in my house.

"You're having all the parties here from now on," Alec said.

"I've set a bad precedent," I said. "Doesn't it look amazing though?"

"Even I'm impressed," Adam said.

"Will you do my engagement party?" Angela asked.

"I didn't know you were seeing anyone," I said.

"I'm not, but you never know. Maybe I'll meet Mr. Right tonight."

"You know almost everyone who's coming, except for the plus ones, and they're off-limits." Alec glared at her. "You do know they're off-limits, right?"

Angela stuck her tongue out.

I laughed. "I promise to do your party. Now, all of you, go home and get cleaned up."

"See you in an hour," Alec said and hugged me. "Thanks again for this. Caroline's going to love it."

"She deserves it after all she's been through," I said as I scooted them out the door.

My cell phone rang from somewhere in the living room. I thought about letting it go to voice mail but realized it could be someone with questions about the party. I hunted my phone down and answered it just in time.

"Grace, it's Marci," she said in a whisper when I picked up. "You need to get over here now. They're transferring Johnny for the research study tonight. He's leaving in half an hour."

"I can't leave now. The engagement party's tonight," I said, trying to subdue my panic.

"I know. I'm going to try to make it after my shift, but if you don't come now, you'll miss him," she said.

"I'll try to reach Adam and Alec. They're supposed to be here soon. Try to stall."

"There's not much I can do, but I'll try," she said and hung up.

I called Alec, but it went to her voice mail. I tried Adam next with the same result. In a panic, I wrote a note on bright pink paper and stuck it on the cake table, hoping they'd see it. Alec had a spare key, so I knew they'd be able to get in. I grabbed my purse and headed out the door to the hospital, praying that Alec would forgive me.

⊨ ⊨

They were loading Johnny into the ambulance when I arrived.

"Wait up," I told the driver, "I want to say good-bye."

"You do know this is the comatose baby, right? Baby John Doe?"

"I know who it is," I said, getting annoyed. "Don't call him that."

He gave me a look and said, "Fine, but make it quick. We've got a schedule."

I leaned in and gave Johnny a kiss on the forehead. He looked so small and vulnerable. I brushed his palm, and he squeezed my finger. It was still the only way he ever reacted to me. "I'll be coming soon. Don't worry. Mommy will be there for you. I love you."

I kissed him again and pulled my hand away, trying not to lose control. I stepped back and watched the driver close the doors. As they drove off, Dr. Carter came out with Kinsley.

"I'm glad you made it in time," Dr. Carter said. "Did Marci call you?"

"Thank you, yes," I said and turned to Kinsley. "What do you think you're doing sneaking him out of here under the cover of darkness? The least you could have done was given me some warning."

"Why would I need to tell you? You don't have any consideration in his situation. Just because you've deluded yourself into thinking you're his mother doesn't mean it's true," he said and crossed his arms.

I stepped toward him. "How dare you!"

Dr. Carter stepped between us. "I tried to get in touch, but there wasn't time. I'm in communication with the head of the study in Baltimore. I'm trying to get you a temporary transfer there. He said you could have important insight because you're so close to Johnny."

"You mean I can go with him? And for the length of the study?" I asked thrilled at the prospect.

"Against my better judgment," Kinsley said. "You know my feelings in the matter."

"Fortunately, it's not up to you," I said. "And what do you know about it? Have you spent any time with Johnny? He's just a dollar sign to you."

"That's not fair, and I know far more about it than you realize. I'm the one who has to look at the big picture."

People were staring at us, so Dr. Carter said, "Let's go discuss this in my office. I'm sure we can work it out."

"I can't. I'm late for an event. I'll contact you in the morning," Kinsley said and went back inside.

Once he was out of earshot, I said, "That hyena!" I paced in small circles, trying to compose myself. I'd done my best to avoid Kinsley, but it only took three seconds for him to get to me. I took a deep breath and said, "I have to go too. I appreciate what you're doing, Dr. Carter. What do you think my chances are for a transfer?"

"I'd say good, and, please, call me Brad. They don't want to lose you right when you're going back on as charge nurse, but they know the stint in Baltimore will be temporary. They're looking at Alec Covington to fill in while you're gone. Can she handle it?"

"Piece of cake. I have full confidence in her, but she'll be reluctant to leave the ID team."

"Like I said, it'll be temporary," Brad said.

"Speaking of cake, I'm supposed to be throwing an engagement party for Caroline. Would you like to join us?"

"Thank you, but I have a patient I need to look in on."

"You're a conscientious doctor, Brad. Thanks for your attention to Johnny. I know everyone thinks it's hopeless, but you don't treat him that way."

"That's because that's not what I think. I'm anxious to see the results of the study. I'm hoping for positive news."

"Me too. Well, I'd better get going to my own party. I'll come by first thing in the morning."

"See you then. Go and enjoy yourself. You deserve it," he said and walked in through the sliding doors.

I was a nervous wreck on the way home. I was worried about Johnny, and I had an idea of how furious Alec would be. She'd left three messages and about twenty texts. Alec and Adam were clearing away some dishes when I rushed into the kitchen from the garage. Sounds of the happy guests floated in from the living room. The mood in the kitchen was just the opposite. Adam and Alec stopped and stared when they saw me.

"I'm so sorry. When Marci called, I tried to reach you, but it was too late. It was unavoidable, Alec. Please forgive me?"

Alec went into the living room without answering.

I started after her, but Adam stopped me and said, "We'll deal with it later. For now, let's paste on our smiles and make the best of it for Caroline and Jared. Why don't you go get changed?"

I nodded and followed him out of the kitchen. The guests all seemed to understand when I said I'd been called to the hospital. They were mostly medical professionals, and they all knew what it was like to be called away at the worst times. Alec refused to make eye contact with me for the rest of the party. I mingled and tried to ignore her, refusing to let her ruin it for me.

After the last of the guests had gone, I stepped in front of Alec, blocking her from leaving the room and said, "Talk to me."

"How's Johnny?" Alec asked. Her toned oozed with sarcasm.

"That's a long story. We'll talk about it if you honestly want to know, but right now, we need to deal with us. You have a right to be angry, but you're not leaving until we settle this."

"I asked about Johnny because I wondered what could have happened to make you leave when you were about to host a party. Wasn't there anyone in the entire hospital to handle the crisis? Was he on the verge of death? What was so critical that you couldn't wait fifteen minutes for us to get here? I've put up with a lot for you. I've always been there for you, and this is how you repay me?"

I lowered myself into a chair and cradled my head in my hands. I'd expected her reaction and I felt bad, but I had an obligation to Johnny too. There was no way she'd understand my feelings toward him.

Before I could decide what to say, Adam knelt next to me and put his hand on my shoulder. "Does this have to do with the research study?"

"Yes," I said, but it came out like a croak.

"I figured that was the case when I saw your note. Did they transport him tonight?"

"Yes," I said again.

"I'm glad you got to say good-bye," he said. "What were those skunks doing, sending him at night?"

Alec crossed her arms. "Adam, what are you talking about? Did you know why Grace left? Why didn't you tell me?"

"If you want answers, sit down and stop barking at me," Adam said. "You're acting like a child, and you're going to feel stupid when I tell you."

Alec's mouth dropped open. Adam obviously hadn't ever spoken to her that way. He started to say something, but I held up my hand to stop him.

"Let me tell her, Adam. The last thing I want is for this to come between you two." I turned to her. "I got a call from the hospital about fifteen minutes before you were supposed to get here. Marci told me that they were transferring Johnny to Baltimore Regional for the pediatric neurological research study. I didn't think Kinsley had the gall to send him off behind my back. He's trying to put me in my place."

Alec knelt next to Adam and took my hands. "I'm sorry. I'm such an idiot," she said. "I should have known that you wouldn't bug out without good reason. I should be asking for forgiveness, not the other way around."

I shook my head and said, "I owed you more than to just take off, but that might be the last time I'll ever see Johnny."

Alec handed me a tissue and said, "This was only a party, and it turned out fine without you."

"I've been so excited about it, and Kinsley ruined it. This is his fault. He ruins everything," I said and blew my nose.

Adam helped Alec up, and they went to the sofa. He put his arm around her. I was relieved to see things were back to normal.

Alec saw me watching them and smiled. "I know this is hard for you, and don't get mad, but I can kind of see where Kinsley's coming from," she said. "Parenthood's always a challenge, but being the mother of a child like Johnny can consume your life. You've seen the fatigue and despair on the faces of parents of chronically ill children. They didn't choose to have sick children, but once they have them, it's forever. They can't choose to put the burden down when it gets too hard. You don't have to choose this."

"Don't you think I know that?"

She ignored me and said, "If you adopt Johnny, it'll mean missing weddings, birthdays, and holidays. You've already spent several nights pacing the PICU. I know you love Johnny, but maybe you should be more realistic."

There was truth in what she'd said. I waited several seconds before saying, "Would you be saying this if I were Johnny's biological mother or even adopted mother?"

"Of course not," she said without hesitating.

"Then depending on what happens with the study, and as soon as the powers that be allow it, I'll start the adoption process," I said. "Then I'll be Johnny's real mother."

"But Johnny's not your son now, and he might never be. I'd hate to see you get sucked into his life only to have it end in disaster. I don't think you should go to Baltimore."

I was shocked. I got up and walked to the window because I couldn't look at her. Alec always said she had my back, but she was taking my enemy's side. I turned to face her. "You sound like Kinsley. You obviously don't know me after all."

"The opposite is true. I'm saying it because I do know you. I'm not saying give up your plans of adopting Johnny someday, if he comes out of the coma. I'm saying take a break from him. Step back for a while to get a better perspective."

I walked back to my chair and sank into it. "I'm sorry you feel that way, but you're wrong. Johnny needs me more than he ever has. If I abandon him now, what kind of mother will I make?"

"I'm sorry, Alec, but I agree with Grace," Adam said. Alec started to protest, but he stopped her. "Going to Baltimore will be the best way for her to find out what she's up against."

Alec gave Adam the look of death, but he just shrugged. "It's how I feel," he said.

"I talked to Brad Carter. He's hoping the study head in Baltimore will bring me on board. If they agree, Kinsley should too, but I doubt he will," I said.

"I'll do what I can to help Brad get you transferred with Johnny," Adam said.

Alec slumped back in defeat. "I hope you two know what you're doing. I'm trying to protect you; that's all."

"I know, but we've been through this. I know the risks. It's my choice to take them."

She nodded, and I remembered what Brad had told me about her.

"I should tell you, my going to Baltimore will affect you too. They're planning on you filling in for me while I'm gone."

"Me? Why? I've never been a supervisor," she said. She tried to act shocked, but I could tell she was pleased.

"You have to start somewhere. You'll be fine, but just don't do too well, or they may not want me back. Kinsley already hates me. All he needs is another reason to get rid of me. Have fun working with him, by the way," I said and shook my head.

That eased the tension, but Alec's attitude still disturbed me. I felt betrayed. I wanted to trust that she had my best interests at heart, but she had to know that Johnny was an integral part of my best interests. If she didn't understand that, then I was way off about where we stood.

As if reading my mind, she said, "I can see the wheels spinning in your brain. You need to know one thing. I made a commitment as your friend to support you in any way I can. I stand by that. I just needed to make sure that you're not so caught up with Johnny that you're missing the reality of the long term."

"Every day since Johnny came into my life, I've waited for the call telling me he was gone. I've also known every day that they could find his family. I get it, Alec. It's an insane situation, but I'm choosing that insanity. I don't know how to convince you that I'm not going into this blind. Please, once and for all, tell me you believe that."

"Fine, I'm convinced," she said. "I won't bring it up again."

"Let's put this behind us and finish the party. I hid some cake in the kitchen, just in case," Adam said.

Alec followed him into the kitchen. My day that had started out so well had gone south in a hurry. I hoped it wasn't an omen of things to come. I lifted my glass and said, "To chapter two."

⇥ ⇤

Brad and Adam convinced Kinsley to let me go to Baltimore when the doctor running the study approved the request. I packed in a hurry, excited to be with Johnny again. I hadn't been able to focus on anything since he'd gone. Two days later, I was ready for Alec to take me to the train station.

She hugged me on the platform and said, "I'm going to miss you and Johnny. I hope it goes well. I'll be sending positive vibes your way, and I'll try to come up a few times if I can."

"I'd love that. Are you ready to take on the IM floor?"

"I know the ropes pretty well by now. You've trained me well. It'll be fine," she said.

"Call any time."

"I will. Take care of yourself. See you soon."

We hugged and Alec walked away without looking back. I'd miss her, but I was sure she'd be relieved to have Johnny and me out of the way for a while so she could spend more time with Adam. I knew how she felt. I was looking forward to having Johnny all to myself. I found an empty row and took the seat by the window. I'd never been to Baltimore, and even though I knew I would be spending the majority of my time with Johnny, I was looking forward to a change of scenery. I grabbed a few travel brochures in the train station and browsed through them as the train pulled away.

CHAPTER TEN

Whenever he moved close, I forgot how to breathe. He smelled like a clean breeze over the ocean, and he was so tall and confident. He leaned in to examine Johnny, and I imagined running my fingers through his thick salt-and-pepper hair. Lost in my fantasy, I missed his question, so I just nodded. I had to get out of the room before I said something to make a fool of myself. I excused myself and left, hopefully without arousing suspicion.

I found the closest restroom and locked myself in a stall. Meeting Dr. Jay Morgan two hours earlier had turned me into a dreamy-eyed schoolgirl. He was a renowned pediatric neurologist. His books were benchmarks in the field. He was the head of Johnny's research study, so I'd be spending the bulk of my time working with him.

My reaction to him confused me. I hadn't had the slightest interest in men since escaping my marriage, and I'd never been affected by a man that way, not even Danny. I'd seen handsome men but only noticed them with casual detachment. There wasn't anything casual about my reaction to Dr. Morgan. I closed my eyes, leaned against the cool metal of the stall door, and surrendered to the sensation.

Dr. Morgan was leaving Johnny's room when I walked out of the restroom ten minutes later. He saw me in the hallway and motioned for me to wait. My emotions erupted again at the sight of him. I was tempted to retreat back into my hiding place but resisted the urge. As he drew closer, I tried to convince myself that he was just another doctor, but it didn't work. He was the man of my dreams.

"You're pale," Dr. Morgan said. "Is everything all right?"

"Oh, I'm fine. Just worn out from the trip here," I said.

"You should go back to your room and get a good night's sleep. Johnny will be well looked after here."

"I think I'll do that, Dr. Morgan."

"Please, call me Jay," he said and extended his hand. "I was looking for you to see if you'd be available for lunch tomorrow. I'd like to discuss Johnny's case with you. I'm sure you have valuable insights."

My legs went weak again. "I'd love to," I said before I could stop the words from tumbling out of my mouth.

He took a business card from an engraved silver case and pressed it into my hand. "Call my extension around noon. I'll meet you after rounds and take you to a bistro I like. The cafeteria food here is terrible."

"I like it," a nurse who was walking by said, "but not all of us have such uppity tastes."

Jay smiled and shook his head.

"Until tomorrow then," I said and watched longingly as he walked away, wondering how I'd survive until I saw him again.

⚔ ⚔

I'd been assigned an apartment in staff housing, and when I woke the next morning, my first thoughts were of Jay, not Johnny. I got up and tried on every outfit I'd brought, hoping to find something that would be good enough. I hadn't planned to socialize while I was in Baltimore, so I'd only brought uniforms and casual clothes. Nothing was right, and I was tempted to wait for the local mall to open and find something there. I came to my senses before I followed through on that plan, though. Jay hadn't said anything about our meeting being a date. It was a lunch to discuss Johnny's case. I settled on a pair of jeans, blouse, and jacket, and left to see my boy.

On my way to Johnny's room, I tried to convince myself that I was being ridiculous about Jay, but my gut still knotted up at the thought of seeing him. I was pleased and disappointed to find Johnny alone, tranquil and oblivious as always. I scolded myself for allowing my juvenile fantasizing to take priority over him. He was the reason I was in Baltimore. I checked his chart and saw that the nurse had already been in to bathe and change him. I picked him up and brushed my cheek against his. I thought I felt him cuddle against me, but it was probably just wishful thinking.

I sat with Johnny cradled in my arms and hummed while I considered our situation. I was looking forward to my lunch for more than just a chance to be with Jay. I wanted to pick his brain and find out how he planned to focus his study. I was desperate for a glimmer of hope. I'd heard stories of people waking up after years in a vegetative state, but they'd always been adults. I was encouraged by the knowledge that babies' brains grow and develop at a much faster rate than adults, but I didn't know if that meant they healed faster too. If so, then why was Johnny still asleep after more than five months?

I laid Johnny back in his bed and started making notes about his history. As I wrote, I realized Johnny would be a year old soon. I wished we were in Richmond so I could have a party for him. I was sure the staff in Baltimore would think I was certifiable if I did it there. I decided to just bring in a few decorations and a new quilt and called Jay's extension to let him know I was ready to go.

⇥⊢ ⊣⇤

"You must have gotten a good night's sleep," Jay said as he walked me to the physician's parking lot. "You look lovely."

"Thank you," I said, pleased that he'd noticed.

He held out his hand to help me into his black convertible.

And you're drop-dead gorgeous, I thought as he walked around to his side of the car.

He took me to a trendy bistro and gave me excellent suggestions on what to order. I was sure I'd never eaten in such an expensive restaurant. He made small talk while we waited for our food, effortlessly making me feel at ease. While we ate, he questioned me about Johnny. I rambled on for most of the meal, thrilled to discuss my favorite topic.

"I'm impressed," Jay said when I'd finished. "You've obviously done your homework. The information will help when I go over his initial test results."

I was flattered and took a bite of food so he wouldn't see me smiling.

"It's clear that you have more than a professional involvement with Johnny. Describe your relationship with him," he said.

I panicked, not knowing how I could describe my relationship with Johnny to someone like Jay. I wiped my mouth to stall while I thought of what to say. I didn't know what he'd heard about me. For all I knew, he'd spoken with Kinsley. I decided to be direct, figuring he'd find out anyway. "I intend to adopt him," I said, looking him in the eye.

"Adopt him? What, you mean if he regains consciousness?" he asked, clearly trying to hide his shock.

I squared my shoulders and said, "No, I plan to start the process when we get back to Richmond."

It was Jay's turn to stall. He calmly wiped his mouth with his napkin before laying it neatly on his lap. "I know we've just met, and I can't pretend to know your motivations. I can see that you're an intelligent woman, but you must understand how irrational that is, even if he does recover. I'm sorry to be so blunt."

"Don't apologize. I get the same reaction from everyone. I know people think I'm crazy to want this, but it's not an impulsive decision. Maybe I'll explain my motivation, as you called it, at some point."

"I don't think you're crazy, just misguided. For now, I'll respect your reasons. I don't agree with them though. From what little I've seen, I expect that you may be in for disappointment."

Strike one, I thought. At least the truth was out. I wouldn't have to pretend with him. I tried to ask him a few questions about Johnny, but he stopped me.

"I don't want to make any more assumptions. Once the initial testing is done, we'll compile the results and consider treatment options. I'll make sure to keep you in the loop."

"Thank you, Jay. I know you're not obligated to do that."

"My pleasure," he said and flashed a smile that paralyzed my legs. "We'd better get back to the hospital. Do you mind if we go straight there, or do you need to go back to your apartment?"

"Straight there is fine. I'm here to watch after Johnny after all," I said.

He held out his hand to help me up. I was grateful since my legs were still like cooked spaghetti. As we walked, he softly laid his hand on my back to guide me to the car. His touch was so light that I wondered if I were imagining it. He held my hand just a second too long when he helped me into the car. My skin tingled under his touch. He was all business on the drive back to the hospital though. I scolded myself for reading motivations into his actions that clearly weren't there.

☞ ☜

My life settled into a new normal in the days that followed. I spent most of my time with Johnny. Even though I was assisting in a minor roll with the study, there wasn't much for me to do. I wasn't used to sitting around, so I had to be creative to keep myself occupied. Jay was true to his word and kept me involved in Johnny's care. Progress was slow. Johnny wasn't the only patient in the study, and Jay had other patients too. Sometimes I went for a few days at a time without seeing him. He showed nothing but familiar professionalism with me, but I still looked forward to every glimpse of him.

I became acquainted with a few of the nurses and tried to dig for information on Jay without being too obvious. I learned that he and his ex-wife had divorced years earlier. They had two successful daughters who lived in the area. They came to visit him at the hospital occasionally, but I never saw them. The nurses considered Jay one of the most eligible bachelors in the city. He'd traveled the world and authored several books and articles. A man like Jay would forget a woman like me the minute I was out of sight. I'd been foolish to think he'd ever be interested in me. I contented myself with admiring him from afar.

Two weeks after my lunch with Jay, I went back to Johnny's room after dinner. I was getting antsy in my little apartment. Alec had recommended a novel she liked, but I was having a hard time getting into it. I'd read the same page for the third time when I heard a tap on Johnny's door and looked up to see Jay peeking in.

"You're here late," he said and came in.

"Had to get out of my apartment. I can read here as well as there. You're here late too," I said.

"I had a surgical patient with complications," he said. "She just turned the corner for the better. I've been neglecting Johnny, so I thought I'd check in."

"There's no change that I can see. Are there any new results?" I asked.

"Yes, and some are minimally encouraging. Don't get your hopes up though. We're a long way from knowing exactly what his prognosis or treatment plan will be."

"Thanks for letting me know. I'm used to not getting my hopes up when it comes to Johnny."

An awkward silence followed. I was sure he was searching for a polite way to escape. To make it easy on him, I said, "Well, I'm sure you probably want to get home."

He didn't respond but just stood there studying me. After several seconds, he said, "Are you planning to stay much longer? I'd be happy to give you a ride home."

His offer was the last thing I expected. I had given him an out, but he missed it. It hadn't occurred to me that he actually wanted to spend time with me. Not wanting to be rude after his kind offer, I said, "I'm ready to go now, but you don't have to do that. My apartment's only a few blocks away."

"You shouldn't be walking alone this late. Please, I'd be happy to take you. Maybe we can get to know each other better. I'll just go close up my office."

He left before I could say anything. I stared after him in shocked silence, wondering if I'd fallen asleep. I pinched my cheeks to make sure. Convinced I was awake, I grabbed my tote bag, kissed Johnny, and followed Jay to his office before he changed his mind.

⚔

I gave Jay directions to my apartment and showed him where to park. He didn't say a word until we got inside. "Is this where they stuck you? I'll have to do something about that."

114

Not sure why he cared, I said, "No, please don't. This is fine. It's only temporary, and I'd rather not move again. I'm settled in here."

He looked skeptical but didn't say anything. I didn't have anything to offer but herb tea and water, so I sat on the sofa and motioned for him to take the recliner. He hesitated slightly before sitting. I'd never seen that side of Jay. He was the kind of man who took command of a room just by walking into it. If I hadn't known better, I'd have said he was timid.

"I don't know much about you other than you want to adopt Johnny," he said.

The one thing I wish you'd forget, I thought.

"Tell me about yourself."

"Not much to tell. I grew up in Nebraska and Iowa. I moved to Richmond in my early twenties. I've been there ever since, working in the same hospital. I'm charge nurse on the IM floor, which you probably knew."

"I did," he said.

When he didn't go on, I said, "Johnny showing up in the ER is the only interesting thing that's happened in my adult life. That's it," I said and sat back.

"I'm sure there's more to it than that, like why you decided to get involved in Johnny's situation," he said.

Two weeks earlier, I'd have given anything to have Jay alone in my apartment, but I found myself wishing he'd leave. He was asking questions too complicated for our new friendship. I searched for a way to divert the conversation without being too obvious. I finally said, "It's complicated. I'm not comfortable talking about myself, especially with someone I hardly know."

He stood and said, "You're right. I'm sorry. It's just such an unusual situation. You don't owe me an explanation. I'll go if you'd like."

"Sit down," I said. "You don't have to leave. I'm sure we can find something else to talk about."

He threw his head back and laughed—a warm, smooth laugh, like melted chocolate flowing in a fountain. He sat down next to me on the sofa instead of in the recliner. "You're right," he said. "I'm sorry for prying. You'll learn that I'm a very direct person, but that doesn't mean everyone's business is mine. Let's start again. Is this your first time in Baltimore?"

Relieved, I laughed too. "Yes, and I like it already. The campus is beautiful. I've picked a few sights I'd like to see before I go back to Richmond."

"I'd be happy to show you around," Jay said.

"You don't have to do that," I said, afraid he thought I was fishing for an offer. "I know how busy you are, and you have a life here. You must have better things to do than be my tour guide."

"The offer was genuine. It's refreshing to have someone closer to my age to talk to, and you seem like a unique person, Grace Ward. I meant it when I said I'd like to get to know you better."

"If you insist, I accept. What do you recommend that we do first?" I asked.

"Actually, I was going to ask a favor. My niece has a lead role in *Othello* with a local theater company. Would you mind going with me? I know it's not what you had in mind for sightseeing, but I'd rather not go alone."

"I'd be happy to. Sounds fun," I said, pleased that he was willing to introduce me to family.

"You're just being kind, but thanks. We'll grab a quick dinner beforehand. For now, I'll leave you in peace," he said and stood.

I walked him to the door and thanked him for the ride.

"My pleasure," he said and looked in my eyes, and I had no doubt what he was thinking

"See you tomorrow," I said.

"Looking forward to it."

I watched him until he passed the streetlight, and darkness enveloped him. I locked my door and got ready for bed. As I brushed my teeth and undressed, I tried to make sense of my encounter with Jay. In the two weeks since we'd had lunch, he hardly acknowledged me, and next he asked me out. I wondered if it was just convenient because he stumbled upon me in Johnny's room. Was I only fresh meat on the market to Jay? In the end, I quashed my suspicions and decided it didn't matter. I told myself to enjoy the attention while it lasted. I was sure it wouldn't be long.

⊷⊹⊶

When I got to Johnny's room the next morning, I found him with EEG leads attached to his head. A nurse I didn't recognize was checking his vitals. Jay hadn't mentioned starting any new tests.

"Is there a problem?" I asked.

"No. Dr. Morgan has ordered continuous EEG. It's part of Johnny's diagnostic plan."

"I guess I missed that," I said and walked to Johnny's bed.

I felt sorry for my poor baby with all those leads stuck to him, even though he'd had many EEGs by that point. I should have been used to it. I comforted myself knowing that Jay would gather valuable data as a result.

"Is Dr. Morgan looking for something in particular?" I asked.

"You'll have to ask him, ma'am."

"Okay, thanks. I'll do that when he comes in."

"He was already in. You just missed him," she said and left.

I wanted to see if Jay would act differently toward me after our conversation in my apartment. I was disappointed that I'd have to wait to find out. I began my daily routine of massaging Johnny's legs and arms hoping Jay would come back in that day. He didn't.

I didn't see him the next day or the one after that either, even though I'd gone to the hospital earlier that morning to catch him. I could see from Johnny's chart that Jay had been there. I began to think he was deliberately avoiding me. I unloaded my feelings

117

on Johnny since I didn't have anyone else to talk to. At least he couldn't interrupt or contradict me like Alec would have. I decided that Jay must like to keep people guessing. It dulled my attraction to him slightly. I hated games.

When I hadn't seen or heard from Jay by Friday afternoon, I concluded that he only invited me to the play on an impulse and later regretted it. I spent the day in Johnny's room and was packing to go to the cafeteria when Jay finally came in.

"There you are," he said, like I'd been hiding from him.

"I'm always here," I said, not hiding my irritation. Where else would I have been but in Johnny's room?

"Not always. I've been missing you all week. I thought you were trying to avoid me," he said and winked.

I wondered what kind of game he was playing and thought avoiding him might be a good idea.

"No. I thought the same about you," I said. "We must have bad timing. Are we still on for the play tomorrow?" I wanted to make him squirm or see if he'd try to get out of our date.

"Of course," he said. "You haven't changed your mind, have you?"

"No, but I haven't heard from you since Tuesday. You haven't even given me the details yet," I said, keeping myself guarded.

"You're right. I've had a killer week, but that's no excuse. I'm not making a very good impression, am I?" When I shrugged, he said, "Can we start again?"

He flashed his melted-chocolate smile, and my caution melted too. I'd been too quick to judge him. "No need," I said and smiled back. I put my tote bag down and sat in the rocking chair. "Just because I'm sitting around doing nothing doesn't mean you are too. I have too much time to think, and I'm not used to that. I rarely have a free minute at home. I understand the demands on your time." I realized that I was rambling and stopped talking.

Jay smiled. "That doesn't mean I should ignore you. The play starts at seven. Can I pick you up at five?"

"My only other plans are sitting here with Johnny, so five is fine."

"Thanks for understanding," he said. "I promise not to neglect you again."

He walked to Johnny's bed and took out his pen light. He lifted each of Johnny's eyelids and shined the light on his pupils. "Hmm," he said. Next, he ran his finger along Johnny's palm. Nothing happened. He tried again. Same result.

I felt a twinge of panic. I got up and went to Jay's side. "Let me try," I said. I placed my index finger on Johnny's palm, and he squeezed. I breathed a sigh of relief and gently pulled my finger free. I turned to Jay and said, "Try again."

Jay imitated what I'd done, but Johnny didn't grab on. "You do it now," he said.

I repeated what I'd done the first time, and Johnny closed his fingers around mine. "Jay, what's happening? Could he possibly know it's me?"

"No," Jay said. Without another word, he stepped out of the room. He came back ten seconds later with a research nurse named Alice in tow. "Brush your finger across his palm," Jay said.

She looked at him like she hadn't heard right. "Go ahead," he said, nodding.

Alice brushed Johnny's palm just as we'd done. Johnny's hand twitched, but he didn't squeeze her finger. She started to lift her hand, but Jay told her to wait. She waited for ten seconds, and then glanced at Jay. He nodded again, and she lifted her hand up.

"Try again, Grace," Jay said.

When I touched Johnny's palm, he grabbed my finger.

Jay stepped back and said, "That's not possible. It's got to be a coincidence, a fluke."

"He knows it's me, Jay. Can't it be possible?"

"No, it can't. It's a reflex action. There's no such thing as a selective reflex."

"Do you still need me?" Alice asked.

I'd forgotten she was there. I think our exchange made her uncomfortable. Jay cocked his head toward the door, and she left, clearly relieved to get away.

"Maybe on a deep subconscious level, he recognizes my touch," I said, irritated at Jay's inability to admit it wasn't a coincidence.

"I've never come across or even heard of such a thing, at least not at his level of vegetative state. I have to look into it, but don't get your hopes up. His other responses don't support his being able to distinguish who's touching his hand. He shouldn't be able to squeeze your hand at all." As if to emphasize his point, he touched Johnny's palm again, and nothing.

"Johnny's responded to me that way since his first day in my hospital. None of us thought he'd survive for a week, let alone months. He shouldn't still be alive. There's something unique happening here." I let Johnny grasp my finger again. I knew the truth. Johnny knew exactly who I was.

Jay studied me for several seconds before smiling. "He's not the only one who's unique. I think we're on the verge of an adventure. I'll see you tomorrow."

He walked out and left me staring after him again. "Definitely going to keep me guessing," I said to Johnny and then gave my sweet boy a kiss on the cheek.

⇒+ +⇐

Except for a change to khakis, I wore the same outfit as I had for my lunch with Jay. I made a mental note to go clothes shopping the next day so I'd be prepared for any future dates. He arrived at a little after five wearing khakis and a polo shirt. He even made ordinary clothes look amazing. I wondered again how he could be interested in me.

We had dinner at a Greek restaurant. I'd never eaten Greek food and hoped I'd like it. Jay ordered Greek salad, dolmades, lamb souvlaki, and pita bread with tzatziki sauce for both of us. After a few bites, I told him Greek food was my new favorite.

"I never thought I'd like anything better than Italian food," I said.

"You should go to the Mediterranean," he said. "You'd be in heaven."

The thought of my taking a trip like that made me laugh. I'd never even been out of the United States, not even to Canada. Other than Nebraska and my crisis trip from Des Moines to Richmond, I'd only been to a few other nearby cities for conferences. To prevent Jay from discovering how boring I was, I asked him how many countries he'd visited.

"Too many to count. I've been to every continent except Antarctica, but I plan to get there in the next year or so," he said.

"That sounds like the last place I'd want to go. I'm always cold. Just thinking about going there makes me shiver." I wrapped my arms around myself.

"It's all about having the right clothes and equipment. I learned that when I went to Greenland to see the northern lights. I stayed warm the whole time. It was spectacular, by the way."

He was matter-of-fact when he said it. He wasn't trying to impress me but was only making a point. I felt the need to impress him, though. I was like the poor country cousin compared to him. I took advantage of the opening he gave me and said, "I didn't know people took trips to Greenland, but I've seen the northern lights too, in Iowa. Not very exotic, but I'll never forget it."

"Neither will I. See, there's something we share," he said. He kept watching me but didn't say anything else.

To keep the conversation going, I said, "At least we have one thing in common."

"How do we know what we have in common? I know next to nothing about you. I'm looking forward to the discovery."

I glanced at my watch to deflect him again. "We'd better get going to make the play on time," I said.

"Why do you always change the subject when it gets personal?"

"I told you the other day, it makes me uncomfortable. I'm used to keeping people at arm's length," I said.

"Why?" he said. He was like a dog with a bone.

"Long story, and we do have to get to the play." I pointed to my watch.

"Fine, I'll let it go for now, but I'm not giving up until I learn all your secrets."

Alec had said those very words to me once. Opening up to her had been worth it. I hoped it would be with Jay too. "Give it time. You'll know when I'm ready." I stood to go.

"Off to the adventure, then," he said and placed my hand in the crook of his arm.

＝≒⊩ ⊩≒＝

Jay kept his arm around my chair during the play but was careful not to touch my shoulders. I was grateful that he'd gotten the message at dinner and respected my boundaries. I loved feeling him close, but I was in foreign territory and wanted to ease into it.

I enjoyed the play. Jay's niece was a talented actor. He took me backstage afterward to meet her.

"Bravo, Melissa," he said and kissed her cheek. "You were brilliant." He turned to me and said, "This is my friend Grace."

Melissa gave him a questioning look. She clearly wasn't used to seeing her uncle out with someone like me. She shook my hand and said, "It's nice to meet you. How do you two know each other?"

"Grace is here from Richmond assisting in one of my research studies. She has an interesting story," Jay said.

"She doesn't want to hear about that," I said. "You did a wonderful job. I was impressed."

"I hope the critics agree," Melissa said. "I'm moving to New York after I finish school in the spring. I'll need some good reviews for my résumé."

"I'm sure they loved it too," I said.

"I agree, but we'll let you get back to your cast celebration now. See you soon." Jay kissed her cheek again.

Melissa waved good-bye as she ran back to join the other actors. Jay led me out through the stage door. As we walked to the car, he said, "They'll eat her alive in New York. My sister shelters her."

"She's young and confident. I can't imagine wanting to get into such a cutthroat career, but she seems to know what she's doing," I said. "She has the talent. I'm sure she'll be fine."

"I've forgotten what it's like to be young and feel like you'll conquer the world. Remember what that was like?"

I smiled and looked at the ground as we walked. I had different memories. By the time I was Melissa's age, I'd been through hell and was on my way to Richmond. I was glad she was living life the way it was meant to be lived.

We were quiet as Jay drove me home. I had a much better time than I'd expected but wasn't sure what came next. After the incident with Johnny the previous day and my refusal to open up, I was afraid Jay was done with me. While he walked me to the door, I said, "I enjoyed this. Thanks for inviting me."

"My pleasure," he said. "Can I see you again? Are you free next Friday?"

"Since you and Johnny are the only people I know in Baltimore, I'd have to say yes."

"Did you happen to bring any evening wear?" he asked.

I gave a small laugh and said, "I'm not even sure what evening wear is. Why?"

He leaned closer to me. "I have tickets to the Baltimore Symphony, and I'd like to take you. There's a guest conductor I've wanted to see."

"You don't have a date?" I asked.

"Good question." He laughed. "I guilted one of my daughters into going with me, but I know she'd rather not."

"In that case, I can pick up something to wear. I'd love to go," I said and smiled.

"Good, it's settled then. I'll see you Monday," he said and kissed my cheek before turning to leave.

I touched the spot he'd kissed with the back of my hand. Keep 'em guessing, I thought as I went inside.

⇌ ⇋

The following week was uneventful, but I felt like a character from a fairy tale while I dressed for my date with Jay on Friday night. I'd gone to a boutique and asked the salesclerk to help me pick out an appropriate outfit. She chose a little black dress that cost five times what I'd ever spent on clothing, but it looked great on me, so I bought it. I found a pair of shoes with heels just high enough that I wouldn't fall and break my neck but would make me a little taller for Jay. I got my hair done and had a manicure. When I was ready, I admired myself in the bathroom mirror and decided I didn't look half-bad. I hoped Jay would agree.

He arrived in a tailored Italian suit. I nearly fainted at the sight of him. I sneaked glances at him from the corner of my eye through the entire concert, and tried to imagine what he looked like under that gorgeous suit. At one point, he whispered a comment about the conductor. I quivered at the warmth of his breath on my neck. For the first time in my life, I understood what infatuation meant and why it made people crazy. It was unsettling and exhilarating at the same time.

We went to a French restaurant after the concert. In true Jay style, he ordered just the right dishes for our five-course dinner. He finished before me and watched while I ate my dessert. His scrutiny made me uneasy.

"Why are you staring at me? Do I have food on my face?" I asked.

"No, I'm just admiring the view." He took my hand and held it in both of his. He had long, slender fingers, but his hands were strong and warm.

Surgeon's hands, I thought.

"You aren't like anyone I've ever known. The women I meet are superficial and self-absorbed. You're genuine and honest. You have no idea how attractive you are. That's your charm. You're smart too. It's a rare combination."

"I'm glad it's kind of dark in here so you can't see me blushing," I said and held my napkin up to my face.

Jay laughed. "See? You're proving my point. You look stunning tonight."

"Well, thank you. That's kind of you to say."

"It's honest of me to say."

I smiled and took another bite of dessert to stop the conversation.

Jay paid the bill as soon as I finished and hurried me to the car. I invited him in when we got to my apartment. We sat on the sofa and talked for an hour before I started to yawn.

"I'm keeping you up," Jay said. "You've had a long day. I should go."

"I don't want you to think that you're boring me. I'm having a wonderful time. I'm just not used to staying up so late."

Jay stood and led me to the doorway. He pulled me close and kissed me passionately. "I'll see you in the morning," he said, brushing his lips on my neck.

"Yes, the morning," I said, slurring my words. I closed the door behind him and leaned against it for support. I'm in big trouble, I thought.

⇒+ +⇐

The weeks that followed passed in a dream. I spent my days caring for Johnny with Jay and my nights in Jay's arms. He regaled me with stories of his adventures traveling the world. He took me to expensive restaurants, plays, and art exhibits. He introduced me into Baltimore society, exposing me to a world I'd hardly known existed. I kept bugging Alec for advice on how to navigate my new environment. She warned me to be on my guard and not get taken in. I didn't have the heart to tell her it was too late for that. I'd never imagined that a man like Jay could want me, especially when he could have the pick of any woman he knew. Emotion overcame reason, and I found myself falling in love.

Jay saw his daughters on a regular basis, and after about a month, he introduced them to me. They were charming and confident like their father. They seemed to take the fact that their father was seeing me in stride, and I wondered how many other women he'd introduced them to. I worked up the courage to ask one of his nurses if a relationship like ours were typical for Jay. She told me that even though he had frequent relationships, they didn't usually last long. She'd never seen him in a relationship like ours. I chose to believe her, hoping that she wasn't just being polite.

Jay was determined to learn about me too. In his artful way, he nudged me to unfold the secrets of my past life to him, one by one. I told him about my childhood and that I'd come to terms with it years before. The truth about my past didn't scare him off. He was kind and supportive. The only truth I held back was my disastrous marriage to Danny. Jay knew I was divorced, and thought he could relate because he was too, but I couldn't bring myself to tell him the traumatic details. It had all happened so long before and had nothing to do with our present relationship. I figured it wouldn't matter anyway. Jay Morgan would forget I existed the minute I left for Richmond.

The only clouds that marred that time for me were Jay's refusal to discuss my future with Johnny and rare instances of Jay's arrogant behavior that disturbed me. He was always kind and respectful with me, but a few times I'd caught him treating the staff in ways that I thought were harsh or dismissive. I mentioned it once, but he just laughed it off and said he'd try to do better. I rationalized that it would be difficult for a renowned neurosurgeon like Jay not to be arrogant and tried to ignore it. I convinced myself that I was just gun-shy and was being too critical. No one is perfect, I told myself.

Jay took me to his house for the first time after we'd been seeing each other for a month. He said he was tired of my tiny, austere apartment. Being in his house had unnerved me at first. The ultra-modern decor wasn't my favorite, but it was the walls and shelves covered with proof of Jay's accomplishments and status that intimidated me. They were glaring reminders that he was out of my league. When I pointed it out, he said, "That old junk? Just ignore it," and brushed it aside. I did my best to pretend it wasn't there, but it was hard to overlook.

We had decided to stay in for dinner that night. We stopped at the market to buy the ingredients on our way back from the hospital. It felt nice to do something ordinary with Jay for once. After he gave me a tour of the house, we went to the kitchen to fix our meal.

I was chopping onions when I looked up to see Jay staring at me. "What's wrong? Am I not doing this right? I told you I'm not the best cook." Without a word, he set my knife on the counter and took my hands. "Now you'll smell like onions too."

"I think I'm in love with you," he said. I was glad he had my hands, or I would have fallen over. "Did I upset you? All the color drained out of your face."

"No. I'm glad, but you caught me off guard. I'm in love with you too," I said.

He smiled and pulled me closer. "I wasn't sure until I saw you cutting those onions. I love everything you do. There's something magnetic about you that I can't resist. I felt it the first time I saw you."

He kissed me deeply in a way he never had. I pulled away to catch my breath and pressed my cheek against his chest. "I feel the same way about you. I've never reacted the way I do with you to anyone else. You have me in your spell."

"Let's skip dinner. I don't want to let go of you," he said. He squeezed me tighter.

I pulled free of his arms and said, "It's almost ready, and I'm hungry. Besides, we have the whole evening together."

He kissed me again and handed me the knife. "Fine. I'll have to satisfy myself with watching you slice onions."

"I love you," I said and winked at him.

While we finished cooking and eating our dinner, I tried not to think about the complications that might arise with this new level in our relationship. I savored my good fortune of having a man like Jay Morgan to love me and planned to make the most of it while it lasted.

I hurried to the hospital the next morning to tell Johnny what had happened and to ease my guilt for neglecting him to spend so much time with Jay. As I approached his room, I hoped that it would be the day Johnny regained consciousness, as the last puzzle piece to my new happiness. I found him unconscious like the day before and every day before that. To keep from getting discouraged, I massaged Johnny's legs and told him my news.

Jay came in smiling an hour later. He kissed me and said, "I haven't stopped thinking about you since last night. It's making it hard to do my work. What have you done to me?"

"I could ask the same question. I love you," I said. "That feels great to say."

"Love you too. Now we better get back to work. I have news for you. It's not much, and I don't want to get your hopes up, but look at Johnny's latest EEG and MRI."

He held up his tablet so that I could read the screen. Both results showed slightly improved brain activity. It wasn't much, but it was the first sign of improvement Johnny had shown.

"Is this happening on its own or as a result of something you're doing?" I asked without taking my eyes from the screen.

"Both, I think, even though we haven't done much. There isn't much we can do, as you know. If this is true recovery, I would expect steady progress from here. It may just be an anomaly. I'll be watching closely in the next few days."

I hugged Jay. "This news comes at the perfect time. I knew he'd start getting better eventually."

Jay gently pushed me away and said, "Hang on before you get too excited. I just said it may be an anomaly. This is why I hesitated to show you the results. You have a blind spot when it comes to Johnny."

"Maybe, but what's the harm? He needs someone fighting for him. He can't do it himself, so why not me?" I asked. If it had been any other day, Jay's comment would have offended me, but I knew he loved me and was probably concerned about me. I shook it off and smiled. "It doesn't matter if I have a blind spot or not. Johnny will recover, or he won't. How we feel about it makes no difference."

"True. Now, I have to go back to work, my beautiful girl. I won't be able to see you tonight. I have meetings."

"Don't worry about it. I'll stay here and read. We'll have the whole weekend, right?" I said. I was bothered and a little confused by my relief to have time away from Jay. I decided to think about that later and gave him a lingering kiss. "See you in the morning."

"You can count on it," he said and left.

Johnny's brain activity showed slight improvement two more times, but then the progress stopped. No one could figure it out, not even Jay. My frustration grew along with my determination. My gut told me Johnny just needed more time, and all I could do was hope that Jay would be willing to give him that.

CHAPTER ELEVEN

Jay and I were snuggling on his den sofa one night after we'd been dating for over two months. The den was the one room in Jay's house I liked. It was intimate and cozy. I was at ease there. We'd ordered one of my favorite romantic comedies on pay-per-view but missed most of it. I nestled closer to Jay and kissed his cheek. He leaned in and brushed his lips on my neck the way I loved. As he kissed me, he moved his hand to the front of my blouse and started to unbutton it. He slipped his hand in the opening and caressed my skin. I shivered at his touch.

"Grace, stay here with me," he whispered. "It would be so much easier. Let's move your things over in the morning."

He shifted his weight so that he was partially on top of me. His words and the movement startled me back to my senses. Had he just asked me to move in with him? Fiery panic welled up in my gut.

"No, stop it, Danny!" I struggled out from under him and moved to the opposite side of the room. I turned away to button my blouse.

Jay groaned behind me. "Who's Danny?" he asked.

"What?" I asked, turning to face him.

"You called me Danny. Who's that? One of your former lovers?" He sounded as confused as I felt.

"I called you Danny?" I asked, not able to believe what he was saying. I'd never told him Danny's name. How else could he have known? "I'm sorry, Jay. I don't know why I said that. Danny is my ex-husband."

"Ex-husband? What's going on here?"

I hesitated, not knowing what to say. The truth would mean telling my whole story. I only had seconds to decide. To stall I said, "I panicked when you asked me to move in with you. You did ask me to move in, didn't you?"

"Yes, I did. Is the idea so terrifying that it calls up your ex and sends you scurrying away? I'll ask one more time: What's going on?"

It sounded more like a command than a question, but I did owe him an explanation. I sighed in resignation and sat down, still shocked at what I'd done. Without looking at Jay, I said, "You know about my past, but not everything. Some of it was too painful to tell. You'll view me differently if I tell you, and you'll pity me. I don't want your pity."

"It's worse than what you told me about your father?"

"Yes. Worse." I stopped, needing to breathe before I bared my soul to him. After recounting the details, I said. "Since I escaped him, I've isolated myself from intimate relationships. You're the only man I've been with other than Danny, and I left him over twenty years ago. I never expected to fall in love with anyone. I never knew what love was until I met you, but this is happening so fast."

Jay pulled me into his arms and kissed the top of my head. "I'm sick at the thought of anyone hurting you. You're the kindest person I've ever known. Danny's lucky he's not here."

I sat up and faced him. "See, you're pitying me. It was twenty years ago. I would have said I was over it until I called you Danny. I rarely think about it now."

"I wish you'd told me sooner. I would have respected your feelings. I'm not Danny," he said.

I relaxed against him. "I know. I thought I had everything under control. That was my first mistake. I was planning to tell you if our relationship got serious. I do feel better now that it's out there though."

Jay lifted my face to his and kissed me again. He pulled back after a few seconds, and said, "I'm glad you feel better, and I promise I won't pity you. You're too strong for that. Now, to change the subject, I noticed that in spite of what just happened, you still haven't answered me."

I looked him in the eye. "You always tell me how much you admire my honesty, so here's the truth: after what happened with Danny, I promised myself that I'd never live with a man unless we were married. Any man who truly loved me would have to be willing to make that commitment. I know it's an old-fashioned concept, but it's nonnegotiable with me."

Jay paused for several seconds before he said, "Then marry me."

I locked eyes with him, trying to gage if he was serious, but before I could I started to giggle.

Jay pulled away and crossed his arms. "Not the reaction I'd hoped for," he said.

"You caught me off guard. I was expecting you to break up with me." I fell against the sofa and laughed again. It was one of those nervous laughs, the kind not far removed from crying. As soon as I was able to stop, Jay scowled and set me off again. I finally sat up and took a few gulps of water, hoping it would help me get a grip.

Jay shook his head and said, "Who else but Grace Ward would laugh at a marriage proposal? And why would you think I was breaking up with you?"

I swallowed my last sip and said, "Regretting you asked me yet?" He shook his head again.

I took his hand and squeezed it between my hands. "I was afraid you'd think I wasn't worth it with all my baggage. But you need to know that I wasn't fishing for a proposal. I just wanted to help you understand why I can't move in with you."

"I didn't propose because of what you said. I've been thinking about it for a few weeks. I was waiting for the right time. I guess this wasn't it," Jay said and rubbed his forehead.

"No, I guess not." I took three deep breaths to keep from laughing again. "You know how much I love you, but it's only been two and a half months. That's too soon to be considering marriage."

"According to whom? At my age, I don't need a year or even a month to know. When I want something, I go for it. You know that. I've never felt this way for anyone either, not even my ex-wife. Johnny's study is almost over. He'll be going back to Richmond. I'm not letting you get away."

"You're serious about this?" I asked.

"Yes, believe me. Do I have any chance, or is it hopeless?"

"I don't know. There's a lot to consider. How can I just pick up my life and move here? What about my job? What about Johnny?" I got up and started pacing. The thought of moving to Baltimore permanently seemed too overwhelming to imagine.

"What's Johnny got to do with this?" he asked.

"Johnny has a great deal to do with this. I'm not going to just abandon him. I haven't changed my mind about adopting him."

Jay sat forward with his shoulders hunched, staring at the floor. "There's next to no chance of him surviving, let alone regaining consciousness. When are you going to accept that? It's time to prepare for the worst."

I stared at him without speaking. What he said about Johnny was the last thing I needed to hear. I'd had enough emotional upheaval for one day.

Jay lifted his head. "I know that look. I think I've lost this round."

"I need time to think. It's late, and I want to decide with the right body part. I should go."

Jay kissed me again. "Fine," he said. "I'll take you home, but don't take too long to make up your mind. I'm ready to wake up next to you for the rest of my life."

⚔

I called Alec early the next morning to catch her before she left for work. "Hi, Alec, it's Grace," I said when she answered.

"I'm so relieved. I was starting to get worried. Didn't you get my messages?"

"I did. I'm sorry I didn't call sooner. I've been busy."

"Work or pleasure?"

"Both, but maybe a little more of the latter."

"I'm glad to hear it. How's the fabulous Dr. Jay?" Alec said, teasing me.

"I wish you wouldn't call him that," I said. "He's fine. In fact, he's the reason I'm calling. I need to talk to you, but not over the phone."

"Sounds serious. Is everything okay?" she asked.

"Everything's fine, but I need to use you as a sounding board. I know it's short notice, but can you drive up today and spend the weekend? I wouldn't ask if it weren't important."

"I can. In fact, this is the perfect weekend for me to go. Adam's going to Denver for a few days on family business. I was just going to hang out here. I'll leave after work."

"You have no idea how happy I am to hear that. See you tonight."

With that settled, I got dressed to go to the hospital. Jay had promised to keep his distance for a few days. Knowing his schedule and that he would have already finished rounds, I planned to go visit Johnny. I wanted nothing more than to be near Jay, but my ability to think rationally shrunk in proportion to my proximity to him. Alec had no idea how much I needed her to keep me in line.

⛬

I met Alec at the door with a hug. We hadn't seen each other in several weeks, and I was glad to see her standing in my doorway. "I was getting worried," I said. "Why are you so late?"

"The traffic was terrible. I'd forgotten how bad I-95 is on Fridays. I'm glad I made it. I hope you didn't wait on me to get dinner. I ate on the way."

"No, I had a sandwich in Johnny's room earlier," I said.

She took my hands and stepped back. "You look great. I'm loving the new outfit and hairdo. Now that the small talk's out of the way, what's going on?"

We were still in the doorway, so I took Alec's suitcase and motioned her toward the sofa. I sat on the loveseat facing her. "I'm so glad you're here. It's been awful not having anyone to talk to."

"I've been dying of curiosity. You were so cryptic on the phone," Alec said and leaned back, looking like a psychiatrist waiting for me to spill. All she needed was a notepad.

I smiled at her, relieved she was there. Alec was the one person in the world who understood me.

"Well, as you know, Jay and I have been seeing each other since about a week after I got here," I said. "I couldn't resist him. Isn't he gorgeous?" I'd texted her a picture the week before. "He's everything I used to wish for in a man."

"Yes, very distinguished," Alec said.

"It was all so out of the blue. The last thing on my mind when I came here was that I'd become involved with a man. My better judgment screamed against it too, but my heart wouldn't listen," I said.

"That's like what happened with Adam and me. I sure wasn't looking for a relationship when I met him."

I nodded, remembering how hard she'd fought her feelings for Adam. "It's too bad we can't plan who we fall in love with or when. It sure would have saved me years of anguish."

"Fall in love with? You're in love with Jay?" Alec asked, and sat forward on the edge of the couch.

I nodded and looked away in embarrassment.

"This is great. I thought your relationship was casual. I had no idea you were in love with him. When did this happen?"

"About five seconds after I met him," I said. "I kept it from you because I just planned to enjoy it while it lasted and then walk away. That's not an option anymore. He's asked me to stay and marry him."

She came and sat next to me. "Marry him? You're kidding. What did you say?"

"I haven't answered yet. There's more to it than a simple proposal. There's Johnny to consider. He's supposed to go back to Richmond in a few weeks. That's why I needed to talk to you. Tell me what to do, Alec. Should I stay here with the man I love in a secure and promising life, or should I go back to Richmond for the child I love and want to raise? There are so many uncertainties if I go, but Johnny is a part of me. I can't abandon him now."

She squeezed my hand and said, "Why didn't you tell me all of this sooner? I can't imagine what you've been going through."

"Everything spun out of control before I knew what was happening."

Alec sat back and pulled her hair back like she always did when she was concentrating. It was good to see some things hadn't changed. "I know it's probably pointless to ask, but is there any chance of Jay transferring to Richmond?"

"And give up a top position at one of the premier hospitals in the world? Not a chance. He's worked for years to get where he is.

Leaving here is out of the question, and I wouldn't ask him to. His daughters are here too."

Alec turned to face me. "Can't you go back to Richmond until the adoption is final, and then bring Johnny here? Would Jay wait for you?"

I got up and started pacing. I didn't want to tell her that Jay thought my plans to adopt Johnny were crazy, even though she'd once felt the same way. I was still hoping to change his mind like I had with her. Instead, I said, "If I'm able to adopt Johnny, it could take several months to a year. I don't want to be pulled between Johnny and Jay all the time. This is going to be hard enough without having my heart torn in two. Why isn't anything ever easy for me?"

"Being in love doesn't always hurt, you know. What does Jay think about your plans for Johnny?"

To stall, I walked to the kitchenette and started loading the dishwasher. It was clear from the look on Alec's face that she knew exactly what I was doing. I loaded the last mug and said, "He admires my devotion but believes I'm setting myself up for heartbreak. He knows more about Johnny's condition than anyone, but he still can't give me any definitive answers." I was sugarcoating it, but I didn't want to lie to her. "It seems like one week things are good, and the next, they're hopeless. I can hardly keep up with it. It's so frustrating. He says I should forget about Johnny until, or if, he comes out of the coma. He doesn't think that's going to happen though."

"I remember six weeks ago he was saying there was a possibility for Johnny to regain consciousness. What happened to change his mind?"

I sat down and stared at my feet. "I don't want to talk about Johnny right now," I said softly. "I need you to help me figure out what to do about Jay."

She took a deep breath and said, "You know how I feel about Johnny, and I can't believe I'm going to say this, but after all the loss and pain you've suffered, don't you deserve to think of your own happiness for once? Adam and I can look after Johnny. If he regains consciousness, you can come to Richmond and start the adoption process. I'm not trying to get rid of you. I'd miss you so much, but it would make me happier than anything to see you have the love you deserve."

I nodded. "I've told myself the same thing a hundred times, but the honest truth is that I can't leave Johnny. I was miserable when we were only apart for a few days. Besides, you and Adam have your own lives. You didn't sign on to take care of Johnny. It wouldn't be fair. I've taken on that responsibility. It comes down to a question of who needs me more, Johnny or Jay. The answer to that is clear."

"What about what Grace needs?" she asked.

"I don't have the luxury to be that selfish," I said.

"Selfish? No one would call marrying the man you love selfish, but I get it. Don't count Jay out yet. You don't have to break it off with him when you go. Richmond is only three hours away. I can't stand the idea of you giving up the best thing that's ever happened to you. I know what it's like to fall in love with the perfect man."

"I do love him, but he's not the best thing that ever happened to me. I have a great life in Richmond. I have Adam and you and Johnny. I know it's not the same thing, but until I met Jay, I was content. He isn't going anywhere. If it's meant to happen, it will."

"Not many women in this world would pass up a man like Jay," she said and shook her head.

I agreed with her but couldn't see a way to have the best of both worlds. "Don't make me into a saint. Just because I know this is the right choice doesn't mean it's easy. I don't want to live without Jay, but if he can't accept that Johnny is an important part of my life, then maybe there's no room for him. I haven't given up though. He's a father. Maybe he'll understand."

"I don't know the guy, so I can't say, but for your sake, I hope he does. When are you going to tell him?" she asked.

I sighed and said, "On Monday. He gave me the weekend to think it over."

"You'd better be on that phone to me the minute it's done," Alec said.

"I promise," I said and got up again. "Let's forget about this for now and make plans for our weekend. We'll start by going to see Johnny in the morning, if that's all right with you."

"I'd love to see him. I'd better get to bed now, though, or I won't be able to get up before noon."

We made up my sofa with extra sheets and blankets that Alec had brought, and then we both got ready for bed. Alec was asleep two minutes after she turned off her light, but I was wide awake. My conversation with her had left me with more questions than answers. I stewed over it for three hours until an idea struck me. I kicked myself for not having thought of it sooner. I decided not to tell Alec. I wanted to see what Jay thought first. Satisfied with my solution, I turned out the light and went to sleep.

Wanting to be on neutral ground, I asked Jay to meet me at the park near the hospital on Monday afternoon. It was a frigid April day. The sky was gray, and a crisp breeze was blowing. I pulled my jacket around my neck and looked around, hoping we'd be alone. I got there before Jay, so I walked along the trail and practiced the speech I'd gone over a thousand times. When it was time, I went to our favorite bench to wait. Jay, who was punctual to a fault, appeared right on time. He took my hand to help me up and enveloped me in his arms. My determination melted at the feel of him. I longed to tell him I'd never let him go, but he pulled away and led me to the bench.

"That's promising," he said and kissed me. "These past few days have been torture. Please tell me you have an answer."

My brain turned to mush, and the words of my speech vanished. I looked into his eyes and said, "Yes, I'll marry you, Jay."

He smiled, and his joy shone in his eyes. He kissed me again, but I pulled away.

When I could get my mouth to form the words, I said, "But I have some conditions."

Jay groaned and sat back. "Not conditions," he said. "Is this about Johnny? You know how I feel about that, but—"

"Just listen." Regaining control of my senses, I took a few breaths and said, "I'm confused about what you told me about him. Not long ago you were encouraged by his progress. Now suddenly, you're convinced there's no hope for him?"

"It's not suddenly. I've been telling you all along, but you refused to listen. I hope you're listening now. I'm going to recommend that Johnny be removed from life support." His tone became more tense and accusatory with each word. I backed away out of instinct.

I hardly recognized the face staring back at me. He'd become a stranger who was going to sign Johnny's death warrant. I wanted to shake him and beg him to reconsider, but I knew it was pointless.

"The fact that you still want to adopt Johnny makes me rethink everything I know about you. I get that he's an abandoned orphan who fell in your lap, but I thought you'd get over this little fantasy of playing house with Johnny by now. If you want to be a mother, go find a kid who's not brain-dead." Having put the final nail in his argument, he sat back and crossed his arms over his chest.

I stood and squared my shoulders. "Then I guess it's for the best that you proposed when you did. Our masks are off, and we see each other for who we truly are. You've saved me from a terrible mistake."

Jay stood and faced me. "You're right. It *is* for the best. I used to think you were so smart. You're nothing but a fool." He glared at me and stalked off without looking back.

I dropped to my knees in the middle of the park and sobbed, not caring who saw me. Jay had crushed all my dreams for a happy family with one master stroke.

⊷⊶

I walked around for two hours but finally got so cold that I made my way back to my apartment. I'd known since I met with Jay that he might reject my idea, but I never imagined he'd try to destroy me. I dialed Alec's number knowing she must be dying to hear from me. I drummed my fingers on the table while I waited for her to answer.

"Hello?" Alec said, stifling a yawn.

"It's me. I'm sorry to call so late," I said.

"My shift was grueling today, and I just got out of the bath. What's wrong? You sound terrible," she said. It was comforting to hear the concern in her voice.

"I am terrible. It didn't go well with Jay. In fact, it was worse than I could have imagined." Tears threatened again, but I fought them off.

"What happened? I thought you were going to say yes," she said.

"I did, but I told him it was on the condition that he accept my plan to adopt Johnny. He went ballistic and called me a fool for having any hope for Johnny."

"Ouch," Alec said. "That must have been devastating."

That's putting it mildly, I thought. "It's worse than when Johnny got sick during the quarantine. Worse than my suspension. I wish I were there with you. I want to come home." I started crying, too exhausted to hold back.

"I wish you were too. You'll be here soon." The line went quiet, and I thought we'd lost the connection. Then I heard what sounded like blankets rustling. "Sorry. I was getting comfortable," she said.

"Honestly, none of this makes sense to me. If Jay thinks there's no hope for Johnny, why would that stop him from marrying you? If he's right, it'll be a moot point. If you're right, then Johnny will get better, and you go on from there. It's not as though your situation with Johnny was a secret. He's known from the beginning."

I blew my nose and grabbed a clean tissue. "It doesn't make sense to me either. You should have seen him. He was furious. I'm still not sure how it all went so wrong. All I can think is that he never really loved me."

"See, that doesn't make sense either," she said. "Why did he propose? Why wasn't he willing to wait to see what happened with Johnny first?"

"I haven't told you everything. Jay is going to recommend removing Johnny from life support."

The line went quiet again, but I knew she was probably digesting what I'd said.

"I don't even know what to say to that," she said. "For some reason, I can't get rid of the feeling that there's something deeper going on. Aside from what's happening between the two of you, I find it hard to believe that any physician, no matter how revered, can say unequivocally that there's no hope for Johnny. Do you have access to all the records?"

"Yes," I said, not sure what she was getting at. "Jay's been giving me copies of everything. I don't have his final report, but I'm not sure it's even finished yet."

"Compile everything you have from the day Johnny got to Baltimore. Speak with some of the other researchers. I know that this is Jay's project, but maybe someone else has a different opinion."

"What good will that do?" I asked. My head was pounding from all the crying. The idea of doing what Alec suggested seemed overwhelming. I just wanted to take a pain reliever and forget the day had ever happened.

"Hear me out," she said. "Maybe you'll come across some info that will explain Jay's behavior. At the least, it might help you learn why Jay reacted the way he did. If he's right, it might help prepare you for the worst too."

She had a good point. Doing what Alec said might help me make sense of everything. "I'll think about it," I said.

"I hate to bring up another stinky subject, but have you thought of how Kinsley will react if Jay files a report recommending removing life support? Kinsley wouldn't hesitate for a second."

I groaned and said, "Not until now, thank you very much."

"I'm sorry for bringing it up. I guess that's a little too much after the day you've had." When I didn't respond, she said, "Take a hot bath and get some sleep. I'll call you in the morning when we both have clearer heads."

"Don't worry about upsetting me. I count on your honesty, even if you're telling me what I don't want to hear. Thanks for listening and trying to help."

"I've always got your back."

Even after a long bath, I couldn't asleep. What Alec had said was true. Jay had been encouraged by the early test results. If he'd discovered something recently, he hadn't shared it with me. I wondered if he had been protecting me, but I wasn't some naïve child. Then again, I realized that maybe he had tried to tell me, and I wouldn't listen. The more I tried to make sense of Jay's behavior, the more confused I got.

After two agonizing hours, I decided to do what I'd done the day after Johnny came into my life. I went to him. As soon as I saw my sweet boy lying peacefully in his crib, my thoughts cleared, and I knew what I had to do. I brushed my finger against his palm, and he squeezed. "That's right, Johnny. Keep fighting. Help me prove Jay wrong."

I waited for Jay in his office three days later. He'd texted me several times and left voice messages, but I'd ignored them. There was nothing he could say to take back what he'd done. I was there for Johnny, nothing more. I held the draft of his final report along with an inch-thick file in a manila folder. I'd listened to Alec for once and had used the time to study Johnny's medical records from Jay's study as well as similar cases. I also spoke with some of the nurses and researchers. They were reluctant to talk to me, but when I told them I was only trying to educate myself about patients like Johnny, they cooperated. I compiled my conclusions and waited to confront Jay with the results.

Jay stopped in the doorway when he saw me but then came right for me. He took the folder from my hands without a word and set it on the desk. Then he took my hands to help me up and pulled me into his arms. He caught me off guard, and before I could resist, he lifted my chin to kiss me. His lips were warm and inviting. I'd been so engrossed in my research that I hadn't realized how much I missed him. I forgot why I came to see him. I forgot Johnny and the rest of the world. All I knew was the comfort of being in his arms.

"I've missed you," he said and brushed his lips on my neck. "Please tell me you're here to say you've changed your mind."

His words brought me back to my senses. I struggled free and grabbed the back of the chair for support.

He stepped forward, but I held up my hand to stop him. "No, Jay, please don't," I said.

"What's going on?" he asked, the hurt and confusion clear in his eyes.

That got me fired up. He had no right to be hurt. I was the injured party. I wasn't his victim though. My days of being a victim were over. I picked up the file and sat down. "I'm sorry. I shouldn't have allowed that," I said and straightened my blouse. "Nothing's changed. I came here to talk about Johnny's case before I go back to Richmond."

"If nothing's changed, why didn't you stop me? What are you trying to do to me, you vixen?"

"So what am I, then, Jay? A fool or a vixen?"

He flinched, and I savored the moment, knowing I'd gained some ground. Dealing with Jay reminded me of my bouts with Kinsley, without the kissing part, of course.

"Please sit down and stop glaring at me," I said. "I'm here about Johnny's case."

He stared at me for a few more seconds before saying, "Why haven't you returned my calls?" Without waiting for an answer, he walked around his huge mahogany desk and dropped into his leather chair. "I've been trying to apologize. I don't know what came over me in the park. You know that wasn't the real me. I was just so hurt. Please forgive me."

"You were hurt? I didn't do anything. That was all on you." Talking about our encounter in the park brought it all back, and my burst of courage fizzled slightly. I reminded myself that I was there for Johnny, not myself. I sat up straighter and said, "You may feel bad about what you did, but the fact that you could treat me that way is all I need to know. You destroyed any chance of a future for us. I may forgive you in time, but that doesn't mean I'll ever want a life with you."

"Fine," he said. "If you're incapable of forgiveness, so be it. I'm not going to beg. Now, what's all this about Johnny's case?" His eyes became guarded, and he sat back with his arms crossed.

Determined not to let him intimidate me, I said, "I've been going over all the test results and reports from Johnny's study, as well as other recent studies. I've also read the draft of your conclusions. I'm hoping to convince you to reevaluate your conclusions before you submit your report. I found discrepancies."

"Are you telling me that because you've read a few test results and some medical records, you think you know more about

Johnny's case than I do? You're just a nurse. I've devoted weeks to this study. There aren't discrepancies. You just can't bring yourself to accept reality," he said.

"I may not be a doctor, but you always told me how intelligent I am. I understand the implications, but I know Johnny. I expected the documentation to prove you right, but it didn't. All I'm asking is that you look at my findings. If you don't think they have merit, show me why. Then you can toss the file if you want. Otherwise, I intend to dispute your final report."

"Can you honestly believe I would publish a flawed report? I wouldn't risk my career or a child's life."

I looked down and rubbed my forehead with my fingers. I tried to make sense of how just days before we were talking about marriage, and now we were arguing across his desk as enemies. I looked him in the eye. "After the other day, I'm not sure what you're capable of, but what do you have to lose by reading my findings? If you're afraid of a mere nurse showing you up, you don't need to worry. No one else knows about this. You can tell people that on the final evaluation, you found new information. You'll be praised for preventing a medical tragedy."

"I can't believe we're having this conversation. I'm looking at a stranger. I still love you, even now. I thought you loved me too. What's happened to you?"

I stood and dropped the file on Jay's desk. "*You* happened to me, Jay, but this has nothing to do with us. What are you going to do about Johnny's case?"

"It's a waste of time, but out of my love for you, I'll look at the file. I'm busy, so it might take a few days to get to it. Then we'll meet and talk about Johnny's case and what's going to happen between us before you leave."

"Thank you. That means a great deal to me. Call me after you've read my findings, and we'll talk—about everything." I walked out without looking back. I'd won round one, but I knew I had a long way to go. I prayed for the strength to go the distance.

⇥⊹⇤

I waited for Jay's call for three days. After breakfast on the fourth day, I went to see Johnny before going to find Jay. I was lost in thought as I opened Johnny's door. It took a few seconds to register that he wasn't there. His crib was empty and freshly made. All the decorations and other items I'd placed in his room were in a box on the table. I ran to the nurses' station to find out what was going on. No one would look me in the eye.

"Heather, where's Johnny?" I asked.

"He's on his way back to Richmond. Dr. Morgan submitted his findings yesterday and notified the administration there that Johnny was going back today. I was going to call you, but Dr. Morgan said you knew what was going on."

I leaned on the counter for support and said, "Can you get me a copy of his report?"

"Yes, I can e-mail it to you." She handed me a notepad to write down my e-mail address.

I started to go after I wrote it down but turned back to Heather instead. "Have you read the report?"

Heather shook her head.

"Well, then have you noticed any changes in Dr. Morgan's conclusions or decisions about Johnny?" I asked.

Heather hesitated before saying, "It's not my place to notice. I'm just here to do my job."

I stormed off in a blind rage. I wasn't angry with Heather. I knew it was all Jay's doing. I went back to my apartment and threw everything into my suitcases. After I packed, I got on my laptop and booked the next commuter flight to Richmond. It cost a fortune, but I didn't care. As I was about to call Alec, the phone rang. It was her calling me.

She started talking in a rush before I could get a word in. "Johnny's here. Why didn't you tell me he was coming back today?"

"I just found out. Jay did this behind my back. I was just about to get a cab to the airport. I get in at seven."

"I'll pick you up and fill you in on what's happening here. Please tell me you made backups of your research," she said.

"Of course, for all the good it'll do. Jay already submitted his case study," I said, confused at why she'd asked.

"Good, and I know. Don't worry about that. I'll see you in a few hours."

She hung up before I could ask what she was talking about. I stared at my phone like it could give me answers. After a few seconds, I called a cab and waited on the front step for it to come, wondering what my life held next.

CHAPTER TWELVE

My flight was smooth in contrast to my internal turbulence. I was relieved to see Alec waiting for me at the baggage claim. Once we were in the car, she said, "Johnny's settled in his old room. That's the good news. You aren't going to like what else I have to tell you."

"It can't be worse than what I've been through this week."

Alec squeezed my arm and gave me a sad smile. I was comforted to know that I wouldn't have to deal with my problems alone anymore.

"Adam was livid when I told him what Jay did to you. We all were," she said.

"What do you mean 'we all'? Who else knows about Jay and me?" I felt rising dread that my troubles were the current topic of hospital gossip.

Alec ignored my question and said, "Adam got suspicious when I told him what happened with you and Jay, especially after he and Brad Carter saw your report."

"Brad Carter? He knows about this, too? I should be asking who doesn't know," I said.

She tapped my arm. "Just listen. Adam is friends with Pete Sanders. They go way back. He doesn't know you and Adam are friends or about his involvement with Johnny."

Pete Sanders was Kinsley's executive assistant. I'd never met him and had only seen his name on paperwork that passed through Kinsley's office. I hadn't known that Adam knew him. I was surprised that he didn't know that Adam and I were friends.

I was about to interrupt her again, but before I could, she said, "Adam and Pete went to dinner the other night, and Pete had a little too much to drink. He blabbed that Kinsley is an old crony of the chief of staff in Baltimore. According to Pete, Kinsley pulled strings to make sure Johnny's study had the result they wanted. The chief of staff at Baltimore Regional is retiring this year, and if Pete has his story straight, he promised the position to none other than our Dr. Jay Morgan if he'd cooperate. Can you believe that?"

"Wait, what?" I said, totally confused by what she was saying.

"I'm trying to tell you that Jay was coerced into making sure Johnny's study came out the way Kinsley wanted. Adam didn't believe it either. He thought Pete was making stuff up to get attention, but he seemed really nervous when he was telling Adam."

I laughed and said, "Oh, come on, Alec. Do you actually believe this? It's like something from a bad crime show. Jay didn't change Johnny's prognosis until recently, and he seemed positive about Johnny's chances at first. Why would he have done that?"

"I'll tell you in two words: Grace Ward. Adam said that maybe Jay had a conscience at first and refused to cooperate, especially after he became involved with you. When he saw that you wouldn't give up on Johnny and things went south between you, he probably figured he had nothing to lose. He may have even thought that with Johnny out of the way, you'd marry him."

Hearing her say that did make some sense. It would also explain Jay's bizarre reaction to my wanting to adopt Johnny. When the implications of what she was saying hit me, I shook my head. "I've seen my share of insanity in this life, but this is just too crazy. I could believe it of Kinsley, who sees everything in terms of dollars and cents. Maybe he's fed up with footing some of the bill for Johnny. And I never met the chief of staff in Baltimore, so I can't speak for him, but even after everything Jay did to me, I can't believe that he would stoop this low. It's more than my relationship with him. I watched him work for over two months. He genuinely cares about his patients. No one's that good of an actor, and we're talking about a child's life here. On top of all that, I'm planning to adopt Johnny. That takes the problem off their shoulders."

"How can you say that after what Jay pulled today? He ignored your report and sneaked Johnny out of there right under your nose. And the hospital would have to pay for Johnny until the adoption was final. Like you said, it takes up to a year. Paul's not sure it's even going to be possible."

I remembered how furious I'd been earlier that day, and my certainty wavered. How much did I know about Jay? I rubbed my forehead to calm my growing headache. "I'm exhausted, and this is too much to think about now. I want to see Johnny and then go home to my own bed. Can't we forget Jay and everything that happened in Baltimore? I was planning to start the adoption papers tomorrow. Can't we focus on that and not on trying to take down the bistate medical establishment?"

We rode along in silence for a few minutes until Alec said, "I'm sorry to dump this on you the second you're in the car, but you may not have much time. It can wait until morning though." She was quiet again for a few minutes but finally said, "I've missed you. I love Adam, but he's terrible at girl talk. Let's get dinner tomorrow after I get off. We'll catch up then."

I nodded but didn't say anything. I looked out the window as we neared the city, grateful to see the Richmond skyline welcoming me home.

⋙ ⋘

I'd never been so happy to walk through my front door. My time in Baltimore had changed me, but my little house was like an old friend welcoming me in with open arms. It was my safe place.

I went straight to bed when I got home. My back was thrilled to get reacquainted with my comfy mattress. After a great night's sleep, I got up to tackle the pile of mail waiting on the kitchen table. Alec had been picking it up and mailing it to me in weekly batches, but she hadn't sent the last one. She had given it to me on the way back from the airport. Other than another letter from Aunt Jenny begging me to come for a visit, the rest was junk and bills. I paid the bills and put Aunt Jenny's letter aside to deal with later, not having the energy to think of another excuse to put her off.

With that out of the way, I did a full inspection of the house. I'd had a cleaning service coming in every two weeks, and I was impressed with the job they had done. The house was cleaner than it had been when I was taking care of it. I was about to e-mail them to thank them and cancel their service but changed my mind and asked if they would keep coming. I could easily afford it and not having to do the heavy cleaning would free up time for me to spend with Johnny. They e-mailed right back saying they'd be happy to keep me as a client.

With my morning shaping up nicely, I went to take a long, relaxing shower. The phone rang two minutes after I started, but I ignored it. I assumed it was Alec wanting to light a fire under me. I cursed when it rang for the third time and turned off the water. Dripping all over the carpet, I grabbed my cell off my bed and checked the caller ID. It was Alec as I suspected, but I knew that not even she would be so insistent if it weren't important.

"Couldn't whatever this is wait two minutes, Alec? I was in the shower," I said without bothering to say hello.

"No, it can't," she said in a rush. "It's bad. Kinsley must have passed Jay's report to DSS. They've filed a petition to remove Johnny from life support. Get over here. Now!" she said and hung up.

I sank down to the wet carpet and stared at my phone, waiting for it to tell me I'd heard wrong. The blank screen stared back in silence. I started to shiver and feared I was going into shock. I dried off and dressed as fast as I could. Nothing mattered but getting to my Johnny.

Alec and Serena Davis were in Johnny's room when I got there. Johnny's feeding tube was still in, so I had made it in time. I turned to Serena and said, "Tell me what's happening. How could this happen so fast? Jay just filed his report yesterday."

"I don't know about that," she said. "All I know is that the Department of Social Services petitioned the court for permission to remove Johnny from life support. A courier delivered a copy of the court papers a few minutes before I left my office. I came as soon as I read it. They're saying that, based on the study results, he's brain-dead, and they're merely keeping his body alive. I was completely blindsided."

I grabbed the rail on Johnny's crib for support. "They're going to kill him? He's costing too much to keep alive, so they're just going to kill him?" I said. "What happens now? How do we fight this?"

"Listen to me," Serena said, putting her hands on my shoulders. "Don't panic yet. We're a long way from them removing life support."

I broke free of her grasp. "After all I've done, it comes to this. After fighting for him and caring for him for so long, I'm supposed to stand by and watch them murder him? That's what this is, you know. It's murder."

Alec stepped toward me and said, "No one is asking you to just stand by. The first thing we need to do is talk to Paul. He'll walk us through the process."

I calmed down when she mentioned Paul. He knew what was at stake. We could trust him to fight along with us for Johnny.

"Don't take too long," Serena said. "There is a process, but I have a feeling Kinsley will put pressure on my department to rush this before word gets out. They'll do anything to avoid the negative publicity."

Hearing her say "my department" made me realize the position Serena was in. Her office had ordered the petition. "You need to stay out of this," I told her. "You'd be risking too much to help us. You'd be going against your employer."

"Don't worry about me. Kinsley did go over my head, but I'm still Johnny's assigned caseworker. I'm his advocate. There are things I can do from my end. Just let me do my job. Speaking of which, I need to get back to the office, but I'll keep in touch. I meant what I said. Don't panic. I'm not."

I nodded, and she squeezed my hand on her way out. I walked to Johnny and caressed his cheek. He was so peaceful. I'd have given anything to know that feeling.

"Kinsley's going to pull the plug on him, Alec," I said without turning around. "Can't Johnny and I have one moment of peace in our rotten lives? Maybe we'd all have been better off if I'd never gone to see Johnny that first day."

"Don't say that. Johnny wouldn't be better off, and neither would you. Are you saying that what happened that day wasn't real? It's what's been driving you all these months. You said it gave you a reason to live. You were so sure," Alex said and put her hand on my shoulder.

"I believed it was real. I'm not sure of anything anymore. I thought Jay was a good man too. I was in love with him. I considered marrying him. How can he do this to us?"

Alec turned me to face her and said, "I told you in the car last night. He's being extorted," Alec said. "We have your report. We have to use it against them."

I groaned and said, "Not that again. You want me to prove that administrators from two prestigious hospitals coerced a well-respected, world-renowned neurologist into falsifying research-study results. I'm not strong enough to do that. If I tried and failed, Johnny would die. I couldn't live with that. Besides, who would believe me over Jay?"

"If you do nothing, Johnny definitely dies. Face it, that report is your only weapon. What choice do you have?"

I took the satin corner of Johnny's blanket and rubbed it between my fingers. "I only have one picture of my mother. It's of my brothers and me having a picnic with her in a park. I've thought of going back to find that park, but it's probably buried under a strip mall by now," I said with a half grin.

"It was before Mama got cancer. I felt safe and protected, like nothing bad would ever happen to me again. Fate had a few punches left of course, but I didn't know it that day. That day, my life was perfect. My mother had given me a precious gift of pure happiness. Since Johnny came into my life, I've hoped to be able to give him that someday. In spite of what happened between Johnny and me that first day, I need to do this for his sake and to honor my mother. I can't let them take that away. I'll do it. I'll fight them. It's a matter of wounded pride for Jay and a matter of money for the hospital. For Johnny and me, it's a matter of life and death."

Alec looked at me with tears on her cheeks. The only other time I'd seen her cry was during the quarantine. I was comforted to know she felt what I did.

"I'm proud of you. I know what a sacrifice this is, but they don't know what they're up against with you. You have more strength than you know, and we'll be beside you. The first thing we need to do is call Paul."

Alec reached for her purse and bumped a table next to the rocking chair. Johnny's chart crashed to the floor. He flinched at the sound.

"Did you see that?" Alec asked.

"I did," I said. "Was it coincidence or response to the sound?"

Alec picked up the chart and dropped it again. Johnny flailed his arms like a startled newborn.

"It was the sound! He's never done that. Get Dr. Carter in here," I said.

As Alec ran out of the room, I slapped Johnny's chart on the table. He reacted again and gave a hoarse cry. His nurse rushed into the room to see what was going on. Brad and Alec came in while I was explaining what happened.

I took Brad's hand and pulled him toward Johnny. "He's definitely responding to sounds."

"It might be nothing more than an involuntary defensive reaction, but I need to examine him to know for sure," Brad said. "This *is* new though. I need to run some tests. If the results are positive, Kinsley might request an independent exam for a second opinion because of the timing. I'll contact you as soon as I'm finished." He paused before saying, "I just got the news about the DSS petition. I was on my way to convince you to take action on your report. Now, God willing, that won't be necessary."

"We'll leave you to work, then." I tugged on Alec's arm to get her to follow me. When we were in the hallway, I said, "Johnny hasn't shown any change since he got here. Do you realize what this means? He might be coming out of it. Jay's wrong. This changes everything."

Alec led me to some chairs and sat down. She patted the chair next to her, but I was too excited to sit. Alec shrugged and said, "I agree it's encouraging, but don't get your hopes up too much yet. Like Brad said, it could be instinctive."

I stopped pacing and stared at her. Sometimes I didn't want Alec to be the voice of reason. I knew in my gut that something was happening with Johnny, and I refused to let her discourage me.

"You were the one telling me to fight a few minutes ago. Now you're telling me to back down. Which is it?"

"Please sit down. Your pacing drives me crazy."

I sat next to her but stared at the opposite wall.

"I'm not telling you to back down. I want you to take Jay and Kinsley down. I'm just saying that you need to hold off on getting too excited about Johnny until you hear from Brad. I want you to be right about him; just take a breath. You've been through a lot in the last twenty-four hours."

I thought about the previous day and couldn't believe it had only been twenty-fours since I'd discovered that Jay had filed his report and sent Johnny back to Richmond. I took a breath and said, "I am right about Johnny, but I'll wait for Brad to confirm it. In the meantime, don't talk about this to anyone but Adam and Paul. If Brad has positive news, it might be enough to get DSS to put the petition on hold. It might give me time to start the adoption too. If they won't hold off, maybe I'll hold a press conference."

"Go, Grace!" Alec did a fist pump. "You do realize you'd lose your job for that, though?"

"I hope I do. How can I work for Kinsley if he could pull something like this? There are other hospitals in this city."

"That's lucky because we might all be looking for new jobs by next week," she said.

"They can't fire all of us, but it's not going to come to that. Trust me. Johnny's going to wake up."

⚔️ ⚔️

I hadn't slept much, so I gave myself a few extra minutes in bed the following morning to make sense of the events of the previous few days. Little more than a week had passed since Jay had proposed. I contemplated the course of events from that day to the previous evening when Alec and I had dinner with Paul and Adam. Paul was encouraged by the news of Johnny but told us that if Brad's test results were negative, our only hope was my report. He said Brad would have to rewrite and submit it as evidence at the petition hearing since my opinion didn't carry any legal weight. I was kicking myself for holding off on adopting Johnny. If I'd started the process before I went to Baltimore, Jay and Kinsley wouldn't have any control over Johnny's fate. As it stood, his life was in the hands of my two biggest enemies.

The first thing I did when I forced myself to get up was check my phone messages, hoping there was one from Brad. When I saw that he hadn't called, I got dressed and went to the hospital to find out what was going on.

I'd avoided Kinsley the day before and wasn't sure if he knew I was back, so I didn't have to go to work. I knew that would only last for another day or two. With Johnny back in Richmond, Kinsley would know I was there too. The big question was whether he was even going to want me back. Alec said he hadn't mentioned anything to her about me returning as supervisor. I decided to tackle one problem at a time and take care of Johnny first.

⚔️ ⚔️

I saw Brad at the nurses' station as I was heading to Johnny's room. He waved me over and said, "I was just about to call you. The news is good. Johnny is responding to stimuli, and he's making sounds. I got the preliminary results to Kinsley as fast as I could. Just as I suspected, he wants a second opinion. You're not going to like this, but he sent for Dr. Morgan. He'll be here tonight. I'm meeting him first thing in the morning."

"So fast?" I said, shocked that Jay would drop everything to run to Richmond. I dreaded the thought of seeing him but said, "That's the best and worst news I've ever had at one time. At least your tests will force him to have an open mind."

"That's what we're all hoping. I have to run, but I promise to keep you updated," he said as he walked away.

I checked in on Johnny next, but he was the same as always. I tried to get a response from him by clapping my hands, but nothing happened. I put my finger in his palm, and he grasped it, just like always. I was relieved to see that hadn't changed.

I left him to rest and took the elevator to the IM floor. I found Alec working at my desk. She started to get up when she saw me, but I waved her down and sat on the sofa. I told her what Brad had said about Jay.

"I know it's the last thing you want to hear, but you have to see Jay and convince him to update his report," she said.

"You're right. It's the last thing I want. I'm willing to do anything to save Johnny, but what makes you think he'll listen to me?"

She leaned back and pressed her fingertips together. She was suited to that chair. I wondered if it was a sign that it was time to turn it over to her permanently.

"Because, he loves you," she said, drawing me out of my thoughts.

I shook my head. "No, that can't be true. If rejecting him wasn't bad enough, I wrote a report that contradicted his results. That's a huge blow to a man like Jay. I'm sure he hates me by now."

Alec eyed me before saying, "Do you still love him?"

I hadn't allowed myself to consider that question. I was afraid to face the answer. "I honestly don't know. You can't feel so deeply for someone and be over it a week later. I'm positive he's not the man for me, but that doesn't mean I don't still have feelings for him."

"You just proved my point. If you can't get over it in a week, neither can he." She got up and sat next to me. "I hate having to ask you to face him. I wouldn't for any reason but to save Johnny's life, but you might be the only person with the power to convince him. Yesterday you committed to fighting Jay and Kinsley. This is your battleground."

I nodded, knowing she was right, but the thought of confronting Jay terrified me. Only the thought of saving Johnny gave me the courage. I had to ignore my fears and do battle for my son. "I'll be waiting for him when he's done with Brad, but you better be there for me afterward. Knowing you've got my back is the only way I'll survive it."

"Text me when it's over, and we'll meet here. You can do this. You've overcome much worse."

I hugged her and got up to leave. It was time to prepare to face Goliath.

⟞⟊ ⟋⟝

I listened quietly in the doorway as Jay discussed Johnny's condition with Brad. My breath quickened, and my knees went weak at the sight of Jay. I cursed fate for the hundredth time for making me fall in love with the one man who had the power to shatter my life. When the conversation was winding down, I tapped on the open door, and both doctors turned toward me. Jay's face was a mixture of alarm and pleasure at seeing me. Brad excused himself and glanced at me as he pulled the door closed on his way out.

Jay and I sized each other up for what seemed like an eternity until he said, "Hello, Grace. It's wonderful to see you." I just nodded, so he went on in a rush. "I never planned for any of this to happen. I think of you every day. I'm sorry for what I did before you left Baltimore. You didn't deserve that. I acted out of my pain at losing you. I've started to call you a hundred times, but I didn't know what to say, and I doubted you'd talk to me anyway."

"I appreciate your saying that, but your words don't mean anything to me now. I fell in love with a cardboard caricature of you. I don't want anything to do with the flesh and blood Dr. Jay Morgan that I see now."

"You're wrong. I *am* the man you saw working on Johnny's study. Believe what you saw then, not what came later. You have no idea the kind of pressure I was under."

"Then enlighten me," I said and leaned against the door jamb with my arms folded.

Jay rubbed his forehead. "I can't talk about it here. Come to my hotel tonight. I'm seeing a play with a friend, but I'll be back by ten thirty." He took the paper hotel-key holder from his pocket and handed it to me. "That's where I'm staying. Please, come see me. We need to talk, and not just about this," he said and gestured toward Johnny. "We need to talk about us."

"There's no 'us,' and there's nothing to talk about," I said and turned to Johnny. "I'm only here for Johnny. You have the chance to redeem yourself with me on that score. Johnny is progressing. It's slow, but it's progress. Will you at least admit now that your findings might be wrong?"

"Dr. Carter brought me up-to-date, but it's too soon for me to form an opinion. I do promise to have an open mind."

"Well, that's a start. I'll have to hold on to that for now." I gave Jay a long, penetrating look before I turned and walked out.

My legs nearly buckled as I made my dramatic exit. Somehow, I managed to stay upright until I was out of Jay's sight. I went to the nurses' lounge and texted Alec.

She found me twenty minutes later with my feet propped up and an icepack over my eyes. She lifted the ice and said, "Headache? That bad, huh?"

I moaned and sat up. "Actually, it went much better than I'd expected. Jay apologized, and I managed to get the last word. I'm glad he can't see me now."

"You're brave. See? I said you could do it," she said and sat down.

"I don't know if it's bravery when I didn't have any other choice. Jay promised to keep an open mind though."

"That's hard to believe from the Fabulous Dr. Jay."

I smiled at her nickname for him and said, "There's something else I have to tell you. I'm resigning today. I'm giving two weeks' notice, and I'm going to recommend you to replace me. Are you interested?"

"Of course, but aren't you going to wait until after the hearing?"

"How can I?" I sat up and slammed the icepack on the coffee table, making Alec jump. "Kinsley should have quashed the petition the minute he had Brad's report. Instead, he called in Jay, the very doctor who falsified the findings in the first place. I'm sure he intends to go forward with Johnny's execution regardless of what Jay says."

"You might be right, but if Paul and Adam find the evidence they need to prove what these people are up to, they'll all be gone," she said. "You shouldn't let them drive you away."

"They shouldn't be here now." I picked up the icepack, put it on my forehead, and sat back with a sigh. "I get that the hospital is a business, but it's supposed to be about saving lives, not paying homage to the almighty dollar."

"Have you forgotten that this is the same institution that took you off the street and saved your life?" she asked.

"No, I haven't forgotten, but seeing what it's become, I have no choice but to leave."

Alec got up and grabbed two water bottles from the fridge. She handed me one. "Do you have another job lined up?"

I thanked her for the water and said, "I have two interviews next week. I hope I can still count on a few people here for excellent references."

"Of course, not that I think you'll need it. I'll miss having you here to help me with every minuscule problem or listen to me gossip. At least you'll still be coming to visit Johnny."

"If we win, I'm going to move him to another facility as soon as the adoption's final. I've started looking for a place."

"Not *if* we win, when we win," she said and tapped my arm. When I didn't say anything, she put her arm around my shoulder. "Promise me we won't drift apart. I can't imagine my life without you."

"You'd be fine," I said. "You have Adam. Besides, you tell me all the time that we're family. We're bound together. You'll be Auntie Alec to Johnny."

"That would be an honor," she said and got up. "I have to get back. Don't get discouraged. Things are turning our way. I feel it."

I smiled and watched her walk away, praying that she was right.

CHAPTER THIRTEEN

I thought about going to check on Johnny after talking to Alec but remembered that Jay was probably with him. I went home to start working on my resignation letter instead. I took out my laptop and stared at the blank screen, not knowing where to start. My thoughts wandered to Jay. My reaction to seeing him again had lingered, and I was frustrated at not being able to control myself when it came to him. What I told Alec was the truth: Jay wasn't the man for me, but I was obviously still in love with him. As hard as I tried to deny it, I couldn't. My own heart betrayed me.

I closed my laptop and fixed myself some lunch as a distraction. I didn't really have an appetite. After three bites, I tossed my sandwich on the plate and grabbed a pad to jot down some notes for my resignation letter. I imagined how happy Kinsley would be when he read it, and I hated the thought of giving him any pleasure. I took comfort in the fact that I wouldn't ever have to see him again after I left.

I sighed and lifted the lid on my laptop again. As I typed, I knew that, in spite of Kinsley, resigning was the right thing to do. It wouldn't be easy though. I was sad to leave my job. I had spent some of the happiest years of my life there. In the days before Johnny, I had planned to stay until I retired, and then do some traveling. I should have known that it was pointless to plan for my future.

The phone rang and startled me out of my musings. I glanced at the screen to see who it was, and a picture of my brother popped up. "Hi, Carl," I said. "It's been a while. How's it going?"

"Going great for me, but imagine my surprise to see my baby sister's face on the evening news."

"On the news? What are you talking about?" I tried to mask the tremor in my voice.

"I saw your picture on the news. I turned it on when I got home from work, and there you were. They were interviewing some doctor who said you're trying to adopt a brain-dead boy and that you're spreading lies about some doctors and hospital administrators. What the hell's going on, Squirt?"

I felt the old panic coming on and took a slow, deep breath. "I told you about Johnny a few months ago, remember? I *am* planning to adopt him, but he's not brain-dead. The hospital wants to pull the plug on him even though he's starting to recover. Do you remember the name of the person they interviewed?"

"I don't remember the name, but he's some muckity-muck doctor from Baltimore. I knew you spent time there, so that stuck in my mind."

I got up and hunted for my TV remote. When I found it, I pressed the power button and clicked to the local news channel. They'd already moved on to another story. "Was it Jay Morgan?" I asked.

"Yeah, I think that was it," he said.

I flipped to a few more channels, but couldn't find anything. "What they're saying's a lie," I said. "You have to trust me. They're trying to stop me from getting in their way. I'm sorry to cut this short, but I need to make some calls. Thanks for calling, Carl. I'll be in touch."

"No problem, Squirt, and good luck," he said.

As soon as I hung up, the phone rang again. It was Paul. He'd been watching the news on his tablet during lunch and had seen the news report too. He told me to get to his office as soon as I could.

⊨ ⊨

When I got to Paul's office, Alec and Brad were already there. It was a sure sign of how serious the situation was that they'd all leave the hospital during their shifts.

"They're making a preemptive strike to sway public opinion in favor of taking Johnny off life support. We've got to get the truth out there as fast as we can," Paul said as soon as I sat down. "I have a few connections at some local stations. I'll try to set up an interview. This is a good human-interest story, and I'm sure people still remember when Johnny first showed up at the hospital. Grace, do you have any recent video of Johnny?"

I held up my hands and said, "Wait a second. What happened with Jay? Why is he targeting me and saying I'm spreading false reports? I don't understand what's happening here."

Brad squirmed in his chair and looked away.

"What, Brad? Tell me," I said.

"Dr. Morgan gave his results directly to Kinsley without consulting with me. He's refusing to give me access, saying it's evidence for the hearing. He didn't spend much time with Johnny. My opinion is that he doesn't have any intention of changing his findings," he said.

"And he must have told Kinsley about your report. It's making them nervous," Paul said.

"Kinsley's not a hyena; he's a snake," Alec said. "And Jay's worse. Paul, is there anything you can do to get a hold of what he gave Kinsley?"

"Doubtful, but I'm looking into avenues to fight the DSS petition. I'm going to brainstorm with some colleagues to see what we can come up with. Our hope is that the hospital won't want the negative publicity if their ploy doesn't work. I know the DA in Baltimore. I'm going to try to convince him to file charges for medical fraud against Dr. Morgan too. Unfortunately, even if he agrees, that will take too long to be any help for Johnny."

No one spoke when Paul finished. I rubbed my forehead and stared at the floor. Without looking up, I said, "Am I the only one who sees that this is hopeless?"

Paul came beside me and put his hand on my shoulder. "It might seem that way, but these things can change on a dime. I've had too many cases where I ran up against a wall and had it tumble down at the last minute. This isn't over. Trust me on that."

I looked up at him. "That's what I told my brother when he called to tell me about the news report. I should practice what I preach. I do trust you, Paul. You know that. There's just too much that we have no control over, and Johnny's life is in the middle of it."

"It's despicable that they're using the two of you as pawns. We have to stay tough and not let them think they're getting to us. Let's talk in the morning. In the meantime, put this on my shoulders, and let me go to work," Paul said.

I hugged him and said, "I'm leaving it in your more-than-capable hands. Thank you for taking this on. We couldn't make it through without you."

As we walked to the parking garage, Alec said, "Come stay with me for a few days. The press will probably be crawling all over your house soon, and I hate the thought of your being alone to deal with this."

"I'll only agree if we can just forget about this tonight. I need a break for a few hours."

"I promise," she said. "We'll rent movies and stuff ourselves with pizza and cannoli." She handed me a key to her apartment. "Go home and pack a bag. I'll meet you at my apartment as soon as I get off work."

"I will, but I want to say good night to Johnny first. I'll come over after that."

She smiled and squeezed my hand. "You heard what Paul said. We have to stay tough."

I nodded. "I will. See you in a few."

⚔ ⚔

I rocked Johnny and gently stroked his corn-silk hair. In spite of what Paul and Alec had said, the hopelessness of his situation was tearing me apart. I racked my brain for a way to stop Jay. I'd overcome too much to lose now. My father had beaten me. Danny had beaten me. Life had almost beaten me. No more, I thought. I had to remember my vow to stop being a victim.

Holding Johnny in my arms calmed me, and my thoughts began to clear. As I searched his angelic face, a tiny thread of an idea came to me and wove itself together in my mind. As I rocked him, I planned my strategy. It would be a daring risk, but I had to take it. I saw no other way out, and I had nothing left to lose.

I gently laid Johnny back in his crib and smoothed my skirt. "Open your eyes, Johnny dear. You have to wake up," I said. "For both of us. Son, I need your help. It's time to wake up."

⚔ ⚔

I pulled up to the curb across the street from Jay's hotel and turned off the engine. I looked at the picture of Johnny I had taped to the dashboard for courage, and I settled in to wait. A cab pulled in front of the hotel thirty minutes later, and Jay got out. He paid the driver and walked confidently into the hotel, oblivious of what was coming. I forced myself to wait five minutes before following him inside.

I found his room and knocked.

After what felt like an hour, he said, "Who's there?"

"It's Grace. I need to see you," I said, trying to keep my voice upbeat.

He didn't respond for a few seconds. It hadn't occurred to me that he might not open the door. I was going to have my say, even if I had to yell through the door.

"That's not a good idea," he finally said. "Like you said this morning, we have nothing left to say to each other."

"Please, Jay. Don't make me stand out in the hall making a fool of myself."

The lock turned after a few more seconds of silence. He opened the door and stood there in the thick, deep red terrycloth robe I'd always loved to see him wear. Uninvited memories of our nights together flooded over me. I imagined myself encircled in his protective arms, my face pressed into the soft cloth against his chest. I could tell by his eyes that he shared my memory. We stood transfixed in the doorway for several seconds until he took my hand and pulled me inside. He closed the door behind us but blocked me from going further into the room.

"I assume you're here to beg me to change my mind about Johnny again," he said. His stern tone shattered my romantic delusion and reminded me why I was there.

"I'm through begging. I'm here to demand that you reexamine Johnny and produce a truthful report of your findings."

"Have you lost your mind? You're not in a position to demand anything of me."

"My evidence says otherwise," I said, squaring my shoulders.

Jay flinched but said, "Evidence? There's no evidence. I think you should go."

As he reached around me for the door, I said, "I'm going to ruin you if you don't do what I ask."

He froze for an instant but then turned and walked to the sitting area. Crossing his arms, he said, "Don't be so dramatic. Are you planning to scare me into confessing to some conspiracy?"

"That's exactly what I'm going to do. Kinsley convinced your chief of staff to coerce you into falsifying Johnny's records to show that his case was hopeless. They did it by dangling the chief-of-staff position in front of you. Kinsley then used your report to get the DSS to petition the court to remove Johnny from life support. How am I doing so far?" I asked, crossing my arms too.

The color drained from Jay's face, and beads of sweat glistened on his forehead. He breathed deeply a few times through his nose but kept his composure. "That's a good fantasy. Did your lawyer send you here to frighten me with these lies?"

"No one sent me. In fact, no one knows I'm here. I'm tired of playing it safe with you, and time's running out for Johnny. Would you like me to go on?"

"Go ahead. This is entertaining," he said and sat down on the sofa, feigning nonchalance.

"I have witnesses who'll testify to what I've said. I also have medical evidence proving that you falsified the results. Several people are aware of this, so if you try to stop me, it won't matter. I've taken steps to protect my evidence. We have Brad Carter's recent test results too. You have no choice. Change your results, or we're going to file charges against you and expose you along with everyone else involved in this crime."

Jay leaned forward and massaged his forehead. I hoped I'd punched through his wall of arrogance.

Before he had time to recover, I started in on him again. "Even though they got you to go along with their scheme, I haven't been able to figure out why it worked. Some people, like my father and ex-husband, are born rotten. Others are capable of goodness but can't seem to overcome their own self-interest, like you. Even after everything you've done, I still think you were once a good and caring doctor. What happened? Does your career mean more to you than a child's life?"

I glared at him and could tell he was shaken. My plan was working. I stood over him, waiting for his next move.

He finally sat forward, but kept his eyes lowered. "I guess I have nothing to lose by telling you that you're right. If you ever repeat what I'm about to say, I'll deny it, but you might as well know the truth."

I sat in a chair facing Jay and remained silent, wishing I'd thought to turn on the voice recorder on my phone.

"I was coerced into cooperating," he said. "Blackmailed would be more accurate, but I didn't do it for a promotion. I never would have done that. It hurts that you think I would."

His shoulders were slumped. He looked like a beaten man. I searched for the confident, or maybe arrogant, Jay I'd loved, but only found a pathetic figure.

He looked me in the eye. "I did it because I had no choice. I've never told anyone this, but a few years ago, I made a terrible mistake, and a child died."

I was stunned by his confession. "What happened?"

"I got an emergency call during a charitable event where I'd had a few drinks. The patient was a young girl, an accident victim. I treated her when I should have turned it over to a colleague. I didn't feel impaired, but I missed a cerebral hemorrhage. The girl died. I'm not sure if it was human error or the alcohol, but I haven't touched a drink since."

"You were going to marry me without telling me this? You rejected me because of Johnny when you were hiding a secret like this? I don't know what to think." I stared at him, trying to recover from the shock. "How did you keep your medical license?"

"The hospital vouched for me to avoid a lawsuit from the parents. They've held it over me since then. When the situation came up with Johnny, they threatened to expose me if I didn't cooperate."

I'd assumed that he'd acted out of pride and self-interest. The idea of blackmail never occurred to me. "How could they expose you without revealing their part in it? They're in as deep as you are."

"These are powerful people. It's my word against theirs, like the two of us now. Before Johnny arrived, they convinced me that his case was hopeless. I wanted them to be right, but, in time, I discovered they weren't. Johnny started to progress. You saw it too. I'm sure that was in your report."

"What do you mean, 'I'm sure'? Didn't you read it?" I asked, furious all over again.

"No. I didn't. I tossed out it the second you were out of my office. It wouldn't have mattered. By then I had no choice but to continue the charade. I never expected things to go this far. My first hope was that Johnny would regain consciousness. When he didn't, I rushed to send him back here and put this mess out of my mind."

"This mess? Is that all Johnny and I are to you, some mess to get rid of?" I was outraged. I stood up and stepped toward him.

He held up his hands in surrender. "You know what I mean. It would have been so much easier to have faced that lawsuit back then than face medical fraud and attempted-murder charges now. They told me they'd protect me and that there was little risk. I've been powerless to stop it from spiraling out of control, especially since Brad Carter can prove Johnny's getting better."

"Powerless? Is that what you tell yourself so you can sleep at night?" Seeing the perfect opening, I moved next to him on the sofa and put my hand on his arm. "You have all the power you need. You can make 'this mess' go away right now. Examine Johnny again and report that he's improving. He is improving, Jay. Soon it'll be obvious to everyone. Your blackmailers can't force you to go along with your original results when it becomes apparent that he's recovering.

If DSS withdraws their petition, I can adopt him. The state and hospital won't be responsible for him anymore. That's what this has all been about. Let him live, and I'll take him off their hands."

"You make it sound so simple. Based on my findings, some of the people involved in this believe that keeping Johnny alive would be inhumane. They wouldn't accept the truth now." He covered his face with his hands and sighed. He looked exhausted.

"You may be right," I said, "but how will you know if you never take a stand?" I got up and paced in circles. It was time to go in for the kill. "You've been running in fear for too long. You can end this now. If you don't, they'll always have this power over you. Your life will never be yours. If that's not enough to make you act, think of your daughters. Is this the legacy you want to leave them?"

I stopped and faced Jay. He was watching me intently. I waited for my words to sink in.

"You have to think of Johnny. I know the risks you'd be taking for an orphaned child whose future is anything but certain. You think I'm asking the impossible, but if there's the slightest chance he'll recover, you're obligated to act. This could be a win for all of us."

I sat down and waited for Jay's reaction. The future for the three of us teetered on the cliff's edge. Jay's decision could pull us to a life of safety on solid ground or plunge us onto the jagged rocks below. I held my breath and prayed that this man who held my fate would have the moral courage to do the right thing.

Jay stood and took his turn pacing. After a minute, he stopped with his back to me and said, "I do want my life back. It might destroy my career and reputation, but I'll reexamine Johnny in the morning. I can't promise you that it'll make any difference, but I promise to be honest. The hearing is scheduled for tomorrow at twelve. They're rushing it through to avoid the media circus. It may be too late for me to do anything now."

I gasped. Paul hadn't told us that the hearing was already scheduled. All I could guess was that he found out after our meeting.

I had turned off my phone before going to Jay's hotel because I knew Alec would be calling to find out where I was. I wondered if Paul had tried to call too.

I put those thoughts out of my mind and focused on what Jay had just said. I walked to him and took his hands. "I came here tonight not knowing what to expect. I was afraid you'd slam the door in my face before I got started. Having you agree to see Johnny again is far more than I could have hoped. This is right, Jay. You won't regret it."

Jay took my elbow and pulled me into his arms before I could stop him. I allowed him to hold me and buried my face into the soft cloth of his robe. He brushed his lips against my ear and in a husky whisper, said, "Stay with me tonight. You know we should be together. I don't want to be alone. I need you. Please, stay."

I held still, afraid to move and spoil the moment. A part of me longed to stay with him forever, but too much was at stake.

Reluctantly, I stepped back. "I want that more than you can know, but not now. We'll talk when this is behind us. Neither of us is in any condition to make that kind of decision now." Jay started to protest, but I put my fingers to his lips. "I'm leaving now. By this time tomorrow, our lives will have changed forever. We can both be happy and free of this nightmare. Go to sleep thinking of that. I'll see you in the morning."

I picked up my purse and kissed him on the cheek before leaving without looking back. Once outside, I leaned against my car for support and waited for the strength to return to my legs. I climbed into the driver's seat and looked at the picture of Johnny. I had achieved my objective and much more. I had conquered the fabulous Dr. Jay Morgan. "It worked," I told the sleeping image of Johnny. "You're going to live and become my son. Now you have to wake up!"

⊷⊱ ⊰⊶

Alec met me at her door with a hug. "Where have you been? Paul and I have been calling you. I even contacted the hospital, but no one had seen you."

Adam walked in from the kitchen before I could answer and said, "Oh good, she found you. Alec's been in a panic. Where have you been?"

I untangled myself from Alec. "I couldn't tell you where I was going because I knew you'd try to stop me. I'm sorry I made you worry, but there was something I had to do. I'll tell you the whole story, but I need to call Paul first. Wait for me here. I'll be back in a few minutes."

I called Paul from the guest room to tell him what had happened with Jay. He answered on the fourth ring. "I'm sorry to call so late, but it's urgent."

"I wasn't asleep. I've been here waiting for Adam to call and tell me they found you. You gave us a scare. What's going on?" he asked and yawned.

"First off, I know about the hearing tomorrow. Jay told me," I said and cringed while I waited for him to answer.

"Jay told you? Did you go see Jay?" His voice rose with each word.

"I went to convince him to reexamine Johnny and submit a new report. He agreed to do it. I can't explain now, but it's your turn to trust me. After he sees Johnny, he's going to try to get the hearing stopped or at least postponed."

"I wish that were true, but he's playing you. I'm surprised you fell for it after everything he's done."

"You won't say that when you hear what he told me," I said, not surprised by his skepticism.

"Before you tell me, I have news for you. I was able to schedule an interview for us on all the local network affiliates for tomorrow's morning news cycle. The first one's at six thirty. Their crews are all coming to my office."

The door opened, and Alec peeked her head in. "What's going on?" she mouthed, and I waved her in.

"I can't do that, Paul," I said. "If Jay gets the petition thrown out or postponed, the interview will be pointless. Besides, you never said anything about my doing an interview. I can't go on TV."

"What interview?" Alec asked. "Put it on speaker phone."

"Is that Alec? Tell her I want her there with you," Paul said. "People don't care what I have to say. You're the one they care about, and it's the fastest way to get the truth out there. They can tape the interviews as planned and show them at noon if it comes to that. If the situation changes, we'll go back and do a second interview. It's too late to cancel at this point, and canceling is a bad idea."

What Paul said made sense, but I dreaded the idea of being on the news. I agreed to do it but hoped it wouldn't have to air. "I hope you know what you're doing," I said.

"I'll trust you if you trust me. Now, tell me what Jay said."

I explained my encounter with Jay. Paul and Alec interrupted every two seconds with questions. When I finished, Paul whistled and said, "You've got guts. I'll give you that. Do you believe him?"

"Why would he make up a story like that? It makes him look terrible," I said.

"You didn't record the conversation, did you?" he asked. "If not, it's just a case of 'he said, she said.' He'd be able to deny everything."

"No, I thought of it too late, and that's exactly what he said he'd do. At least it gives you a starting point for your investigation. I don't want to worry about that until we get rid of this petition," I said.

"Right. First things first. I'll see you in my office at six, and you come too, Alec," Paul said and hung up.

As soon as I put my phone down, Alec said, "Are you out of your mind? Who knows what Jay is capable of? He could have hurt you."

"Jay is a lot of things, but he's not violent. What's done is done, and I got what I needed. I've turned the tables. Jay will have to file new results. DSS will have to withdraw the petition, and I'll be able to adopt Johnny. The nightmare is almost over."

Adam tapped on the door. "Can I come in? I'm dying to know what's going on."

Alec snickered. "I saw you listening on the other side of the door."

"You caught me." He dropped onto the bed next to Alec.

"I'm sure you must have an opinion too," I said to Adam.

"Of course. You know how much we all hope Jay's telling the truth, but I don't trust that guy. Don't get your hopes up until we see his report. Paul's right to be skeptical."

"At least this gives Johnny a chance. That wouldn't be the case if I hadn't gone to Jay. Now I'm going to bed. We have to get up in a few hours." I stood up to shoo them out.

Adam got up and kissed me on the cheek. "I'm going to the interview too. No way I'm missing that. See you bright and early."

Alec raised her eyebrows and glanced at me as she followed Adam out. I shut the door behind them and got undressed. I refused to let myself think about Jay. I was out five minutes later.

CHAPTER FOURTEEN

P ress vans were lined up along the street in front of Paul's building when Alec and I got there the next morning. We wove our
way among them to get to the entrance. I was relieved that the
filming had been scheduled before most of the surrounding busi-
nesses were open, to avoid curious onlookers.

We stepped inside to find the foyer transformed. The furniture
was rearranged, and technical equipment was set up around the
room.

Paul came toward us, careful to step over the cables taped to
the floor. "I was afraid you weren't going to show," he said. "Adam's
already here."

"That's my fault," Alec said. "I was nervous about the interview
and was awake until two. I slept through my alarm. It's a good
thing Grace was there. She did try to back out, by the way."

I glared at her. "Only for a few seconds. I made a commitment
to you. After all you've done for me, there was no way I was going
to let you down."

Paul smiled. "I appreciate that. Now, let me introduce you to everyone, and we'll get started."

Paul was friends with the producer, who, after introductions, gave us instructions and asked us to be seated. Paul went over what to expect, and we went over ways to answer the questions and what to avoid. My heart was pounding so hard by the time we got started that I was afraid everyone would notice when they watched.

I recognized the first interviewer, Charlotte Graves, from the news show I usually watched in the morning. She must have noticed my nerves, because she sat next to me and chatted casually for a few minutes. She knew what she was doing, because I was calm by the time the interview began.

After introducing the segment, she directed her first question to me. "Grace, I'm told you've been caring for the child you've named Johnny for several months now. Is that true?"

Easy one, I thought and forced my mouth to form the words. "Yes. Since he has no parent or guardian, I've been acting in that role in an unofficial capacity. I was in the planning stages of adopting him when the Department of Social Services issued their petition."

Charlotte explained the petition to the camera and said, "Haven't experts declared him brain-dead with no chance of recovery?"

"One expert I know has declared that. He'll be reexamining Johnny this morning. The doctor who's been treating Johnny since he came to the hospital has had different results. We're hoping those will be submitted as evidence at the hearing later today." I said, growing more confident. "Our hope is that DSS will withdraw the petition before the hearing takes place."

"So you believe a local physician over a world-renowned expert in the field who ran a two-month research study that included Johnny? If so, why?" she asked.

My confidence wavered, and I wasn't sure how to answer. I had no evidence to prove that Jay had falsified his results, so I couldn't mention that. I had no way to prove that Brad was right. Before I could answer, Paul came to my rescue and said, "Johnny has shown drastic improvement since Dr. Morgan filed his initial results. We're hoping he'll see that as he does the exam this morning."

"I see," Charlotte said. "But Dr. Morgan said in an interview last night that he did an exam yesterday and saw no change. Would one day make enough of a difference to do another one?"

Her tone had changed, and she was going on the offensive. Even though I knew the media thrived on conspiracy, I'd gotten the impression she was on our side. I stared at the camera at a loss.

It was Alec's turn to rescue me. "Yes," she said, "it can. Even hours can make a difference, especially with a child this young. Those of us who spend a great deal of time with Johnny have seen him start to recover before our eyes. We're confident that the improvement will be obvious to Dr. Morgan too."

"For the child's sake, we all hope so too," Charlotte said, clearly trying to hide her irritation at not having won that round. She turned back to me and said, "I've read reports that you're trying to adopt Johnny because you're unable to have children. Why have you waited until now to make this step in such a challenging situation?"

My jaw dropped at that. I was shocked that she had such personal information about me and that she could have gotten it so quickly. I shook my head and was about to respond, but Paul waved his hands at her and said, "Let's stop there. I have an agreement prohibiting personal attacks on Ms. Ward."

"How is that an attack?" Charlotte asked. "I understood that it was common knowledge that you can't have children," she said, turning to me.

"It's okay, Paul," I said and squeezed his hand. Turning to Charlotte, I said, "I don't know how you found that out, but it's not exactly common knowledge. I'll answer the question though. It's true that I'm unable to have children, but that's only a small part of why I'm doing this. The main reason is because it's right. For whatever reason, Johnny has no one in this world to care for him. When he recovers, I want him to know that he has someone to love him."

"That's admirable," she said, "but how will you be able to afford the medical bills on a nurse's salary? And how do you intend to keep working after taking on such a huge burden? His medical bills must be astronomical, and you're divorced, correct?"

Paul started to interrupt again, but I help up my hand to stop him. He threw up his hands in defeat and sat back with his arms crossed. "I am divorced, but I've made wise financial decisions in my life and am capable of supporting Johnny. There will also be multiple avenues of assistance available from federal and state agencies. I've had time to investigate this and understand exactly what's involved."

"Very well," Charlotte said. "Now, let's talk about the allegations made by Dr. Morgan that you're spreading lies about doctors and hospital administrators. Do you know what he meant by that?" she asked, finally getting to what I knew she'd been wanting to ask all along.

Paul answered before I could say anything. "We have no idea what Dr. Morgan is alluding to. You'll have to ask him. All we're concerned with here is saving the life of a child. We believe he's been misdiagnosed, and we're doing our best to get that remedied before a tragic mistake takes place."

"We're all behind you in hoping this matter is resolved in the best way for everyone involved," Charlotte said and wrapped up the interview.

Her crew was out of there in a flash, and the next one got set up. While they were doing that, I told Paul and Alec that I thought the interview had been terrible and hadn't done much to help Johnny.

"I thought it went great," Paul said. "Trust me, if I hadn't been friends with the producer, it would have been much worse. Once they edit it and add music and video and photos of Johnny, it'll be great."

Alec nodded, and Adam came up and said, "That went great. Ready for round two?"

"Sure didn't seem that way to me," I said. "I'll have to take your word for it."

The next interviewer asked us to take our places on the sofa, and we started again. The next two interviews followed the same line of questioning, but the third interviewer was much kinder, and I decided to switch to watching his news show instead.

It was almost eight by the time we were wrapping up. Alec saw that I kept glancing at my watch. "You have somewhere to be?" she asked.

"I'm dying to know what happened with Jay and Johnny. Let's go," I said.

I thanked Paul and said good-bye to everyone before racing out the door, grateful that we weren't far from the hospital.

⊷ ⊶

Alec and I went straight to Johnny's room, but Jay wasn't there. I asked around the pediatrics floor, but no one had seen him. It was eight thirty, and I was getting concerned. Jay should have been in and done by then. Johnny's diaper was wet, and he hadn't been bathed. I started to do it myself, but Alec told me to go see if Jay was in the cafeteria.

He wasn't there either. I headed back to Johnny's room, hoping Jay had shown up while I was gone, but Alec was still alone with Johnny.

"I'm going to call him. We were up late last night. Maybe he overslept," I said.

183

The call went to his voice mail, so I tried calling the room directly. Jay didn't answer. I called the front desk and said, "Dr. Jay Morgan was in room 301 last night, but he's not answering. Do you know if he left the hotel?"

"He checked out a day early, at five o'clock, ma'am," the desk clerk told me.

I tried Jay's cell again, and then called his house. Alec raised her eyebrows at me, and I said, "I'll try his office."

The phone rang several times, and then forwarded to his receptionist. "We haven't heard from him since he left for Richmond, but we aren't expecting him until Monday. I'll leave a message that you called," she said.

I turned to Alec and said, "Where could he be? I'm not sure what to do."

She finished changing Johnny and handed him to me. "I'm sure he's in the hospital somewhere. You know how it is around here. No one pays attention to doctors coming and going."

Her comment made me realize that he'd have to have help with the tests. I called a few techs, but they hadn't seen him either.

"Maybe he's in Kinsley's office. They've probably got their heads together scheming," she said.

I handed Johnny back to her and said, "Stay here."

I ran for the elevator and went to Kinsley's office. I turned the door knob, not caring what he'd think if it opened. It was locked, so I went down the hall to the boardroom. It was locked too. I sat on a chair in the hall and tried to figure out my next move. In my desperation, I decided to call Jay's daughters. The first didn't answer, but the second picked up. Sherry told me that he had a fishing lodge in the mountains and sometimes went there without telling anyone.

"The lodge doesn't have a phone or cell service," she said. "He goes there when he doesn't want to be bothered." She hesitated when I asked where it was. "I'm not sure I should tell you. He told us what happened between the two of you."

"Thanks anyway," I said. "It doesn't matter now. Please ask him to call if you hear from him."

I hung up and went back to Johnny's room. I updated Alec and said, "I don't understand this. He promised to be here. Do you think something could have happened to him?"

"No, other than he chickened out and ran away," she said.

"Don't say that. You weren't there last night. He was telling the truth. I'm not that gullible, you know."

Alec put Johnny in the crib before sitting in the rocking chair. "I'm not saying you are. Maybe he meant what he said last night but then came to his senses. If he's so brave and honest, why did he go along with the deception after that child's death in the first place? And look what he did to you in Baltimore."

I turned away from Alec and rubbed my forehead.

"I'm sorry. I know you're scared. You know better than anyone what Jay's capable of."

I sat on the floor next to her and said, "Don't apologize, and thanks for not saying 'I told you so.' We're all feeling the strain. What are we going to do? The hearing is in three hours."

"We need to call Paul and find Brad. This is worse than bad," she said and put her hand on my shoulder.

"You don't have to tell me. I've screwed it all up again. You call Paul and Brad. I have to find Jay. Without his testimony at the hearing, Johnny has no chance." I got up and faced her. "I'm going to the hotel to see if he left me a message. I still can't believe he would just leave without saying anything. I'll meet you at the courthouse."

"Good idea. Maybe there's a simple explanation. Be careful, and call me as soon as you know anything."

⋙⊹ ⊹⋘

When I asked the hotel clerk about a message from Jay, she told me that he hadn't left any messages. She hesitated slightly and looked around before saying, "He did say something strange before he left. When I said, 'Come back and see us,' he said, 'I'll never be here again.' I thought he meant to our hotel, so I asked if there'd been a problem. He said, 'I'm never coming back to Richmond.' He had a strange look on his face when he said it. Kind of dazed, you know. That's why I remembered. It was eerie. He walked out after that."

I thanked her and went back to my car. I called the hospital again to make sure Jay hadn't shown up. He wasn't there. I dialed Paul's number next. I was ashamed of myself for trusting Jay and putting Johnny in jeopardy.

"Alec told me what happened." Paul said when he answered. "This is one time I wish I hadn't been right, but we can still do some damage control. I hope you aren't blaming yourself."

"Of course I'm blaming myself," I said, wondering how he could even ask that. "Jay begged me to stay the night. If I had, he wouldn't have been able to sneak away. Now it's too late." I broke down.

"Don't say that. This is all on Jay and Kinsley. We're right where we were before you went to Jay. Nothing's changed. I've prepared for the hearing. I have copies of Brad's results, and he's going to testify. We have video too. The judge will see reason. We have a good chance, so pull yourself together and come to the courthouse. I need to update you on our strategy."

I agreed to meet Paul to placate him but had no intention of going to the hearing. Even though Paul was optimistic, I had no doubt of the outcome. The limits of my courage were exhausted, and I didn't have the strength to watch the judge hand down Johnny's execution order. I left the hotel and drove out of the city, needing to get away from the noise and carefree busyness surrounding me. I drove aimlessly on empty back roads for two hours before pulling into a park along the James River. When I turned off the ignition, the dashboard clock read 1:07 p.m., and I had to assume that the hearing had ended. I expected a call from Alec or Paul any second. I wanted to know, and I didn't.

I turned the car on and lifted my trembling hand to the radio button. I found a continuous news station and sat back to listen, desperately hoping that Johnny's story hadn't made the news.

The newscaster reported the traffic and weather before the local news started. My mouth went dry, and my heart pounded. I decided I'd rather hear the news from Alec and reached up to turn the radio off, but before I could the newscaster said, "In local news, a judge has approved a petition from the Virginia Department of Social Services to authorize removal of life support from a four-teen-month-old child in a Richmond hospital. The child, simply named Baby John Doe, has been a ward of the Commonwealth of Virginia since being abandoned in a local emergency room eight months ago. The judge approved the petition based on the medical findings of Dr. Jay Morgan, one of the country's leading pediatric neurologists, who declared the child brain-dead. Dr. Morgan could not be reached for comment."

The walls of the car closed in, and I needed to get air. I stumbled from the car and staggered for ten feet before vomiting onto the asphalt. The mess splattered my shoes and pant legs. I wiped my mouth on my coat sleeve and blindly headed for the river. Even though it was spring, the day was chilly and gray. Patches of frost lingered on shaded grassy areas. I climbed onto a large boulder, oblivious of the fact that I was ruining my best suit.

I looked out over the tumbling water. This is where it all started, I thought bitterly, remembering police photos of the spot where that couple had pulled Johnny from the river. I imagined my life without Johnny, what it would have been if they'd left him to die. Empty and loveless, I was certain. I wouldn't have traded the chance to love Johnny, even if it meant losing him.

I knelt on the rocks and tried just as hard to imagine my life ahead without him. I had changed. I had people who cared about me, but it was Johnny who gave my life purpose. My future rose up as a dark void before me. Sobs racked my body until I feared the pain would tear me apart.

"I failed him," I cried, but my words fell on the damp air. What more could I have done? I cursed fate and wept out my bitterness. The pain of loss and past failures flooded over me with this ultimate failure. I got off my knees and stumbled to the edge of the rock.

The water level was higher than normal from recent rain storms. The cold, muddy water surged by below my feet, and I imagined stepping off the edge. Without Johnny, no one needed me. When Johnny was gone, I would just be in the way. I slid my feet forward another inch and shuddered as twigs and leaves swept by in the roiling river below.

What I was contemplating went against everything I'd been taught to believe. Even in my darkest hours with Danny, I hadn't considered ending it all.

"Are you there?" I yelled to the heavens, praying for the prince on a cloud from my childhood to swoop down and rescue me. Only silence answered. Bile rose in my throat again, so I took three quick breaths and searched my heart for answers. Had finding Johnny been nothing more than a coincidence and not part of some greater plan? If that were true, what would it matter if I stepped from the rock?

I willed my feet forward, but they didn't obey. I longed for the freedom that would come if I took that step, but my survival instinct was strong. Through the din of the war raging in my mind, I heard a whisper of a voice carried on the wind. I looked over my shoulder but didn't see anyone. I scanned the landscape one more time before turning back to the river. I was alone.

I knew I had to act or I'd give in to instinct and pull away from the edge. I tried to coax my feet to move, but they stayed cemented in place. I leaned forward, but instead of falling, I was yanked violently backward onto the rocks. My hip and elbow struck hard. Pain shot through my body and brought me to my senses. A man dressed in a green uniform lay next to me on the boulder. I scrambled to my feet and backed away.

"What do you think you're doing?" I shouted at him.

"I should be asking you that," he said and got up, rubbing his shoulder.

"None of your business," I said.

He stepped toward me, and I held up my hands to block him. "Stay back," I said.

"I wanted to make sure you're all right," he said, stopping where he was and holding his hands up in surrender. "I'm Ryan Walker. I work for the state park service. I saw your car in the parking lot and was afraid someone might be on the river. Looks like I was right."

I limped to a tall boulder nearby and leaned against it. I rubbed my hip and noticed blood seeping through my sleeve at the elbow. Ryan asked if he could sit next to me. I nodded.

"Will you allow me to treat your injuries?"

Too weak to protest, I nodded again.

He asked me to remove my suit coat. "I have a first-aid kit on my four-wheeler just over there," he said and pointed toward it. "Will you come with me to get it?"

I nodded again and followed him to the four-wheeler. While he gathered his supplies, I took off my jacket and rolled up the sleeve of my blouse. Drops of blood splashed onto my pant leg. I numbly watched the pattern of the spreading stain and wondered why I had followed Ryan. What difference did a few cuts and bruises matter compared to what I was facing?

He came back and examined my wounds. I took the chance to get a better look at him. He looked my age or a little older. He had short-cropped brown hair with touches of gray at the temples. He had a rugged look but a kind and open face. The muscles in his arms were toned and solid. Definitely an outdoorsman.

"That's quite a gash," he said. "You need a doctor to treat that."

I turned away at the thought of doctors and hospitals and began to cry softly. "I know. I'm a nurse. Why did you stop me? Why didn't you just let me go?"

"I couldn't do that, ma'am. There's nothing in this world so terrible to be worth taking your life," he said as he put a butterfly bandage on my arm.

"Trust me. There are plenty of things terrible enough. You'd know that if you'd lived my life." I wiped my tears with my other arm.

"I don't know your life, but I do know life. I don't live in a vacuum. Tell me what brought you to the edge of that boulder. Help me understand. Maybe I can help." He stopped working on my arm and looked into my eyes with genuine concern.

I shook my head and said, "No one can help. It's too late. The child I love is going to be killed because small, ruthless cowards want him to die, and I'm powerless to stop it."

"He's going to be murdered? Can't we call the police?" Ryan pulled his phone from his pocket.

I pushed his hand down and said, "Have you heard of the boy in a coma that they want to take off life support?"

He nodded. "I've heard the story on the news." He studied my face. "Now I know why you look familiar. You're the woman trying to adopt him. I heard on the news that he's been declared brain-dead."

"That's a lie!" I cried, and Ryan backed away from the force of my reaction. "I'm sorry. I'm not exactly myself today," I said. "The boy is starting to regain consciousness and respond to the world around him. For reasons that would take too long to explain, the doctor who was going to testify to that at the hearing ran off today. No one knows where he is."

"This is a tragic situation, and I'm sure you care for the boy, but I still don't see why you're here. Why aren't you with him? He needs you in the time he has left." He took my arm and gently taped gauze over the bandage.

"There are others to take care of him. I can't stand by and watch him die of thirst or starvation. Once he's gone, I'll have nothing to live for." I looked down at my vomit- and blood-stained shoes and wondered why I was telling a stranger my deepest feelings.

"That can't be true," he said. "You must have friends and family who care for you and who need you."

"I don't have much family and just a few friends. They'd hardly notice I was gone." I knew it wasn't true as soon as I said it, but I felt I had to justify my behavior.

"I'm sure you're wrong. Anyone who would do what you've done for this boy must be pretty incredible. I don't think I'd have done it. It took enormous courage and selflessness. I'm sure you're worth much more than you give yourself credit for."

Without looking up, I said, "My life has been a long chain of unending tragedy. I'm too tired to do it anymore. Life is nothing but grief and pain. Please, go away, and leave me alone."

"I'm not going to do that, and I don't think you're big enough to fight me off."

I looked up at Ryan.

He nodded and finished bandaging my arm. When he was done, he put his hand on my shoulder. "What's your name?"

"Grace," I said, avoiding his eyes.

"Beautiful and timely name. It's an honor to meet you, Grace. I'm determined to help you. Please, don't push me away."

"I already told you, it's too late." My tears threatened again.

"Maybe it's too late for the child," Ryan said, "but not for you. Do you think it's a coincidence that I found you when I did?"

"Yes, I do," I said without hesitating. "Why? Do you think some 'higher power' led you here?"

"That's exactly what I think. I didn't plan to check this part of the river today, but a little voice in my head kept nagging at me to come here. As soon as I saw your car, I had a feeling someone was in trouble. I didn't know what to expect, but I had to find out. The voice prodded me on until I found you. Didn't you hear me call out to you?"

"I thought I heard something, but I couldn't see you," I said, wondering who this man was to say such things.

"I would've been too late if you hadn't turned toward the sound. I almost didn't make it as it was. Something guided me to you."

"Maybe you just got lucky," I said and backed away, not wanting to hear more.

"Grace, stop. I need to get you out of here. You're shivering and need to see a doctor. Will you take me to meet Johnny?"

"I can't," I said and started to move away again. "I'm not as strong and brave as you think. It would kill me to see him."

"No, it won't," he said, following me. "Look, I'll follow you to the hospital in my truck, and we'll go see Johnny. We'll stop by the ER afterward. I'm not going to leave you here, so you don't have a choice."

He extended his hand. I took it reluctantly. He took me to the parking lot on his four-wheeler and gave me directions to where he'd parked his truck. I climbed in my car, not sure why I'd agreed to go with him. The radio was still on when I started the car. The newscaster was repeating the story about Johnny. I was about to turn it off when the newscaster said, "We're transferring you now to a live statement from a hospital-administration official."

There was a second of silence before Kinsley began speaking. "We strive in every way to dedicate our resources to saving lives. On rare occasions, in spite of our best efforts, that isn't possible. Such is the case with Baby John Doe, affectionately known to us here as Johnny. As many of you know, he was abandoned in our emergency room several months ago in a vegetative state. He hasn't shown any improvement since that time. After repeated tests and examinations by some of the country's top physicians, the court has approved a petition by the Department of Social Services to remove Johnny from life support. We're deeply saddened to have to take this action, but we know it is in the child's best interests. We plan to cooperate fully."

"How can you live with yourself?" I said and switched it off. I drove to the hospital on autopilot. An hour earlier, I thought I'd be gone and never see Johnny again. Six hours before that, I couldn't wait to see him. Now Ryan had to force me to go back. I'd do what Ryan wanted, but time beyond that was black nothingness. I'd reverted to the battered young wife, traveling on a bus to Richmond.

⊶⊷

I pulled into the parking garage and waited for Ryan to join me. News crews and curious spectators were crowded together behind a yellow-tape barrier at the main hospital entrance. Vultures, I thought, sickened by the sight of them waiting for Johnny to die.

I got out of the car and walked toward Ryan's truck. He climbed out and motioned for me to lead the way. When we got within fifteen yards, I grabbed his arm, forcing him to stop. "I can't do it," I said. "I have to get out of here."

Ryan gently took my shoulders and turned me to face him. "We don't have to go in this way. Isn't there a staff entrance? Can you get someone to let us in?"

"I have an ID badge." I took it out of my purse and held it up to show him. "I work here, or at least I think I still work here. I'm not even sure what day this is."

"Show me where we need to go," he said and nudged me forward. "We need to find out what's happening."

"I know exactly what's happening. These ghouls are here to watch Johnny die."

"We don't know if this has anything to do with Johnny. The sooner we go in, the sooner it'll be over."

I allowed Ryan to push me gently ahead and started for the staff parking lot. I walked with my head down, concentrating on making my feet move. Five minutes later, we were inside, and I ran for the elevator. I sighed when the doors slid shut, leaving us in silence. I closed my eyes and leaned against the cold metal wall, trying to calm my pounding heart. Ryan patted my arm but stayed quiet.

A quiet beep sounded when we reached our floor. I stayed frozen against the elevator wall. Ryan held the door open and tried to coax me out. "You're almost there. You're going to see Johnny, your boy. He's waiting. Just a few more feet."

Hearing Johnny's name calmed me and gave me courage to step into the hallway. Johnny had given me so much. I owed him my love and caring. I straightened to my full five foot one inch and stepped resolutely into the hallway.

As I led Ryan to Johnny's room, we approached a small group crowded around the nurses' station. Alec broke from the group when she saw me. She stopped a hug in midair when she saw my bandaged arm and torn, dirty clothing.

"What happened to you? Were you in an accident?" she asked, taking my hands.

"Something like that," I said. "I'll explain later. Why is everyone standing around out here? How's Johnny? Did they already remove his feeding tube?"

Her eyes glistened at the mention of Johnny's name. "No, not yet, but he's the same. Paul says it'll take a day or two for the paperwork to be processed. We came here to give Johnny, and one another, moral support. It's not working. I feel worse. Why weren't you at the hearing? I've been imagining—dead in a ditch."

You weren't far off, I thought.

Ryan cleared his throat and said, "I think it's time I got going. Thanks for bringing me here."

"Oh, no you don't," I said and took his elbow. "You're not going anywhere until you've seen Johnny." As we passed Alec, I said, "This is Ryan—uh, I'm sorry. I don't know your last name."

"Walker," Ryan said.

"Ryan Walker. He's the angel who saved my life today," I said.

"I was just doing my job. It was my privilege to help," he said.

"It looks like we're all in your debt, Ryan," Adam said, coming forward and shaking his hand. He glanced at me with raised eyebrows. "I look forward to hearing this story."

"That'll have to wait," I said and pushed Adam out of the way. I was afraid Ryan might tell them more than I wanted them to know, and I was anxious to see Johnny and get it over with. "Ryan came here to meet Johnny, so that's what we're going to do." I took his elbow again and pulled him down the corridor.

The instant I saw Johnny lying helpless in his crib, my resolve wavered. I summoned what courage I had left and went to him. I gently stroked his soft head while my tears dripped onto the sheet beside him.

Ryan stood beside me and said, "I can't believe he's the child from the news. I see why you're so fond of him. He's a beautiful boy. It's strange to think he's totally unaware of what awaits him."

"Take a good look," I said in a hoarse whisper. "He'll be gone in a few days." I wiped my tears and went to the rocking chair. "It wasn't supposed to end this way, you know. I've been caring for him almost from the moment he came here. I've planned and dreamed of the day he would come home as my son. Can you understand what drove me to the river today? I don't know how to go on living without him."

"I know we just met, but I think I've learned something about you today. You have a supportive group of friends out there," he said, pointing to the door. "They obviously care about you. Why do you think they'll turn their backs on you now? Let them help you. You don't have to go through it alone."

I nodded, knowing Ryan was right. My friends had proved their devotion to me countless times, especially Alec.

"You have a great deal of love to give," Ryan said. "I told you at the river that someone could come along who'll need you as much as Johnny. You might even help someone without knowing it. We all do sometimes."

"My days as a Good Samaritan are finished. The trade-off's not worth it. I can't go through this again. It almost killed me this time." I closed my eyes.

"Do you regret helping Johnny?" Ryan asked.

"I asked myself that question earlier. I'm grateful to have known Johnny, but if someone had told me this was how it would end, I probably would have walked away. I've lost almost everyone that I've loved. I can't do it again," I said.

"I'm glad that not everyone feels that way. If they did, no one would ever help anyone. We'd all be lonely and suffering. Is that the kind of world you want to live in? Hasn't anyone ever helped you out in a time of need—before today, I mean?"

Ryan's question caught me off guard. I'd been too absorbed in my own pain to think of anyone else. Where would I have been if my friends hadn't come to my rescue? Where would I have been without my mother or Andrew or my grandparents? Many people had sacrificed for me. It hadn't been easy for them, yet there I was, saying I'd never help anyone again because it might be hard.

"Yes, I've been helped, in profound ways and more times than I can count. I *am* deeply grateful for that." I rubbed my arm. "This is too deep for me right now. My whole body is throbbing, and I need to focus on surviving the next few days without worrying about what will happen beyond that."

"Fair enough," Ryan said. "I didn't mean to pressure you."

I stood and tenderly placed my hand on his arm. "Don't apologize to me. I owe you my life. I haven't even said thank you. It's impossible to express that kind of gratitude, but thank you for listening to that little voice in your head. You must be an angel."

He put his hand over mine. "Don't thank me. I meant what I said. It's been my privilege to be part of this. I'm just an average guy doing his job."

"What you did today was anything but average. How can I ever repay you?"

"You can repay me by promising that you'll never attempt that again. I'd like to do what I can to help. Would it be too much to ask that we stay in touch? I'd like to know you're all right."

"Nothing would be too much for you to ask. How could I not stay in touch with my guardian angel? Now, I have another favor to ask," I said. "I have no right to ask, but would you mind if we keep what happened at the river between us? Answer me honestly. If that makes you uncomfortable, I'll understand."

"You mean when I saved you from slipping off that rock into the river? That's what happened, isn't it?"

I breathed a sigh of relief. "I'm in your debt again."

"You were desperate. Who am I to judge? You promise not to do that ever again, right?"

I looked into his eyes and saw the same concern I'd seen at the river. "Yes, never again."

He took a card from his wallet and pressed it into my hand. "Hold on to this, and call me when you have time or when you need me or just want to talk. I have to get back now to see if I can save any more damsels in distress," he said and patted my hand.

"I'll show you the quickest way out." I led him into the hallway.

CHAPTER FIFTEEN

After walking Ryan out, I went back to Alec and Adam, knowing I had explaining to do. They both turned and stared at me when they saw me coming toward them. Paul was on his cell phone by the nurses' station but hung up when he saw me. The rest of the group that had been there earlier was gone, probably to get back to work.

When I reached them, we all waited for the first one to speak. It was Alec, of course. "Tell me what really happened," she said and crossed her arms.

"First, I need someone to treat my arm. Then I'm going home to take a shower."

"I'll take you home for fresh supplies," Alec said. "We'll go back to my apartment and pick your car up in the morning."

I was sure Alec had offered so she could get me alone to grill me on the gritty details, but I was still grateful. I hadn't decided how much I would tell her, but I'd have to give some explanation.

"Let's go to the ER. I'll stitch you up, but then you're getting a complete exam," Adam said and headed down the hall.

Paul patted my shoulder. "I'll call first thing in the morning. You and I have a lot to talk about."

I nodded and followed Adam to the elevator with Alec close behind. Adam insisted on doing x-rays and checking out every inch of me after he stitched my arm. When he was satisfied that I was well enough to leave, he kissed Alec and went to the ID unit. Alec and I left the hospital and walked to her car in silence. Once we were inside, she refused to go anywhere until I promised to start talking.

"I promise," I said, "but please, let's go. I'm starving and filthy, and I want to go home."

Alec nodded and turned the key.

I'd decided not to keep anything back from her. She was crying softly by the time I finished my story. I handed her a tissue.

She wiped her face with one hand as best she could. "Why didn't you call me? I had no idea what you were going through. The thought of you alone when you heard the news kills me." She smiled weakly and said, "Sorry. Poor choice of words."

"I wasn't alone, Alec. Someone was looking out for me," I said and looked out the window, still trying to make sense of what Ryan had said. We rode along in silence until I got up the courage to ask her the question that was nagging at me. "Alec, do you feel differently about me because of what I did today?"

Alec didn't answer right away. She found a safe place to pull off the road and turned the car off. "I've never understood how anyone could commit suicide. It's not something any of us likes to think about, is it? A girl I went to high school with killed herself. I didn't know her very well, but I knew her well enough to see that she had emotional problems. I felt pity for her and the friends and family she left behind. Of course, in my work as a nurse, I've seen people who have attempted suicide, but I've seldom known the circumstances that drove them to such a desperate act. I've heard that the majority of people who attempt suicide contemplate it for a long time before they act. What happened to you today is nothing like those situations. First, you never would have gone through with it."

I started to protest, but Alec held up her hand to stop me. "Second, you've been in some pretty desperate situations in your life, and you've never seriously considered it before. Most people probably would have in your place. We'll never know what would have happened if Ryan hadn't come along. If you had wanted to jump, you'd have done it in spite of him. All that matters is that you're here now. We all have a difficult time ahead of us. Put what happened on hold for now. We don't ever need to speak of it again."

"I don't deserve you," I said quietly. "I'm so relieved. You're right about what happened. I was on the edge of that rock, but I couldn't move, like my feet were glued down. I panicked when I heard that news report. I've heard about people doing crazy things when they get shocking news, but I never thought I'd be one of them. I can't pretend it didn't happen, but you can't imagine how relieved I am that Ryan was there. No matter what happens with Johnny, I'm going to face it and go on. It'll be the hardest thing I've ever had to do, but I have you to get me through it."

"I'll keep your secret too, even from Adam, and I'll be here for as long as it takes," Alec said and pulled back onto the road.

I woke early the next morning but didn't get up right away. My arm throbbed, and I ached all over. At least I'm still here, I thought. I went over the events of the previous day in my mind. It was hard to comprehend that it had only been twenty-four hours since I'd gone to the hospital blindly believing my troubles were almost over. One day later, the worst was about to happen.

I thought of my mother's last days. I'd been old enough to understand that my mother was dying of cancer but knew little of what that meant. I understood exactly what was going to happen to Johnny. I prayed that the meds and coma would be enough to dull his pain while he slowly died of dehydration. I also hoped he wouldn't linger. Paul still believed that getting the truth out to the public would make a difference, but I knew it was too late for Johnny. Anyone who had the power to save him would have already acted.

I dragged myself out of bed and slowly dressed. The important thing was to keep Johnny as comfortable as possible. How many times in my career had I said that to my patients and their families? "We'll make them as comfortable as possible." I was learning that those words didn't give any comfort at all. When I was ready, I stood facing the door, knowing that once I walked through, there would be no going back. As I reached for the knob, a faint tapping came from the other side.

"Come in," I said.

Alec came in wearing a baggy T-shirt and pajama shorts. "I wasn't sure if you were up yet. I was awake all night and finally gave up. Did you sleep?"

"Yes, surprisingly, I did, even though I woke up early. I guess I was exhausted after all the upheaval yesterday. I'm sorry you didn't sleep," I said.

"That's life. I'll sleep later."

I pulled my hair back in a clip. "That's the right attitude. Now, it's time to go face this."

"I'll throw on some jeans and meet you out front in thirty," she said and shuffled off to get dressed.

⚔ ⚔

I was in my usual spot by Johnny's bed an hour later. Alec left to check on news about the legal paperwork and left me alone with him. The nurse had already been in to bathe and dress him. I was relieved to see that everyone was going on with business as usual. I sang to him for a while, gently stroking his soft head as we rocked. He lay peacefully in my arms, blissfully unaware of what was coming.

Alec peeked her head in the door twenty minutes later to tell me that Paul was waiting for me in the hallway. I reluctantly put Johnny into his crib. From the look on Paul's face when I walked out, I knew the news wasn't good.

"For once the court has managed to speed up the process, and the paperwork is ready," Paul said, looking like he was fighting back tears. "They'll be sending it over soon. I estimate that they'll take Johnny off life support sometime after noon today. I'm so sorry. I wish I could stop this. I failed you both. I was hoping the interview would make a difference."

"Don't apologize, Paul. It's not your fault. If anything, I blame myself. I scared Jay off," I said, fighting my own tears. "Has anyone heard from that snake, by the way?"

"Not that I know of, and I told you not to blame yourself. The court already had Jay's report and deposition. He probably wouldn't have gone to the hearing either way," Paul said.

I sighed. "I wish it were over. I'm going to sit with Johnny until lunchtime. I'd rather not be in the room when they come in to do the deed. After that, I'm staying with him until the end."

"I have to be in court, but don't hesitate to call if you need anything. I'll check my phone on breaks and come back in the afternoon."

"I promise to be here. No more running away," I said as he walked away.

<hr/>

Brad came up and followed me in as I turned to go back to Johnny. I watched silently while he gave Johnny a brief exam. "How long do you think it'll take?" I asked.

"How long will what take?" Brad said without looking up.

"For him to die."

Brad turned to face me. He looked tired. He dealt with illness and death on a regular basis, but Johnny's case had taken a toll on him. He was in his early forties and of average height. He wasn't strikingly handsome like Jay, but attractive. He had relaxed, easy manners and made people feel comfortable around him. That definitely wasn't like Jay. Jay commanded attention when he walked into a room. Brad was just as happy if no one noticed him. I'd learned the hard way that I'd much rather know a man like Brad.

He fidgeted under my scrutiny and said, "You know I can't give you a definite answer, but I don't think it'll take long, probably less than two days. As you know, children become dehydrated much faster than adults do. For his sake and ours, I hope he goes quickly."

"How am I supposed to sit here and watch this? I'm committed to stay with him, but I don't think I'm strong enough. I'm scared, Brad."

"You're a nurse. You've seen patients die. I know this is different, but maybe you have to detach yourself from the situation and deal with it as a medical professional. Bring your years of training and experience into play," he said and went back to examining Johnny.

"You make it sound simple. You want me to turn off my feelings, just like that?" I snapped my fingers.

Johnny flinched, and we eyed each other knowingly. Brad took off his gloves and said, "We've known each other for a long time. I remember the old you. You could choose to behave that way now."

"I'm not that person anymore, and I won't pretend to be."

Brad shook his head. "What I'm saying is, it might help you get through this. You think of yourself as his mother, but he's not your son. He's just another patient we're treating in our hospital."

I got up and went to his side. As we looked down on Johnny, I said, "That may help you cope, but it's too late for me. I understand what you're trying to do, and I appreciate it, but I'll always think of

Johnny as my son. I know people don't understand how I can feel this way about a child who's been unconscious since I've known him, but I've had a connection to him since that first day. I can't sever that now. I'm no different than any mother about to lose her child."

"I'm not trying to minimize your feelings for Johnny. I was hoping to find a way to soften the blow."

"Nothing can do that now," I said and took Johnny's hand.

Brad nodded and took out his laptop to make some notes in Johnny's chart. "I don't know why I'm bothering to do this," he said.

"How is he doing, Brad?" I asked. "Not that it matters, but are you surprised he hasn't improved more in the last few days?"

"I am," he said. "I was encouraged with his progress last week. I honestly thought he would have regained consciousness by now. He's even having sleep cycles. If he had another week, I think he'd become fully conscious. Here, look," he said and handed me his laptop.

I read through his notes and test results for several minutes before handing it back to him. "How did Jay get away with declaring him brain-dead? Didn't you submit your findings to the court too?"

"Yes, but so much is still left up to interpretation in these cases. When there's a doctor with Jay's level of expertise involved, everyone naturally defers to him."

"But your findings were exactly the opposite. Why didn't the judge think that was suspicious? I don't understand how this happened," I said.

"I don't even know if the judge looked at my report. It all happened so quickly. I think she'd made her decision by the time the hearing started." Brad patted my shoulder and said, "I have other patients to see. I can't forget them because of what's going on. I'll come back after I've finished my afternoon appointments."

"Thanks for taking the time to talk this out with me. It doesn't change anything, but it helped." I gave him a weak smile.

Brad smiled back, but the smile didn't reach his eyes. He walked out, leaving me alone with Johnny again. His eyes were open, but he just stared vacantly at the ceiling. I waved my hand across his face.

"I told you it was time to wake up, Son. Be a good little boy and mind your mommy now. Your life depends on it," I said and kissed his cheek.

Johnny didn't respond but continued to stare. I sat down and took out my tablet to read. I read the same page three times but had no idea what it said. I started again, trying harder to focus on the words but got the same result. I gave up and tossed the tablet back into my bag. It was too early for lunch, so I decided to go for a walk. Since I'd be at the hospital for the foreseeable future, I knew I should take advantage of the fresh air and exercise while I could. It was warmer than it been the day before, and the sun was out. I hoped to draw strength from the warmth.

⇥ ⇤

I wound aimlessly along the streets for an hour before finding a bench near the state capitol grounds. I watched as mothers cheerfully pushed their children in strollers or chased them on the lawn. Joggers and bikers passed by on the sidewalk, enjoying the spring weather. Bright white blossoms blazed on the dogwood trees. I would have relished the scene on any other day and hoped there would be a day when I could do the same in my future.

I stayed for another hour until deciding it was time to get back. I groaned as I stood. My hip was still stiff from its encounter with the boulder, so it took longer than usual to get back to the hospital. My stomach growled as I walked through the doors fifteen minutes later, and I realized I hadn't eaten for hours. I went to the cafeteria, loaded my tray, and sat alone to eat.

I ate slowly, stalling as long as I could, still afraid to face what lay before me. I thought of Johnny and my promise to stay with him. Pushing my fears aside, I put my tray away and went to the elevator. The sound of excited voices floated in as the doors opened on Johnny's floor. I'd expected a mournful silence, not cheerful celebration. I stepped out to find the same group from the day before, but they were laughing and patting one another on the backs. Alec spotted me and smothered me in a crushing hug.

I pushed her off and said, "What is this, Alec? Did the judge change her mind?"

"You'd know if you'd stop running off without telling us where you're going. We've been looking all over for you." She tried to hug me again.

I ducked out of the way. "I went for a walk and had some lunch. What's happening?"

"Johnny's awake, Grace! He's awake!" she cried.

Adam came up beside her. "It's true. Johnny's regained consciousness. When Brad was removing his feeding tube, Johnny started following him with his eyes. He's still in with him. We've had everyone out looking for you, again."

Before Adam could say more, I pushed past him and ran to Johnny's room. Brad was leaning over the crib, blocking my view. He turned when he heard me and said, "Grace! Where have you been?"

I ignored his question, transfixed on the scene behind him. Johnny was propped up on a pillow, watching us intently. I brushed by Brad and knelt at Johnny's bedside. We stared at each other wide-eyed until I said, "Hello, Johnny," in a broken whisper.

He made a soft gurgling sound and smiled at me with a crooked grin. It was too much. I laid my head on the rail and broke into sobs.

Brad let me cry it out and then helped me up.

"It's true," I said, never taking my eyes from Johnny. "How could this happen? We were just here three hours ago."

Brad shrugged. "I told you he only needed a little more time. I guess three hours was enough. It's the most astounding thing I've seen in all my years as a physician."

"How is he? What's his prognosis? Can I hold him?" I asked in a rush.

Brad chuckled. "I'll answer the last, first. Of course, you can hold him. Move slowly. I'm not sure how he'll react to you."

I lifted Johnny and sat in the rocking chair with him cradled on my lap. He nestled against me and closed his eyes.

"Well, that answers that," Brad said. "As for his prognosis, he has a long road ahead, but I'm hopeful. At least he'll live to travel that road." He paused, and I smiled at the emotion in his voice. "I think he's able to swallow, but he has to learn how to eat. His heart and lung issues will be ongoing concerns. I've done some minor preliminary tests on his hearing and vision. They seem fine, but we'll need to do in-depth testing. He was approximately six months old when he came here. His cognitive abilities may have regressed or stayed the same. It'll be some time before we know if he'll be able to speak or even understand speech. There's no way to know yet if he'll be able to walk."

"He does understand us," I said, still smiling. "I told him before I went out that he needed to wake up, and he did."

The door opened, and Adam and Alec came in. "I couldn't hold her back anymore," Adam said.

"Like you weren't dying to get in here too," Alec said and knelt next to my chair. "This isn't what I expected though."

"He smiled at me," I told her through quivering lips. "I think he's sleeping now."

I tenderly laid him in his crib and went into the hallway with the other three following behind. Brad asked if any of the nurses had time to sit with Johnny in case he woke up. They all answered yes at once.

"I think it would be better if one of you went in at a time," he said. "We don't want to overwhelm the poor little guy. There will be plenty of time for you to all have a turn. Besides, don't some of you have other patients?"

They groaned collectively and picked numbers to see who would go first. The winner did a victory dance and went to Johnny's room.

"What happens now?" I asked. "Has anyone called Paul or Serena?"

"I called Paul a few minutes ago," Adam said. "He's making the necessary calls before he comes here. He said he'd tell Serena."

"Is there any danger of him becoming comatose again?" Alec asked Brad.

"It's unlikely, but in his case, I can't rule it out. He's alert and responsive. I need to do an EEG and CT scan. I'll schedule the tests as soon as I get authorization," he said.

"What do you mean get authorization? He's awake," I said.

"By law, I can't treat him until the judge reverses her ruling. We can't even give him anything to eat or drink until we straighten this out. Admin is scrambling to figure out how to deal with it. They'd better hurry."

"This is ludicrous. You may not be able to do anything for him, but I can," I said and stomped my foot. "I don't work here anymore, so Kinsley can't stop me. Do you think he can take a bottle of formula?"

"I don't see why not," Brad said, "but don't tell anyone that came from me. You may not work here, but I still do."

"I'll pick up a few things for him at the store so you don't have to leave. Back in a jiff," Alec said and tore off down the hall.

CHAPTER SIXTEEN

I went to Johnny after Alec left. He was still sleeping. I was tempted to wake him up and wondered if that was how new mothers
felt while their babies slept. I watched him sleep until Paul came in
with Alec thirty minutes later. Johnny heard the commotion and
woke up. He looked around frantically and then did something
we'd never seen him do: he cried. It was the most beautiful sound
I'd ever heard. Paul turned away, but not before I saw him wipe a
tear off his cheek.

"That's amazing," Alec said, not trying to hide her tears.

I picked Johnny up and tried to soothe him, but he cried louder.
"Quick, fix him a bottle," I said to Alec. "He's probably starving."

While Alec prepared his bottle, I put him in the crib and
changed his diaper. He quieted for a few seconds before starting
to howl again. I picked him up and walked around the room patting his back, but it didn't help. Alec thrust the bottle at me, and
I tried to get Johnny to take it. He tossed his head back and forth,
refusing to allow the nipple into his mouth, and screamed louder.

Paul, who had been standing silently by the door, took Johnny and the bottle from me. He cradled Johnny in his arm and put a few drops of milk on his tongue. Johnny smacked his lips and opened up for more. Paul gave him a few more drops and then slid the nipple into his mouth. As soon as it touched the roof of his mouth, Johnny's instincts kicked in, and he started to suck ravenously. Alec and I stared at Paul wide-eyed.

"I'm always the one who gets our kids to take a bottle when they're fussy," he said, smiling proudly. "I guess it's a gift." He gazed down at Johnny and brushed a lock of hair from his forehead. "I left here thinking this was the worst day of my life. After Adam called, I couldn't wait to get here to see for myself if it was true. I know that Johnny waking up has nothing to do with me, but I'm so grateful. Do you remember what I said a few days ago about walls tumbling down when things looked hopeless? It looks like Johnny tore the wall down himself."

"He did what we couldn't," I said. "What happens to him now?"

"I called Serena. She says it's chaos at DSS. They'll probably have Brad reexamine him and submit his new findings. After that, the judge will reverse her decision. They'll have some serious damage control to do. Then we go back to square one, and you adopt Johnny. I'm sure they'll hurry it up and not stand in your way. If all goes well, you'll be Johnny's mother before we know it."

I was too overwhelmed to speak.

Alec squeezed my hand. "What about Jay and his cronies? Do they just walk away now, unpunished for what they did?" she asked Paul.

"I'll do whatever it takes to make them pay for their crimes, but that comes later. I heard on my way in that the hospital is holding a press conference this afternoon. They'll probably twist things around to come out looking like heroes," Paul said.

"Nothing matters to me but being with Johnny. Promise that you'll do what you can to keep us out of the limelight. I'd hate to see Johnny become a circus sideshow," I said.

"I'll do my best to protect you, but you need to be prepared for the worst. Johnny's a major headline again. It'll be impossible to avoid the media forever."

Johnny squirmed. Paul held up the empty bottle before handing him back to me. "Now that this fellow has a full tummy, I'll place him in your capable hands. I need to find out the latest anyway. I'll let you know about the press conference."

Brad walked in as Paul was about to leave. "I came to warn you to expect company. The judge, someone from DSS, their lawyer, and a neurologist from another hospital are on their way over. I guess they want to see Johnny for themselves. I'm amazed that they're coming so quickly."

"Sure, now they come," I said and rolled my eyes. "I'm glad, though. I want to get this over with so we can get the adoption started."

"I think I'll stick around to watch the circus. This should be good," Paul said and leaned against the windowsill.

I showed Brad the empty bottle. "Alec and I couldn't get him to take it, but Paul got him going. He's a pro. Johnny seems to be taking all this in stride."

"We'll have to see how he tolerates the formula. We'll start him on soft solids after that," Brad said.

The door opened, and the legal entourage walked in. Serena came in last and winked at me.

"Let me introduce Judge Brackman; Mr. Gains, legal counsel for DSS; and Dr. Foster," Serena said.

We all squeezed against the wall in the small room and introduced ourselves too. I laid Johnny in his crib, and he started to whimper as soon as I stepped away. The judge moved closer and asked Serena to verify that he was Baby John Doe.

"Yes, your Honor. That's him," Serena said.

Johnny started to cry and flail his arms. I tried to comfort him. He quieted down after a few seconds and smiled at me. Judge Brackman raised her eyebrows.

"Dr. Carter," Judge Brackman said, turning to Brad, "it seems I should have paid closer attention to your findings. I've learned something valuable today. Please reexamine the child and submit your results to me. Dr. Foster, do you concur with that decision?"

"I've seen all I need to. It's obvious this child isn't clinically brain-dead. He's not even in a vegetative state. I'll gladly defer to Dr. Carter," Dr. Foster said.

Judge Brackman turned next to the DSS lawyer. He nodded. "Very well," she said. "Pending submission of Dr. Carter's findings, I'll assume that the Department of Social Services will withdraw its petition. This child will then be under its jurisdiction again. Since I've seen what I came for, I'll be going now."

She left the room, and Mr. Gains and Dr. Foster followed.

Serena said, "Go ahead without me. I'll join you shortly."

We waited until the group was out of earshot to begin celebrating. Alec picked Johnny up and squeezed him tightly, scaring him into another round of crying. Brad and Paul patted each other on the backs, and Serena hugged me.

When Serena caught her breath, she said, "I need to drag Johnny's case folder out of the closed file. Hurry up with those tests, Brad. Your report is the one thing holding us back."

"I promise to set speed records on this one," he said as he left to schedule Johnny's tests.

Serena told me she'd be in touch, and she and Paul followed Brad out.

"It's happening, Alec," I said. "Everything I've wanted. Tell me I'm not dreaming. I'm afraid I'll wake up."

Johnny lay quietly in Alec's arms, following her with his eyes. She sat with him in the rocking chair and said, "It's real. Soon you'll be taking this sweet boy home as your son. Last night when I couldn't sleep, I was thinking about what you told me in the parking lot the night Johnny went in the ID unit. It was the first time I started to believe you could be Johnny's mother someday. Then Jay came along with the mess with Kinsley, and Judge Brackman issued her ruling. I was confused and hopeless and had a minicrisis of my own last night. It wasn't as dramatic as yours, but it was just as real. You and I just gave up too soon."

Alec's words reminded me of Ryan. "I have to call him. He doesn't know about Johnny," I said and got up to find my phone. I stopped before I reached my purse and turned to Alec. "What if Ryan hadn't been at the river? What if I had—"

"Don't say it," Alec said, holding up her hand. "No 'what ifs.' Focus on what's happening now. You're here with Johnny. He's going to live. Just be grateful for that."

I took a deep breath. "You always know what to say. I won't allow myself to think that way." I fumbled in my purse for Ryan's card. "Can I go to your office to call him?"

"It's weird to hear you call it my office," she said and crinkled her nose. "It'll always be your office to me, so you don't even need to ask."

I laughed. "Thanks, and please stay with Johnny until I get back. Promise?"

"You couldn't tear me away," she said.

I went to my old office to call Ryan. It felt like a hundred years had passed since I'd been there, instead of just a few days. I couldn't bring myself to sit at the desk and went to the sofa.

When Ryan answered, I said, "This is Grace. I have unbelievable news." I told him about Johnny and asked how soon he could come to the hospital.

"It's incredible. More than incredible. What's the word for more than incredible?" he asked.

I laughed and said, "There aren't words."

"Well, I'm thrilled! I'll come after dinner and stay as long as you can put up with me."

"Thank you. Stay as long as you'd like," I said, strangely pleased at the thought of seeing him again. "The hospital's holding a press conference this afternoon, but I don't know the time yet. Will you be able to watch it?"

"I'll record it if I'm not home in time. I can't get over this. It's the last news I expected today."

"It's a miracle. There's no other way to describe it. You'll see for yourself."

"You don't have to convince me. I already know," he said.

The line went quiet for a few seconds, and I thought the call had dropped. I was about to see if he was still on when he said, "I'm looking forward to seeing both of you. Until then."

The line clicked, but I stared at the phone for a while longer. I was baffled at how he could be looking forward to seeing me. The guy had stopped me from killing myself only one day earlier. In the end, I decided that he was being polite and that I'd probably never see him again, even though I secretly hoped that wouldn't be true. I wondered again at this enigma of a man who had come into my life. I smiled as I slipped my phone into my pocket and went to be with my son.

Johnny wasn't in his room when I got back from calling Ryan. Alec had waited for me and said they'd taken him to begin the tests. I was disappointed. I wanted to stay with him through the ordeal. I started to go find out where Johnny was when Paul came in and told us that the press conference was starting in fifteen minutes.

"Adam has gone down to save seats, so we should go," he said.

Since I wouldn't be allowed in if Johnny was getting an MRI, I reluctantly followed Paul and Alec to the first-floor conference room. Adam had grabbed four seats near the front.

"This is where I saw you for the first time," Alec told me. "You intimidated me. I never would have imagined that we'd end up as best friends."

I smiled and nodded. I'd been remembering the same thing and marveled at the changes in our lives since then. I wouldn't have traded it for anything.

A door opened at the front of the room, and Brad walked in with Kinsley and the hospital's public-relations rep. They took their seats at a table behind the microphone. Brad looked like he'd rather be under the table. If Jay had been there, he'd be eating up the attention. Brad did anything he could to avoid it. Brad's wife is a fortunate woman, I thought. I smiled at Brad to encourage him, and he winked at me.

The PR rep stepped to the microphone and said, "I'll make a brief statement before I take questions. A child known as Baby John Doe, who is under our care and is a ward of the state, has been in a persistent vegetative state for approximately eight months. After intense and lengthy medical examinations and treatments, a neurological specialist determined that he was, in fact, brain-dead. Based on those findings, and after much deliberation, the Department of Social Services and this hospital concluded that the most humane action would be to remove him from life support rather than keep his body alive. This was an extremely difficult decision to make and was not taken lightly."

I huffed at that and poked Alec in the ribs with my elbow. Alec rolled her eyes.

"Consequently," he continued, "the DSS filed a petition to gain permission to remove him from life support. Yesterday, Judge Beatrice Brackman approved that petition, and we received the order to remove the child from life support this morning. At approximately twelve thirty this afternoon, a nurse on staff entered the child's room to comply with the order. It soon became clear to her that he was fully conscious. She carried out her duty before contacting Dr. Bradley Carter, seated here behind me."

Brad gave a weak smile and nodded.

"Dr. Carter has directed the child's care since he arrived here. He examined Baby John Doe and concluded that he had, in fact, regained consciousness."

The reporters gave a collective gasp. Several raised their hands.

The PR rep motioned for them to lower their hands. "I'll begin taking questions when I conclude my statement. I'm aware that many of you came here expecting the news that the child had passed away. It's with great relief and pleasure that we announce that not only is he alive and conscious, but his prognosis is positive. Judge Brackman visited him a few hours ago and has dismissed the DSS petition. We'll now take questions."

He took his seat next to Brad. Almost every hand in the room went up. Kinsley randomly picked a reporter to ask the first question.

"You're saying this child is fine after almost eight months in a coma?"

"I'll ask Dr. Carter to answer that question," Kinsley said.

Brad cleared his throat and leaned into the microphone. "Johnny, as we call him, is not fine. He'll most likely suffer lifelong complications due to his time in a comatose state. However, he is fully conscious and aware of his surroundings. Chances are good that he'll live a long, if not challenging, life."

The reporter raised his hand again and said, "I have a follow-up question. How is it possible that you declared him brain-dead a few days ago and now he's fully conscious?"

Brad sat up straighter, and the color returned to his face.

Here we go, I thought.

"Let me make it clear to you all that I was not the physician who declared Johnny brain-dead. Dr. Jay Morgan, a leading pediatric neurologist, was the doctor who made that declaration."

"Where is Dr. Morgan?" the reporter asked.

Several others nodded.

"I'm unaware of Dr. Morgan's whereabouts. I haven't seen him for three days," Brad said.

"Let's keep the questions focused on Johnny's recovery," Kinsley said.

He called on another reporter who said, "But how could two neurologists come to two completely opposite conclusions?"

Brad said, "I can't speak for Dr. Morgan, but these cases are often subjective."

"Well, you obviously got it right," the reporter said. "Maybe Dr. Morgan isn't as big an expert as he's made out to be."

Several reporters laughed, and I was the loving the direction the discussion was headed.

Kinsley spoke up. "You're free to contact Dr. Morgan and ask him these questions. We're here to take questions solely about Johnny's recovery."

I cringed at hearing him use Johnny's name. He had no right. He was responsible for sending Johnny to Jay to seal Johnny's death warrant. No wonder Kinsley wanted to dodge their questions.

Another reporter asked, "What happens to the child now? How soon will he be released from the hospital?"

"I'll take the first question, and Dr. Carter can address the second," Kinsley said. "He remains a ward of the state. When we release him from the hospital, the Department of Social Services will place him in foster care. Our hope is that his parents will hear the news of his recovery and step forward to claim him. If that doesn't happen, he'll remain in foster care unless he's adopted."

I wanted to grab the microphone and strangle Kinsley with the cord. He knew perfectly well that I was trying to adopt Johnny.

Alec squeezed my hand.

I took a deep breath, forcing myself to be patient. He'll get his, I told myself.

Several reporters raised their hands again, but Kinsley ignored then and motioned to Brad to answer the rest of the question.

"It's far too soon for us to know when Johnny will be able to leave the hospital. I'll do everything in my power to make sure he's strong enough before he's released."

A reporter raised his hand and said, "What can you tell us about Grace Ward? There are reports that she's trying to adopt Baby John Doe."

"Please refer to him as Johnny," Brad said, and the reporter nodded.

Before Brad could answer, Kinsley broke in and said, "We're not authorized to answer that question. She's here if you'd like to ask her yourself. Grace, will you come forward, please?"

I glared wide-eyed at Kinsley and shook my head. Paul had promised to protect our privacy, but Kinsley didn't care in the least about that. The reporters were looking around, trying to find me, and I wanted to crawl under my chair. Paul leaned over and whispered that he'd handle it. He walked to the front of the room.

"My name is Paul Pierno," he said. "I'm an attorney representing Ms. Ward. You may address your questions to me. Ms. Ward was in the process of adopting Johnny when the DSS filed their petition. She intends to continue with those plans now."

Every hand in the room went up. Paul called on a reporter near the front. She said, "If Ms. Ward was trying to adopt him, why did the DSS file the petition? Why not let her do it and remove him from their responsibility?"

"I can't speak for the motives of the DSS, but I don't hold them accountable." Paul paused for a few seconds, and the room grew quiet. When all eyes were glued to him, he said, "I believe DSS is unaware that Dr. Morgan was pressured by his superiors to declare Johnny was brain-dead. We have evidence supporting this, and I'm currently conducting an investigation into the matter."

The room erupted into chaos.

The PR rep pushed Paul away from the microphone and said, "The conference is concluded. Please clear the room as quickly as possible."

A reporter spotted me and said, "That's her. There's Grace Ward."

The mob rushed me. Adam and Alec each grabbed an arm and pulled me out a side door. We managed to climb into the elevator before the doors closed.

⇥⇤

We went to Adam's office to wait for Paul and Brad. Brad got there first.

The second he was through the door, I said, "Where's Paul?" through clenched teeth.

He held up his hands and said, "He's talking to reporters in the parking lot. After you ran out, the security guards chased everyone outside. I figured you'd be here."

"Why would he do that?" I asked. "I nearly got trampled."

"I'm glad he did it," Adam said. "I was getting tired of Kinsley's lies. You did great, Brad, by the way."

"You did," I said, "but that's not the point. They'll be hounding us now. Paul could have waited until the story about Johnny died down." I rubbed my forehead and paced back and forth. "I'm really steamed."

"Paul's doing damage control, so that might help, but the press would have been after you either way," Brad said.

I groaned. "As if I don't have enough to deal with. I wanted to keep Johnny's life private. That'll be impossible now."

"It would've been impossible anyway," Alec said. "The whole country knows about Johnny. Stay on with me until the craziness dies down. You'll be closer to Johnny that way too."

"Thanks for the offer, but I'm staying here. Brad, can you get a bed moved into Johnny's room?"

"Yes, I'll take care of it," he said and squeezed my shoulder.

I picked up my purse and started to go but stopped when Paul stepped sheepishly into the room. I pushed him against the wall by his shoulders and pinned him there.

Paul was nearly twice my size, but he didn't try to resist.

"How could you do this to me? A few hours ago, you said you'd protect us. Is this your idea of protecting us?"

Paul gently removed my hands from his chest.

I pulled free and turned my back on him.

"I don't blame you for being angry, but I may have actually done you a favor," he said.

I spun around to face him. "A favor?"

"Yes, a favor," he said, looking me in the eye. "When I was talking to those reporters in the parking lot, they weren't asking about you. They wanted to know about Jay. I put them on his scent. That doesn't mean they won't be back, but I may have bought you and Johnny some time to start your life together in peace."

I took a few deep breaths, letting what Paul said sink in. The idea of the media hounding Jay, wherever he was, made me smile. They wouldn't give up until they found him. He'd had his chance to help them and come clean, but he'd blown it. He was going to pay for what he'd done.

"I hope you're right," I said, "but that was a big risk to take. It's going to get ugly once they start digging. I hope I can count on you to do a better job running interference than you did today."

"I will; trust me. This will be the best thing in the end. You'll see."

I gave a slight nod and picked up my purse again. Alec and I left the men to talk strategy, and we headed back upstairs. Ryan was sitting on a chair in the hallway outside Johnny's room when we got there and stood as we approached. I'd forgotten about him in the excitement.

"I'm so sorry, Ryan. I hope you haven't been waiting long. Things got out of hand at the press conference," I said and shook his hand.

"I've been hearing the buzz from here. What happened?" he asked, still grasping my hand.

"Long story. Can we talk about it later? I want you to meet Johnny first," I said, reluctantly pulling my hand free.

"I've already been in to see him. He's sleeping now, but he was all smiles when I went in. Hard to believe he's the same child I saw yesterday. To be honest, I thought he'd be gone by now. Shows what I know. I've never been happier to be wrong," he said.

"Even with all our medical knowledge, it's impossible to predict what will happen. I wonder how many people have had the plug pulled when they were a day, or even hours, away from waking up," I said. The thought broke my heart. Even though I knew that removing life support was the right decision for the sake of some patients, I cringed to think how often medicine may have gotten it wrong.

Alec cleared her throat. "These questions are too big to tackle now. Let's go pick up your things now since Johnny's asleep. Maybe he'll be awake when we get back."

"Ryan, you remember my friend Alec from yesterday," I said. "She's my other guardian angel. I told her the truth about what happened at the river."

"We're more than best friends," Alec said, shaking Ryan's hand. "We're sisters. I'll always be in your debt for bringing her back to me."

Ryan shifted his feet. "I'm honored to have a small part in this. I'm glad Grace has someone like you in her life," he said, glancing at me.

"Do you mind if I talk to Ryan for a few minutes before we go?" I asked Alec.

"No, that's fine. I'll check to see if Johnny needs anything else. See you in a few," she said and went into Johnny's room.

CHAPTER SEVENTEEN

I led Ryan down the hall to a small chapel. I was relieved that it was empty. We sat on a pew near the back. He watched me from the corner of his eye. He started to fidget and was about to get up, but I put my hand on his arm to stop him.

He relaxed and said, "Well? You told Alec you wanted to talk to me."

"I'm not sure how to start," I said, moving my hand to my lap. "Do you grasp the magnitude of what's happened in the last two days? I'm talking about all of it, not only Johnny waking up. I wouldn't have believed it if I hadn't been part of it."

"Of course I understand. I knew it the minute I saw you perched on the edge of that rock," he said and looked into my eyes.

I clenched my hands together. "If you hadn't been there, or if you'd come one minute later..." I wrapped my arms around myself and shivered. "I wouldn't ever have seen Johnny awake. He would have been left alone and defenseless in the world. Who knows what could have happened to him?"

Ryan put his hand on my arm. "That didn't happen. Don't torture yourself. You're here, and Johnny's awake. That's what matters."

"Alec told me the same thing. You're both right, and I know I should listen, but it's hard. Good things rarely happen in my life. When they do, I have trouble accepting it. I've never known happiness like this was possible. I'm glad you're here to share it with me. You were the first person I called with the news."

Ryan stood and walked to a small stained-glass window. He kept his back to me and pretended to study it. After a few minutes, he took a breath and turned back to face me. "I was elated when you called to ask me to come to the hospital. You've been on my mind since the river," he said.

"I bet I have," I said and winced. "It's not every day you rescue a crazy lady at the river."

"That's not what I mean. I haven't so much as looked at another woman in the two years since my wife died, and you didn't exactly make the best first impression by any stretch." He shook his head.

I shivered again. "I'm still mortified by the memory of it. It's going to take time to work through it, but in my opinion, the world's a magnificent place today."

He smiled. "I couldn't agree more."

I patted the pew next to me and said, "You know my deepest, darkest secrets, but I hardly know anything about you. Sit down, and tell me about yourself."

"Isn't Alec waiting for you?"

"She's with Johnny. She's fine."

He hesitated before sitting down. "If you insist," he said. "I have to warn you, though. My life is plain boring. What do you want to know?"

"Start with your family. Tell me about your wife," I said.

Ryan looked down at his clasped hands before answering. "She died of cancer. It's still hard to believe she's gone sometimes."

"I'm so sorry. My mother died of cancer when I was a child. It's a terrible way to lose someone."

"She had an aggressive form of cancer and went quickly, which was a blessing in the end. She was in a lot of pain. We have three grown children, a son and two fraternal twin daughters who barely act or look like sisters. Our son, Mark, is the eldest and got married six months ago. He and his wife Valerie live here in Richmond. The girls, Jennifer and Stephanie, are away at school. They come home on their breaks," he said with pride showing in his eyes.

"Have you lived in Richmond all your life? You don't have an accent," I said.

"My wife would have laughed at that question. I was in the Marines, and we moved a lot, including overseas. When I retired, we settled here because this is where my wife's family is. That was when I started working for the park service."

"Where are you from originally?" I hoped he wouldn't think I was nosy, but I found myself craving every detail of his life.

"If I tell you, you have to tell me about yourself," he said.

"That's fair," I said, smiling.

"I'm from Yakima, Washington. It's a small town near Seattle. I bet you've never heard of it."

"I've heard of it, but I don't know anything about it."

"It's a beautiful place at the base of the Cascade Mountains. That's where I got my love of the outdoors. I grew up canoeing, kayaking, camping, and mountain climbing."

"Sounds nice. You'll have to talk to Adam. He's from Colorado, and he goes on about that stuff all the time." I laughed.

"I hope I get the chance. Now it's your turn."

"I was born in a little town south of Lincoln, Nebraska. My family lived on a farm when I was born, but later we sold it and moved to Lincoln. My mother's parents were there. A few years after my mother died, I went to live with my aunt and uncle in Des Moines." Describing my childhood that way made it sound normal, when it had been anything but. I wondered what he'd think if he knew the truth.

Ryan eyed me like he was waiting for more. When I didn't go on, he said, "How did you end up here?"

"That's too long a story to go into now, but I've been in Richmond for over twenty years. I have two older brothers who were in the army. One died in the Gulf War. The other retired and lives in Atlanta with his family. That's all the family I have. As you know, I don't have children, or I didn't until today," I said.

Without warning, Ryan reached out and took my hand.

I looked at our intertwined fingers for a few seconds and said, "I was hoping you'd do that."

He smiled. "I know there couldn't be a worse time for this, but I'd like to get to know you better. If my kids knew how we met, they'd think I was the one who's crazy, but I feel drawn to you. I want to protect you and take care of you," he said and shook his head. "Wow, could that have sounded more patronizing?"

I smiled. "I happen to need someone to take care of me right now, but you might change your mind once you know more about me. My life is...complicated."

"I've noticed, but I'm pretty sure it won't ever be worse than yesterday."

"It won't, not even close," I said, and my lip trembled. "We have nowhere to go but up. Having you show up in my life is an added gift, and I'm grateful. All I ask is that you give me time to figure things out with Johnny. I'll be spending most of my time here until we have a timeline on his recovery. I need to be with him, but you'll know where to find me. After that we'll see where our path leads."

"I'll try not to be a pest. Promise you'll tell me if I'm getting on your nerves," he said.

"I have a feeling that won't happen," I said. "For now, I'd better get back to Alec. She's probably given up on me by now."

Ryan nodded, but neither of us moved, reluctant to let go of the moment. I was afraid it would never come again.

He raised my hand and brushed it with his lips. "I'd better go," he said and cleared his throat.

I gently pulled my hand away and said, "Give me a few days. I'll call you."

Ryan gave a quick nod and left without looking back.

⇥+⇤

"What took you so long?" Alec asked when I walked into Johnny's room after talking to Ryan.

Johnny was still sleeping, so I motioned for her to follow me into the hallway. It felt strange to worry about waking Johnny up after not having to worry about it for so long.

"I'm not ready to talk about that. I'm not sure I could explain it. When I'm ready to talk, you'll be the first," I told her.

"Fair enough," she said. "Let's get going."

I checked with the nurses to make sure that Johnny wouldn't be alone while I was gone. When I was satisfied they had it covered, I followed Alec to her car. On the way, we talked about everything that had happened in the previous weeks. I told Alec that I felt like I'd lived multiple lifetimes since Jay had proposed to me. Some of it was worse than anything I'd ever known, but that was all forgotten in the joy of having Johnny alive and awake.

When I told Alec that, she said, "Then maybe this is the best time to tell you something I've been keeping from you. If Johnny hadn't survived, it wouldn't have mattered. Now that he's going to live, you need to know."

"What now, Alec? I've been to heaven and hell and back in the last few weeks. I'm on top of the mountain. Will telling me ruin that?" I asked.

"Not sure," she said. "I've debated all day whether or not to tell you, but I realized that if it came out that I knew and didn't tell you, you'd be furious. So, here goes. A few weeks after that couple dumped Johnny in the ER, an FBI agent came to see him. I happened to be in the PICU visiting Johnny at the time. I told him I was on duty the night Johnny came in, and he shared a suspicion he had about who Johnny was. He asked me not to tell anyone. I'm not sure why he told me."

"Was it Grant Erikson?" I asked, recalling my conversation with him in Johnny's room months earlier.

"Maybe. I don't remember his name," she said.

"What did he tell you?" I asked, ignoring the growing dread in the pit of my stomach.

"He told me that six months earlier, he'd been working in New Mexico before transferring to Richmond. Before he left, a couple kidnapped a newborn boy from a hospital. He didn't give me any of the details but said they never found any leads, and the three of them disappeared. When Johnny showed up here, he had a strong hunch that he was the kidnapped baby. All he had was the hospital photo taken about an hour after the kidnapped baby was born. You know how fast their looks change. It was impossible to tell if Johnny was the same child."

"Stop, Alec. Please, just stop talking," I said and gripped the armrest.

"No, you need to hear the rest," she said. "He came back to see Johnny a few weeks later and came to look for me. He said he tried to talk his superiors into letting him contact the boy's parents, but they refused. They didn't want to get the parents' hopes up based on a random hunch. Johnny has the same common blood type as the parents, but the agent's boss didn't want to go to the trouble and expense to run the DNA. They told him to get back to his other cases, so he had to let the matter drop. I could tell it bothered him."

"How could you have kept this from me?" I asked her. I was shaking uncontrollably and felt light-headed.

"I shouldn't have kept it from you, and I regret waiting so long. I never saw the point when Johnny's future was so uncertain. I should have told you, even though we thought Johnny wouldn't survive." Alec glanced at me. "Your face is white as a sheet. Say something."

"You knew what I've been through the last few days. You couldn't have picked a worse time to tell me," I said.

"I put it out of my mind until last night. That's the truth. I was thinking that if Johnny was that same baby, he would die without his parents ever knowing what happened to him. Then at the press conference, I wondered if his parents might be watching. I almost told you then but chickened out. This is the first chance I've had since then. Nothing's happened after all this time. Maybe they found that boy and he's back with his parents. Your knowing changes nothing."

I pressed my forehead against the cool window glass. "Let me out. Let me out of this car."

"Don't do this," Alec said and started to cry.

I swung around to face her. "What did you expect? If there's any chance that Johnny is that couple's son, I'm obligated to find out. Can't you see that? What if you had a baby and someone kidnapped it? You'd move heaven and earth to find him. You know you would. Have you ever even thought about what those people have gone through?"

"Of course I have, but what are the odds of Johnny being their child? That agent could've contacted you at any time with his suspicions. Johnny's story's been all over the news. That has to mean something," she said.

"I've got to tell Paul. He has to do something about this. How can I adopt Johnny if he's someone else's son?"

"Paul knows," she said and sniffed.

"What? So you thought it was all right to tell him and not me? What's wrong with you?" I said, getting angrier by the second.

"I told him before the interview. I know it was only local, but there was a chance it could have been picked up nationally."

I went back to my deep breathing. "What did Paul say?"

"He went to the FBI, but that agent wasn't there. The person he talked to told him to forget it. They never believed Johnny was the same child, and they stopped investigating both cases months ago. They never had enough evidence for either. Paul let it drop."

"You two did this behind my back?" I asked, shocked that they had both betrayed me.

"You were going through enough trauma. What difference would it have made? There's nothing you can do."

"Then why tell me? Why not take it to your grave? If Johnny isn't that kidnapped child, then why tell me?"

"I did it to protect you! There's still a microscopic kernel of doubt. With the media crawling all over Johnny's story, I was afraid someone else might make the connection. I wanted you to hear this from me in case someone came forward."

I turned back to the window and stared into the darkness beyond. Without facing Alec, I said, "I knew it was too perfect. That should have been a red flag. Why couldn't you have left me in blissful ignorance, even if for just a day? Now Johnny isn't mine. He'll never be mine."

Alec pulled into my driveway and turned off the ignition. She got out, walked to my car door and yanked it open. "Get out!" she said.

I obeyed and faced her. She put her hands on my shoulders and said, "Stop this now! We've never known where Johnny came from, but we knew someone out there gave birth to him. None of that has changed. I'm not going to apologize for telling you. Maybe I could have timed it better."

"Oh, you think?" I said, trying to break free.

"Quiet!" she said, not letting me get away. "Johnny is your son. A day ago, we were sitting a deathwatch over him. Now you get to adopt him. This changes nothing! Take that boy home when the time comes, and love him the way that only you can. Give him the life he, and you, deserve. Put this from your mind and be his mother. If I ever hear you say again that he's not yours, I may have to smack you."

She dropped her hands, and I backed away from the force of her words. As we glared at each other, the truth of her words sank in. I threw my arms around her and sobbed on her shoulder.

When I finally pulled myself together, I backed away and said, "I need some major therapy or maybe just some new friends."

A smile broke on Alec's face, and we burst out laughing.

I leaned against the car and took another deep breath. "You have terrible timing. I can't say I'm glad you told me, but I needed to know. For now, I'll park this in the back of my mind with the rest of the mess and focus on Johnny. That's as much as I can handle."

"I'm glad to hear that. I hope you won't let this be a wedge between us."

"It won't. I'm going to be mad at you for a while, but as you told Ryan, we're sisters. Nothing will ever change that."

I left Alec waiting in the car and went inside. I hesitated as I stepped into the kitchen. Everything was exactly as I'd left it. A teacup and spoon rested in the sink, patiently waiting to be washed. A loaf of moldy bread sat on the counter. I threw it away and looked in the fridge to see what other food I should toss. My answering machine sat on the counter next to the fridge. The message indicator was flashing, so I pushed the play button and leaned against the counter to listen.

The first few messages were ordinary calls about everyday things. That life seemed years ago and far away. The next several messages were from Adam, Alec, and Paul, trying to find me. I erased those, not wanting to dwell on the events surrounding them.

There was one message from a concerned neighbor and a few from reporters wanting to interview me. I skipped those to deal with later. There was one call from Ryan. I smiled at the memory of our encounter in the hospital chapel earlier. I briefly savored the moment before pushing play again. The voice in the next message froze my blood. I played it through and then rewound it to listen again.

"Grace," he said, speaking in a whisper. "It's Jay. I don't have much time. I didn't bother calling your cell because I knew you wouldn't answer. I have to see you. I heard about Johnny, and I saw the press conference. Give me a chance to explain. People are looking for me. We need to meet. Please, I'm begging you. I've got to make you understand. Call my daughters when you're ready to talk. I'll be waiting."

I pressed the stop button and stepped back. My heart pounded. How dare he call me? I thought. I had almost lost my life because of him. My thoughts flashed back to the horrible scene at the river. He was the cause of my pain and despair but had the gall to beg for my help. I never thought I'd hear the fabulous Dr. Jay beg for anything. It must have killed him to make that call. I knew his deepest, darkest secrets. There wasn't anything he could do to change that, but that didn't mean I wanted him hurt. If any of what he'd told me was true, he could be in real danger, but I wasn't sure what I could do to help him.

I had a decision to make. Johnny was going to live. He'd soon be my son in spite of the wisp of a shadow on our future. I had dear friends in my life who cared for me, and now maybe Ryan too. Jay didn't belong in that future. He failed me when I needed him most, but I still almost felt sorry for him. Almost. I jotted down the information to give to Paul in the morning. With that done, I pressed the delete button and erased Dr. Jay Morgan from my life.

CHAPTER EIGHTEEN

Life with Johnny awake was not exactly what I'd dreamed. While I couldn't have loved him more if he were my own flesh and blood, my instant initiation into life as a mother of a special-needs child was rocky. Added to those challenges was the fact that none of us, not even Brad, knew what to expect from Johnny from day to day. Some days he cried for hours despite our best efforts to comfort him. Other times, he slept for twenty-four hours at a stretch. I tried to catch naps when I could but had a hard time sleeping knowing he could wake up screaming at any moment. Working him into a normal sleep-wake cycle took some doing.

Johnny's initial injuries and long months in a coma left him with ongoing pulmonary, brain, and neuromuscular problems. His left side, including his face, was partially paralyzed when he first woke up, but with therapy and reduced brain inflammation, he regained some movement. He still smiled with half a grin that I found adorable. Brad was hopeful that Johnny might be able to walk with assistance someday. I joked that we'd have matching limps.

Johnny had a constant cough, and his oxygen levels sometimes dropped when he was overactive. Almost drowning and
being intubated for so long had left scar tissue behind. His pul-
monologist hoped that once Johnny built up muscle tone, his
lung function would improve. In the meantime, we controlled
the problem with medications and breathing treatments. Johnny
was no fan of those and fought me when I tried to put his face
mask on.

On the plus side, Johnny's cognitive abilities, hearing, and vision were good. He responded well when we spoke to him and
chattered incoherently most of the time he was awake. He loved
his stroller rides around the hospital grounds and smiled at everyone we passed. He also had a ravenous appetite and was gain-
ing weight quickly. He gobbled up his baby-food spaghetti with
gusto, and Alec said that was a sure sign he was supposed to be
my son.

A clear picture formed of what my life as Johnny's mother
would be. Once Johnny was released from the hospital, we'd
have trips to the physical therapist, speech therapist, and occu-
pational therapists a few times a week. The idea of my going back
to work before Johnny started school was out of the question.
I reconsidered accepting some of the interview requests I kept
getting.

I was so exhausted after the first two weeks that Brad refused to
let me stay in Johnny's room 24/7. I refused to leave Johnny alone
at night, so we reached a compromise by allowing anyone who was
willing to take a turn sleeping in Johnny's room. Pleased with my
brilliant idea, I created a rotating schedule and went home to my
own bed for the first time in two weeks.

Alec volunteered for the first shift with Johnny. That meant I
could rest knowing he was in her capable hands. I thought I'd drop
off the minute my head hit the pillow that night, but I lay there
staring at the clock as the minutes crawled by. I finally turned on

a boring documentary on my tablet and waited for sleep to come. I woke six hours later with the tablet stuck to my cheek, but I was ready to tackle another day in my new role as a mother.

During that time, Serena and I had been meeting every few days to work on Johnny's adoption. After the petition fiasco, DSS was bending over backward to expedite the process. Serena was hopeful that it would only take three months for Johnny to become my legal son. That coincided with when Brad thought Johnny would be able to leave the hospital. In the meantime, I became his foster mother. My dream of taking Johnny home to start our new life as a family was becoming a reality. With Ryan and Alec's help, I converted the room across the hall from mine into a bedroom for Johnny and counted the days until he'd be there.

Happy as I was, clouds hovered over my bliss. Foremost, I was concerned about our financial future. Since I'd never submitted my resignation, I was still employed at the hospital. With Johnny taking all my time, I couldn't go back to work. I applied for a leave of absence because I wasn't entitled to family leave until the adoption was final. Kinsley granted it without question. I put off my decision of whether to remain working at the hospital until Kinsley's fate was decided. Pete Saunders had told Adam that the board was breathing down Kinsley's neck, so I hoped it would only be a matter of time until he was gone.

The other cloud was Jay. Paul had passed on the information from Jay's call to his contact in Baltimore. Jay had shown up back at his own house two weeks after he had run away. Paul's contact kept him updated on the investigation. Jay made a preemptive strike by confessing to his involvement in the death of the young girl. The medical board suspended his license and was considering revoking it permanently. Paul told me they'd likely put him on probation, because it was impossible to prove that he'd caused the girl's death. The family wasn't pressing charges, but they were suing him for malpractice.

Jay was also facing charges for his role in Johnny's case, but Paul said that would be just as hard to prove because there had also been a chance Johnny wouldn't recover, and Jay's superiors had been blackmailing him. That made Jay a victim of sorts. The thought of Jay as a victim made me laugh. He had never been a victim in his life. He'd had the option to admit his wrongdoing from the beginning but had chosen the coward's way out.

Paul prodded me to sue Jay and the hospital as soon as the adoption was final, but I wasn't sure I would. I'd been so proud of myself for putting Jay behind me that I hated the thought of facing him in court. Paul assured me that Jay would most likely settle out of court, but all I wanted was to focus on was my life with Johnny.

I took comfort in the fact that Jay and Kinsley's careers were destroyed, and they'd pay a high price. My only enticement to sue was that if I won, I could get financial help to offset the cost of Johnny's care that the state wouldn't cover. I tucked those thoughts away and focused on bringing my boy home.

Another bright spot in my life was Ryan. I hesitated to call him after our talk in the chapel, even though I felt a spark between us. I had a hard time separating those feelings from the intense emotions I'd experienced the previous few days. All I saw when I thought of Ryan was the scene at the river. He knew my deepest secret, but I hardly knew anything about him. It felt like I'd met him in my bare skin.

I started meeting with a counselor to work through everything from Jay to Johnny to Ryan. When I disclosed the episode at the river, my counselor said my behavior was understandable in light of the circumstances. I told her I was horrified by what I'd almost done, and she said that was a healthy reaction and a good sign. She cautioned me to take it slow with Ryan but that I should be candid with him from the start.

⊱⋅ ⋅⊰

I called Ryan as soon as I left my counselor's office that day.

"I was afraid I'd never hear from you again," he said. "I haven't stopped thinking about you since our talk in the chapel."

"I've been thinking about you too, but life's been crazy," I said, making excuses. So much for being candid, I thought. "Would you be up to meeting me at Juliana's Bakery on Saturday morning? We'll start simple." I held my breath while I waited for his answer.

"Juliana's is my favorite," he said, and I let out my breath. "How'd you know? I'd love to meet you there. Is eight too early?"

"No, I'll just have to make sure someone is with Johnny. See you Saturday," I said and hung up. Hearing his warm and friendly voice had made me laugh at myself for being afraid to call him. I went back to the hospital, anxious for Saturday to come.

⊱⋅ ⋅⊰

Ryan walked into Juliana's five seconds after me. We picked out our favorite pastries and went to an empty table by the window. After some small talk, I poured out my heart, leaving nothing out. I didn't want to keep secrets from him like I'd done with Alec and Jay. If he rejected me after knowing the truth, I could walk away with no regrets.

While I spoke, Ryan studied me intently with his sparkling blue eyes. He was the first man I'd known to have a balanced mixture of boy next door and rugged confidence.

"Now you know the whole me," I said when I finished. "I owe you my life, but you owe me nothing. I won't think any less of you if you leave now."

Ryan laughed. "You say that like you want me to go. Do you?" When I shook my head, he took my hands and said, "Good, because I wasn't going to leave anyway. Knowing the whole you, as you call it, only makes me want you more. You're the most intriguing person I've ever met."

The feel of my hands in his sent tingles up my arms. I wanted nothing more than to sit there and relish the feeling, but I had to clear up one more issue. "I don't want your pity. I don't want you to try to fix me," I said. "Aside from Jay and Johnny, the rest happened many years ago. I've moved past it. I want us to be on equal footing, but is that possible after how we met? You seem like such a normal guy. I'm a lot to take on."

Ryan sat back and crossed his arms. "I don't want to do those things. You say I'm a normal guy. What's normal? I told you at the river that I don't live in a vacuum. I haven't had troubles like yours, but I was in the Marines, remember? I've killed people in combat, Grace. I was a sniper. It took time to cope with that afterward, but I worked through it. It was what I had to do, but that's only a part of who I am, and I don't regret it." He put his hand on my cheek and tenderly caressed it with his thumb. "I don't see you as a victim or the desperate woman on the edge of the rocks. I see you as the hero who fought to save Johnny's life."

I was speechless. Ryan was a giant in my eyes compared to Jay. I was able to be myself with him, something I'd never been able to do that with Jay. I'd always felt inferior to him, and looking back, I realized Jay had wanted it that way. Ryan was relaxed and down to earth and treated me as his equal. As I sat in that bakery, I became certain that I'd never been in love with Jay but had only been dazzled and infatuated.

Ryan and I talked about everyday things and laughed at the same stupid jokes. The crowning jewel was that when I talked about Johnny, he was attentive and enthusiastic. When he said he admired my devotion to Johnny, I knew Ryan was the man for me.

⇒⊰ ⊱⇐

Not long after Ryan and I started going out, he took time off to help me navigate the adoption process and prepare to be Johnny's mother. We grew closer each day, and I began to wonder how I'd ever survived without him. Even after he went back to work, we spent every free minute together. Adam and Ryan hit it off from the beginning, and Alec gave him her stamp of approval, which was no small thing.

Johnny was the last piece of the puzzle, but I had no worry on that score. Johnny's face lit up every time Ryan walked into the room. He held up his good arm as a sign to be picked up and flashed his crooked grin. Ryan ate it up, and I began to consider him a part of our family.

While Ryan and I were painting Johnny's room after dinner one night, I got up the courage to ask him if he'd told his kids about me and how we'd met.

"Yes, I have," he said, "but I just told them I met you through work. They've been asking to meet you and Johnny. The girls even said they'd drive home one weekend to do it. They never want to do that, so this is big."

"How did they react when you told them who I am? Had they heard about Johnny on the news?" I was nervous about meeting them and worried that they wouldn't like me or that when we met, it would be all about what they'd seen in the media.

"The girls are thrilled that I'm seeing someone. They were pushing me to start dating and even wanted to sign me up for a dating site. Mark had reservations at first, but he's fine with it now," he said.

"Should we set a time for me to meet them? Do I have to meet them all at once?"

"Don't worry; they'll love you," he said and wiped a dot of paint off my nose.

My stomach knotted. "I guess the sooner we get it over with, the better," I said.

Ryan laughed. "That's the spirit. They want to meet Johnny too. Would you mind?"

Hearing that gave me an idea. "Bring them to the hospital so they can meet Johnny and me together. We're a package deal, after all. Maybe not all of them at once though."

"I'll see if Mark and Valerie want to come this weekend. Jennifer and Stephanie are off on a road trip with some girlfriends. They'll be back next week. We'll set up a time then. They'll be jealous that Mark got to meet you first," he said and chuckled. "I'm glad you want to get to know my kids. We're a package deal too."

He pulled me into his arms and smeared paint all over my T-shirt.

"If they're anything like you, it'll be a delight," I said with more confidence than I felt.

I was a nervous wreck while I waited in Johnny's hospital room for Ryan to show up with Mark and Valerie three days later. I asked Ryan to let them know what to expect, and I hoped it would be one of Johnny's good days. He'd settled into regular sleep cycles and rarely had hours-long crying jags by then, but those were only the first small steps.

I was rocking Johnny and trying to calm my nerves when Ryan walked in with Mark and Valerie. Mark was a carbon copy of Ryan, down to the warm smile and sparkling blue eyes. All he lacked was the touch of gray hair at his temples. He came directly toward me and shook my hand. Johnny held his arm up to be picked up. Without thinking twice, Mark took him from me and said, "You must be Johnny." He was rewarded with one of Johnny's biggest crooked grins.

Valerie was more reserved and stayed back. She was only slightly taller than I was and had my same fair skin, but her hair was black and straight. The combination was striking. She waited for about a minute before clearing her throat to distract Ryan and Mark from fawning over Johnny. Ryan turned and started toward her, but I beat him to it. I held out my hand and said, "I'm Grace. It's nice to meet you."

"Valerie. Those two become goofs around babies," she said, pointing her thumb at Mark.

"It's a good thing," Ryan said. "They announced in the car today that they're making me a grandpa." He hugged Valerie and beamed.

"Congratulations," I said and kissed her cheek.

She thanked me and asked if she could hold Johnny.

"Good luck getting him away from Mark," Ryan said.

Valerie took Johnny from Mark and carried him to the rocking chair. Mark leaned over them, making silly noises with his mouth, and Johnny giggled. Ryan and I stepped back to admire the scene.

"They'll make great parents," Ryan said.

I kissed him and said, "Congratulations to you too. They're wonderful. You've clearly done a great job with Mark."

"That was mostly him and my wife," he said, "but I'll take a little credit. He was easy to raise."

I nodded and wondered why I'd been so afraid to meet them. "I can't wait to meet the girls. I hope it goes this well," I said.

Ryan laughed and said, "Just wait. You ain't seen nothing yet."

⊰⊱

Ryan brought the girls to the hospital two weeks later. Stephanie burst in, hugged me, and went straight to Johnny's crib. He backed up with wide eyes for a second before grinning at her.

She turned to me and said, "Oh please, you have to let me hold him."

I smiled and nodded.

"Just be careful," Ryan said. "He doesn't like jerky movements."

Stephanie dismissed Ryan's comment with a wave and said, "I got this." She picked Johnny up and did a little dance around the room with him. When he giggled, she looked at Ryan and said, "See? He likes me."

Ryan rubbed his forehead and said, "Grace, that's Stephanie."

I turned to Jennifer. She rolled her eyes and held out her hand to me. "Sorry about her," she said. "Stephanie does everything big. She's like a human tornado sometimes."

"Don't worry," I said and smiled. "I have a friend like that."

Jennifer walked to Stephanie and asked for a turn to hold Johnny. She was a few inches taller than Stephanie but had a slender build. She had lighter hair and green eyes too. I assumed she took after her mother. Stephanie had a stockier build like Ryan's and was clearly an athlete. While she and Jennifer bickered over who got to hold Johnny, Ryan leaned over to me and said, "I tried to warn you."

I put my hand over my mouth and tried not to laugh. "They must have been a handful," I said.

"They've always been full of energy. Raising twins isn't easy, but they're good girls. They make me laugh and keep me young. They took their mother's death hard, but Stephanie's bouncing back.

243

It's taking Jennifer a little longer." He put his hand on my shoulder and said, "I'm hoping you two become close. Maybe you can help her in ways I can't."

"I hope so too," I said and put my hand over his.

When Johnny's lower lip started to quiver, Jennifer took him to the rocking chair and tried to shush him. He cuddled against her and closed his eyes.

"You sweet thing," Stephanie said.

"Are you feeling superfluous?" Ryan asked.

I laughed and said, "You two must be looking forward to being aunts."

Stephanie turned and said, "We can't wait. We wouldn't mind being stepsisters either." She kissed the top of Johnny's head.

Ryan's face turned bright red. He sighed and rubbed his forehead. I grinned at him, knowing that the girls and I were going to get along just fine.

⚒⚒

Ryan and I had dinner with his family later that day. They were relaxed and welcoming. By the end of the night, I felt like a member of the family and wondered at Stephanie's comment from earlier. I wanted to ask Ryan about it while he drove me home, but I was afraid that Stephanie spoke out on her own.

Ryan came in with me and led me to the sofa. "So, what do you think of my family?" he asked.

"I love them," I said. "You are a fortunate man."

"Yes I am." He kissed me. After a few seconds, he said, "I'm not sure if this is the right time, but I have something I've been wanting to say. You know how I am about speaking my mind."

I nodded, knowing I could always count on Ryan to be honest with me. Knowing that didn't prepare me for what came next though.

He caressed my cheek with the back of his hand and said, "I love you, Grace Ward." When I gasped and put my hand over my mouth, he pulled away and said, "I knew it was too soon. Now I've scared you off. You don't have to say it back. I just wanted you to know."

I pulled him closer and said, "You caught me off guard, that's all. I've been waiting for the right time to tell you too, but I kept chickening out. I love you too, Ryan Walker."

"I am a fortunate man." He kissed me again before pulling back and looking into my eyes. "Now what do we do?" he asked.

I'd been expecting some deeply romantic comment, so I laughed at his question. "If you don't know, I certainly don't," I said. "Why don't we kiss good night, wake up happier tomorrow, and go from there."

"Reasonable plan," he said and stood, offering his hand to help me up. When we got to the door, he said, "I do love you, and I'm not going anywhere. Sleep well knowing that."

He kissed me on the way out. I closed the door behind him and sighed. There'd been little to trust in my life, but I was certain in my trust for Ryan. Meeting his family and seeing them interact had solidified that for me. I fell asleep confident that no matter where my future led, I wouldn't walk the road alone.

⊷⊱ ⊰⊶

I woke the next morning thinking of Ryan and smiled. The warm memory faded two seconds later when I felt the pounding in my head. I got up to take some ibuprofen and realized I had a sore, swollen throat too. I ran the thermometer across my forehead, afraid to read the results. It registered 100.6 degrees. I groaned and pulled out the list to see who my backup for staying with Johnny was. It was an off-duty nurse named Allison. I dialed her number and got worried on the fourth ring, but she answered as I was about to hang up.

"Can you stay with Johnny today? I'm sick and can't go to the hospital," I said.

"Oh no, I'm sick too," she said in a raspy voice.

"I'm so sorry," I said. "You rest and get better. I'll find someone else."

I called three more people from the list. Two were sick and one was out of town. Alec, Adam, and Ryan were all working. Trying not to panic, I called Brad to check on Johnny. When he assured me that Johnny was fine, I racked my brain for someone else to call. I was about to give up and ask the peds nurses to cover as best they could, but Stephanie's face popped into my mind. I called Ryan to get her number and ask if he thought she'd want to help.

Ryan answered with a croak.

"You're not sick, too?" I asked, already knowing the answer.

"I am," he said and sneezed. "I feel like death."

I explained what was happening and asked about the girls.

"They're fine so far, but we were with them all day yesterday. It might just be a matter of time," he said. "On the plus side, Stephanie has the constitution of a horse. She never gets sick."

"It might be worth the risk," I said. "She could wear a mask and gloves. Will Jennifer be offended if I don't ask her too? I might need her tomorrow."

"No, she'll insist on staying here to take care of me. Maybe you should come over too," he said and went into a coughing spasm.

"I'm going to use all my strength to get to the doctor. You should too. Alec will be over here fussing over me as soon as she gets off work anyway. We probably ought to keep our distance for a few days," I said, sad to be separated from him right after declaring our love to each other.

"I hate to admit it, but I agree. The phone will have to do."

We hung up, and I called Stephanie. She answered and said, "Dad already told me. I'm sorry you're sick, but I'd love to help with Johnny. Jen says she'll go tomorrow if you need her to."

Relieved, I gave her detailed instructions and told her the nurses would help too. I asked her to thank Jennifer and tell her I'd call after I'd seen the doctor.

My doctor was booked up, so I dragged myself to urgent care where I found out I had a virus that was going around. I'd hoped it was bacterial so I could take antibiotics and be better in a day. I talked the doctor into giving me an antiviral even though I knew they didn't always work and that I could be sick for days.

I spent the next two days in a fever haze but started to feel better after that. It was agony to stay away from Johnny, but I knew I could still be contagious for another forty-eight hours. I contented myself knowing that Stephanie was taking good care of him. Jennifer woke up with a fever on the second day and hadn't gotten a turn with Johnny. Ryan told me she was heartbroken. I called and told her not to worry. She'd have plenty of chances to help with him in the future.

I woke up the sixth morning feeling like my old self. I showered and disinfected my house so I wouldn't carry the infection to the hospital. My excitement grew the closer I got to my Johnny. It was the longest I'd been parted from him since the quarantine. I put on a mask and gloves before I went into his room. I went in to find Stephanie holding a box filled with Johnny's belongings. His quilt was folded up in the crib, and Johnny was wearing an outfit I'd bought him the week before. His face lit up when he saw me, so I scooped him up and held him close.

"I've missed you," I said, as he struggled to get loose. I turned to Stephanie and said, "What's all this about? Is Dr. Carter moving Johnny to another room?"

"In a way," she said, and winked.

Brad walked in before I could ask what she meant. He smiled when he saw me and said, "Good to see you back in the world of the living. How are you feeling?" He shined a light in my eyes and asked me to pull down the mask and stick out my tongue.

I did as he asked and said, "What's going on?"

Instead of answering, he put on gloves and felt the glands in my neck.

I pushed his hands away, and said, "I'm fine. Are you moving Johnny?"

Johnny reached up and grabbed a hold of his light.

Brad handed it to him and said, "Yes, I'm moving him, but not to another hospital room. He's going home with you today, if you're up for that."

Johnny tried to stick the light in my mouth.

I gently pushed his hand away. "I can take Johnny home? Today? Why didn't you tell me?"

"Alec spied out your house while you were sick and said you'd be ready for Johnny as soon as you were well. She made me promise not to say anything. She said you'd be here today, so I asked Stephanie to pack up Johnny's things. If you don't feel strong enough, we can wait another day or so." He patted the top of Johnny's head to distract him while he retrieved the light.

My legs wobbled, so I dropped into the rocking chair with Johnny on my lap. As I stroked his hair, I said, "You mean it, Brad? Johnny's ready to come home with me?"

"Yes, but not until Serena gets here and we finish up the paper work. Johnny's ready to go, and I'd like him out of here before the virus gets him. You've already had it, so he'll be safer there with you," he said.

I tried to thank him, but the words caught in my throat. I grabbed a tissue and blew my nose. Johnny giggled, and I cried even more. Stephanie took Johnny from me and danced around the room. He squealed in delight.

"You're going home with Mama today," she said, and he squealed again. "I think he understands."

Brad started to contradict her but was interrupted when Serena walked in with Alec following her, carrying a car seat. I ran to Alec and hugged her. When she pulled away, I said, "Why didn't you tell me? I would have been a lot less miserable if I'd known I'd be bringing Johnny home soon."

She laughed. "You know me and surprises. I hoped to get here before you to see the look on your face when you got the news." She studied me for a second. "What do you know? It's still there."

Serena came up and hugged me too. When I thanked her for all her help and support, she said, "Don't thank me yet. We still have a long way to go, but I'm thrilled that Johnny is ready to go home. It's time he learned about life outside of a hospital. I'll be coming with you to do a final home check, and then I think we'll only need one more home visit before the adoption."

"I'm coming too," Alec said. "You're not getting out of here without me."

Stephanie tapped me on the shoulder and said, "Can I come?"

"I'll tell you what: come over tonight with your dad and Jen, if she's well enough. I don't want to overwhelm Johnny."

She looked disappointed but nodded. "We'll bring some dinner to celebrate. I'll call Dad right now," she said and went into the hallway.

I started laughing and crying at the same time. "It's incredible. I worried this would never come. Now that it's happening, I can't believe it's real. Let's get the paperwork started. I want to get out of here. If I ever see this room again, it'll be too soon."

Serena opened her briefcase and pulled out a stack of papers. While I signed and she explained the legal considerations, Brad printed off Johnny's discharge papers and had a nurse bring in Johnny's temporary oxygen concentrator and nebulizer. He gave me the lists of Johnny's prescriptions and told me he had already called them in to the pharmacy.

An hour later, I pushed Johnny's stroller to the parking lot with the troop following behind, carrying all the gear. My eyes were too blurry with tears to strap Johnny into the car seat, so Alec had to do it with Serena looking on.

Alec drove my car so I could sit in the back with Johnny. He started to scream the second I put him in the car seat. He quieted to a whimper when we started moving and was soon gazing, wide-eyed, out the window. I took him on a tour of the house when we got there, explaining every room in detail. Our last stop was Johnny's bedroom. I laid him in the crib with his favorite quilt and rubbed his back. He was asleep two minutes later.

Alec stopped in the doorway and said, "I've never seen any-thing more beautiful. I need a picture." She took out her phone and whispered for me to smile. She didn't have to tell me. I felt like I'd never stop smiling again.

CHAPTER NINETEEN

Having Johnny home with me made life easier in some ways, and monumentally more difficult in others. I loved not having to sit in the hospital room for hours every day and had fun playing with him on the floor of his room or in the park. Mealtimes were special too, especially when Ryan was with us.

On the other hand, our days were filled with repeated trips to various doctors and therapists. Johnny never got used to the car seat and screamed every time I strapped him in. That made for some nerve-racking car rides. It was also always a struggle to get Johnny to take his medicine and do his therapy exercises, but that all paled in comparison to my joy at being Johnny's mother, and I had no regrets.

I had to remind myself of that on occasion, like the day when Johnny decided he'd had enough of getting his diaper changed. He tossed his upper body from side to side in a valiant attempt to escape. I won the battle and taped down the second tab just as the doorbell rang.

"That's Serena," I told him as I pulled up his pants and lifted him off the changing table. "Let's go show her what a good boy you are."

Serena visited us more often than her usual cases. When I asked her one day if she'd been ordered to keep a closer eye on us, she laughed and said she came because she liked to. When I opened the door that afternoon, she didn't look like she was there for a pleasure visit.

I invited her in and said, "How bad is it?"

She sat in the armchair and said, "You'll want to sit down."

I put Johnny on a blanket on the floor and sat on the sofa across from her. I leaned forward and ordered myself to keep breathing.

"I have good news and bad," she said. "Good news first. Kinsley got fired. The board brought someone in on a temporary basis until they find a permanent replacement. I thought you'd want to know."

I sighed and sat back. "Finally! I hope it's only the first step on his road to ruin."

"I'm sure it is, but I can't comment on that because of the ongoing criminal investigation," she said.

I considered Serena as more than Johnny's caseworker. She was my friend, but that made our relationship tricky at times. "Give me the bad news," I said.

"It has to do with your background investigation," she said and looked down at her clasped hands.

"My background? I thought that was completed," I said in confusion. I wouldn't have been allowed to bring Johnny home otherwise. I racked my brain for what could have come up. The only thing I'd worried about was what had happened at the river, but Ryan and Alec were the only two who knew. They would never have betrayed my confidence.

Serena interrupted my thoughts and said, "It was completed, but new information has come forward. As Kinsley's last official act, he submitted an affidavit detailing your actions during the quarantine. He claims you're unfit to be Johnny's mother because you acted without regard to Johnny's life or safety."

I jumped up and started pacing. "The Hyena. I should have known. He's just doing this to get revenge." I stopped pacing and faced her. "The board cleared me. I served my probation. How much can this hurt me?"

"I can't answer that, but this isn't the same as trying to keep your job. This is about a child's welfare, placing him in a safe and loving home." I started to protest, but she held up her hand and said, "We all know that's you. If this were solely up to me, I'd dismiss this. In my mind, it proves your devotion to Johnny, but others may not see it that way. They could consider it reckless, at the very least. The decision is in the hands of my superiors and, ultimately, the judge who presides over the case. You need to contact Paul, and soon."

I covered my face with my hands and sank onto the couch. The adoption had been sailing through without a glitch. It should have been a warning sign. And Kinsley! I should have anticipated that he'd interfere. He hated me. I thought back to the days after Kinsley suspended me. The board hadn't fired me like he'd wanted, and they put him in his place. His plan to get rid of Johnny had backfired. He'd been biding his time, waiting to strike, and he'd wielded his last weapon like a pro.

"How can I fight this? They have my confession. They'll have my personnel file," I said, searching desperately for a way out.

Serena picked Johnny up and sat next to me. "We already had that," she said. "This isn't over. The opinion at DSS is in your favor. They're not looking for ways to stop the adoption. Talk to Paul. He'll guide you in the right direction."

Johnny grabbed a handful of my hair and shoved it in his mouth. I tried to pry it free, but Johnny pulled harder. I slipped my index finger into his fist and freed my hair. Johnny squeezed my finger and looked up at me with his crooked grin.

"I won't give him up. After all the trauma and sacrifice, I won't give him up. He's my son. I love him. I won't give him up," I said and tightened my arms around him.

Serena handed Johnny to me and got up to leave. The sadness in her eyes betrayed her worry. "You've been through the worst. We'll overcome this too."

After she left, I put Johnny in his high chair with some snacks and called Paul. When he didn't answer, I assumed he was in court and left him a message. I called Ryan, but he didn't answer either. I didn't leave a message. I put Johnny down for his nap and climbed into my bed, letting the fear and despair take hold. I'd proved to everyone that I'd do anything for Johnny. What more did I have to give? I was tired of fighting and wondered if Johnny would be better off with someone else.

That was the frame of mind Ryan found me in three hours later. I was on the bed in my dark bedroom. I heard Johnny jabbering happily in his crib when he first woke up from his nap, but the jabbering turned to whining. Ryan rescued him and came into my bedroom, carrying him.

Ryan flipped on the light, and said, "Get up. There's no time to feel sorry for yourself. Paul's on his way, and I brought dinner."

I put my arm over my eyes and said, "Go away." Then I sat up and glared at him. "How'd you find out what was going on?"

"I'm not going anywhere, and Paul called when you didn't answer your phone. Alec called five minutes later. She heard about Kinsley at work and told me how you reacted after he suspended you. She ordered me to get over here because she couldn't leave work. So, I'm here to get you back on your feet, so come on. On your feet!" he said.

I groaned and rolled away from him. "What's the point? I surrender. Kinsley wins."

"Nonsense," he said.

He put Johnny in the playpen, which Johnny wasn't too thrilled about, so he started wailing. Ryan grabbed the container of dry cereal off my dresser and tossed it into the playpen. Johnny picked it up and forgot about crying. While he tried to figure how to open it with one hand, Ryan pulled the covers off me and sat down on the bed.

He rubbed his hand on my back and said, "You know I'm not leaving until I see your old fighting spark. I'm just as stubborn as you are, so you might as well give in now."

I rolled over to face him. "I appreciate what you're trying to do, but it's too late. I don't have any more fight left in me. It's over, Ryan. They should just take Johnny away now." I put my hands over my face and started to cry.

Ryan pulled my hands away. "I know. You've been through more than most people would endure in ten lifetimes, but you have to go a little further. You're almost there, but you're not alone. I'm not abandoning you, and neither will anyone else. Let us help you help Johnny. Doesn't he deserve that?" Ryan handed me a tissue.

I wiped my face. "Of course, but I don't have control over this. What can I do? And what will happen to Johnny if I lose? No one will ever love him like I do."

Without hesitation, Ryan said, "I'll adopt him."

"I'm being serious." I looked away.

"So am I," he said softly.

I looked into his eyes and saw that he meant it. "You would do that? Have you thought that through?"

"The whole way here. I love you and Johnny and so do my kids. We would do anything for you." He tenderly placed his hand on my cheek. "When are you going to accept that you're both a part of our family? This is what families do."

I took his face in my hands and kissed him. "Are you real or just an amazing dream?"

"Want me to pinch you?" he asked, and I laughed.

"I'll pass on that. I don't deserve you," I said and kissed him again.

He helped me up. "That's settled. Now come have some of your favorite Italian food, and I have a surprise."

"Juliana's?" I asked. When he nodded, I said, "I guess I can face anything with the help of Superman and cannoli."

Paul showed up as we finished eating. I was glad Ryan had thought to bring enough dessert for him, since I knew he was a fan of Juliana's too. As I handed Paul a second cannoli, the door flew open, and Alec burst in, followed by Adam, carrying a box from Juliana's. She laughed when she saw our box on the table.

"Great minds and all that," she said and sat down next to me.

I hugged her. "What are you doing here?"

"We're second string in case Ryan wasn't enough," Adam said and shoved half of a cannoli in his mouth.

"Enough for what?" I asked.

"Of a cheerleader," Alec said. "Let me guess, after you talked to Serena, you went to bed, pulled the covers over your head, and waited for the sky to fall."

"Nailed it," Ryan said. "Does she know you or what?"

"I'm so glad you all have me all figured out," I said, irritated with their teasing. "We're facing a serious problem, and you are all having a laugh at my expense."

"You're right. We're sorry," Alec said. "You know we love you, or else why would we be here offering moral support? So, Paul, what's the plan of action?"

Paul swallowed his food and said, "Not much of a plan. I'll send a copy of the board-hearing transcript to DSS in the morning. Since Serena was already here and knows the whole story of your breaking quarantine, they probably won't want to interview you again. It wouldn't hurt to get a few more character references from people you've worked with at the hospital. Other than that, there's not much else to do. The judge who presides over the case will review the new material and probably question you at the finalization hearing."

"So we won't know anything until then?" I asked. "Waiting for two months to find out will be torture."

"If DSS decides it's a big enough issue to disqualify you, we'll know within a week. I'd be shocked if that happened. They're still reeling from having filed the petition against Johnny. What you did is small potatoes. I think Serena is overreacting," Paul said.

"But what if you're underreacting? What happens if the judge rules against me?" I asked.

"That's not going to happen, but if it did, DSS would take Johnny away from you, and he'd go into the foster system until Ryan adopts him," Paul said.

"Ryan? He's not going to adopt Johnny. I am. Adam and I already decided," Alec said and crossed her arms.

"We didn't know Ryan was willing to adopt Johnny," Adam said. "As great a mother as I know you'll make, I think it would be better for Ryan to adopt him."

I sat in quiet awe as I listened to the conversation around me. The selflessness of my friends was breathtaking. I glanced at Johnny in his high chair. He was trying his best to grab the dessert box off the counter. I took him out of his chair and sat at the table with him on my lap. No one noticed in the heat of their discussion.

"I can't believe you're taking his side," Alec said. "Besides, he might be too old."

"Hey," Ryan said, "that was uncalled for."

"I'm not taking sides. Think about it, Alec. Can't you see why it would be better for Ryan to adopt him?" Adam said and cocked his head at me.

Alec looked at me and then Ryan, and back at me again. "Oh, you're right. That would be better."

"I'm glad you got that settled, but the discussion was pointless," Paul said. "Grace is going to adopt Johnny. I'm right. You'll see."

They all turned their eyes on me. I just nodded and smiled. I wanted to believe Paul, but there was no way he could be sure. For once, I decided to let things play out the way they would. After all, what choice did I have?

I was running late to meet Paul at the courthouse two months later. Johnny decided he didn't want to wear clothes that morning, so he screamed and fought me while I tried to dress him. He howled even louder when I put him in the playpen in my room so I could get in the shower. I stared down at him with my hands on my hips and wondered if all eighteen-month-olds acted that way. My phone rang in the midst of the chaos, and I frowned until I saw that it was Ryan.

"Please tell me you're on your way," I said, continuing to put on mascara.

"Five minutes out. Rough morning?" he asked.

"Is it too late to change my mind about today?"

He chuckled. "You don't mean that. I'll be there in a sec to rescue you."

"Not soon enough," I said and hung up. I picked Johnny up and tried everything to calm him, but every time I started to lower him into the playpen, he screamed. In a flash of genius, I handed him my phone with a photo of Ryan open on the screen. He quieted immediately and chatted contentedly with Ryan's picture. I put him in the playpen and threw my clothes on as fast as I could. I heard tapping on my bedroom door as I finished getting dressed.

"Aw, the man himself," I said, as Ryan came in.

Johnny squealed in delight when Ryan picked him up and swung him around.

"That's it; you're moving in here," I said and froze, wishing I could suck the words back into my mouth. I glanced at Ryan to see if he'd caught what I said.

He was staring at me, but then he smiled and said, "If you insist."

I gave a nervous laugh and threw things into the diaper bag. When it was packed, I carried it and the stroller to the car. While Ryan put Johnny in his car seat, I loaded the trunk, pretending nothing had happened. Johnny rescued me from having to talk about it by screaming the entire way to court.

Paul, Alec, and Adam were waiting for us in the lobby when we arrived. Alec hugged me and said, "How are you doing, Mama? I was awake all night. I bet you didn't sleep a wink."

"You'd lose that bet," I said. "Johnny and I both slept through the night for the first time since...ever. He must have sensed this was his big day. I'm a nervous wreck now, though." I turned to Paul. "Please, run me through this again."

"Relax. Brackman is the judge," he said. "She insisted on being the one to preside. We're familiar with her, so that's good. The hearing will take place in her chambers. Serena's waiting for us there. The judge will ask a few questions, including about your breaking quarantine, I'm sure, but that's a good thing. It'll give you a chance to explain your actions in person. Then she'll sign the adoption order. That's it. We're a few minutes late. We should get going."

As we started moving, Brad ran up behind us.

"Just in time," Adam said, shaking his hand. "We were afraid you weren't going to make it."

"I wouldn't have missed this for anything short of death," he said. "Had to sneak away. Glad I made it in time."

I smiled and squeezed his hand. "Me too," I said.

Once we were all sworn in, Judge Brackman asked Serena, Paul, Ryan, and me to stand in front of her desk, with Ryan holding Johnny.

Judge Brackman looked at me and said, "Presiding at these occasions is my favorite duty, but never more so than today. I shudder to think that this day almost didn't occur. I remember my distress at having to approve the petition to remove Johnny from life support." She paused and shook her head. "Officiating at this occasion is the highlight of my career. I considered holding it in the open courtroom, but I didn't want to turn this into a spectacle. I'm sure you've all had enough of media intrusion."

We all nodded in agreement. It was the understatement of the year, and I was grateful she'd decided to hold the hearing in private with only my dearest friends present. Alec sat behind me. I turned and smiled at her. She smiled back, and her lower lip quivered. I looked away to keep from crying too.

"Ms. Ward," Judge Brackman said, "I'd like to ask you a few questions to make sure you understand the seriousness of what we're doing here today. If I agree to sign the adoption order, Johnny will be as much your son as if you'd given birth to him. Do you understand this?"

That did it. The feeble dam holding back my tears crumbled and let loose the flood. Serena handed me a tissue and kept one for herself. As Ryan reached for my hand and entwined his fingers in mine, I could hear Alec sobbing quietly behind me.

"Take a moment, Ms. Ward. There's no rush," Judge Brackman said.

I took a deep breath and shook my head. "No," I said, "let's keep going. In answer to your question, I do understand how serious this is. If you knew my life story, you wouldn't have needed to ask. There's nothing in the world I want more than to be Johnny's mother." I blew my nose and smiled at her.

"I believe you. You've proved it to all of us in this room through your selfless sacrifice on Johnny's behalf. There is an issue we need to discuss, however. I'd like to hear, in your own words, what happened the night you broke the hospital quarantine," she said and sat back with her arms crossed.

It was my chance to give the statement that I practiced and refined for two months, but my mind went blank. Paul glanced at me with raised eyebrows, and whispered, "Just give her the statement you practiced," but that didn't help. I couldn't remember what to say.

"Is there a problem, Ms. Ward?" Judge Brackman asked. I shook my head, and she said, "Please respond aloud."

"I had a statement prepared, but all I can think to say is that I did it because I love Johnny. I hated being separated from him, and I'd promised not to leave him alone, but they wouldn't let me see him. I was desperate. I had to get to my baby, and nothing else mattered to me. That's the truth. That's why I broke quarantine," I said and started to cry again.

Judge Brackman didn't respond to my outburst right away but sat staring at me with her arms folded. When I regained my composure enough to look up, I searched her eyes but couldn't gauge what she was thinking.

After another full minute of keeping me in agony, she said, "If I'd never met you and knew nothing of Johnny's story, I might have my reservations, but that's not the case. I see no reason to deny this adoption based on this incident alone. I believe it was a small moment of indiscretion and that you've learned from it. As I stated before, you've more than proved your devotion to Johnny since."

There was a collective sigh of relief in the room. Paul had been right that the incident wouldn't be enough to prevent the adoption. As usual, I should have trusted him instead of only envisioning the worst-case scenario. I wondered if I'd learned as much as Judge Brackman thought I had.

She saved me from having to ponder that by saying, "You'll have unique challenges as Johnny's mother, but as a medical professional and a strong, loving woman, I know you're up to the task. In light of that, I hereby grant this adoption order." She picked up a pen to sign it. "Some parents like to take a picture of me signing the order. I'll pause if you'd like to do that."

Alec had her phone ready before the words were out of Judge Brackman's mouth. After Alec took the picture, the judge signed the order and held it up for us to see. "Congratulations, Ms. Ward. Johnny is now your legal son."

I took Johnny from Ryan and squeezed him to me. He looked up and put his hand on my cheek, touching my tears. "I love you, my little man," I whispered. "You're mine forever."

Ryan put his arms around us and kissed my cheek. When Johnny giggled, Ryan kissed him too.

Judge Brackman cleared her throat, so we turned to face her. "The last order of business is to let you know that a new birth certificate will be issued. Since we don't have access to Johnny's original birth certificate, we need to know the name you've chosen for him."

Without hesitation, I said, "Jonathan James Ward."

"Lovely," she said and jotted the name on a paper. "We are adjourned." She tapped her gavel and walked around the desk to join us. "May I get some pictures with you?"

We all congratulated one another and took several pictures. Johnny got cranky, and not even Ryan could quiet him, so we decided it was time to go.

As we were leaving, Serena asked me the significance of Johnny's name. "I get the Jonathan part, but what is James for? Was that your father's name?" she asked.

Alec beat me to it. "It's for the James River," she said and looked at me knowingly.

"I love that," Serena said. "Now he's officially tied to this place."

"That he is," I said and smiled.

CHAPTER TWENTY

R yan called me the following Friday and ordered me to clear my calendar because he was taking me out.

"Oh yes, I'll have to cancel my myriad of social events." I laughed. "Besides, who's going to babysit Johnny now that the girls are back at school? Man, I miss them, and not just for the babysitting."

"Me too," Ryan said. "It's always too quiet the first few weeks they're away, and Mark and Valerie are so busy with their own lives. I'm glad I have you and Johnny this time. But as for a babysitter, Alec's going to do it."

"Alec? She'd rather be out with Adam on a Friday night, not babysitting," I said.

"Adam's fishing with Paul and some other college buddies, so she's free," he said.

"Then I'd love to go out with you. I could use a break and some adult conversation."

"Exactly my thought," he said. "Be ready at eight, and dress up a little."

"Dress up?" I asked. Ryan didn't like anything fancier than jeans most of the time, which was fine with me. I thought it would be fun to get dressed up for him though. "Where are you taking me?"

"That's a surprise. See you tonight. Love you," he said and hung up.

I spent the day in happy anticipation, and not even Johnny's little bouts of fussiness got me down. Alec got there at six to help me get ready. She knew where Ryan was taking me, but I couldn't pry it out of her.

"I promised not to ruin it," she said. "You'll love it. Trust me."

We dug through my closet to find the right dress. The only positive thing left from time with Jay was that I took more care of my appearance. That gave Alec and me a much bigger selection. She reached in the back and pulled out the black dress I'd worn on my first formal date with Jay. I thought I'd thrown it out.

Alec held it up. "This is cute. Wear this."

I took it from her and threw it on the floor. "Not that one." I climbed back into the closet.

"Oh, must be a Jay holdover," Alec said and followed me in.

We settled on a formfitting maroon silk blouse and knee-length black pencil skirt. I had bought the outfit in Baltimore, but it didn't have any significance with Jay. Alec pulled my hair up in a style I liked and advised me on my makeup. I added a necklace and earring set Ryan had given me for my birthday and stood back to admire myself in the full-length mirror.

With my eyes glistening, I said, "I couldn't have imagined being dressed like this a year ago or having a man like Ryan to love me or being a mother. I saw the course of my life stretching out as sterile, lonely, and safe. I didn't believe I was worthy of a life like the one I have now. Andrew tried to tell me. I wish I'd listened sooner."

Alec wiped a tear off her cheek with the back of her hand. "Stop that, or we'll have to redo your makeup, and Ryan's going to be here any minute."

I laughed at her and went to say good night to Johnny. We'd carried his high chair into my room and put Johnny in it with some fruit chews to keep him occupied while I got ready. I lifted him out and gave him a tight squeeze and peck on the cheek.

"You be good for Auntie Alec." I handed him to her before he got me all sticky.

"He's always an angel for me, aren't you?" she said.

He gurgled incoherently and jammed his sticky hand in his mouth.

The doorbell rang, and I ran as fast as I could in my heels to answer it.

I opened the door and said, "Why didn't you just come in?"

"And miss the chance to admire you in the doorway?" Ryan put his arms around my waist. "It was worth it. You're stunning."

I kissed him. "You're not so bad yourself. Let me get a better look." I stepped back and eyed him up and down. He was wearing a black tailored suit that I'd never seen. He looked amazing. "Where have you been hiding that?" I asked.

"I didn't want to let you see it because I was afraid you'd keep making me wear it," he said and turned in a circle. "Like it?"

In answer, I pulled him close and kissed him. "Maybe we should skip dinner."

Alec walked into the living room carrying Johnny and cleared her throat. "Oh no you don't. There will be time for that later," she said and opened the door. Johnny reached for Ryan and started crying when Alec pulled him away. "None of that. You're too sticky for Ryan to hold you tonight."

Ryan ducked out the door, and I said, "Have fun," and gave her a little wave on my way out.

Ryan took me to the highest-rated Italian restaurant near the canal walk in the city. I'd only been there once with Alec and had nearly choked on the prices. When I protested, Ryan shushed me and opened my menu. We decided on a five-course meal for two that culminated in cannoli. We ate slowly and laughed and talked about everything. I couldn't remember a date where I'd been more content.

It was a nice night, so we walked along the canal after dinner. When we reached a secluded spot, Ryan stopped and turned me to face him. He took my hands, and said, "You are stunning, and not only your looks. I thought my life was over after Marie died, but then you fell into my path."

"Literally," I said and smiled.

Ryan laughed. "We have the most unique 'How did you two meet?' story out there. But don't change the subject. You brought me back from an edge of sorts too. Life is vibrant with you. I'd never felt this way, and I want to capture this feeling forever, which is why I brought you here." He let go of my hands and reached into his chest pocket. When he pulled his hand out, it held a small black box. He took my left hand and said, "I can't let you get away, Grace Ward. How would you like to marry me?"

"Yes, yes, more than you'll ever know," I said.

He opened the box and held up the ring. It was beautiful but had faint scratches and nicks on the band and had an antique style.

"It's lovely. Where did you get it?" I asked.

"It was my grandmother's ring. Dad gave it to me when she died. It was after Marie and I were married, so we just put it in the safe. I've been planning to give it to you since I decided to propose. Nanna was very dear to me. You remind me of her."

He slipped the ring on my finger, but I could hardly see it through my tears.

"That's wonderful. I'm honored," I said. "Just when I think you can't surprise me. I'm not the only one who's stunning, Ryan Walker."

"Well, there is more," he said. "I told Serena and Paul I wanted to marry you and adopt Johnny. Since your adoption was just final, I didn't know how that would work. They said it was no problem. They've been doing the background work. I swore them to secrecy. You know I would have adopted Johnny if it hadn't worked out for you. Since it did, I want to ask your permission to adopt him too and give him our name. If you want Johnny to keep your name, I'll understand and be his stepfather, but, if you're willing, I'd love to become his full-fledged father."

He held his breath, waiting for my answer.

I hesitated for a second to make him squirm. "Of course, you crazy goose. I assumed that's what would happen if I married you. You're Johnny's favorite person in the world."

He threw his arms around me and held me tight. After a few seconds, he pulled away. "So you've thought about marrying me? For how long?"

"Since our breakfast at Juliana's. It took you long enough to ask," I said and kissed the tip of his nose.

"I was giving you time to settle in with Johnny and recover from everything you'd been through. It was hard keeping it a secret from you."

"How many people know about this?" I asked.

"Just about everyone. I even told Johnny, but he's good at keeping secrets."

Ryan placed my hand in the crook of his elbow and led me to the car. When he opened my door, I turned to him and said, "I'd given up dreaming that life held any of this in store for me. Now, I have a beautiful child and soon, the perfect husband, and a new family. Thank you for this. Truly, thank you."

Ryan didn't speak, but his eyes glistened as he gazed at me. No words were needed as he put his hands on my cheeks and touched his forehead to mine.

◆════◆

Alec jumped up when we got home and said, "Do you have something to show me?"

I held up the ring for her.

"It's gorgeous. Congratulations, both of you," she said and kissed each of us on the cheek. She looked at Ryan and said, "Did she agree about Johnny?" When he nodded, she said, "I told you she would." She picked up her purse and walked to the door. "I'm going to get out of here and give you two some alone time. Call me first thing in the morning," she said to me. "I want every detail."

"You got it," I said and closed the door behind her.

Ryan took me to the sofa and pulled me onto his lap. He loosened my hair and drew me close with his hand still in my hair. He brushed his lips on mine and moved down to my neck.

I closed my eyes and shivered. "I like alone time," I said.

I lowered my face to Ryan, but jumped when Johnny's cry sounded through the baby monitor. I leaned back and groaned. "We're never going to get alone time," I said.

Ryan kissed me once more and slid me off his lap onto the sofa. "I'll go," he said. "And don't worry, we have the rest of our lives to enjoy alone time."

I admired the view as my handsome fiancé walked away to take care of my son and marveled at the joy that had come into my life. I remembered what I'd told Alec in front of the mirror earlier and felt Andrew smiling down on me. "Thank you for sending the love my way, old friend," I said, and blew a kiss to heaven.

◆════◆

The months after our engagement passed in a busy blur. We set a date for three months later and decided on a small church wedding with just friends and family. We also decided that Ryan should move into my house to avoid disruption to Johnny's routine. He started moving his things over a little at a time. I woke one morning thinking how strange it was to see a man's things in my bedroom. It was a strange I could get used to.

Ryan's house was paid for, and it held too many memories to sell it, so he offered it to Mark and Valerie. They were thrilled to accept. With the baby coming, they'd been looking for something bigger than their two-bedroom apartment, and Mark loved the idea of raising his family in the neighborhood he'd grown up in. The only condition was that he and Valerie had to allow the girls to stay whenever they came home from school. They gladly agreed.

I woke on the day of the wedding to the sounds of a shrieking child dragging me from my blissful dream world back to reality. It was still dark out, and I wondered why Johnny was awake at five thirty. He usually slept until at least seven. A clap of thunder rattled the house as I climbed out of bed, and I had my answer. Johnny was terrified of thunder, and I couldn't blame him.

I threw on my robe and went to his room. I untangled him from his blankets and carried him around the room, gently bouncing him and singing softly into his ear. When the storm quieted, I dressed him and snuggled with him on the window seat. He sat on my lap and watched the wet birds flit through the trees with rapt attention. A ray of sunlight split the clouds and streamed through the window, reflecting off Johnny's corn-silk hair. I sighed in contentment.

Johnny looked up at me. "Mama," he said and gave me a crooked grin.

"That's right, sweetie. I'm Mama," I said and kissed the top of his head. Johnny had started calling me Mama months earlier, but I still got a thrill each time he said it.

He began to wiggle to get down, so I put him on the floor. He dragged himself arm over arm in his military crawl to the toy truck that Ryan had given him the week before. He held it up with his good hand to show me and said, "Kuck." When I nodded, he said, "Pop Pop."

"That's right, Johnny. Papa gave you the truck," I said and chuckled at his nickname for Ryan. He'd tried to teach Johnny to call him Papa, but it came out Pop Pop.

Johnny sat up and ran the truck back and forth across the carpet, making engine noises. I let him play while I dozed in the rocking chair. At seven, I carried him to the kitchen for breakfast. The phone rang as I was strapping him into the highchair.

"Good morning, Miss Grace. How are you this fine morning?" Ryan said.

"Just perfect, but how did you know I'd be up this early?" I asked.

"Thunderstorm. I figured Johnny would be awake, so you'd be up too," he said.

I turned on the speaker phone and said, "You must be psychic. I'm about to feed him breakfast."

"You shouldn't be doing that today. It's your wedding day," he said cheerfully.

"What a coincidence. It's your wedding day too." I laughed.

Johnny laughed along even though he had no idea what was so funny.

Ryan said, "I thought Alec was taking Johnny this morning so that you could get ready for your big day."

I handed Johnny a spoon to eat his cereal. He scooped some of it into his mouth and spit half back out, which he thought was hilarious. I grabbed a towel to wipe his face. "It's still early. She'll be here around ten. Did the girls get in all right last night?"

"Yes, and they're already up making plans for nails and hair. They're acting like kids on Christmas morning," he said.

"Tell them they can come over as soon as they want. I'm excited to see them, and it's going to take a lot of work to get me looking like a beautiful bride." Johnny spit the next bite of cereal at me. I took the bowl away and put some apple pieces on his tray. He gleefully stuffed them into his mouth.

"I doubt that," Ryan said. "I bet you look beautiful right now."

"I should take that bet," I said and wiped the cereal off my robe.

"Maybe I should come over and find out," Ryan said, lowering his voice. Jen and Stephanie protested in the background. "I've been informed that I'm not allowed to see you until the wedding, so I guess I'll never know."

"You'll have a pretty good idea when you see me in the morning." I looked at my reflection in the toaster. My hair was a tangled knot sticking out in all directions.

Ryan's voice grew soft. "I can't wait to wake up next to my beautiful bride."

"I love you, Mr. Walker," I said.

"I love you more, the future Mrs. Walker."

"I love you most," I said and laughed.

"I loved you first."

The girls groaned in the background, and I laughed again. "I'll see you in a few hours. You'll have to survive until then."

"I hope so. Love you," he said and hung up.

⇥ ⇤

Later that day, I rested my hand in Ryan's as we knelt at the altar. I'd expected to be nervous, but I was calm in the knowledge that I was doing the right thing. All that was missing was Andrew, but I felt his presence there.

It seemed a lifetime had passed since Ryan rescued me from the precipice. I'd been so certain my life was ending, but as I looked into Ryan's eyes, I prayed in gratitude that because of him, it was only the beginning.

CHAPTER TWENTY-ONE

Four months after our wedding, Ryan and Adam talked Alec and me into letting them go away for a rock-climbing weekend. Alec said she'd only agree on the condition that she could come stay with me for a girl's weekend, and I happily agreed.

When I opened the door for Alec, she bounced in and waved her left hand in front of my face. "Notice anything new?"

I took her hand to examine the engagement ring. The diamond was huge and sparkled in the living-room light. I hugged her and said, "Finally! I never thought he'd get up the courage to do it." I pulled her toward the sofa. "Tell me all about it."

"We've been talking about it for ages, but I think seeing you and Ryan get married was the push he needed. I had no idea it was coming. He invited me over for dinner last night. I thought it was because he was going away for the weekend. I tried to talk to him into coming to my apartment, because we all know about Adam's cooking," she said.

"No wonder he's marrying you. It all makes sense now," I said and laughed.

She gave me a little slap on the arm. "Stop that and listen. He answered the door wearing a tux. He catered an amazing dinner and even hired a string quartet. Of course, I figured out what was going on by then and couldn't eat fast enough. When we finished, he sent them all away and got on one knee."

"He did not," I said. "I thought you two were too modern for things like that."

She scowled at me. "Quit interrupting. You know, he even called Dad to ask for my hand. Can you believe that? What's even more amazing is that Dad gave his approval. Anyway, Adam said he loved me before he met me. I'm not sure what that means, but I'll have our whole lives to find out."

I squeezed her hand and said, "Congratulations, Alec. I've never seen two people more suited for each other."

Alec was about to say something but stopped when my phone buzzed. We looked at it and she said, "I thought we said no phones tonight."

"I just kept it on for emergencies," I said. "I don't recognize the number though. I should answer it"

Alec pushed my arm down to stop me. "If it's important, they'll leave a message."

After the phone stopped buzzing, I waited for the voice-mail alert. Whoever called didn't leave a message. "Must not be important. So, back to you. Have you set a date?"

The phone buzzed again before she answered.

"I'm going to answer it, or they'll keep bugging me," I said. I slid my finger across the screen and said, "Hello?"

"Is this Grace Ward?" a woman's voice asked.

"Who is this?" I asked instead.

"Who I am doesn't matter. If this is Grace Ward, I'm calling to tell you that today is your son's second birthday."

I hung up and threw the phone on the floor.

"Why'd you do that?" Alec asked and picked up the phone. She looked at the number. "Who was it?" When I shook my head, she said, "We can look up the number online."

The phone rang again. I was terrified to answer, but I had to know how the woman knew about Johnny. I swiped my finger again and waited.

"Look, are you Grace Ward or not?" the woman asked. She sounded agitated.

Not wanting to make her angry, I said, "It's Walker now. What do you want?"

"Oh, right," she said. "Congratulations on your marriage. I hope yours goes better than mine. But I'm not calling about that. I called to tell you that I know who your son really is and how he got here. His parents are still alive."

The words hit me like a punch in the gut. I couldn't catch my breath, and the room started to go black. My medical training kicked in, and I forced myself to take a deep breath.

"What's wrong? Put it on speaker," Alec said and took the phone from me. She turned on the speaker and set it on the coffee table.

"How do you know that?" I croaked into the phone.

"Know what?" Alec whispered, but I waved her off.

"I was with your son on the day he was born, two years ago to-day. I was with him for the first six months of his life. I know who his parents are and where they live. I'm willing to tell you," she said.

"What, for a price, you mean?" I asked.

"Don't say anything else," Alec told me. "This is some wacko trying to extort you. I'm hanging up."

Alec grabbed for the phone, but the woman said, "Who is that? Alec Covington? I wouldn't do that if I were you."

Alec looked at me with wide eyes. That woman knew everything about me. My terror rose at the thought that she'd been watching me.

I pushed Alec's hand away. "It's okay. We're listening," I said into the phone and squeezed Alec's hands to keep mine from trembling.

"I don't want anything from you. I've followed Johnny's life since the day my husband dragged me away from your ER. I watched you fight for him. I've watched you care for him. I want to make amends for the terrible things I've done. The doctors told me I couldn't have children. My ex-husband and I had been trying for years, but nothing happened. We wanted to adopt a baby, but we couldn't afford it, and my husband had a criminal record."

"I know how adoption works," I said, cutting her off. "Don't try to make me feel sorry for you."

"Then maybe you'll understand how desperate we were. I don't know which one of us got the idea first, but we decided to kidnap a newborn from a hospital. I was a nurse and knew my way around, so we just had to wait for our chance. Kyle's parents, I mean Johnny's parents, presented the perfect opportunity, and we took it. I took Johnny from the nursery on the day he was born."

"So he was kidnapped!" Alec said. "Agent Erikson was right."

"You already knew? How could you have known?" the woman asked.

I shook my head at Alec to stop her from volunteering any more information. "Just a suspicion. We didn't know for sure," I said into the phone. "How did you get away with it?"

"Easy, but that doesn't matter. All you need to know is that we brought him to Richmond to raise as our own son. We loved him and took good care of him until the day of the flood. We were trying to escape in our boat, but it capsized. I didn't want to leave Kyle in the ER, but Rick forced me to. We went into hiding until we were sure that no one knew we were responsible."

"I can't believe this. How could you do such a horrible thing?" I said, still reminding myself to breathe.

"Believe it, lady. It's true. We were on the move together for a while, but the guilt tore us apart. I left Rick and made my way here. He'd kill me if he knew I was talking to you. I've watched Kyle from a distance all this time. I feel like he's still a part of my life. I know I have no claim to him, but I want him to be happy and grow up where he belongs. His parents need to know he's alive and well. I'll tell you where to find them if you do exactly what I say."

I sank to my knees and gripped the table for support. I wanted to smash the phone and pretend I'd never heard that woman speaking pain into my ear, but I couldn't do that to Johnny or his parents. All that time not knowing where their baby was or if he was even alive. If what she was saying were true, I'd lose Johnny, but I had to get him back to them. Johnny had a right to know who he was, who his real parents were.

I jumped when the woman said, "You still there, Grace?"

"I'm here," I whispered.

Alec put her hand on my shoulder, reminding me I wasn't alone.

"I know you're shocked, and you probably don't believe me, but it's true. I can give you the names and address of his family."

"What's your name?" I asked.

"My name is Jody, but knowing won't do you any good. You'll never find me. I'm going far away from here now that Kyle's with you, and I don't need to worry. I'm going to find a place to have a real life of my own and bury this forever."

"You think you can just escape unpunished? You can't run away from the terrible crimes you've committed, the lives you've destroyed. We'll find you. We'll never stop hunting you until you pay for what you've done!" I said and got up off the floor.

"Pay? Don't you think I've paid for this for the past eighteen months, always living in hiding, fear, and regret? I've done my time and paid the price. If you don't promise to leave me alone, I won't tell you where to find his family. I'll just disappear, and you and your precious Johnny will never know," she said.

I could hear the agitation in her voice. I had to act before she hung up. I could say I'd leave Jody alone and then go to the authorities after I had the information and let them handle it. I was afraid she could do something to hurt us if I went back on my word, but I had to take the risk.

"What's your answer?" she whispered.

"I promise that I won't go to the FBI until you have time to get away. If you've watched me all this time as you claim, then you know that all that matters to me is Johnny's happiness and safety."

"I do know, or I wouldn't have called. Fine, in a few days, you'll receive an envelope containing all the information you need. I'll be long gone by then. No one will know where to look for me. When I drop that letter in the mail, this is over for me, but I'll never forget Kyle. For a time, he was my son too."

I heard a click, and the line went dead. My mind reeled in a haze of fear and confusion. My first memory of Johnny in the ER with Jody and Rick flashed in my mind. They almost killed him. They kidnapped him. He wasn't my son. Fear gave way to a terror that crept over me like a suffocating fog. As I reached for Alec, she grew dim and then faded into blackness.

⊶ ⊷

My eyelids felt like they were made of lead when I forced them open. The ceiling above me blurred in and out of focus, so I blinked a few times to clear my eyes.

"There you are," Ryan said. "Can you see me?"

I rolled my eyes to the right. Ryan leaned over me by the side of the hospital bed. I tried to sit up, but the room faded, so I dropped back down onto the pillows. I couldn't remember what had happened or how I'd gotten there.

"Water," I croaked through desert-dry lips. Ryan put his hand under my head and lifted me to take a sip from a straw in a Styrofoam cup. When he laid me back down, I said, "Why am I here?"

He sat on the edge of the bed and took my hand. "What's the last thing you remember?"

I searched my mind for anything that gave me context. "You and Adam leaving to go rock climbing," I said.

He brushed a lock of hair from my forehead. "That was twelve hours ago. You don't remember the phone call from Jody?"

At hearing the name, memories of the night before flooded back. I struggled to get up again, to get to Johnny. "Where is he? Where's Johnny?" As Ryan gently pushed me back down, I realized that my head was pounding. "What happened to my head?"

"Johnny's safe. Alec and Adam have him right out in the hallway. I'll tell them to bring him in when you prove to me you can handle it," he said. "You passed out from the shock and whacked your head on the coffee table. You have a concussion and five stitches."

That explained the headache. I pushed the button to raise the head of the bed and asked Ryan for another sip of water. "I'm feeling better," I said. "I want to see Johnny, and please get something for my headache."

Ryan told Alec and Adam to bring Johnny in. He reached for me as soon as Alec was close to the bed, and she almost dropped him. She laid Johnny in the crook of my arm. He ignored me and grabbed the remote that worked the bed and started pushing buttons. When the bed moved, he giggled and pushed the button again.

I closed my eyes to fight the nausea and said, "Please find something else for him to play with."

Adam pulled Johnny's favorite truck out of the diaper bag and handed it to him. Johnny dropped the remote and stuck the truck in his mouth.

I mouthed a thank you to Adam. He leaned over me and opened my eyes to shine his penlight at my pupils. "How's your pain?" he asked.

"Excruciating," I said. "That light's not helping."

"Be right back," he said and went out to find my doctor.

Alec and Ryan were standing at the end of the bed staring at me. "Are either of you going to say anything?" I asked and put my hand up just in time to deflect Johnny from banging his truck on my forehead.

Ryan picked him up and said, "Let's put you in the stroller, buddy." He strapped him in and pulled a pack of fruit chews from his pocket.

That's my Ryan, I thought, always prepared.

He sat in the chair next to my bed gave me some more water.

Alec leaned against the windowsill and crossed her arms. "When you blacked out, I called an ambulance and hightailed it over here with Johnny. I called Adam and Ryan on the way and told them to get back here. I didn't black out and hit my head, but I've been a wreck since the phone call. That was terrifying. I still think we should call the cops, but Ryan and Adam agree with you that we should wait."

"They're right," I said. "We can't risk her finding out if we alert the police."

"She probably already mailed it. Besides, even if she's in the parking lot, the police could come in plain clothes, and she'd never know they were coming to see you," she said. "I'm scared. I don't want to leave here knowing she's been watching us. It's creepy." She shivered.

"Then sleep in your office," I snapped at her. I was in no mood to argue.

Adam came back with Dr. Aggarwal, a new neurology resident who was on call. I'd only met him once and thought he looked fifteen years old. He shined his light in my eyes like Adam had done.

"How's the nausea?" he asked.

"Nauseating," I said.

"Good to see a sense of humor," he said. "I'll order something for the pain and nausea, and I'm keeping you overnight. Call the nurse if you need me." He rushed out.

I looked at Alec, and she said, "No need to ask. I'll take Johnny to my office."

"I'm sorry," I said and started to cry, which only made my headache worse. "What are we going to do, Ryan?" I squeezed his hand between mine. "I'm losing him. After everything I've been through, I'm losing Johnny."

Ryan kissed my forehead. "I know, sweetheart. Let's wait for the letter and take it a day at a time from there. I'm staying here tonight. We'll get through this together."

Adam said, "You should handle the letter with surgical gloves when it comes and put it in a plastic bag."

"I was thinking the same thing," Ryan said. "From what Grace says about this Jody person, she probably knows better than to leave fingerprints, but you never know. Hopefully the FBI can find enough evidence to go after her."

"She'll be out of the country by the time you notify them," Alec said. "She's dodged the authorities for a long time."

"That'll be the FBI's problem. I want Jody and Rick caught, but my priority is Johnny. I can't think beyond that," I said.

⊶ ⊷

Dr. Aggarwal released me the next morning, so we went home to everything just as Alec and I had left it, including the bloodstain on the living-room carpet. I'd wanted to go to a hotel, thinking it would be safer, but Ryan convinced me that Jody could have hurt us or tried to take Johnny at any time, but she hadn't. Even so, I agreed with Alec that the thought that Jody could be watching us was creepy.

I jumped out of my skin when the mail came the following Monday. I looked out the window for the hundredth time and finally saw the mail truck driving off. I ran to the mailbox and didn't wait until I got inside the house to rifle through it. It was nothing but junk and bills. The letter wasn't there. Ryan had warned me that it might take a few days. Jody could have mailed it from anywhere. I should have listened to him, but I'd convinced myself the letter would come that day. I was angry and disappointed, but I had no one to blame but myself.

Ryan came home from work an hour later to find me still sitting on the sofa with the pile of mail on my lap. "I take it the letter didn't come," he said. "Why aren't you wearing gloves? You were supposed to wear gloves."

"Who cares about the stupid gloves?" I said and pushed the pile of mail onto the floor. "She wouldn't be stupid enough to leave her fingerprints on it."

"Whoa, excuse me. I'm just trying to help catch a kidnapper," he said and knelt down to pick up the pile of mail.

"I'm sorry. You didn't deserve that, but this waiting is torture," I said. "How am I going to survive until that letter comes? What if doesn't come? What if she decided not to risk sending it? Maybe we should go to the FBI and take our chances that they'll put the pieces together and find Johnny's parents."

Ryan sat next to me and said, "That's too big a risk, and we only need to wait another day or so. Besides, why would Jody have gone to the trouble to call if she didn't plan to send the letter? You're getting worked up over something that hasn't happened. You can't freak out every time the letter doesn't come."

I sighed. "I'll try to get a grip, but tomorrow, you're getting the mail."

Sounds of Johnny crying came over the baby monitor.

"It's a deal. I'll cook dinner. You take care of that," Ryan said, pointing to the baby monitor.

I nodded and went to Johnny's room. His face lit up when I opened the door. "Mama," he said and held his hand up to me.

I picked him up and held him close. In the days since "the call," I'd started to think in terms of lasts. I wondered when I would give Johnny his last bath or do his exercises with him for the last time. Every time he said Mama, I wondered if that would be the last time I'd hear it. I savored each moment, imprinting it in my mind and on my heart.

Johnny raised his head and planted a sloppy kiss on my cheek. I brushed my hand against it and prayed it wouldn't be the last time.

I pretended to be busy in the kitchen the next day when Ryan came in with the mail. "You can stop the act. It came," he said, and held the envelope up between his gloved fingers.

I wiped my hands on a towel and said, "Don't open it. Get Johnny. We're going to the FBI right now."

"Yes, ma'am," he said and saluted to break the tension.

I glared at him.

"Sorry. I'll just get Johnny then."

We were on our way in record time. I sat in the back and held Johnny's hand. He didn't scream for once but quietly stared out the window.

After we went through the security checkpoint at the FBI office, the security guard asked why we were there. When we explained that we needed to speak with Agent Erikson, he raised his eyebrows and asked us to follow him. He led us to a waiting area and told us to wait.

Three minutes later, Special Agent Scott Michaels walked into the waiting area and introduced himself. "Why are you asking for Agent Erikson?" he asked.

"Because he worked on the case that we're here about," I said. "I met him about eighteen months ago. He said if I ever had more information to contact him."

Agent Michaels rubbed his chin, and said, "I'm sorry to tell you that Agent Erikson died in the line of duty six months ago, but I can try to help you."

When I recovered from my shock at the news of Agent Erikson's death, I looked at Ryan, not sure what to do. He nodded and said, "Go ahead. Tell him."

I took a deep breath and told him Johnny's story from the beginning. When I finished, I held up the envelope in the plastic bag for him.

He took the bag. "You should have come to us immediately, but I'm glad you came at all. I understand what you risked by coming here."

"We wanted to make sure she was telling the truth," I said. "I was afraid if we came to you before we got the letter, she wouldn't send it."

"No need to explain." He looked at Johnny and smiled. "I remember hearing about him on the news, and I helped in the initial investigation. Agent Erikson was adamant about Johnny being the kidnapped child. His hunch was right. This case is one tragedy after another."

"Like my life," I said under my breath.

"What's that?" he asked. When I shook my head, he said, "Let's go to the conference room."

We followed him down a long hallway.

When we were settled in the conference room, he put on gloves and said, "Let's open this and see what it says."

He read the letter and I could tell that Jody had been true to her word. He told us she'd listed the names of Craig and Samantha Stuart with their address in Albuquerque. She also gave the name of the hospital and the date that she and her husband had kidnapped Johnny two years earlier. Agent Michaels pulled open kidnapping cases on his computer and found the one from Albuquerque that fit the time frame.

He read the file for several seconds and then rubbed his chin again. "Like I said, tragic. There's a kidnapping that fits."

I slumped against Ryan and cried on his shoulder.

Agent Michaels looked away and said, "Now, don't do that. This doesn't prove that Johnny is the missing baby. Jody may have heard about the kidnapping, and she's using the information to torment you."

I glanced at Agent Michaels. It was clear he didn't believe that any more than I did. Jody hadn't asked for money or anything else. She had nothing to gain by causing us trouble.

"We'll take a DNA sample from Johnny and compare it to the sample on file from the Stuarts. We won't notify the family until we're certain, in case this turns into a dead end."

I sat up and pulled a hankie out of my purse, glad that I'd thought to bring it. Tissues weren't going to cut it.

Ryan put his arm around me and said, "How long will this take?"

"At least a few days, but I'll try to rush it and contact you as soon as the results come in. In the meantime, go home and continue on with your lives as before. This may turn out to be nothing more than a hoax." He stood and walked around his desk to face us. "I'll lead you back to the lobby."

As we followed Agent Michaels back down the long, tiled hallways, Johnny chatted happily in his stroller. I was grateful he was too young to comprehend the massive upheaval we were about to face. Agent Michaels had told us to go on as before, but that life had been wiped away. Johnny was no longer my son. He belonged to Craig and Samantha Stuart of Albuquerque, New Mexico.

⊶ ⊷

I wanted to sit in the front seat with Ryan on the way home, so I gave Johnny a sippy cup filled with juice to keep him happy. Ryan and I rode in silence for the first few miles. I turned away from him and looked out the window, not wanting him to see my tears.

"You have every right to cry. You don't have to hide it from me," he said. "Giving Johnny up will be incredibly hard. We'll have to work through that, but this isn't only about us and our future with Johnny."

I wiped my face with the hankie and looked at him. "You're talking about the Stuarts. As much as I want them to have their son back, it doesn't mean I won't mourn losing him. I don't know if I'll ever get over it." I took his hand.

"You will. We will. Johnny's not dying, and you're so much stronger than you give yourself credit for. Focus on the extraordinary thing you've done for Johnny. You were Johnny's mother when he needed you. You've loved and protected him and prepared him to return home. I hope that won't get lost in this." Ryan squeezed my hand. "Don't let the sadness erase the time you had with him and what you gave each other."

I pondered what he'd said, and I wanted to follow his advice, but I wasn't sure I had the strength to do it, at least not at that moment. He was right to remind me that Johnny wasn't dying, just going back to his true home. "Do you think his parents will let me be a part of his life?" I asked.

"I guarantee it. If they won't, they don't deserve Johnny," he said as he pulled into our driveway. "It's time to tell Paul about this."

"Will you do it? I'm not sure I want to hear what he has to say," I said and climbed out of the car. "I'll call Alec. She must be going crazy waiting to hear."

Ryan took Johnny out of his seat and followed me into the house. I hugged them both when we got inside before heading to our room to call Alec.

CHAPTER TWENTY-TWO

I heard from Agent Michaels two days later, right after Ryan had driven off to go work. Johnny's DNA matched the Stuarts'. At long last, we knew Johnny's true identity. I was glad that his parents would finally know the truth too, but the news carried me one step closer to losing him.

Agent Michaels said that an agent in Albuquerque was in the process of contacting the Stuarts and that he'd get back to us to make arrangements for a meeting. I called Ryan as soon as I hung up with Agent Michaels. Ryan told me he'd call out of work and turn the car around.

I wanted Ryan by my side, but I was strangely calm after getting the news. It reminded me of how patients react after getting the news that they have a terminal illness. Sometimes the waiting is worse than the news.

Ryan and I spent that morning playing with Johnny and waiting to hear from Agent Michaels. Ryan insisted on calling Paul, even though I wanted to wait, hoping to postpone the inevitable. Paul came as soon as he got out of court and waited with us. He sat on the floor, getting fuzz all over his good suit, and played cars with Johnny. Serena came to the door twenty minutes later. Her eyes and nose were red and swollen.

She hugged me and said, "I just heard. Rough trip driving here. My emotions are all over the map. I'm thrilled that the Stuarts' long nightmare is over, but my heart is broken for you." She blew her nose, and Johnny giggled, which made her start crying again. "This is what I get for getting too close to my clients."

I took her hand and led her to the sofa. "It's been a long road," I said, "a long, crooked, torn up, detour-filled road, but it's led right where it should."

"You're taking this better than I am," Serena said.

"Seriously, what's up with you?" Ryan asked. "This calm, collected version of Grace scares me."

Adam and Alec walked through the door before I had a chance to respond.

"Don't you ever knock?" Ryan asked.

"We're family. Family doesn't have to knock," Alec said and kissed Ryan's cheek. "Well, here we all are again." She shooed Ryan off the sofa and sat next to me.

Serena noticed Alec's ring and congratulated them on their engagement. We talked about their wedding plans while we waited for the phone to ring. When the conversation petered out, we made lame attempts at small talk, carefully avoiding the topic on our minds. After half an hour, I couldn't take the waiting and got up to pace.

"Now, there's the Grace I know and love," Ryan said.

I ignored him and continued pacing. When the doorbell rang, I told everyone to stay where they were and went to the door. I expected our usual delivery guy but found Agent Michaels on the stoop holding our pizzas.

"He was coming up the drive when I got here. I hope you don't mind," he said and handed me the boxes.

I peeked around him and said, "Did you pay him?"

"Yes. You can repay me by giving me a slice," he said and followed me in.

"Have all you want," I said as I put the pizzas on the table. "What are you doing here? We were expecting you to call."

He looked me in the eye. "I thought it would be better to deliver my news in person."

I nodded and introduced him to the crowd in the living room. Ryan got up to shake Agent Michaels's hand and give him his chair.

He started to insist that we eat first, but I held up my hand to stop him. "That can wait. Tell us what you came to say."

"I'm glad you're here, Ms. Davis. This involves you, and possibly you, Mr. Pierno."

Serena and Paul nodded.

"Our agent in Albuquerque has spoken with Mr. Stuart. He was shocked and elated that his son is alive, as he should be." He paused and took a breath. "But there's another tragedy connected with Johnny's story. His mother died giving birth to him, so Mr. Stuart lost his wife and son on the same day."

We stared at Agent Michaels in stunned silence. Alec and Serena started crying quietly behind me, but I was numb. To prepare myself to give Johnny to the Stuarts, I'd imagined him going home to the loving arms of his mother. With her gone, who would nurture and love him as only a mother could? Who would take my place?

As if reading my mind, Agent Michaels said, "Mr. Stuart remarried two months ago."

Ryan came behind me and put his hands on my shoulders. "It's nice to get one bright spot of news. What happens now?"

"Mr. Stuart is making arrangements to fly here. He's coming alone and wants to meet Johnny for the first time without you present, Mrs. Walker," he said, avoiding my eyes.

Alec jumped up and said, "Why? Grace is the one who's done everything for Johnny. He wouldn't even be alive if not for her."

Serena reached up and touched Alec's arm. "This is pretty common. We can meet with him at my office," she said to Agent Michaels.

"I understand his not wanting the Walkers there for the first meeting, but I won't allow my clients to be pushed aside. Alec's right, he wouldn't have survived without Grace," Paul told Agent Michaels.

"I'd never let that happen," Serena said. "Let us get this first meeting out of the way and go from there."

"When? When will this happen?" I asked. My earlier calm vanished as I felt Johnny slipping away from me.

"As early as tomorrow," Agent Michaels said.

I lifted my chin and squared my shoulders. "That's settled then. Let's eat before it gets cold," I said and opened the first box.

⋙⋘

Serena called at ten the next morning to tell me that she'd be by at around four to pick up Johnny. She assured me that it was a small first step. She said that there would be another hearing to nullify the adoption and that Mr. Stuart and his wife would need time to learn how to care for Johnny and rearrange their lives. I told her I'd have Johnny ready at four and hung up, not caring if it was the first step or not. The longer the process dragged out, the more excruciating it would be to let go.

Serena showed up right on time. I held Johnny while she buckled his car seat in her car. I warned her to be prepared for the screaming.

When it was time to go, she reached her hands toward Johnny, but I turned away and held him tighter. "We'll be back in two hours," she said.

I sighed and kissed the top of his head. "Here you go," I said, turning to hand him to her.

The second he was in her arms, I went into the house without a word and locked the door. It was time to get used to an existence without Johnny.

⚔

I'd been a little premature in getting used to life without Johnny. Serena had been right about a first step, and the process dragged along at a snail's pace. Mr. Stuart stayed for three days on that first visit, and spent an hour or two with Johnny each day. According to Serena, Johnny didn't take to his father well. All Mr. Stuart wanted was to hug and squeeze Johnny, but he would have none of that.

He promised Serena that on his next visit, he'd spend time getting to know us. That happened two weeks later. He came with Paul and Serena and brought his wife, Kristin.

I studied them while Paul made the introductions. Craig was average-looking, with light-brown hair and a medium build. I didn't see much of Johnny in him, other than his smile. He had a kind face, and I hoped Johnny would have that too. Kristin looked much younger than Craig. She was beautiful in a Hollywood way, and I could see how Craig had fallen for her. She seemed nice but didn't look too happy to be there. I thought back to how Ryan's kids had reacted to Johnny the first time, and it made me love them more.

Once we were seated, Craig said, "Before you bring Johnny, I have some things I need to say. For two years I lived in agony, not knowing if my son was alive or dead, not knowing if he was safe. When my phone rang six weeks ago, I couldn't imagine the joy that call would bring." His lip trembled, so he stopped and took a breath. He glanced at me. "I own this joy to you. I was overwhelmed when I heard the story of what you did for Johnny. It's miraculous.

291

There's no way to thank you enough or repay you. I'll make sure to tell Johnny all about it as he grows up."

"You don't need to thank me, but you can repay us by loving Johnny like we have. If I know he's loved, I'll be able to bear losing him," I said.

Craig's lip trembled and he nodded. "You have my promise on that."

"I'll get Johnny," Ryan said. He wiped his cheek as he walked by.

After Craig introduced Johnny to Kristin, I asked how they met.

"Kristin is my best friend's sister. I never would have survived Sam's death and losing Johnny without them. Kristin and I became closer as she helped me through my grief. Before we knew it, we realized we couldn't live without each other. Some people were surprised at how soon we got married after Sam's death, but it was right for us," Craig said and squeezed Kristin's hand.

"We have other news too. We just found out I'm expecting," Kristin said and beamed.

"That's great news," Ryan said. "Johnny will have a little brother or sister."

Kristin smiled, but the smile didn't reach her eyes. I wondered if she wasn't as thrilled about Johnny as Craig was.

Johnny did better with Craig in familiar surroundings. Craig listened intently while Ryan and I explained Johnny's likes, dislikes, and quirks. He moved more slowly around Johnny and gave him the chance to warm up to him. By the end of the visit, Johnny sat on Craig's lap, chatting happily away.

Kristin didn't do so well, which didn't surprise me. She seemed terrified of Johnny and sat stiff as a statue while she held him. I didn't hold it against her. The situation must have been overwhelming. I just hoped she'd warm up to him in a hurry.

There was a tap on the door an hour after Craig and Kristin arrived, and Alec walked in. "I'm sorry to interrupt," she said, "but

I've known Johnny as long as Grace. I helped treat him the night he was left in the ER. I'm Auntie Alec."

I shook my head and motioned for her to come in. Johnny held his arm out to her as soon as he saw her. "Do you mind?" she asked Craig. "I'll just hold him for a minute."

"That's fine," Craig said and handed Johnny to her. It was clear he wasn't too happy about it.

After Craig and Kristin left with Johnny, I asked Alec what she was up to.

"I had to check them out. They're taking our Johnny from us," she said.

"He's their Johnny. We all have to get that into our heads," Ryan said.

"Did you see the way Craig looked at me when I asked to hold Johnny? Daggers," Alec said.

"Not exactly daggers," I said. "And what did you expect? He's had to wait two years to meet his son."

"I'm glad to hear you defending Craig. I was afraid you thought of him as the enemy," Ryan said.

"Of course not, but just because it's right that Johnny should go with them doesn't mean it's not hard for me to let him go," I said. "I'm doing my best."

Alec put her arm around my shoulder. "I'm proud of you, and you're right, Ryan, he is Craig's Johnny. He's not Kristin's Johnny though. Did you see how scared she was of him?"

"I did, and it disturbed me. Not the loving mother I'd hoped for Johnny," I said.

"Give her time. She has a lot to take on all at once: a new husband, a special-needs son, and she just found out she's pregnant. I'd be freaking out too," Ryan said.

"When you put it that way...," I said. I felt guilty for judging Kristin. "This will be an adjustment for all of us."

⇥ ⇤

Craig and Kristin stayed in town for a week. They took Johnny to their hotel room one afternoon to see how he'd do without familiar faces around. He lasted for two hours before he started crying for me. Craig was pleased to be making progress and told us he wanted to keep Johnny overnight on his next visit. I thought it was too soon, but Craig was Johnny's father, so I couldn't deny him time with his son.

Craig made arrangements to stay for a month on his next visit. He owned an architectural firm and was between projects, so he could stay as long as he wanted. He took a room in an extended-stay hotel with a full kitchen and separate bedroom. Kristin couldn't get the time off from the PR firm where she worked, so she didn't come with him. I was sure she wasn't sad about that.

Craig kept Johnny with him for longer periods of time the first week until he felt ready to keep him overnight. They both did fine, but I was secretly disappointed. I stayed awake all night waiting for Craig to call and say he was bringing Johnny home. Craig brought Johnny back the following afternoon and said he wanted to try two nights the next time. When things went well again, Craig called and told us he was going to keep Johnny for a week. I reluctantly handed over Johnny's medications and gave Craig the schedule for visits to the therapist, still secretly hoping that it would be too much for him. That didn't happen.

I suddenly found myself with hours of free time to fill. I cleaned out closets and cupboards, organized my desk, and even painted my bedroom. When I ran out of things to do around the house, I started looking for a job.

Paul called on the fifth day and told us that Craig had been talking to a lawyer who had scheduled the date for a hearing to nullify the adoption.

"So fast?" I asked when Paul told me it would be in ten days.

"After Craig's first visit, you told me you wanted this over with as soon as possible. Now that it's moving forward, you say it's too fast," he said. "Are you ever satisfied?"

"That's because at the beginning, Johnny was still sleeping in my house. What happens after the hearing?"

"Craig and Kristin will take Johnny home," he said, and the line went quiet.

"He *is* home," I said, trying to keep my voice from breaking.

"We've been through this. I thought you were coming to grips with the idea of Johnny going away," he said.

I sighed. "I thought I was too, but I'm beginning to think I never will be. My only hope is that Craig will agree to let us visit and that he'll keep us posted on how Johnny's doing."

"Those decisions are his. The court won't have any say in them, but I'm sure he'll agree to that. I know how grateful he is for what you've done for his son."

I was too tired to speculate anymore. We had no choice but to abide by Craig's decision. I thanked Paul for letting me know and said we'd see him at the hearing. I hung up and turned back to the job-classifieds page on my laptop.

We all stood when Judge Brackman entered her chambers. As she took her seat and called the hearing to order, I fought off memories of the last time I'd been in that room. I stood in a daze as she spoke with Craig and explained what was taking place. I didn't need her to explain. All I knew was that Johnny would soon be ripped from my arms and given back to his father. I didn't blame Craig or Judge Brackman. Craig deserved the joy I'd known to have Johnny as my son. Judge Brackman was just doing her job. We'd been denied the chance to face the real culprits, and it was tragically unfair.

Judge Brackman cleared her throat and said, "This is the most unusual case I've seen in all my years on the bench. Even though some of you here will know sadness as a result of my actions, we can all agree that justice is being done here in putting the Stuart family to rights. Before I make my final ruling, Mr. Stuart has requested the opportunity to make a statement."

Craig opened a folded piece of paper with trembling hands. He glanced at me and nodded. When I gave him a weak smile, he turned back to the paper and began to read. "I know this is a difficult day for the Walker family, but I want them to know that it's one of the happiest days of my life. I'm grateful for all you've done for us. I will always be indebted to you, and when Johnny is older, I'll tell him the story of what a woman named Grace did for us."

Craig folded the paper and put it in his pocket. I nodded and mouthed a thank you to him. Ryan put his arm around my shoulder and said, "Hear, hear."

And with that, Judge Brackman tapped her gavel and adjourned the hearing. Serena gave us a moment to say good-bye to Johnny before she took him from me and handed him to Craig. Johnny reached for me, but Craig turned away and walked out.

"Craig would like a moment with you in the lobby," Serena said.

By the time we caught up with him, Johnny was in the stroller sucking on a sippy cup.

"I appreciate your sending Johnny's things to my hotel," Craig said. "I'd planned to pick them up, but this made things easier. I've already mailed the boxes home."

When I didn't respond, Ryan said, "We were glad to help. Grace and I are wondering what your plan is going forward, as far as we're concerned. I know you'll need time to get settled, but we wanted to know how soon we can come for a visit."

Craig's eyes widened, and he said, "Didn't Serena explain our wishes to you?"

"No, this all happened so fast. We haven't had a chance to talk to her," I said.

Craig fidgeted for a few seconds. "I meant everything I said in the hearing, but Kristin and I have decided that it would be best for Johnny if we make a clean break. Seeing you come and go would only cause confusion. I know this isn't what you hoped for, but it's about what's best for Johnny. I'll give you occasional updates, but that's going to be the extent of our contact."

My hands tightened into fists. I looked at Ryan. His face was red, and his jaw was clenched. It was the most anger I'd even seen him show.

"You can't be serious," I said. "You're just going to drag Johnny away to a strange home with strange people and never let him see me again? He'll think I died!" My voice rose with each word, and people started to stare.

Ryan took a step toward Craig and said, "You said you could never repay Grace, but you're doing the opposite. You're punishing her. She didn't have to report that call from Jody. She could have kept it secret, and you never would have known what happened to your son. This is how you repay her, by denying her access to him?"

Craig stepped back. "I've been studying about child psychology. They say that with a child Johnny's age, this is the best way to do it. I agree, and it's what we want. Kristin and I are just starting our lives and family together, and now we have Johnny. We want to do that without outside influences."

"You got it from a book?" I said. "A book! Johnny's not some test subject. He's a person. You can't do this to him. To us. We're not some interference. We're his parents." The tears I'd fought all morning won out.

"Please don't," Craig said. "I'm sorry. Maybe when Johnny's older. Give us time. You'll have a new grandchild. He'll fill the void left by Johnny."

"No, no. You can't do this us," I cried.

Ryan put his arms around me and gently pulled me back. "We'll respect your wishes, but you're making a big mistake. I don't know how you can do this to us."

Craig's lip trembled, but Kristin stood by him, emotionless. "We gave it a lot of thought. We believe it's for the best," he said.

Craig slowly turned and gripped the stroller handles. He gave us one last look and pushed Johnny out the door. I couldn't move. I couldn't breathe. I wanted to wake up and find out it had only been a nightmare. Johnny was gone. My baby was gone, and I'd never see him again.

Ryan got me out of bed a month later and told me I'd moped long enough. He said it was time to go out and discover my next adventure. I decided to treat myself to breakfast at Juliana's and a day of touring museums. He thought a day in the city was just what I needed and even offered to come with me, but his eyes glazed over at the thought of spending hours strolling through museums. I let him off the hook and went alone. I needed the solitude. I had a lot to figure out. Ryan said his next adventure was to start cleaning out Johnny's room and turn it back into an office. I was sure what he meant was turn it into a man cave.

It was a beautiful spring morning and reminded me of the day I'd gone for my walk when Johnny was taken off life support. I'd been certain that was my last day with him, but I'd been blessed to have him for another whole year. At least the second time he'd gone with his father, who loved him and wanted the best for him. Life without Johnny would be a long, difficult adjustment, but I could survive knowing Johnny would be loved.

After breakfast, I drove to the canal walk and found the spot where Ryan had proposed to me. My first step to recovery was reminding myself that I wasn't alone and that I had the perfect man to spend my life with. I teared up as I remembered the joy I'd felt that night and pledged to find my way back again. Ryan had given me so much. He deserved a life of joy too.

My next stop was the Virginia Historical Society. I hadn't been there in years, and they were hosting an exhibit I'd wanted to see. I took my time, reading each placard and sign. As I walked to my car four hours later, I turned on my phone to check my messages. There were three texts from Ryan, one wishing me a good day and two asking me to bring dinner home and where were his glasses? I grinned at that last one. Ryan was an intelligent and capable man, but he couldn't ever keep track of anything.

The next text was from Serena. It read, "Get to my office NOW!" She had sent it forty-five minutes earlier. Serena was generally so reserved, so her text had me concerned. I texted back that I was on my way and drove to her office.

I made my way from the parking garage to the street as fast as I could. When I was a block away from Serena's building, I heard someone call my name. I looked around but didn't recognize anyone on the busy street. I started walking again but only made it a few steps when someone yelled, "Grace!" I turned to see Craig Stuart rushing toward me through the crowd. I stopped in the middle of the sidewalk and waited for him to reach me. Without a word, he took my arm and led me into an alley.

I pulled my arm free and backed away. "What are you doing here, Craig? You're supposed to be in Albuquerque."

Craig put his hands on his knees to catch his breath. Without looking up, he said, "It didn't work. It didn't work out with Johnny."

"What are you saying? Why were you chasing me down a sidewalk?" I asked, trying to understand. "How did you find me?"

Craig leaned against one of the buildings and slid to the ground. He rested his head in his hands and said, "I'm saying that I'm giving Johnny to you. He's miserable. He cries all the time and won't sleep. He's exhausted. I'm exhausted." He started to sob.

"He just needs time. We warned you this could happen. He doesn't understand. Just give him time."

"He calls out for you all day. You're his mother. He needs you," he said, trying to get control.

I imagined Johnny confused and not understanding why I never came when he called, and my heart ached. "Let me go back with you and stay until he's settled. He'll get used to you, just like he got used to being in the hotel. You shouldn't have taken him away so abruptly. He wasn't ready."

Craig looked up and said, "No, you don't understand. Kristin threatened to leave if I keep Johnny. She never wanted this, never wanted him. She was too afraid to tell me when she saw how happy I was that Johnny is alive. I thought my long nightmare was over. I never considered Kristin's feelings. She didn't sign up for a handicapped two-year-old when she married me. She wants to focus on our baby and others to come. She doesn't want Johnny." He broke down again.

Tears rolled down my face as I watched him. How could anyone not want Johnny? It was inconceivable to me. "So, you're choosing Kristin over Johnny, your own flesh and blood?" I said.

His shoulders shook, and I regretted what I'd said. He was in an impossible situation. As much as I wanted Johnny back, I hated witnessing Craig's misery. I wondered how different things would have turned out if Jody had called six months earlier.

"I'm sorry, Craig. That wasn't fair," I whispered. "Just give them time. He'll forget me. Kristin's his mother now. He'll come to love her in time, and she'll love him."

He climbed to his feet and wiped his face on his shirt. "She's not a bad person. She's not. This has all been so overwhelming.

We hadn't planned to have children right away, but she got pregnant. We're happy, but when this happened, Kristin got overwhelmed. I love Johnny. I see my Samantha every time I look at him." He reached into his shirt pocket and pulled out a photo. "This is her. Here, you take it. Give it to Johnny when he's old enough."

I studied the picture, and Johnny's eyes looked back at me. He had Samantha's coloring and blond hair too. She was beautiful.

"We had a hard time getting pregnant. Samantha had two miscarriages. We walked on eggshells through her pregnancy with Johnny. She made it to term and went into labor while I was at work. She called an ambulance, but the paramedics found her in a pool of blood by the front door. The placenta had ruptured. They kept her alive long enough to deliver Johnny. I went straight to her when I got to the hospital, but it was too late, too late to say goodbye. By the time I got up the strength to tear myself away and go to the nursery, Johnny was gone. The first time I saw him was in Serena's office."

He said the words in monotone, as if he'd spoken them a thousand times and was weary from the telling. I wanted to hold him, to take his pain away. Tragic, I thought, recalling Agent Michael's words.

"If you do this, Craig, there's no going back. You can't do this to me again, but we won't shut you out like you've done to us. You can be a part of Johnny's life, as much as you want," I said.

Craig reached into his other pocket and pulled out an envelope. He shoved it into my hand and said, "No. When I leave here today, you'll never see me again. This is the paper permanently relinquishing my parental rights. Judge Brackman has agreed to reinstate the adoption. Johnny's your son now, forever."

I stared at the paper in my hand and said, "You don't have to do this. You can still be a part of his life. Come visit as often as you want. We won't shut you out. It doesn't have to be either-or."

Craig looked up, and I saw a glimmer of hope in his eyes. "When Johnny's older, tell him about me. Tell him I love him. Tell him I left him because I love him. Call me when he knows, and I'll come."

I nodded and smiled at him. "Where *is* Johnny? What have you done with him?"

"He's with Serena. She told me you were on your way. That's how I found you. Take Johnny home. I'm sorry. I'm so sorry for the pain I've caused. Forgive me," he said and stumbled off toward the street.

I clenched the paper in my hand and ran to Serena's office. Johnny was on her lap, and she was reading his favorite book to him. When he saw me, he lifted his arm and cried, "Mama."

I lifted him up. "That's right, my little man. Mama's here, and it's time for us to go home."

END

ABOUT THE AUTHOR

Eleanor Chance discovered her love of writing with a poetry assignment in the fifth grade. It is a passion that has stayed with her ever since. She was first published in a poetry anthology in middle school. She received an English degree and has worked as an editor, copywriter, and ghostwriter.

Inspiration for her stories comes from her experiences working in a hospital and her appreciation of the natural world.

Eleanor Chance has lived in many different states and four different countries. She speaks Spanish fluently. She currently resides in the Williamsburg, Virginia, area with her husband and is the proud mother of four grown sons.

Connect with Eleanor *at:*
www.eleanorchance.com
eleanor@eleanorchance.com
facebook.com/eleanorachance
twitter.com/eleanorachance